There are few things that can drive a woman crazier than an attractive man who is trying to get into her pants when she is trying to stay loyal to a husband who has lost all interest in sex. All the way to the diner I told myself I was going there to see this guy to discuss the video promotion we were supposed to put together, but I found myself wet between my legs in spite of myself.

In the dark brown air of the Odyssey Diner, we sat across from each other, protected by a fat leathery booth, and saw ourselves over and over again in the angled mirrors that surrounded us. He had ordered drinks before I arrived — seltzers with lime for both of us.

"You *are* real," he said after I took a sip.

Why was it so hard for me to speak? I felt my voice — heavy and far away. "I have to tell you I — I don't know why I feel so strange around you — I keep telling myself it's just my imagination playing tricks, but — why did you say that before — about maybe there was another life?"

"I have no idea. It just came out like someone else said it."

"Do you believe in past lives?"

"Yes, but I don't really care about them," he said. "I'm having enough trouble with this one. I know this sounds like a line —"

"But you were the one who said it. 'Another life' you said, just like that — without even thinking about it. Have we met before?"

"Can we hold hands?" he asked taking mine in his.

"Now wait a minute!" I said. "This is not why I'm here — besides, I'm a married woman and —" He laughed out loud and I never finished. It was a wonderful throaty laugh, full of abandon, and then his eyes burned through me.

℘   ℘   ℘   ℘

MIRROR MIRROR

a novel by

Carol Kafka

Taylor Productions Inc. • New York • NY

Published in the United States by Taylor Productions Inc.
c/o GRM Associates, 290 West End Ave, New York, NY 10023

ISBN: 0-929093-06-2

Cover by Dorothy Wachtenheim
Photo by Stephen W. Buckley

Manufactured in the United States of America

To my father,
Warren Joseph Kafka

R.I.P.

It is the dead,
not the living,
who make the longest demands.

Sophocles

✦ ✦ ✦

*This book is also dedicated with love to Evelyn,
Alison, Stephen, Kathy, Sam,
Taylor and Brianna*

✦

I owe a debt of gratitude to many people for their generosity and support during the writing of this book, and so I thank: James Chemerys, Gerald Cusack, Rita Freedman, Michael Gebbia, Bill Kafka, Bob Kafka, Roseanne Kaplan, James Lee, Carol Liaros, Rosemary Martino, Cheryle Menary, Lori Monastra, Llorraine Neidhardt, Jeanne Nugent, William Packard, Jackie Rumsey, Elaine Thomas, Jack Uzzle, and Tom Wagner.

And I must give special thanks to these extraordinary women: Molly, Carolyn, Dorothy, Marie, and Trudy.
And to my agent and friend, Gloria Mosesson

✦

✦

Prologue

In the dream I discover that my father is alive again — here only for a day after bursting through the cosmos — his soul packed back into his body — coiled there — waiting to uncoil and fly home with moonlight following his ride back home to the spirit world.

I run to see this angel/spirit fallen from the sky, chasing the soul of my father; yes, living still.

And fly through thick and puffy air to the building where he waits — see it through blinding sunlight — enormous structure, dense gargoyle carvings, standing gray in a flat, green meadow. The gargoyle's eyes burn me. At the front door are curving marble steps with water pouring over them, pulling against my ankles as I climb. I try to breathe in air enough so I can speak — or only make a sound, expecting him to hear me and appear — expecting him in the next second, and then in the next. The humming of a thousand cicadas vibrates against me like a touch, but I shake my hair off my shoulders and pretend not to notice.

I float through the huge door, carrying my heavy

manuscript under my arm — the story of my father's life. He moves and breathes, alive in my pages. I slide through a greenish haze and find his room. Oh! I see him in a flash, bending over and stirring a vat of June bugs.

Yes.

At last. As large as —

I teeter on the brink of a hole that suddenly appears in the floor. This does not concern him; he does not reach out to steady me. Oh, please! I clutch blindly as if I could grab the air, as if it is some sort of beast holding the room in place.

The hole in the floor disappears.

"Daddy, I'm Christina," the words ooze out of me as if they were thick taffy. I reach for his hand. He will not take mine. "I'm almost forty-five now," I say. "I know you're only thirty — thirty when you died. That's why you don't know me. I've grown older than you." Does he think I look pretty?

"You'll have to wait," he says, as if I were just anybody. "I'm very busy now." He is tall, fiercely handsome with thick, mahogany hair, curling in all directions. He wears a khaki shirt; he does not look at me.

"I've written a book about you," I say, clearing my throat and holding up the manuscript for him to see. How has he managed to get out of the pages and stand here in front of me?

"Wait in here," he says, pointing to a white room with high ceilings. "I'll come when I'm finished."

No! I want to scream out. Don't leave! Not again — but he slips away. I reach out into the empty air; still seeing the ghost of his soft curly head.

Why doesn't he want to be with me? The ticking of a clock grows louder, faster, hitting me like hail. I turn and turn, searching to the inner circle of myself, stalking

him inside and out through both ends of a telescope . . . here . . . there . . .

He is gone and I plummet into despair.

Doesn't he know?

Now he must go back into the pages and die again.
I have already written that part, so it is clear what will
happen to him. This was our only chance. We will never
have another.

The ticking blends together like the raspy song of
the cicadas. Oh God! Here comes the car. He is in the
old black Ford — the one that killed him right after I was
born. Slumped over the wheel, he cannot move. He
cannot come to me. It is too late again. It is always too
late.

Then I am awake, and the tyranny of my longing
rears itself again.

I see him still.

One

𝒫

The classroom intercom had rung twice during my spectacular vocabulary-roots lesson. I had ignored it. My sophomores sat on the edges of their seats, eager to absorb every jewel of knowledge I could offer.

"Quaerere: to seek," I said. "Say it five times." They did so with the enthusiasm of a colony of slugs.

"Now just look at all the words that come from this root," I went on. "Try to contain yourselves, because this is the exciting part. 'Query, querist, quaestor, quest, question, querulous, inquest, inquiry, acquire, conquer.' Doesn't it make sense to memorize a few hundred roots which will then open the door to thousands of words?" I asked, smiling at them.

"Not really," one of them said. The phone rang again.

"Is she going to put this on the test?"

"What time is this period over?"

"Is a quaestor somebody who goes on a quest?"

"Yeah, like this is really gonna help me when I become a movie star."

"Oh you think you're all that, plus tax."

"Shut your stupid holey mouth."

Maybe I should have tried this lesson on my juniors.

"Mrs. Fitzsimmons," said my key student, "your phone

is ringing."

"I know," I said. "I hear it."

"How can she stand not to answer her phone?"

I hate it when students talk about me as if I weren't there. Am I too old to be a waitress — the only other job I've ever had?

"I can't stand to be interrupted in the middle of a lesson," I said, finally giving in and going to the phone.

"Someone here to see you," said the principal's secretary on the other end. I could sense her blue eyelids jiggling; they were too big for her eyes and never closed at the same time, so one eye was always watching you.

"Why are you interrupting me now?" I said.

Her voice fell into a hush. "Says he has an appointment with Mrs. Christina Fitzsimmons. Sounds like your name to me. Says you sent for him. Something about a video, heh, heh, heh."

Then I remembered. "He's early," I said. "I'm in the middle of a class." I'd been asked to make a video commercial of the school for parents of prospective students; I had called a video service, and then had forgotten that I'd made an appointment for today with one of their reps.

"You're early. She's in the middle of a class," she repeated into space. "This is against our policy. She cannot be interrupted — one of our rules here." A pause. Then her voice came back, keeping time to her winks. "He says since he's early, he'd be delighted to wait," she giggled again and then whispered, "Can you beat that!" I hung up.

"Ms. Fitzsimmons, Anthony put his hand on my tit while you were on the phone," said a bright female student.

Maybe I can sell shoes.

At the end of the period, I walked to the office. A tall man sat forward on his chair in the waiting room, his brown leather jacket slung on the chair post. He wore a khaki shirt and did not see me at first, because he had leaned forward to fix the buckle on his tan leather boot. All I could see was the top of his head — thick dark hair curling in all directions, and my breath caught. He was the same man I had seen over and over in my dream! The man I fancied was my father — a father I had known only a few months in my waking life. I'm going to die, I thought. He finished his buckle, lifted his head, and there I was, gasping at him. All in one motion, he stood, pulled at the waist of his tight jeans and grinned at me. The secretary zapped her jiggling gaze at us.

"Je-sus," he said, more at me than to me. Then he grinned and added, "Didn't know you were there."

"Uh," I said with great deliberation and gripped the door jamb.

"Daniel Wexler from Video Cats." He extended his hand to me.

"Yes. Well. How nice." You jerk, I said to myself. He's going to think you're crazy. "I've looked — through all your material and I'm sure we can use you — your service," I said. We stared at each other. It was embarrassing, but I couldn't look away. I could feel the eyes of the other secretaries who had now joined Miss Eyelid. This is ridiculous; I'm not in a movie.

"I'm sure there are some questions you want me to answer about how we'll do the actual shooting," he said. His grin seemed to suggest he had a secret inside.

"Yes," I said, "certainly. Questions." But could not think of one. "I'm sure there are." He looked so young. Why was he flirting with me? What was he thinking? — probably that I was an old bag. Why should I care? Who was he anyway? Does he like my hair? My face?

"'Course, I know you don't actually want to start until next September, but there's a lot of preliminary stuff . . ." There was a long pause, a lot of deep breathing, and then I knew what he would say next before he spoke.

"Excuse me for saying this," he interrupted himself, "I know I've never met you before, but —"

"You feel like you know me," I said.

He nodded, started to speak, but then hesitated. After a swallow, he said, "Another life?"

I felt myself flush when I realized he was serious. "Yes," I said. His pupils were enormous. I could see myself in them.

"Is there somewhere we can talk?" He shook his jacket off the chair and swung it over his shoulder. Yet somehow we both moved and spoke as if in a trance. "Somewhere maybe where we can eat. I haven't had lunch."

"Come this way," I said and walked out of the office

toward my classroom. "People are listening." Stop gasping, Christina, for heaven's sake. We moved out into the hall and stopped.

"And watching," he laughed.

"I have one more class," I said. "I'll meet you at three-thirty. There's a place on North Street and Grange, called The Odyssey Diner." I pulled myself away from his eyes and was vaguely aware of the grins of the secretaries who now stood in the office doorway with their heads nodding like mechanical dolls. People don't come back from the dead, I told myself as I half-ran down the hall. I remembered seeing a psychic once on a talk show who said that when people die violently, they often come back quickly. But if there is such a thing as reincarnation, people don't come back looking like they did in their last life.

Do they?

There are few things that can drive a woman crazier than an attractive man who is trying to get into her pants when she is trying to stay loyal to a husband who has lost all interest in sex. All the way to the diner I told myself I was going there to see Daniel to discuss the video promotion we were supposed to put together, but I found myself wet between my legs in spite of myself.

In the dark brown air of the Odyssey, we sat across from each other, protected by a fat leathery booth, and saw ourselves over and over again in the angled mirrors that surrounded us. He had ordered drinks before I arrived — seltzers with lime for both of us.

"You *are* real," he said after I took a sip.

Why was it so hard for me to speak? I felt my voice — heavy and far away. "I have to tell you I — I don't know why I feel so strange around you — I keep telling myself it's just my imagination playing tricks, but — why did you say that before — about maybe there was another life?"

"I have no idea. It just came out like someone else said it."

"Do you believe in past lives?"

"Yes, but I don't really care about them," he said. "I'm having enough trouble with this one. I know this sounds like a line —"

"But you were the one who said it. 'Another life' you said, just like that — without even thinking about it. Why?"

"Can we hold hands?" he asked taking mine in his.

"Now wait a minute!" I said. "This is not why I'm here — besides, I'm a married woman and —" He laughed out loud and I never finished. It was a wonderful throaty laugh, full of abandon.

I twisted the edge of the napkin into a tube with my other hand. Music curled out of the juke box. Stop getting sucked in by his charm, I told myself.

But I did not take my hand away.

"Please relax," he said. "After all, this is the eighties. You don't have to stay married. This is a strange connection we have here. I don't feel it often. All I know is that I intend to enjoy it — wherever it goes. Why don't you?"

I hated the fact that I was blushing, and he could see it.

"It can't go anywhere," I said. "After today — this has to be all. I can only see you in school from now on. I thought we only came here to talk about other lives, and as flattering as all this is — "

"I thought we came here to talk about a video," he said, unabashed. "Oh, what a shame you can't just let go! How many chances does life give you?" I saw the clock in my dream — heard the ticking, felt the sting of the insects — quickening — faster — was I going to be too late again?

He signaled the waitress who picked up his cue immediately. It was like being on stage. Everyone noticed him right away.

"I don't like this sandwich. Could you bring me a Swiss cheeseburger instead?" he asked her. "I think the lady is too ethereal for food."

She left. Then he looked at me. "How long have you been married?"

"Twenty years," I said.

"Wonderful. So it's good and stale by now — maybe it's over, but you just haven't said the words yet."

He stunned me; he held my life in front of me for a second, and I could not bear to see the sham of it. I dug my nails into the palms of my hands.

"Excuse me, but this is none of your business. You have no right to say these things to me."

Then he said, "Never saw anyone with hair like yours. Whoever heard of red with gray streaks? And your eyes — extraordinary — so green; so wild."

"It's auburn, and I guess it means that I'm much older than you, and I should get the hell out of here right now." He had thrown his jacket on the far end of the table and I touched the warm leather.

"Does that bother you — to be older?" he asked. We both knew I wasn't going to leave.

"No. I'm forty-five. I mean you — you were born after me," — after he died, I thought, but I could not say it out loud.

"So how many other thirty-eight year olds do you think would die for you right now?"

"Look — you're very — amusing, you really are, but we have to get back on the subject."

"What is the subject? Isn't this a good enough one? Have no fear. I am going to make you the best video promo any school has ever had, Christina, but I hope to see a lot of you during the process — if you want me to. Think of all there is for us to discover — about ourselves." He started to laugh. "Like what I'm supposed to do with this erection that is causing me great distress right now."

"Oh, God," I said, and we both began to laugh.

He looked down into his lap. "Well if that's all you have to say, I guess I'll just have to take it home and put it in the refrigerator." The waitress arrived with his burger, and he took my hand again. "The lady will probably have a bite," he said to the waitress, but never took his eyes off me. "Or two."

"Whatever," she said and left.

"You are the most outrageous —"

"I know, and I'm sure you'll hold it against me, because I'd certainly like to hold this against you." And he glanced back at his lap.

"Call her back here," I said looking toward the waitress. "Ask her to bring a pitcher of cold water to throw on you!" I took my hand back.

"Don't you need some too?"

I looked down at my busy fingers, stroking back and forth on the supple leather of his jacket. I pulled my hand back and picked up my napkin. He was right. I'm surprised I didn't slide right off the seat.

"Are you married?" I asked. "Not that it matters."

"Block and parry. Very good. No. Never been married. A couple of long-term relationships, but never a ring. Girls like to get rings. I guess that's why they left." He bit into the cheeseburger. "Besides, I've really been saving myself for you. Look at the sparks flying around in here. Can you imagine what it will be like?"

"I'm afraid that would be too easy."

"You mean I'm really not going to make love to you today?"

When was the last time I made love? I thought. My husband — in a word — can't get it up anymore. Hasn't touched me in — well, I bet it's over a year — more like a year and a half . . .

"I'm afraid not."

"But you'd like to. I can feel it. I also know that your marriage ain't so good."

"What makes you say that?"

"You'd never have let me get this far." Now he held my hand with one of his and stroked it with the other. I said nothing and stared down at my curled napkin, trying to swallow the pain at the back of my throat. "Well?" he prodded.

"I really have to go. I didn't know that this was going to be all about sex. I don't believe in lightning bolts." By now, all four corners of the napkin were scrolled into curls, and it was starting to shred. But I made no move to go.

"Who was I to you in another life?" he asked, suddenly very serious, his voice soft like warm sun.

And because he reminded me of the man in my dream, I began to tell him about me. "My father died when I was very young," I began. "And because no one would tell me the details, his death was a mystery to me, and it's haunted me all my life. When I was a child, I thought he really wasn't dead, and he'd come back some day. I knew they were keeping something from me — my family, I mean. At the same time, they told me I couldn't miss what I'd never had, and I always did what I was told, so I believed them for years. I trained myself not to miss him, but it didn't work because I still do. In fact I think it's worse now. There obviously is a lot more to it."

"There usually is."

"When I was eighteen I discovered I had a half-brother, but my mother swore me to secrecy. I'm a good girl, I told you; I do what I'm told, goddamnit. So I could not even have the pleasure of telling my friends about him. But I figured that he was the mystery I had imagined all those years. Now I'm not so sure, because the nagging inside persists — nagging that says there has to be more."

"What are you going to do about it?"

"What can I do?" Now I had confetti where the napkin used to be.

"Well if it still bothers you," he said ever so slowly, "search out the mystery and solve it."

"Do you know I still dream of my father. Once I dreamed that my mother was on the phone talking to him, and he was asking her about me. I begged her to let me talk, but she wouldn't give me the phone." I stopped because I could feel tears trying to squeeze out of my eyes. I bit my lip and leaned my chin on my hands so I could partly cover my trembling mouth. "'Give it to me,' I screamed at her, but she hung up."

"It's okay," Daniel said, his eyes soft and accepting.

"After my father died, my mother had to move back into her mother's house. She had three sisters still at home. They all made quite a fuss over me and tried to protect me from any kind of pain — especially anything that would make me feel the loss of him. All those aunts. Once I told them I wanted to go see his grave; they told me it wasn't there any more and quickly changed the subject. They'd do anything to keep me from feeling bad." A few tears finally came down. I smiled and brushed them off.

He said nothing, but picked up a napkin and dried my eyes. He touched me with exquisite tenderness.

"Maybe this is all you need to do," he said.

"I don't like crying. Especially in front of people."

"Think of it as mourning, not crying," he said. "Maybe you need to mourn. Sounds like you never did, because they wouldn't let you."

"I don't know how," I said. "Do you know, I'm almost forty-five, and no one else of any significance in my life has ever died. My grandmother is still alive — in her nineties. I don't know how to mourn. How do you do it?"

"Aren't you already mourning your marriage?"

I gazed at him. "That's a terrible — I mean, just who do you think you are?"

He shrugged. "Someone from another life, I think we agreed?"

"Oh, God — you are —"

He picked up his jacket but then stopped and let it rest on the seat. "I'm sorry," he said, taking my hand. "Don't be upset." Then he kissed my finger tips, and I let him do it.

"A couple of years ago I said to myself, 'How come, if you're not supposed to be able to miss him' — my father, I mean — 'how come there isn't a day that goes by when you don't think about him?' That's when I realized I had been lied to."

"Sounds like you have a lot of work to do."

"I have to go," I said, trying to get up.

But he held me there, and for a second, everything in the room faded but us.

"Is that who you thought I was — your father?"

I could not answer.

"I guess it's possible, if you believe in that sort of thing," he said. "There was a time when I believed in nothing. Then I messed up my life so badly, that now I believe in everything. But the fact is, I'm certainly not your father. I don't know if you think that's good or bad. Rather think of me as a demon lover — something like that — something out of karma that no one can explain."

"The Dark Man — the Minotaur who knows all the secrets. Is that why I feel faint?"

"Do you?"

"Yes."

"Good. So do I. But unfortunately, my love, if you can't see me tonight, this has to be good-bye, because I have to catch the red eye — to do a light show in California. I'll be there for three months. But I'll mail you a work schedule for September, and I'll give you my number in California. And I will think of you every day." His smile seemed to leap out to me. He wrote the number on a fresh napkin. "Are you sure we can't go someplace else now?"

I swallowed hard. "I'm sure."

"You know best," he said and looked away for the first time. Then he said, "Think about your plan to get rid of your father's ghost, and call me. You need to bounce it off someone. I'm not going to call you. You have to call me. Call me any time — collect." He grinned. "I'll try to have some ice ready to throw into my pants, because I'm sure you'll have me in this sorry state even over the phone." Then he leaned forward, and I could not breathe. "Your eyes are green and mine are blue," he said. "Does that mean our children will have turquoise eyes?"

"I really can't believe this — not any part of it!"

But just as I put my hand up to open the door, he called, "Christina!" I turned back to him. "Believe it — and," he paused and lowered his voice, "call," he said, and his blue eyes burned through me.

Two
§

Now I sit here in my new apartment, and it seems light years since I was in that dark diner with him only two months ago. Did it really happen?

The moving man with a stomach so fat you could balance a glass on it smirked a "good luck lady" in a breathy sweat as he closed the door on my piled-high possessions. I open a window to let in the April air and sit amidst the mess of boxes. It seems as if the furniture is trying hard to look like it belongs here; the old upstairs vacuum cleaner from my house, which now will be used to clean only these two rooms, lies on its side, and the dusty cardboard boxes are arranged like the throw of so many dice. I don't move. I wonder what I am doing here. A woman married for twenty years who just walks out? Is that what I did? I see myself in a mirror that rests waiting on the floor, but my head is cut off.

Help! From a crack under the sink, a roach appears, and my skin jitters. Ugh. Couldn't it wait, at least until I unpacked? How can I kill it without the risk of its touching me? My eyes are glued to it as I try to reach behind me for a folded newspaper. Boric acid, my daughter had told me. Boric acid jammed in all the cracks kills them. Living in Manhattan, she is now an experienced roach killer. They don't allow roaches in Bronxville, I had told her. "Yes, they do," she said, "but only if the roach knows other roaches who already live in Bronxville. Recommendations are required."

I slap down on it with all the strength I have, but freak out as a second roach falls from the molding above my head and brushes my shoulder. I throw the newspaper and squished roach out onto the fire escape, while I watch the second roach which is now on the floor. Should I step on it? Run the risk of getting its guts on my shoes? I can always throw the shoes away.

I miss, and it escapes. I don't know where it went, but I can feel it watching me. Oh, please! Now I am certain that I don't belong here.

The sudden wail of a train whistle makes me jump, and I hear the even clap of the wheels as an express commuter gallops through the station, not stopping for anyone. I think of the ten-room house that I left. That still has my husband and no roaches living in it.

I left three weeks ago after the party I threw for my grandmother's ninety-fifth birthday. Although my family drove me wild that night, what they did opened my eyes, I told myself. It was my epiphany. And here I am. Was it a mistake? I don't belong here either. Maybe I should become a bag lady.

The doorbell rings its first greeting.

"Do come up whoever you are!" I say into the intercom and wonder if it was really I who spoke.

Two voices sing out together: "Locksmith!" "Telephone!"

"Yes, yes, I'm here!"

The lumbering elevator carries them up, and I open the door to them. They will make it possible for me to decide whom to let in, to keep out. If Daniel were here, would I let him in?

I wish I had never met him! Maybe I wouldn't be in such distress.

The locksmith has gone. Then the phone man finishes. "It's okay now, lady. You can call any place you want." As he straightens up from his crouch, tools and wires bob from his belt.

"Even California?" I say, tucking my daughter's faded pink shirt in my jeans.

"Hell, Paris, France, if you want. Knock yourself out!"

"Thanks." He leaves looking over his shoulder, hoping I will make a move toward my purse. "Thanks," I say again and close the door. Why should I give him a tip? I don't even know where my purse is.

I can't call Daniel. What would I say? You started me thinking about so many things, I decided to separate from my husband, and now I'm scared that I may have done the wrong thing? I see the box labeled "Personal Papers," and I know that the paper napkin he wrote his number on is filed in there. Don't open it now. No. Calling Daniel must wait.

"And on that note —" I say out loud as the doorbell rings again. Then another roach zigzags across the floor toward the front door. I open it and let the roach out only to have my skin flush with sweat.

"Hi, Aunt Dora," I say, opening the door and trying to smile. "How did you get in downstairs?" How long has she been lurking out of sight like the roaches?

"Christina! What is the matter with you?" She sweeps into my apartment, zigzagging like the roach, as she examines what I have brought here. Her voice has a little gurgle in it, as if she can't quite clear her throat. Please go away and leave me alone. "You should have let me know so I could help. You must be beside yourself." She moves on a glide, as if on insects' legs.

Will boric acid work on her? "That's okay, Aunt Dora. I'm really fine." Stop trying to smile. You don't have to if you don't feel like it. She's not looking at you anyway. Her eyes are sweeping over every inch of the apartment. I suppose I should say "her eye," because only one is real. She had lost the other in a freak accident before I was born. Ever since then she has had a glass eye.

"Well, you can come over for supper tonight. I have a leg of lamb in the oven, and it'll be much too much for me and Granlena." Her thick gray hair sticks out in serpent tendrils which seem to curl and uncurl with each breath. You always have leg of lamb in the oven, and I hate leg of lamb. "Listen, thanks," I say, "but I have a lot to do —"

"And I said I'd help you, didn't I? 'A lot to do,' she

says. My dear, I should show you what a lot to do is." She
sneezes and blows her nose in a hard gust. I am afraid the
glass eye may pop out.

Maybe I can suggest she go to Florida to take care of
that cold. "Aunt Dora, you're very thoughtful, but this is
really something I want to do myself." Now she has finished
her inspection, checking to see which of my possessions I
took with me from my house.

"I can whip a new apartment into shape in no time.
Trust me. Where are the candle sticks I gave you?" She
picks a piece of lint off my sweater.

Hawaii would be even better — it's farther away. "In
that Lord & Taylor box on the floor," I say, twisting out of her
grasp. "Not to worry, Aunt Dora. Charles and I have agreed
it's only a temporary arrangement, until we can work out
some answers."

"What kind of answers? Your mother said something
about wanting to find out some things about — about —
when you were a baby." Now she spots some more lint on my
other sleeve.

"Yes. I need to do some digging into my past —
particularly into things about my father." I sit in my wicker
chair to escape her attack, but she glides across the room to
defuzz my sweater. "Please stop that," I say as she sucks her
teeth.

"Well, I think it's terrible." She is now full throttle.
"And I think you should know that the whole family is very
upset by this. Very." She sneezes again. I look away as she
rubs the lid covering the glass eye. "We've told you over and
over about those days, and that should be enough."

"Well, it isn't enough. It isn't even a drop in the
bucket. What is it you are all trying to hide?"

"Are you kidding? There is nothing — absolutely
nothing to hide at all. We only wanted to prevent you from
being upset by dwelling on unpleasant things — and that is
absolutely all there is to it." Dora stands in the middle of the
room, a tiny Cyclops of sorts.

"Then how come I've always felt there was more? Tell
me. Tell me the whole story all over again." The Cyclops is
about to attack. Get ready.

"Why do you have to go upsetting us? I for one think

it's a disgrace to leave your husband and —"

"What has that got to do with anything?" I say.

"Absolutely everything. Because rocking boats always leads to trouble; so if you want my advice, go home and stop all this nonsense, before you regret it."

"Is that a threat?"

"A warning," she says, dramatically lowering her voice. "You should let me wash that sweater for you."

I can no longer bear to have her here. "Thanks so much for letting me know how you feel. I'm sorry you're so upset." I walk her to the door. "You're going to have to go now."

"You sound like you wish you had the nerve to ask me to leave."

"I'm afraid so," I say, and edge her closer to the door.

"Who do you think you are — a damned reporter? I don't like what I'm seeing here, Christina. I don't like it one bit. Your mother said it sounded like you were taking notes. Next thing you know, you'll be writing a book about us, for God's sake."

What an idea. A book! Not about "us," but about him — my father. Great! I could have hugged her, in spite of everything. Maybe I can write about him and change my own script in the process. Maybe I can hold up a new looking glass and step inside it.

"Thanks so much for everything, Aunt Dora," I say. "We'll talk very soon." And I close the door behind her.

"Well, it's not going to work, do you hear?" she yells even after the door is closed. "You'll see. Oh, aren't you something? You think you're really something, don't you?"

In the past, Dora was always able to distract me from dwelling on thoughts of my father. That must be why she is so furious now, because she can sense that it doesn't work anymore. These distraction techniques were brought into sharp focus only three weeks ago, at my grandmother's birthday party.

My house was packed with relatives, including all my mother's sisters, the aunts who'd helped raise me. Celebration crackled. We would have a perfect party in spite of ourselves. Let's hope the food has no salt, and that no one serves it before Granlena has finished opening her presents. Let's hope no one insults anyone else, or smokes a cigar, or talks about how they feel, or drinks too much. Any infraction of this family's rules, no matter how small, will not be tolerated. Get that?

Suzanne, a seven-year-old great-grandchild, was serving olives wrapped in bacon.

"You're not really going to eat those," said Dora to her sister Julie. "Think of the nitrites! All that pollution in your body!" Suzanne looked hurt, and so Aunt Julie wolfed down three of them very deliberately right in Dora's face. "You may call it pollution, my dear sister, but I call it progress," she said smirking.

Everyone else ignored them and smiled at Suzanne in her little checked apron as she passed her treasure around the living room, her stick-straight hair swishing when she moved. When her tray was empty, she started back for the kitchen, but tripped over the leg of a rocking chair near the door. The tray flew, and she landed on all fours, her right knee banging the door jamb.

My three aunts sprang into action. "Suzanne, Suzanne look what I have!" Tiny Dora, who was only four feet ten and eighty-five pounds, zipped across the room, nabbing a chocolate kiss en route and frantically tearing off the silver paper. "Mmmmm, mmmm, wouldn't you like one?" she said, her curls unrolling as she held Suzanne with her gaze.

"Here, I'll put some ice water on it," said Aunt Babe sticking her fingers in her drink and splashing drops on the sore knee. "Don't cry, Suzanne! Oh, no, no, no you mustn't cry."

"What a good girl!" Aunt Julie chirped, her smile set and rigid. "You know there's a horse named Sweetie Pie who lives down the road from my farm and when you come to see me, I'll make sure you get a ride on him. Okay?"

Suzanne held her knee in a cement grip and looked from one toothy grin to the other, her lip puckering, her tears poking out every now and then.

"How about general anesthesia?" I offered.

Aunt Dora sucked in her breath. "Christina!" she

said.

My childhood rushed at me, whistling through a far-away tunnel. How far would they go to keep someone from feeling bad?

If I had sniveled or twisted a lip when we all lived in that little house in the Bronx, signals must have gone off among these women then, too. If they would go this far for a banged knee, how much more frantic must the action have been to hide something as tormenting as a death?

It was their way of laughing at that God who could bring tragedy again in the stroke of a second. If you kept the diversions flowing, perhaps you could distract even Him.

Now I knew I had to find out the whole story — with all its secrets. How many stories might I have to dredge up? Was there one detail that would unlock all the others? I am certain now that I must write them down, the better to look for clues. And perhaps writing will be a way for me to mourn my father's death. A book it shall be!

The clock will tick off my days; the pages will fall and land in a heap upon the floor.

And on this, the very first night in my new apartment, I dream the dream of my father again.

Three
℘

After the guests had left that fateful party, my husband snapped up ten dirty glasses in the smoky living room, a finger in each one, and began his post-party clean-up frenzy. I was trying to push away thoughts of Daniel, as I wrapped up the leftover food.

"Crap, it's starting to snow. Can you believe it?" he said, loading the dishwasher, wiping the counter tops, and looking out the window at the same time. "How the hell can it snow in April? Trains'll probably be all screwed up tomorrow." It couldn't possibly be snowing where Daniel was. When might he come back to New York?

"Did you see what happened when Suzanne fell?" I said.

"All kids take spills," he said, shrugging. He turned out the light for a second, so that he could see outside better. "Wonder if it's going to stick?"

"No, that's not what I mean. I'm talking about how they wouldn't let her cry when she was hurt. That's what they used to do to me. It's awful." He snapped the lights back on, finished packing every cubic inch of the dishwasher, set the dials, and turned it on.

"They meant well. They were trying to make it easier on her, that's all." The water made a swushing sound. "I'll have to leave my radio on all night to hear the reports."

"They may have meant well, but it's not easier, Charles. It's ten times worse." I could hear the tremor in my voice. Could he hear it over the sound of the dishwasher? "You grow up hiding yourself — from yourself."

He began rinsing the dirty dishes that would have to wait for the next dishwasher load. "You know, you analyze everything too goddamn much. You have a good family. Why can't you just let it go at that?"

"I know they're good," I said. "That's just the point. That's what makes it so insidious."

"Can we hurry and get this finished? I'm tired."

"I'll finish it tomorrow," I said.

"How can you?"

"I'm taking the day off."

"How can you?"

"I'm just doing it, that's all."

"What for?"

"I hate to go to school the day after a party."

"That's absurd."

"Okay, I'm going to the cemetery," I said.

"You drive me crazy, you know that?

"I thought I'd go pick out our graves. How do you look in green?"

"Fuck you," said Charles.

"I should live so long."

"What's that supposed to mean?"

"Look, I have decided to improve my mental health by doing a little research into my father's life, okay? And I thought I'd start with the cemetery."

"This is getting ridiculous," he said. "Now why would you want to go and do anything like that?"

"Look, I'm not really sure why I want to do this, but I thought I would try to fill in some gaps. The grave is one of them. I've never seen it." I hesitated and then turned to look out the window so I didn't have to see the frown on his face, but instead I saw both our reflections in the glass, all glittering from the swirling snow. "Want to come?" I asked.

A look of disgust settled on him like a cloud, and the wrinkles across his forehead extended up to his bald pate. "I don't believe in it," he said,

"In mental health?" I said.

"In visiting graves. My vote is for you not to do it."

"But I didn't ask for a vote. I would just like it if you could understand and kind of stand by m—"

"You are most definitely looking for trouble."

"In which department?"

"Take your pick."

"I'm glad it's snowing," I said.

At six the next morning, the snow was still falling lightly. I was surprised that I felt energized after only four hours of sleep. The stale smell of ashes in the kitchen brought back last night's argument. While I waited for the coffee, I looked out at the woods behind our house. The trees looked so vulnerable in their baby-frail leaves on this April day. The yellow blossoms of the forsythia trembled as if Nature stood aghast at herself. I thought of a story I had written when I was a child about how the four seasons wanted to play with each other but never could, because as soon as one came, one had to leave. Here were two seasons, spring and winter intermingling themselves, sharing their colors. Somehow it did not work.

I found sneakers in the hall closet, put them on with my coat over my robe, and went out into this misfit of seasons. I threw bread for the birds, and wondered how my life had ever come to this point. Here. Now. I'd never planned it. I am the one out of step, I thought. I can no longer conform to my family's rules. But what do I put in their place? A blank page is scary. Shivering, I went back into the house.

Then I heard Charles's shower running. He would come down the stairs soon, outfitted for a North Pole expedition, cursing his way out the front door and all the way to the train station. Whoever heard of a goddamned blizzard in April? Son of a bitch!

By eleven o'clock, the sun had intensified the whiteness into a searing light, so bright I needed sunglasses. I wore high, black, shiny boots, my camel trench coat, and wild terra cotta leggings, (Something I'd never wear in front of Charles) with a coral oversized sweater. I let my hair fall free.

Not exactly a mourning get-up, but a good defense against feeling blue.

Although they really weren't necessary, plows had come through the street. The melting snow dripped everywhere, gleaming in the sun and refracting the light into millions of diamonds. The air had a cold, wet smell. I drove out toward the Sound. Guarded by the Whitestone Bridge, St. Raymond's Cemetery stretched along the roadside, the landmark I remembered from my childhood.

When I was six, Aunt Babe had let something slip once on the way to Jones Beach. She leaned over to me as our distant uncle drove us past the cemetery and whispered, "This is where they buried my grandma, my grandpa, my brother, and guess who else?" she smiled down at me with love in her face, her arm around my shoulder and her hand patting my leg.

"My father?" I guess I had forgotten to whisper.

"What are you telling her?" squealed Aunt Dora from the front seat. "What did you say about that cemetery? Don't listen to Babe, Christina. His grave is nowhere around here." She turned around to face us in the back seat, crossing her good eye toward the glass one. "What do you think you're doing, Babe? Stop scaring her."

"I'm not scared," I protested.

"Never mind, never mind." Dora's voice kept rising, and I knew that meant to keep my mouth shut. "We know what's best for you. Now you just think about that beach and all the waves I'm going to set up for you to jump over."

Although I never admitted it — even to myself — I didn't believe her. I knew in some vague way that he was in there! Had he known we were passing by? Had he wanted us to stop? Now I smiled and stared out the window, as the symmetry of the rows of headstones whizzed by, looking like ghosts standing at attention, sentries over their charges. I fancied they talked to one another at night when no one was there.

The woman in the cemetery office looked as if her face

had never smiled in its long and wrinkled life. She must be anorexic, I thought, staring at her visible bones. Her skirt was three shades of gray and hung unevenly, looking as if it had been made of old curtains gone brittle with age. She looked up my father's name in a huge mildewed book that smelled like death.

"Oooooh yesssss. Carter Shieldsss. Here. Yesssss. December, 1940. Yesss. In the Gentilesco plot." She took a yellowed card out of the book. Her head swayed slowly from side to side, "Tsk, tsk, tsk, tsk what a shame," she said. She looked like a mutant metronome. Had she been here then? Had she been the one who had written his name deep in the recesses of this musty volume before they lowered him in the ground?

She continued her hushed tones, "Firssst, you must find the Old Section. Here," she pointed to the card with her pinkie. "The Row Number. Here. Two Interment Recess Numbers. Yesss. Next to each other." Then she leaned over the counter and spoke in a whisper. "Some of our residents there have been interred for as long as one hundred years."

Residents? Did she really say residents? Did they pay rent? Complain about the drainage? Attend unit dweller meetings? Help!

"I hope I'm back before you call the roll," I said, halfway out the door.

Leaning out of a cart filled with tools, a groundsman directed me to the Old Section, and I began my intrusion amidst ancient trees, saintly angels, and weeping madonnas. The snow did not crunch. There was no sound. I walked from row to row as quiet as an Indian. Then I came to a pedestaled angel stationed at the head of a row, blowing her trumpet, calling me to her charges.

I advanced, reading the names, and touched an old shiny pedestal, once white as porcelain, with "Gentilesco" and several first names of people in my grandmother's family around all four sides. The number matched one on the card the gray lady in the office had given me. The cut letters were rough against the smooth coolness, but nowhere was the name of Carter Shields.

If this was where he was buried, why wasn't his name there? Pain formed itself into lines that ran up and down my arms and legs. Was he going to elude me again? Next to this grave was one bare of any marker. It had only a number on it. Perhaps this is where he was. I'm here, I said. Where are you?

How could they have buried you with no headstone? Yours should be huge and glorious, carved with cherubs and trumpets! Not this! An unmarked grave? Is that all your death amounted to? Are you here? Can you speak to me? A heaviness pushed into me in straight lines, and I wished Daniel were here. Did my father know? Was he watching me from some far off place? I thought I heard the rasp of cicadas; then realized it was a groundsman using a chain saw to prune a tree. I cried all in a gush, until I could no longer bear the lines of pain — up and down — all over me — and I ran all the way back to the car.

"We couldn't afford it," my mother said into the phone. "It was 1940. We had no money. People didn't even have insurance in those days. A headstone was the last thing on my mind."

"Couldn't you have borrowed it from someone?"

"You don't understand, Christina," she said. "You can't even conceive of what it was like — no one had any money. There was no one to borrow it from."

She was right. I could not understand. Perhaps every generation is so handicapped by its own lifestyle that none can ever understand the problems of the previous generation. My own child cannot conceive of a world without computers or even without McDonald's. I could not comprehend not being able to get the money somewhere for something as important as a headstone.

"Well, what about later on, when you had a little money?"

"I never got around to it. Besides I had you to take care of. The question is, why did you have to go there in the first place?" she said, her voice rising.

"I'm tired of having big black spaces in my head where memories should be. I want to know about my father. I'd like you to help me, but if you can't, I'm going to find out one way or another."

"It's not that I don't want to. It's just that I believe in letting the past stay the past. Make do with what you have. It's not going to change the present."

"It might," I said.

"Don't be ridiculous. How could it?"

"We're very different you and I. You used to joke and say they must have switched babies on you in the hospital. Maybe it's not such a joke."

"No my dear, I'm afraid you're stuck with me for a mother. Besides, you look just like your father's family. If you ever saw them you'd see."

"I intend to see them. Do you have any addresses? He had two brothers and a sister?"

"They used to live in Petersburg, Virginia. Do what you have to do. But I suggest you look ahead, not back."

Late that afternoon, I drove to the Forty-Second Street Library where they have all the phone books of the whole nation. There were four "Shields" in Petersburg. I copied down the addresses.

I was sitting in our living room, poised and ready, when Charles came home from work.

"I need to get an apartment, so I can pursue this thing on my own," I managed to get out. Not bad for someone trained to silence.

"Thing? You call it a thing? A thing is making you leave your home? What the hell is finding out about your father's past going to do for you?"

"I don't know. I just know that I have to do it, and I can't do it here."

"Get me a fucking violin!" Charles groaned.

"I'm sorry you can't understand —"

"Understand? Sure I understand. You want to walk out on me, your home —"

"I'm not walking out. I'm just getting an apartment for a while."

"You want to know what I hope? I hope you never come goddamned back. That's what I hope."

Four

℘

I have been in my new apartment for over a month, and I am now fully capable of going to sleep without the lights on. It appears I have also won the boric acid vs. roach war. However, I had to increase my artillery to include Combat traps and a machine that makes sounds inaudible to the human ear but intolerable to roaches. Can you imagine? So far it appears to be working. But what if it didn't? Would I have left by now, rather than live with the little furies?

The days lengthen into May, then June. I look out my fifth floor windows and see parkways and other buildings instead of my back yard with our pool and the woods behind it. But even though I miss the yard and all its beautiful shrubs and plants, I love to hear the exhilarating sounds of the express trains from my apartment. Soon the summer will be here. No more school. How will I survive without a swim in my pool every day? No, I must stay where I am until I have found some answers. My husband calls once in a while to see how I am, and we go out to dinner. He is still angry that I left, and we have little to say. Yet, I recall, he was angry when I was home, too. I tell him and myself that this is only a temporary arrangement, until I've finished the task of my father.

I have made huge holes in the walls where I tried to

hang family photos — including one of my father sitting in a hammock. His head is thrown back and he is laughing. You can almost hear the throatiness of it — feel the wild abandon of him. Since I could not hang it up, I stood it in a frame on the radiator. I wish I had a photo of Daniel.

I also had put a pink candle on the radiator next to the photo which melted and oozed hot wax into an amoeba pattern on the floor — some of which I am still unable to remove. The shower squirts in all directions, because I tried to attach a new Water Pic shower head. Not only can't I get the old one off, I distorted it so that I can't make it work the way it did before I fiddled with it.

My daughter rings the downstairs' buzzer. It is her third visit here. She is now twenty-two and is amazed at how much I have learned in the last few years, because when she was a teen-ager, she had discovered that I knew nothing at all. She is a word-processor/actress, but unfortunately more of the former than the latter.

"Who is it?" I speak into my handy-dandy apartment intercom.

"Sandra Bullock with short hair," she calls. I buzz her in. She is a startling beauty in an updated Annie Hall look except she wears short shorts. Her legs are amazingly long, and must take up at least half of her five-nine frame. Was I ever that pretty? Was I ever that young?

"I like your hat," I say. It is electric blue with a big floppy brim.

"So do I, but it's really too hot." She flings it on the couch and looks up at the holes in the wall above it. "Up to your tricks again?"

"Well, I had a bit of a problem. The man at the store sold me some Spackle and new picture hooks. I just haven't had time to —"

"Why don't you ask Grandmom to help you. You know she could whip this place into shape in one afternoon. The last time I saw her, she was spackling the ceiling in the bathroom."

"Before or after she poured the cement for her driveway?" I say.

"Mom!"

"Look, Melissa, I really want to do this myself. I've

never lived alone in my life."

"That's your trouble," she says, snapping her fingers. "Everyone should have to live alone for a year or so after they finish college — part of a rite of passage."

"Like you're doing?"

"I know you didn't want me to go —"

"But now I know it was the best thing for you."

"Well anyway, I bought you something," she says and hands me a present. "It's for your apartment. Well, not exactly, I mean it is, but mostly it's to bring you luck to find out whatever it is you want to find out. I always thought you were a weak person. Boy was I wrong."

"How nice."

I open the present to find a wooden peasant doll in somewhat the shape of an old-fashioned sock darner. I like touching the smooth shininess of it. What a cheerful thing to give someone! Her painted face smiles through a pink babushka; a little blue apron is painted around her tummy.

"Only you would think of something like this," I say.

"Wait, it gets better." Melissa takes it from me and twists the doll's waist. "She opens. Ta da!"

"Ah, yes, I saw something like this once." Inside her is another doll with a different facial expression and this one is dressed in yellow and green.

"You keep opening and opening and altogether there are six," she says. "Wait till you see the baby." She keeps taking them apart until she comes to the sixth and last, a fat, miniature bowling pin of a doll that does not open. "Don't you just love it? I knew you would. The biggest one, of course, is Granlena. The next is Grandmom, then you, then me! See how we repeat ourselves."

"Is that why they all look alike? Who are the last two?" I ask.

"My daughter to-be and my granddaughter to-be."

"Bite your tongue!"

"Six generations altogether. And you know what? You and I, being numbers four and three will get to know all six before we die. Fate has a way of showing up again."

"God, I hope not." I laugh, knowing there is nothing funny.

"Well, of course it does," she says. "Your father

wasn't there for you.   Neither was mine, even though he's alive." I give her a long hug. "No. Don't go saying it's okay." She pulls away from me. "He was never present. Except to yell and find everything wrong — no, don't say it'll work out either," she can't stop. "I don't want to hear it."

She begins to put the dolls together, lining them up in size order.   "See, we're separate, but we're all connected whether we want to be or not. So call Grandmom. Let her help you. I have to go. Karl is waiting outside to take me back to the city. He has this old, discontinued car called an Impala. Ever hear of it?" She picks up her hat and blows me a kiss.

Of course I've heard of it. I used to own one before you were born, you brat. "Discontinued?" Does she think of me as "discontinued" too?

No one else will ever have such a knack for breezing in and out of my life, leaving me off center and sometimes inside-out.   But she's right.   We are all indissolubly connected, and, oh, how those connections hang on to us, like too much fat around one's middle.   I begin to fit the dolls back into themselves, and as I close each one, I know with certainty that I must recant all the stories I can remember; the blank page is my mirror, terrifying in its possibilities.   I must journey into the underworld — chase the demon lover and bring him back alive. I must see first my own story and then my father's, until the pieces start to fit together, one inside the other.

Do I dare do things my own way?   Oh, Daniel!   I'll send you everything.   Yes, I'd like you to read my stories. Will you urge me to speak?

Perhaps I should start with my mother, especially since Melissa thinks she is so fascinating . . .

Five

℘

    Some mothers cooked, some sewed — mine fixed things. She sure knew how to "make do" in this department. She could take apart a toaster on the dining room table, find the wayward wire, mend it, and put everything back together before I had finished my homework. When she began her work, her eyes shifted gears. Her rhythm became steady, and her concentration moved in like a sigh. She became transfixed on her object, not hearing if anyone spoke to her. Her fingers seemed to get smaller as they slunk into the narrow tunnels of machinery, moving slowly with the precision of a jeweler. When she finished, she would shift out of her trance, and come back into the world where I lived.

    I don't remember my mother in the kitchen. If she did go there, it was not to cook — it was only to repair something. If Granlena had allowed her to go to engineering school, she would probably have been at the top of her class. Aunt Julie told me she begged to go. But the hard times that followed the Depression demanded that she go to work instead. Besides, who ever heard of a lady engineer? She became a dancer after graduating from high school at sixteen (skipped two years in elementary school) and then joined some sort of a tap-dancing troupe that toured the East Coast.

    "Emelia," Granlena had said to her, "be grateful you

have a job. College is for boys."

Marrying my father in 1939 at eighteen saved her from the world of stale bars and ratty costumes. She thought she was safe. But when he died two years later, she had to go back to work, and Granlena had to take care of me.

I think I was about eighteen in 1958, when her boyfriend gave her an aged 1948 Chevrolet coupe. Her first car! It was always parked outside our Bronxville one-bedroom apartment, a place she and I had shared since I was ten.

"Did you play with dolls when you were a little girl?" I asked her one hot evening in late May, when her head was lost inside the hood of the car. It was ten years old and covered with rust spots. She had sanded the rust off the previous week, glued on sheets of fiber glass, and then painted the whole thing herself. A light green. She often had an audience, because she had to do all her work on the street where we lived, a wide avenue lined with Tudor style apartments. Had my father worked on his car too? The black Ford that killed him?

"What?" she said, pulling her head out sideways like a snail coming out of its shell.

"Dolls," I said. "Did you ever play with dolls, like I did? I mean when you were little?"

"Christina, hold this, will you?" she said, handing me a blackened hose with a torn hole in it. Then her arm went full length into the Macy's shopping bag that held all her tools. She came out with electrical tape and stretched it round and round over the hole.

I was distracted by a young man watching us from across the street.

"I had a doll once," she said, "but I don't think I played with it."

"Didn't you like her?" I said. I kept watching the young man.

"It wasn't that I didn't like it," she said. "I just kept taking it apart to see what made the eyes open and close."

She refastened the hose back into the guts of the car, and half of her disappeared again. I bent to look in the rear view mirror (cars in those days had no side mirrors) I pre-tended to fix my hair, but I was watching the young man who started to cross to our side of the street. I wondered if he was going to speak to me or to see what my mother was doing. I moved the mirror, catching his face as he came nearer. I framed his pointy chin, his red-brown hair. There was an odd familiarity about his features, yet I knew I had never seen him before.

"I'm going inside," I said just as the young man stepped up behind me. When I turned to go, we nearly bumped. I looked flush into his face. My toes gripped the bottoms of my white bucks.

"Can't you wait till I'm through?" my mother said, not seeing us. "Only be a minute."

"Hi," I said, dying a little. I always felt I had to fill in the silences people left. It was awful.

"Greetin's," he said. "I was wonderin' if you ladies might know somebody named Shields, supposed to live here," he pointed to our apartment house. "Rang the bell, but no one came." My mother slammed down the hood, and I jumped.

"Who wants to know?" she said, before I could answer. He smiled, and I suddenly realized why he looked so familiar. He looked like me!

"Is your name Christina?" he said.

"Who are you?" my mother demanded, but, some-where in her soul, she knew.

"Pardon, ma'am. Name's Carter Shields, and I'm looking to find my sister." He turned back into my face. "Are you Christina?"

"Yes. Well, I —" some kind of buzzer was going off. "But I don't have —" Electric shocks. "I don't have a brother."

"Just a minute," said my mother, picking up her shopping bag. "You come inside." She strode across the street, and Carter hesitated a moment before following her.

I ran after him. "I'm not supposed to have a brother." Why was she so upset? I could barely control myself.

"Well, I sure am sorry for that, but I am Carter, Miss Christina," he said in his drawl. "I figured by now your mama would have told you. I always knew, so I figured you did too.

I looked straight into his eyes. He was my father incarnate out of the silver frame on my mother's dresser. My father with lighter, unslicked hair and a more narrow jaw. My eyes blurred, and I smeared away my tears. I never cried in front of people. I look so ugly when I cry.

I had tried to make the lies about my father last as long as I could, but they gradually eroded over the years like sand slipping back into the sea.

From the time I was very little, the adults in my family spoke of my father as if he were a god. "People thought he was a movie star, everywhere we went," my mother told me. "You should have seen my cousins at the wedding. They were so jealous! Everyone noticed him — everywhere we went." Her voice was very soft; she covered her sadness well, and I was caught in the spell of her memory. I liked to sit on her lap when we went upstairs at night, and then I would curl her dark pageboy around my fingers; she spoke only of his charm and the wildly glamorous things about him.

Somewhere in my mind where things flash and disappear, I sensed there had to be more to the story, but the resident Greek chorus in our house did much to dispel my doubts.

"Nobody — nobody like him!" agreed Aunt Babe in a falsetto.

"When you were born, he taped snapshots of you to the dashboard of his car," added Aunt Dora, " — said you were the 'purtiest' thing he ever saw."

"Remember that?" said Aunt Julie, "How he used to say 'purtiest'?"

"He sure loved you, you know," said Zizi, my grandmother's sister, who lived on the other side of the Bronx.

"Such a terrible thing when he died." Drum roll at the very least.

"Damn car it was — killed him."

"And you know what?" Now the violins. Aunt Julie loved this part. "You used to sob in your sleep after that. After he died, I mean. You started to do it the night he died; I was in your mother's apartment. I heard you from your crib."

Once in a while I interrupted. "How could I have known if I was only a few months old?"

Then full chorus: "Honey, don't grind your teeth like that."

"Somebody robbed his car after the crash — took his wallet. But the snapshots of you — they were still there."

"And a watch. Wasn't there a watch missing?"

"Of course — Emelia's Christmas present — gone."

"I swear to God, she sobbed in her sleep — all the time after that. As if she knew."

"Don't tell her that. You're dramatizing. Besides it wasn't every night."

"He was some guy!" Applause. Please.

After he died, on December 12, 1940, my mother and I had to move into my grandmother's house near Montefiore Hospital in the Bronx. My mother was only nineteen. We moved into the second floor, which was a tiny apartment. Her three sisters and my grandmother lived downstairs. My aunts were still single. Of course they lived at home. Italian girls did not leave home unless they married (or died). The four sisters went to work every day. Secretaries all. Smart girls. They clicked their way through Grand Central Terminal twice a day. Did my mother have to force herself to keep up, carrying the burden of her loss?

The summer I turned five, I was allowed to run to the corner to meet them at a quarter to six. We walked back to our house, me wearing Mommy's hat, Aunt Dora's white gloves. I was sure I looked spectacular. However, I made a mental note to switch to the hat and gloves of the other two aunts the next night. I had to be careful never to hurt anyone's feelings. I skipped along holding two of the eight manicured hands. A parade of fashion-draped ladies and me, their mascot, going home for dinner. Aunt Julie asked me what I had done that day. It was a cue. I smiled and told her about mushing the tomatoes through the sieve, helping Granlena to make sauce for the macaroni. I knew that my answer could only include pleasant things.

I was not allowed to be unhappy.

*   *   *

Sometimes I pretended that my father came to play with me. And once I invited him to a tea party that I held in the basement. How I wished I never had! I arranged extra chairs around my little wooden play table that he had made for me before I was born. It was stained a deep cherry color and had a decal of a teddy bear in the middle. I sat Raggedy Ann and Andy in the chair next to his, careful not to look at his empty chair. If I did, he might not be there. I sat next to him, and Claudia, my best doll, was on the other side of me.

In the back of the basement was an old folding screen. Behind it was a storage closet where my mother and aunts kept their out-of-season clothes. I never went in it, because it was so dark, but I knew my mother's wedding gown was in there. Today was the day. I held my breath, opened the door fast, ran in and rummaged back through the coats, so many soft monsters bumping my face, until I saw white. I ripped the dress off the hanger, slammed the door, and ran behind the screen. The whole tea party was waiting for me. I had stolen the hair brush from Aunt Julie's drawer, and I brushed out the awful banana curls that Granlena put in my hair every morning. Next came the dress. It was silky-cool moiré and slid over me. I held up the taffeta skirt, so I could walk. "Sing, Claudia," I said.

Claudia had a wooden face and fat wooden legs that clicked together when you picked her up. Today she was ready in her pink organdy dress. First she said, "Here she is!" Then she began to sing "The Blue Danube," which my mother had on a record, and which I thought was the most beautiful song I ever heard.

I came out walking slowly on my toes, my head high and my face all in a smile. I posed and stopped, dancing and dipping my way over to the table, looking straight ahead, as if I didn't know all eyes were on me.

"Come on everybody!" Claudia said to the lesser dolls in the room. "Now we must all sit up and pay attention to the father." I began to move around the table, pouring water into my tiny tea cups, smiling all the while.

"You didn't give your father enough," Claudia said. "He likes more cocoa than that." I concentrated on pouring, careful not to look up, but aware that I was so close to him. Claudia went on. "Give him the big cookie," she said. I reached for the tiny tin that held the four cookies Granlena had given me, and as I opened it, lo and behold, someone (not Claudia) really whispered my name!

I shot a look directly at his chair as fast as a finger snap, and stared at the empty space it held, but I knew I had not imagined it. I dropped the cookies, let the wedding gown collapse around me on the floor, and ran upstairs. I refused to go back until someone came with me, even though I knew I'd get in trouble for the wedding gown, but I never told anyone what happened. Had he really come back? Who had called me?

I was always much happier when I was alone with my grandmother, my wonderful Granlena. She had beautiful brown eyes, veiled by glasses that had made permanent red marks on either side of her nose. She had a way of celebrating me. "Well," she'd say as if the word had two syllables, "look who's here." And she always looked right into my face as if she were taking a picture of me. I could see myself sparkle in her eyes. I loved being there most of the time.

What I didn't like was the feeling of being watched. And there were so many eyes to watch me. Especially Dora's. "I've got eyes in the back of my head," she always said, especially if she caught me doing something I wasn't supposed to. And in my early years, I really thought she did. I didn't know then about her glass eye. She wanted it kept secret — had sworn the others to secrecy. I just thought her eyes were scary — and weird.

Granlena and I went shopping every day, because the food had to be fresh. One of the stops we made on our jaunts was a butcher store that was next to a saloon on Gun Hill Road near the Jerome Avenue el. Joe, the butcher, always gave me a slice of bologna to eat "in my hand." He was a square-shaped man with red hands, and the hair on his chest was as thick as a rug.

The day after I had the tea party with the mysterious whisper, Granlena and I had to go to Joe's for a pot roast. "Hello sweeta pie," he said, trying to sound American. "I finda you surprise." Of course, my surprise was the usual slice of bologna. Then he disappeared into his walk-in refrigerator, slamming the door with a double clank.

I looked up at a huge moose head that he had hanging on the side wall which backed onto the saloon next door. The head had fur and ears and antlers, and, therefore, I knew it had to be real. But where was the rest of him? The huge glass eyes followed me. I had never seen eyes as big as these, not even on the elephants in the Bronx Zoo. I had to keep watching to see if he blinked or changed his position. I wanted to be forewarned, should he decide to come crashing through the wall to eat me. None of the customers in the store seemed to notice him. Remarkable. When Joe came out of his refrigerator, I looked up at him and asked, "Is he in the saloon too?"

"Is who inna saloon?" said Joe.

"Him," I said, pointing to the moose. "The other half." Everyone in the store roared, and Granlena told the story at dinner that night, half choking the words out. They squealed through their laughter.

"Oh, how precious!"

"She actually thought —"

"Oh, no — the other half —"

"Had to be in the next store."

"Oh, my God, she really did?"

Why do adults talk about children as if they're not there?

"So you like the moose?" said Aunt Dora.

"Yes," I said. They laughed more. I laughed too. I was supposed to.

"The moose, the moose, here comes the moose." Julie, the youngest aunt, gnarled her fingers above her head to make antlers.

"He can't come here," I said, still smiling.

"Sure he can," said my mother.

"Here moosie, moosie."

"He can't fit," I offered.

"Then he can live in the basement."

Help! Not my precious basement! It had been my castle, my forest, the tunnel of love, a place for rainy day picnics, and best of all, a theater. It did not matter that it was dingy with exposed pipes, bare bulbs, and a torn linoleum floor.

It was not a place for a moose.

But now that a real moose existed and might actually be down there, my basement became a scary place. I often saw the moose's shadow skulking in the corner of the stairway, and once I thought I saw him looking in a window. My own hiding place became something to hide from.

Was it only a trick? I hoped so, because if they were fooling about the moose, maybe they were fooling me about my father too? Could he still be alive somewhere? I looked at faces everywhere. Strangers on the street. People in the stores. In church. My father was not there.

On rainy days, I often watched by the window. I was sure he would just come walking down the street. He would say it had all been a mistake. He would surely be at the dinner table that very night where he belonged — instead of there being that empty space.

I both feared and ached for him: this god who looked at me from the silver frame on my mother's dresser, his hair slicked with Vaseline, his face slicked with the waxiness of the photographer's touch up. Most questions I had about him went unasked. But sometimes I managed to sneak one in . . .

"Honey, don't think about these things."

"You really can't miss him, you know, because you never knew him."

Once I asked the nun who taught me in school. "Don't say your father is 'dead', dear. Say 'deceased'," she said.

"Does that mean he's dead?"

"We must never question God, Christina."

"Can't I even ask you?" I said. "Why can't I know why my daddy had to die? Everybody else I know has a daddy."

"God loves you more than other people. That's why he took away your father. God gives hardships to people he loves the most." What a dirty trick, Sister Mary Liar. All for thee, sweet Jesus, all for thee.

While I jumped around the kitchen and threw

together some chicken salad sandwiches, I memorized the conversation my mother was having with Carter in the living room.

"What made you decide to come here now?" she asked.

"Well, ma'am, a bunch of my buddies were makin' a trip to New York. I never been here, so I came. I told my Uncle Andy, I was comin', and he gave me your address." I came in with my tray of goodies. "Do you know Uncle Andy, Christina? He's our father's brother." Our father? He actually said "our father"! Carter looked back at my mother. "But I sure am sorry, ma'am. I never meant to cause trouble for —"

"Carter, it's not trouble — it's just a long time ago — it's a lot of hurt I already forgot — it's —" She waved away the rest of her sentence with her hand and went into the bedroom.

"My mama married again and had two more kids, so I got two half brothers," Carter told me. "But they're not any more my own than you are. Hell, blood is blood."

"I think this is the best news I've ever heard," I said.

"I got somethin' for you," Carter said. "When my daddy was thirteen, his mama died." He took something out of his pocket wrapped in tissue paper. "This belonged to his mama, but somehow he wound up with it. He gave it to my mama. Or could be she just took it." He unwrapped a beautiful pink and white cameo brooch set in silver. "She never wears it. It just sits in her drawer, so I knew she'd never miss it," he said.

"You mean she doesn't know — you didn't tell her you took it?"

"Hell no, she'd carry on like a banshee if she did. It should be yours. That's why I took it." He put it into my hands.

I could see right into its shiny pinkness, as if my grandmother's face were hidden in its depths, and I was the only one who could see her. I felt like Alice falling through the looking glass. My mother came out of the bedroom and stood watching us. My hands shook, and my lip was sore from biting it. I tried to open the clasp, but pricked my finger with the pin. My mother took the brooch out of my hands and pinned it on me. "It's only right, since you're his only girl," Carter said. My mother hugged me, and then I hugged Carter. I sucked a dot of blood from my finger.

"There was no reason to tell you," my mother said after I had walked Carter to the train. When I returned, she was painting the wooden step ladder in the kitchen. "Because his people were all in the South, I didn't keep in touch with them. You have no idea what it was like. There was the war."

"Well I hate secrets. They make you feel all alone," I said.

"Maybe, but you have to go on keeping them — especially this one." Her brush went back and forth, making a smushing sound.

"Are you kidding?" I said. "No one is going to blame you now."

"Swear it! Swear it to me," she said urgently. "No one will ever know I married a divorced man."

"Okay, okay," I said. "Don't get upset. I'm sorry. How did Granlena let you do it."

"We never told anyone. We just went to the priest and said we wanted to get married."

"Isn't that a sin?"

"I guess. But ignorance is bliss. We didn't know. We just did it, and no one questioned us. Your father's people were all down south. No one knew him up here."

"I still think you should have told me — at least me," I said. "All this time I really had somebody and didn't know it." She bent too close and got some paint in her hair.

"You had me," she said.

Six
℘

I guess it's no accident that the apartment I am now living in is in the same complex as the one my mother and I moved into when I was ten. Here is where I learned the secret of my brother. Perhaps here is where I will now learn more.

I called my brother, Carter, last week, to tell him of my whereabouts and what I hope to do. We have kept in touch over the years with cards and letters, frequently at first, then less often. I also told him about the four Shields I'd found in the Petersburg phone book. He told me that two of them, Andy and Rob, are my father's brothers, and the third one, Henry, is a cousin. He also suggested that I contact my father's sister, Greta Mae Heinz, who also lives in Petersburg. What hot leads! Who knows? If I can get enough information, maybe I can fill a book!

I sit in my beautiful chair, feet up on my coffee table, Mozart on my stereo, and compose letters to all these people, and it occurs to me once again that I love being alone here. If I were writing these letters at home, I would be wondering if anyone were reading over my shoulder, or if my music bothered anyone. Here, I am so free. Ah.

My mother knew what she was doing, back in 1950. She needed to be alone too. But what courage it must have taken! The day after my tenth birthday, amid leftover balloons and crepe paper streamers, she announced at the supper table that she thought we should sell the house. We were eating in the kitchen, because after Aunt Babe left to get married, the five of us could fit comfortably at the kitchen table.

"I, for one, would like to live in an apartment," she said. I remember how she looked at the ceiling when she said it. I remember the silence in the room that followed. I took a big drink of milk.

"Can I have more potatoes?" I said.

"'May I'," corrected Aunt Julie.

"I don't want to live in a house anymore," my mother went on. "In an apartment, you don't have to bother with upkeep. You don't have to shovel snow and rake leaves."

"Give her the potatoes," said Aunt Dora. No one moved.

" — to say nothing of falling shingles and endless paint jobs," she continued. Aunt Dora's chair scraping on the linoleum gave me the shivers. Then she flung it back, stomped to the other end of the table, picked up a spoonful of potatoes and dumped it in my plate.

"For heaven's sake!" she said to everyone but me. "There, Sweetheart, no one seems to notice you at all."

"How could we ever fit in an apartment?" Aunt Julie said.

"Of course. It's ridiculous," said Aunt Dora, eating with one hand and twirling her curls with the other. "We would need a four-bedroom apartment. Do you realize how expensive that would be? All that rent? We have a perfectly good house here. Christina has room to play."

"This house is a rattletrap, Dora," said Aunt Julie. "You know how much work it needs."

My mother pushed a cherry tomato from one side of her plate to the other. I thought of miniature golf. "I wasn't thinking of all of us in one apartment," she said.

"Do you want more milk, Honey?" said Aunt Dora, gazing hard with her good eye.

"No, I can't finish this," I said. Granlena had not said

anything through all this. In fact she had less and less to say as years went on. Her husband had died in 1938, and she had given her power over to her girls. They now made the money that supported the household.

"Oh, you have to finish it," said Dora. "Just take your time." My grandmother looked at my mother and for less than a second, a signal passed between them. I could see that Granlena already knew whatever it was my mother was about to drop. She had tried it out on her already.

"Hold on," said Aunt Julie. "Would someone tell me what is going on here?"

My mother began coughing. She put her hand up as if to say, "Just a minute."

"Take your time and you'll be able to finish your milk," Aunt Dora told me. My mother's cough subsided enough for her to say, "I think it'd be good if Christina and I lived by ourselves . . ."

"Are you crazy?" Aunt Dora squinted at my mother. "Have you gone absolutely crazy? You think you're going to take her away from Granlena?"

"Emelia can do what she wants," said Granlena.

"Oh, sure," said Dora. "What *she* wants. What about what anyone else wants?" I spilled my milk. My mother slapped me.

Dora drank her coffee to hide her quivering lips. "You are positively terrible," she said getting up, her curls and jowls shaking. Then she got up and hurled her cup into the sink smashing it against two others that were already there.

"Dora," Granlena gasped softly, while the others burst into protests of their own.

We had been so happy yesterday while I was opening my birthday presents. Tonight, however — shouts, a slap, and broken cups. My mother went up to bed early. I was allowed out after supper in the summer as long as I came in when it started to get dark. I bolted for the door as soon as Granlena began the dishes. I never had to help with dishes or any phase of housework. Aunt Dora always told me to go and play, and she would "take care of everything" for me, despite my mother's protests.

I waited until it was good and dark before I came in from playing hide and seek. I was surprised no one came out to get me. The lights were dim. On the way to the stairs, I had to pass Aunt Dora's room. The door was partly open, and her voice, hushed and frantic, snatched at me from the dark. "Ssssst, Christina, in here." She lay face down on her bed. How I wanted to run, but I was caught. I stood in the doorway. "In!" she rasped and leaned way out over the bed so she could push the door closed.

"I have to go up," I protested.

"Just for a minute, Christina. Stay here. I'm so blue — sit down for a minute." I did not know what it meant to be "blue," and I was afraid of the electricity in her voice. Then tears gushed out of her with big, cascading boohoo's, and I wanted to bolt.

"Granlena! Can you come in here?" I called, not knowing what else to do with this fallen pillar.

She flung herself up to a sitting position and covered my mouth with her hand. She was now gushing out great puffs of air, and she heaved for control of both of us. She cradled my head. I could not breathe. I could smell her toothpaste.

"Oh, no, no, no, no, no. You must not call Granlena. She must not know I'm blue. We must not upset her. What will she do without you? — when you move, I mean — to a — to a — separate apartment?" She might have said, to a — labor camp or a ward for Black Plague patients. "You must tell your mother that we must never break up the family. I have done so much to make everything work, and now — this!"

"Aunt Dora . . ."

"Tell her that you don't want to go." I was sure I felt her tendril curls grasping me in the dark.

"Aunt Dora, I have to go to the bathroom." She had to let me go for that, so I wriggled away from her. "I'll come back," I lied. I would get Granlena on some pretext and stand outside Dora's door with her. Granlena would tell me to go upstairs, and I would kiss her good night and go up as if I were following orders.

The following February when the temperature was 9 degrees, we left the Bronx behind and moved into two separate apartments here in Bronxville. My mother and I in one. Granlena, Dora, and Julie in the other. Lucky Babe. She was no longer a care, since she had left to get married, and now her husband had to provide for her. Aunt Dora never mentioned anything about that night again.

It wasn't until I was a grown woman that I understood my mother's need to escape.

Seven

Dear Christina,

      I am as pleased as I can be to hear from you. I never in all these years thought I would ever know Carter's daughter. Yes indeed, you have the right person, me, his sister who has missed him all these years. You are just a lamb to write to us, and we have told everybody down here about your letters to me and Uncle Rob and Uncle Andy. They called me right after they heard from you, because they were so excited. You'll be glad to know there are dozens of cousins all still right here in Petersburg. I said I would write the very same day and tell you how pleased we all are, I declare.

      We are so happy to know you, that we are surely hoping you and your family will come to Virginia, the birthplace of your father's family, and be our guests so that you can meet all your relatives, and so we can fill you in on all the information you need to write a book. Now you just say the word and let us know when you're planning to come, so we can show you what Southern hospitality is all about.

With love and deep affection,
Aunt Greta and Uncle Gordon
(who is my husband, another
"new" uncle for you)

I am the one who is "just thrilled" to get this letter which arrived on a Friday, five days after I sent my letter to her. There is only one more week of school, and already I can taste the summer, sweet and free. I call Charles at the office to tell him about my letter.

"That's nice," he says.

"I'd like to go down there as soon as I can. Do you think you can get some time off?"

"This is your cup of tea, not mine, my dear." I hate it when he says "my dear". "I can take time off, but if I do, I don't want to go to Virginia. Bermuda sounds much better."

"Are you sure?"

"What do you need me for?" he asks.

"I thought you might enjoy it."

"Bullshit! You are so fucked up," he thunders. I wonder how many people in his office hear him. "Call it what it is. You don't need my approval for your project, Christina."

"And obviously I don't have it."

"Let's just say you've decided to put a lot of effort into a rather cliché theme."

"Fine, Charles. I'll go by myself," I say, and hang up before he can respond. I wonder if the day will ever arrive when I will be immune to his coldness. When he can say anything he wants and the bottom of my stomach won't fall out. Why must I always hurt in the wake of him? I go to my file drawer and find Daniel's paper napkin. First I put on a new pair of stone washed jeans that I bought yesterday, along with a tee shirt that has a fringe and silver studs all around the neck. Then I dial Daniel's number, certain I will get an answering machine.

"Hi, it's Christina Fitzsimmons," I manage to say when he answers.

"I knew it was you before I answered, and you don't need to announce your last name."

"How did you know?"

"Felt it, I guess. Felt you."

I can't swallow and I'm trembling a little. "I have a very exciting reason for calling you."

"Did you need a reason?" he asks.

"Oh, please don't say that. Something wonderful just happened, and I wanted to tell you . . ." I am still holding Greta's letter in my hand rolling the edge of it into a diagonal straw. I stop myself.

"Christina?" I can't answer for a second. "Are you okay?" he asks. I untwist the letter.

"I'm fine, fine," I say. "I've been — well I guess — you'd call it mourning. I'm not sure what I call it yet. I wrote to my relatives in Virginia and got the most fantastic letter from my father's sister and she — I have it right here in my hand — and —" I have to stop and bite my lip. "Oh, Daniel, it's really remarkable when you think about it. I just get all filled up, and I — it's quite wonderful even though it took forty-odd years for me to make contact with her."

"Still, you did it. Time never matters. Do you know how much I love the way you say 'wonderful'? Where are you anyway?"

"That's another story you don't know about yet. I needed some space, so I took a little apartment, back where my mother and I used to live. I've decided to write a book about him — my father I mean," I say and wonder what he is wearing.

"Wow!" he says. Maybe he is naked.

" — so I wrote to his sister and brothers, and the sister wrote back and invited me down there. Can you imagine? And oh, Daniel, I've already written something. It's not really anything — I mean, it's kind of — just ideas."

"Well, that is just great! Do you think you'd — Christina, I'd love to read it."

"You would?"

"Yes I really would," he says, " — if you want me to. I'm not a writer, but I'm a great reader," he says.

"Shall I send it?"

"Send away, and give me your address there so I can write you back." I do, and then I get all teary-eyed again as I look at Greta's letter. The 4:30 express whistles through the station, and the steady pulsing clack of the wheels drifts up

and into my window. It is the sound of time. Time con-
densed; time pushed together, much faster than it really is,
and I realize that Daniel is wrong — time does matter.

"I'm so nervous about this, because it will probably
take me twenty years to write this book."

"Yes, but think about it. At sixty-five, at least you'll
have a book. Think of all the people who will be sixty-five
with no book."

I guess I have always felt that a woman who has too
much to say is unlovable. Here is someone who urges me to
speak — someone who wants to cherish my words!

"You certainly have a way of looking at life on a slant,"
I say.

"That's me, always ready to fall off the edge."

"You haven't told me how you are."

"Missing you."

"No, I mean really."

"That's really." There is a long pause, because I can't
think of anything to say to that, and neither can he.

"Send me your stuff," he says. "I'll call you as soon as
I read it. Promise!"

If I hurry, I can still make the post office. I do a
faster-than-normal jog there and back. The exercise feels
good, and I resolve to jog every day this summer.

The days pass and the typewriter clicks away. With
only two more days of school left this June, I am dying to get
into my new summer program of writing and exercise. Daniel
must have my manuscript by now. I wonder what he thinks
of it? Oh, God. Does he know how terrifying it is to let
someone read what you've written? What if he hates it? I
might just die. I speed home to my apartment after school,
change into my sweats and run to the track at the local high
school. I can jog one and a half miles before I feel tired.
Then I walk for two miles, and then walk home.   Today   I
am feeling more energized than ever, probably because of my
imminent freedom from work. I turn the corner, brush past
the tall pine trees in front of my building, and take my keys
out of my back pocket. I lean against the outside door with
my hip, looking down to check the key, and as I turn in to the

lobby steps, I stop short to avoid falling over someone sitting on the entrance steps. Daniel!

"Oh, my God."

"Surprise!"

"Daniel, you really are incredible!"

"No I'm not. I just needed a hug."

And he is holding me, running his hand up and down my back, as we stand in the empty lobby which echoes with a hollow note even when there is no sound.

"So you came three thousand miles for one?"

"Isn't it worth it?" he says.

"Yes," I say. "Oh, yes."

Eight
𝓅

"We'd better go upstairs," I say.

"Not till I finish my hug. I promise not to hug you once we get up there. I won't be able to stop." He kisses my cheek. Then he holds me at arm's length. "You're all wet," he says.

"Jogging."

"Makes you even more sensuous." He has a certain music that swirls around me like an aura. He bends over to pick up a small suitcase. "Actually I had an appointment for a big show at the Waldorf this afternoon. I'm staying at my brother's, but I came here first." We get on the elevator.

I say something inane, like, "Oh, that's nice. I bet he'll be glad to see you." As if I were feeling perfectly normal. As if I were not about to die from the ecstasy of being near him. I am a teenager with a corsage. I have light, jumpy feelings I never thought I could have again. We go into my apartment. The ice cubes are back in my stomach.

"Hey, I like that," he says looking at my seven-hundred dollar, well-curled wicker chair. He traces the filigree pattern with his finger, and I wish he were touching me.

"It was my one extravagance," I say. I can still feel his hand running up and down my back, the rasp of his half-day whiskers on my cheek.

"Look at that will you?   Only you would buy a chair like this."

"I bought it in a little shop in New York."   I want to kiss him lingeringly and then with fiery passion.

"It's a queen's chair.   It's a fan," he says sitting in it.

"Or a peacock's tail.   I just love it."   I want him to rip my clothes off.   My nipples start to itch.   I yearn for his hands on them.   Oh, God.   "Would you like a drink, or something?" I have not so much as looked at another man in twenty years.   Nor have I felt this way for at least eighteen.

"Go take your shower.   I'll help myself.   Then let's go eat somewhere," he says.   A train blows its whistle and beats its way downtown.   "Wow, you get to hear the trains here.   I like that."

"So do I," I say.   Then I make sure the shower is good and cold.

I pray my hair comes out right, and that I can do a good makeup job without taking too long.   He is listening to a trumpet concerto on my stereo when I come out of the bedroom.   His head is back, and his eyes are closed.

"I think I just had a hearing orgasm," he says half to Maurice Andre, half to me.   "I wonder what it feels like to be able to play like that?"

"Probably like you just had a baby."

We drive up to the Tappan Zee Bridge.   The river looks solid as we cross it, mosaicked by the falling sun into a giant strip of marcasite.   Finally we stop at a dark Chinese restaurant in Nyack that overlooks the Hudson.

He clinks my tea cup with his and tells me that I'm beautiful.   Then he says, "Here's to your father, and letting go of him.   How's the book coming?" He suddenly produces my manuscript and puts it on the table.   Where did he have it? Can he pull rabbits out of hats too?

"I thought you'd never ask," I say, trying to act cool.

"I am not going to comment on anything you sent me, because everything you need is here."   He holds up my work.

How did he get it in here without my seeing it? It is still in the envelope that I mailed to him. "Just do it," he says. I cannot eat.

"You really think it's okay?"

"I know so. But you still have to do it."

"Now I'll have the time to work. Tomorrow is my last day of school." The waiter asks me if everything is all right. He looks offended at my nearly full plate.

"The lady is anorexic," Daniel says. "I'm her therapist and we're working on it. I can assure you, I have everything under control." The waiter turns on his heel. "Serves him right for being rude. Want a doggie bag?"

The waiter returns with fortune cookies and oranges after the bus boy has cleared the table. "Maybe you can redeem yourself by eating your fortune cookie," Daniel says.

"Pick it for me."

"I'll not only pick it, I'll read your fortune, how's that?" He pulls out the little slip of paper. "You'll never believe this one. Wow! How do you like that! It says 'Dear Christina.'" I burst out laughing, and he holds it up for me to see, but manages to cover the words. "I swear that's what it says. But wait — it gets better: 'You have to go to bed tonight with the man sitting next to you.'" And the more I choke, the more he is serious. "Would I lie about a thing like that?"

"Oh, Daniel," I finally manage to get out. "You're wonderful."

Through a coal-black night, I drive him to his brother's house. I leave the motor running, and I don't look at him as he reaches back for his suitcase. "I'll see you tomorrow?" he says.

"Is that a question?" He takes my left shoulder in his right hand and turns me toward him. Kissing him is like swimming into a dark euphoric place. We sink together for a long time. His tongue is electrifying. Then I am drowning, and I try to break away. He lets me go, but his energy stays inside me, resounding like a whole note.

"Oh, how I want to make love to you. You are the most sensational woman."

"I'm sorry. I just can't. Not until I decide what is

going to happen with my marriage."

"I'll call you," he says and closes the door. I do not look up. I wonder how I can drive. The car moves without me. I somehow get back to my apartment.

After another shower, I lie awake for hours. A thought echoes over and over in my head. I cannot see him again. I am blinded by my spiraling feelings and have no idea what is happening. I remind myself that I am still married. No. I cannot see him. I have to stop the panic I feel rising up through my windpipe. The next morning I call school to say I won't be in. I have already said good-bye to my students, because yesterday was their last day. I will miss saying good-bye to my colleagues, but this is infinitely more important.

I must get away from Daniel.

At eight o'clock, I call my "new" aunt in Virginia. She is delighted to hear from me, and says that I can come any time at all.

"I'd like to take you up on that and be there tonight," I say. "And I want to take you and Uncle Gordon out to dinner."

"Well, we would sure love that, but I'm afraid Uncle Gordon would never let you pay for his dinner. You know how men are," she says giggling. "Now why don't you just come on down, and we can talk about that when you get here." She puts him on the phone to give me directions. "Men folk love to give directions, I declare," she says before she leaves the phone. I feel like I am in *Gone With the Wind*.

Then I call Daniel, and his brother answers. I just missed Daniel. He is out jogging. I tell him that I'm leaving in a few minutes.

"I'm sorry to be so abrupt, but something came up and I have to leave for Virginia."

"He'll be very disappointed." Has Daniel told him about me?

"Well, it's beyond my control," I say.

"How are you getting there?" his brother asks.

"I'm going to drive."

"Well, good luck. That's a long drive to take by yourself."

*   *   *

I finish packing and remember to take pictures of my daughter out of the album to show Aunt Greta. Then I call my husband and leave a message on the machine telling him where I am going. But my own phone does not ring.

Before I get on the highway, I stop at the corner florist and buy a pink azalea in full bloom for my aunt. The florist wedges it in a cardboard box, which I then wedge in between the seats on the floor in the back. I hope she likes it, and from the sound of her, I think my gift is a safe bet. I try to picture her face when I arrive. Will I look like her?

By nine o'clock, I am well on my way. Lucky for me the Henry Hudson Parkway is finished with the commuter traffic. I approach the toll booth that separates the Bronx from Manhattan and see young men selling the *Times* and the *Daily News*. They stand just ahead of the little dividers that divide the cars into the toll lanes. They wear little multipocketed aprons for making quick change. "Paypa, paypa!" they chant. I have my money for the toll counted out in my hand. "Paypa!" I drop a quarter on the floor of the car and am now in big trouble, because I am in an exact-change lane. I stop. Horns blow. I rummage in my purse for another quarter. Nothing. The paper boys are laughing. Something is wrong. I see a man who looks like Daniel cross the lanes of cars toward me, papers in his hand. More horns blow. In my rear-view mirror, the woman behind me is giving me the finger. Then I see the man who was crossing the lanes again. It *is* Daniel! He hands his papers to one of the kids and jumps into the car. He holds out a handful of change.

"Here, go through." I take the change and the drama of the toll booth is over. "I called your house and got your machine." The hollows in his face go in and out, because he is out of breath. He fills every inch of the car with his spirit.

"There is nobody like you in the world. How did you know where to —"

"My brother told me you were driving, so I gambled that you had to come this way. I had to buy a stack of the kids' papers. I had to sell them or the cops would've chased me." He leans his head sideways on the back of the seat. "Boy, was I glad to see you."

"But what a chance to take!" I say.

"I know. But I like chances," he grins. "We now have at least eight hours with no interruptions. That should give you enough time to come up with an answer — why you are ducking out on me." His long legs make his knees angle high. "Besides I can leave from Richmond airport just as easily as from Kennedy."

"How did you get to the toll booth?"

"My brother drove me."

"Don't you think it's a little strange?"

"I had to see you before I went back. How else could I have caught you?"

"I don't know what to make of you."

"If you want me to leave, you can drop me off before you get on the bridge and I'll take a cab to Kennedy."

"Daniel —"

"Just say the word, and I'll go. Otherwise, you'll have company for your trip. Do you want to be alone?"

"No."

"Good. You can tell me anything you feel like saying. You can talk about your book, where the moon was hiding last night, or the symbolism of the unicorn tapestries." He takes my hand and kisses it. "But I would like you to include why you want to get away from me. As soon as we get on the Jersey Turnpike, let's stop for breakfast. Want me to drive?"

Nine

He seems much more laid back than he was last
night. So am I. He is almost detached. I look at his mouth.
It is as if the kiss never happened. Now there is the tension
of something left unsaid.   I am both relieved and
disappointed. We talk about any number of things, including
the relatives I will visit now, and, yes, even the unicorn
tapestries which we both love and will visit together "some
day." But we avoid the subject of "us." He finds a classical
station and the notes of Schubert slide through the car and
slowly heal the tension we feel. We are almost into Delaware
when a peaceful feeling settles around us like a cloak.   I
reach over and take his hand. The heaviness is gone. He
tells me that when he was in the army guarding Panama, his
buddies used to put baby boa constrictors inside their shirts
to be macho.

"But you're not macho."

"I was eighteen."

"What do you mean?"

"I played the jock-locker-room-mentality game that
lots of guys get into," he says. "Men are really different when
there're no women around."

"Are you saying you put a snake in your shirt too?"

"Of course."

"Daniel!"

"Come on, Christina, didn't you ever do something you've regretted?"

The comfortable conversation is gone, and a terrible memory has taken over.   Something I've regretted?   He should only know!   I see my daughter's face aghast and wretched.   A hateful scene keeps trying to creep out of the dark text of my mind, so strong I can hear it, grating like nails on a blackboard.

"Nothing I can talk about," I say.   "I'd much rather forget about it." I smile trying to push it back in.

"But that's probably what you should be writing about."

"Great idea," I say and hope that's the end of it.

"Well?

"Well, what?"

"What is it?"

"Oh, you mean now? Why do you want to know? Is it so important?" The car speeds along the tawny road. Woods rush by us.   Melissa's face comes back — a ghost in the trees, startling and calling me.   Stop! We approach the Delaware River, reflecting silvery, fierce one o'clock sun.

"It isn't so much that I want to know. I am thinking of it from the point of view of exercise," he says.   "Joyce Carol Oates is a marvelous technician, but I always had the feeling that she doesn't write about things that really touch her. Then I heard her talk about her autistic sister, and I knew my instincts were right.   How come nothing like autism is ever in her books?"

"Are you saying that only subjects that hurt are worth writing about?"

"No, but neither do I think you should leave your guts out of your work. Judging from the way you looked a few minutes ago, and the way you were grinding at that wheel, I think we hit a nerve."

Then I see my husband, lips shaking with anger — way out of control.   "Well, I guess I'll have to try it the next time I face my typewriter."   My own face next appears, powerless, shamed.

"Good idea," he says. He looks at me hard and then turns his gaze out the window graciously backing off. We have passed over the river, and now the woods have taken over the scenery again. I will not look at them. I force my eyes straight ahead, burning the road. I am glad he isn't looking at me. The face of my child will fade if I can get something else going. What? A singalong wouldn't fit in somehow. I forage for a new subject. It will not take shape. I try again, but the nightmare clings like tar. Daniel why did you do this to me? He is still looking out the window. The chord he struck pounds in my head like someone playing wrong notes on the piano. I put on the right hand signal and move over into the right lane.

"I have to stop," I say. He is around me like a fence.

"Okay, ease onto the shoulder and slow." We come to a stop with nothing but trees and bushes for company.

"I'm sorry," I say and reach for tissues in my purse. He holds me and says nothing, as I continue to sob.

Finally I say, "I — I'm getting you — all wet," and try to pull away, but he won't let go. I am still gasping for breath.

"Do you know how long you hold someone when they cry?" he asks. And then, he answers his own question, "As long as it takes."

After a while, the ghosts subside. He touches my hair in soft caresses to calm me. He helps me out of the car and we stand under a willow tree.

"Do you want to tell me?" he asks, touching the leaves.

"No — yes. Do you think I can tell you without it hurting all over again?"

"No." He touches the leaves to my cheek.

"I mean, will it stop hurting after I say it?"

"I don't think anything stops hurting when it's a missing piece. Obviously you have some resolving to do."

"There are no excuses for what happened to Melissa," I say when we get back in the car. "There are lots of reasons, but none of them count. Reasons never amount to much when someone is terribly hurt. Counselors tried to say it was his background that made him treat her the way he did. His mother beat him when he was little. Held his hand over a flame. Held his head under water when he was only five.

That's why he is the way he is. But it really doesn't matter.
If a man abuses his child, it is a crime, and the causes of his
behavior don't cancel out the scars he leaves behind. Not one
bit.

"It probably sounds melodramatic to say that Charles
hated Melissa for most of her life, but it appeared that way to
me and, certainly, to her. If he had any love for her, he had a
funny way of showing it.

"I fit myself into their relationship, forming a triangle
to protect her, but I buckled under the burden of it. How
could a real live in-the-flesh father feel hostile toward his
daughter? I did everything I could to make sure it wasn't
real. I told her how he bragged about her when she was not
present. How much he loved her. I also did everything
possible to make her pleasing to him. I concealed her
shortcomings, choreographed her activities to include special
surprises for Daddy. I cut her hair short, because he said he
liked it that way. I was the ever-ready buffer, the remover of
pain. But I wasn't vigilant enough. She cried almost every
day of her life in the younger years, because of his emotional
cruelty. I dug in, came up with new plans, prayed, got him to
go for counseling, knew it would get better.

"The counseling lasted for about three or four ses-
sions. But I never gave up. Instead I looked for a new plan.
To the outside world, he was charming and kind. People
envied me. I fulfilled the precepts of how to raise a man,
given to me by my female role models. They were careful that
I learn the ten commandments of the care and feeding of this
creature who alone could bring me ultimate happiness.

"'Don't ever argue with a man when he comes home
after a hard day,' Aunt Julie had said when I got married. 'He
has enough competition in the world. He shouldn't have to
compete with you too.'

"Before Melissa was born, he had announced to me
that I would never love him as much after she came. That's
the way it was in his family; ergo, that's the way it must be
with everyone. I was shocked and saddened at this procla-
mation of programmed doom. I made a mental note to work
out a schedule of doing extra things for him, so he wouldn't
feel shortchanged.

"I remember one day, after she had eaten breakfast,

she left the butter out on the kitchen table. It had melted in the sun. He put his face right up to hers and screamed as loud as he could — over and over, until she became faint. 'Don't ever grow up like your mother. She never puts things away. Do you hear me?' I came in on the middle of this.

"Her hands were in front of her face, She was close to hysteria, bawling, 'Okay, Daddy, okay,' over and over. He stopped when I came in. I took her into the bathroom to wash her face. My heart turned over. I wished I could have died. Truly wished it.

"These terrible events did not happen every day. But when something did occur, I would go into a depression for several days. I could not bring myself to talk to Charles about them. When he was out, I always rehearsed what I was going to say; but when he came home, I froze. If I provoked him, he might scream at me too, and I could not bear it. If I said nothing, maybe I'd be safe. I also wanted to protect Melissa from knowing I was unhappy.

"'Don't ever argue in front of your children,' said Granlena long ago. 'They should never know you don't agree.' I kept silent for years.

"After an incident of screaming at her for some trivial thing, Charles was always cheerful and kind. He often brought home a special treat, served it with a flourish, and whistled his way around the house. I was obsessed with worry about the effects of all this on Melissa. But then I would come up with a new plan. I found a course called Parent Effectiveness Training. Thirty-six hours of how to become ideal parents. Charles got an A. Knew all the techniques and could practice them flawlessly on any member of the class. But he could not do them at home.

"Each panacea helped for a short time, but then it was business as usual. Over the years, we went to two other family counselors. But after two or three visits, Charles would not continue. I kept praying. Meanwhile Melissa and I were in private therapy.

"By the time Melissa was a teenager, my efforts to make her think that her father really did love her no longer were successful. I slipped into a new pattern in the triangle. The most I could hope for was to try to keep them away from each other. I tried to induce her to stay out of his way and have as little contact with him as possible. Often it was in vain. It appeared as if she needed some response from him, even a negative one.

"When Melissa was seventeen, she was dating a boy whom Charles hated. He did everything he could to thwart their efforts to see each other. When he found out they were sleeping together, he was wild. 'You don't exist as far as I'm concerned, do you hear that?' he shrieked at her. 'You don't exist!' Then he became very calm. 'I'm divorcing you,' he said. 'If a person can divorce their spouse, why can't I divorce my child? Well, I guess I can.'

"'You bastard!' she said and ran out of the room. He chased her down the hall and hit her so hard, she fell to the floor. I ran behind them. I yelled for him to stop. He had her by the back of the head and pushed her face into the floor so hard — that he — he broke — her nose before I could pull him off her." And I cry all over again.

"The doorbell rang," I continued. "Melissa and I went to her room and cried while he entertained his mother in the kitchen. We were beaten — two women without fathers — from my father who did not exist to hers who tried to make her nonexistent. 'I guess it's time for me to leave home,' Melissa said when she stopped crying. I knew what it was like to be fatherless, and a loving father was the thing I wanted most for my daughter."

"How much of this are you blaming on yourself?" Daniel asks.

"The next day I took her to the doctor. She had to have plastic surgery to repair her face. Charles never spoke of it again. Never even came to see her when she was in the hospital."

I stare out the window for a while. The trees are beautiful — comforting. Then I look back at Daniel who touches my hand and smiles at me. "I've told you his crime," I say. "Mine was that I covered it up. I never exposed him. We told everyone that Melissa fell. I should have protected her from him, starting long, long ago. I blame myself for the lengths I went to hide his cruelty — to neutralize the shame of it, draw a shroud around her pain. If only I had brought it out in the open, the course of our lives would have been so different, and he might have gotten the help he needed too."

"Why do you suppose you're telling me this?"

"Because it's never been told. Because I have always kept the secret of him."

"Just as the secret of your father was kept from you."

"Oh, my God — that's it, isn't it?"

"Could be," Daniel says with such gentleness that I know I love him.

"But I really don't want to face this dragon."

"Yes, I know. 'If onlys' are easy to say. It's much harder to stare down the dragon, as you say."

"I'm sure you think I'm crazy for staying with this man. I wish I could tell you why. Every time I think of leaving him, I go into a kind of terror, and cannot even bear the thought of it. I can't explain it — it's like it's a kind of death."

"But now you have left."

"Not really. We still see each other. Still say it's only temporary. Please don't condemn me for it."

"Have I?" he asks as he speeds through Maryland.

"No, I have."

"I see, well, then you must stop doing that," he says, and we are both silent. Then he asks, "What happened to Melissa after that?"

"I sent her away to my aunt's for the summer, and the following fall she went away to college. She's still trying to heal. Therapy twice a week. I talk to her often. She's trying to forgive us both."

"What does she have to forgive you for?"

"Covering up. That's the roughest part. I thought I was the good parent. I was kind and loving to her, but I still get blamed anyway. Her father was so mean to her and still is. Yet she blames me for not stopping him — for not protecting her from him. But you know, I guess she's right, and that's what hurts the most — my own guilt."

"Why do you suppose he felt such hostility for her?"

"Do you believe in evil?"

"I'm not sure. Maybe it's that simple. Maybe it's his own unresolved oedipal schtick. We had someone in our family like that. The point is, it makes them behave badly and they have no idea why."

"I think Charles is very ill."

"Do you think therapy is the answer?"
"Not if he won't go."

Ten
℘

When we get out of the air-conditioned car at Richmond Airport, the heat assaults us, and we both start to perspire. I agree to call him when I return to New York. Sweat beads on his upper lip, and I taste it when he kisses me good-bye.

"Let's not fall in love," he says. "It's going to make this so complicated." We kiss again. How come I feel his lips in my groin as well as on my mouth?

"We won't," I say, and gasp for air.

The drive to Petersburg is quick and easy, and I am soon parked in front of my aunt's house. It is a sprawling brick ranch set back from the road, with lots of glass everywhere, including a huge, pitched skylight. The street is quiet with sidewalks and an assortment of huge trees. Not exactly what I pictured a house in the South to look like. Did I expect a plantation with fat columns and fields of cotton, my aunt rushing to greet me in a ruffled hoop skirt? I sit for a minute with the motor on, wondering why I am not going in. Crape myrtles on front lawns, much older than the houses they frame, twist their fat branches and raucous-pink clusters around themselves. Were these same trees here when my father was alive?

In the front window, a curtain parts, and a moment

later the front door opens. A tiny woman in a coral sundress and with an enormous amount of auburn hair comes down the front steps. I get out of the car and get slapped again by the heat. She walks very straight, smiling broadly, but there is an energy about her that swirls around her head and eyes.

"Well, my stars, you are a beauty. How you look like Carter!" Aunt Greta says. We hug as comfortably as people who've known each other a long time.

A round man who must be Uncle Gordon stands just inside the doorway. "Look at that," he says. "Look at that!" And he bounds out the door. He is gray-haired with a huge stomach, fleshy jowls, and a mustache in the shape of a bracket. "You two just fit like a cup and saucer," he says. "Little lady, we are just as pleased as punch to have you here." He is wearing a pair of huge, striped Bermuda shorts which stick out around his skinny legs like awnings.

"Hello, Uncle Gordon," I call as he bounces down the steps.

"I kept telling Greta," he punches his words out like bullets, "I wasn't sure you'd come, but lo and behold, here you are." He kisses me and then squeezes me against his stomach in a bear hug. "Couldn't imagine a lady drivin' all that way by herself."

"He thinks we're made of china, I'm afraid," says Greta, laughing at her husband.

"But I made it, didn't I?" I try to catch my breath. He picks up my bag in one hand and holds my hand in his other.

"Well, you surely did, but I was just positive you'd be changing your mind. Thought the phone was gonna ring all day long."

"Christina sure surprised you, but not me. I knew she was coming." We walk into the house, which is decorated all in pastels with lots of flowers everywhere.

"Greta, you call them," Gordon says. "Call those brothers of yours and say we got a real, new, flesh-and-blood relation here, even if she is a Yankee."

"I declare!" says Greta. "Isn't he the limit!"

"When we finish our dinner, they should come over and meet her. How's that sound to you, Miss Christina?"

"It sounds just fine!" I say and kiss him on the cheek.

Imagine! "Miss" Christina!

"I even came home early from work," Gordon goes on.

"And for him to do that — you know it's a special occasion for us," Greta laughs.

"Now, Greta, you know I can't take time away from the business. I own it myself. I'm in parts, Miss Christina. That means I buy machinery for all manner of comp'nies." He wipes sweat from his brow with his handkerchief in spite of the air-conditioning, his sausage fingers sliding over his face. "Last few years, though, my business sure has changed. Everything's Japanese now. Hah! fifty years ago I was shootin' at 'em, now I buy all my parts from 'em. Dirty Japs — don't ever trust one. That's my advice. I can tell you —"

The phone rings, and Greta picks it up. "Well, yes, she sure enough is. It's Rob," she says covering the phone for a second. "Carter's daughter sitting here in my kitchen, just as pretty as she can be. She has his dark red hair, you know." Carter's daughter! No one ever said that before. At least not in front of me.

From where I sit in the kitchen, I can see an enormous mantel clock that looks very old. Gordon follows my gaze while Greta talks to Rob.

"Sure is something, idn't it?" he says, and walks me into the living room. "Here now, we'll make it put on the show for you." He opens the glass dial that covers the face and pushes the hour hand to six. "It's what you call an automaton clock. 'Jever see one?" The chimes ring out mellow and warm, but then two figures, one a knight on horseback, the other a dragon, pop out of trap doors above the dial to face each other in combat. The knight rides forward across a parapet and slays the dragon who tips over and falls through a third trap door below.

·I am spellbound, not only by the delightful surprise of the moving figures, but by something deeper — by the sheer determination of the whole spectacle. Whoever made this must have been so fascinated by evil that he had to create something to overcome it twenty-four times a day.

"How wonderful!" is all I can think of to say. I cannot express to them how moved I am by this masterpiece — this embodiment of success that I wish I could muster in my own life.

"Sure is," says Gordon.

"I can't imagine —" I say. "I mean, I've never seen anything like this —"

"'Course not," he says. "Ain't ever been another like this before. Only one of a kind."

"Your great-grandfather (on my mother's side) was a clock maker and gave this to his bride for a wedding gift, back in Germany." Greta joins in. "See here is his name. The story goes that he made his wife carry all the bags, so he could carry the clock when they came here. Years later, he gave it to my mother and father, soon after they were married, and they engraved Daddy's name under grandpa's."

"But there are no more names," I say. "My father was the first son in the generation after that. Shouldn't his name be there next?"

"Well, his first marriage was kind of peculiar, if you follow what I say," says Gordon. "So he never did get the clock. Andy and Rob didn't seem to mind when Greta got it."

"They didn't care whose it was — so long as Bessie didn't get it," Greta cuts in.

"Who's Bessie?" I ask.

"By God, we keep forgettin' she don't know nothing about this family," Gordon says. "Little lady, you are just going to have to be patient, because sure as I'm standing here, I promise you you'll know as much as you want to before you go on home."

Oh, my dear, dear father! How much must it have hurt you not to get this clock? Was it that you could not succeed in overcoming your own dragons? Will I be able to slay mine?

I try to ask only questions that politeness will allow, and we talk forever through the meal. A story starts to write itself in my head, and I try to slow down my racing thoughts. I decide to sit back and let things unfold.

"The farm where we grew up is not far from here, and we can take you there tomorrow if you like," Greta says. "None of the farming rubbed off on us — except for Rob. Your father hated it — that's for sure. Gordon, fetch me the cream pie in the refrigerator, will you?" She pours coffee. "Or maybe we should have it when the boys get here. Anyway, he and Mama always locked horns over his chores.

Young as I was, I do remember that. He was just a city boy, I guess."

"Couldn't help himself — just like I can't help making money offa the Japs," Gordon says. "What goes around, comes around."

Uncle Rob arrives on the tail end of Gordon's joke, and I am thrilled to see him. He is the youngest brother, still a farmer although he is stiff with arthritis, and looks the most like my father. Puffing constantly on a Camel, he moves and talks in slow motion. I like him immediately. He has slicked his gray crew cut with hair tonic, and it is clear that he is wearing his Sunday best — a black suit that has a hanger mark outlined in dust across the shoulders, heavy black spit-shined shoes, white shirt, and black bow-tie. I can smell the Old Spice and Brylcreem as he kisses me and then holds me at arm's length.

"Well, I never saw the likes of you nohow, nowhere!" he drawls. "Did you ever imagine Carter to have such a beauty? Greta, put some more lights on, so I can see her clear in these eyes." Although his speech is soft and slow, he doesn't pause and holds everyone's attention. Especially mine. "Why is it so danged dark in here? And where do you s'pose is brother Andy? How's about a little bourbon, Gordon? Andy has to see this to believe it. Don't it just kinda make you wish you were twenty years younger?"

"Rob, I think you had better give Christina a little breathing room," Greta cuts in, "before you scare her away from us. After all, she did come down here for a very important reason, and —" The door bell interrupts her, and I get to meet the last brother, Uncle Andy. It is amazing how all three of them resemble each other, and yes, how I resemble them too. Andy is the tallest and wears a blue short-sleeved shirt and navy slacks. His hair is almost white, and his eyes a deep gray.

"Can you believe this, Brother?" says Rob. "Look at this Doll Baby hidden away all these years way up there in Yankee country."

"Brother Rob can slow things down a bit," Andy says. "Pay him no mind. Greta tells me you came here to find out about your father, and I think that is the grandest thing that can happen in this family. Of course, there may be certain things come as a surprise to you." He turns to Greta. "Have you filled her in on any of the dirt?" Greta gives him a frozen smile and shakes her head. "Well, now don't you worry." He turns back to me. "Everything will be just fine."

"So long as I do most of the talking," Rob interrupts. "So long as I tell her the Bessie part."

"All in good time, Rob," Greta says.

"Why can't we all tell her?" says Gordon. "We can all take a turn with Bessie, and Miss Christina'll have several points of view, you follow?"

"It really isn't necessary to dwell on unpleasant things, Rob," Greta says. She fusses with some dried flowers on the table next to where she sits. "There are so many good things we can tell her — about our mama and all. And there's no reason for anyone to be embarrassed, is there? Why there must be dozens of other stories besides — besides the Bessie one." She forces her smile to continue. "Oh, I don't know — this is getting to be so confusing —"

Uncle Andy tries to take charge. "No, no, no, Greta this is a very good thing — of course we aren't going to dwell on anything unpleasant, but sooner or later she has to know. Everyone has to remember there are certain rules of discretion —"

"'Smatter, Brother Andy? Christina ain't no damn reporter," says Rob. "You don't have to keep smiling at her like that. She ain't gonna put you on television."

"Now boys," Greta says.

"Better behave yourself," says Uncle Gordon. Good grief. Are all these lil' ol' relatives fightin' ovah lil' ol' me?

"You want to find out the true story, Doll Baby? I'll tell you everything you need to know. But I ain't gonna tell you while Smilin' Jack here is in the same room with me." The bourbon must be working.

"Listen, Rob —" Andy tries.

"Don't go listenin' Robbin' me," Rob cuts in. "You want to tell her your version? Fine and dandy, boy. I'll just be outa here. But let me tell you, Doll Baby." He switches gears and talks right into my face. "I'll be here tomorrow, eleven-thirty, and I'm taking you out to lunch. Hope y'all don't mind riding in my pickup, because that's all I got now. I'll show you where we grew up and where we got in trouble.

And when I get through, you'll know all the secrets he . . ." he points in Andy's face without even looking at him " . . . he won't even think of telling you."

Then he inches out of his chair, oozes the rest of the liquor down his throat, and walks in slow motion to the door. No one else says a word. "'Bout time we did some real talking. Evenin' Greta, Gordon. Thanks for your hospitality and for letting me see the best thing my eyes ever laid on since I had me that blond vixen between my third wife and the one I got now."

He opens the door and turns back into the room. "What was her name? Vivian I think. Tomorra, Doll Baby, eleven-thirty. Be ready." The door closes behind him, and the silence in the room is so heavy, it feels as if I am bumping up against it even to make the tiniest move.

"Now don't you bother about him," Greta finally says, clearing her throat. "He is just a heap of talk. Believe me, that's all. Let's have our coffee and pie and look at the photos. He'll forget everything by tomorrow."

"Right you are," adds Andy. "Rob is a bit peculiar sometimes." He has brought pictures of my father that I have never seen. He rubs the dusty front of an album with his handkerchief. Then Greta brings out her pictures along with coffee and her cream pie, and the four of us converse easily now that Rob is gone. I learn that their mother died quite unexpectedly when my father was only thirteen, and that he ran away two years later and joined the army.

"He's here," Andy says pointing to a large photo of the four of them. "See if you can pick him out." Of course I do — in a second. There he is — head back, leaning against a tree.

"He's the only one smiling," I say.

"He put on a good show. He was probably dying inside, because this was taken the night after my father's second marriage. The rest of us showed how sad we really were," Greta says. "I'll tell you something else about your father," she goes on. "He ran away plenty, and we never knew where he was or when he was coming back. But you always knew it when he was home!"

"He was a noisy one," Andy cuts in.

"Lots and lots of laughing when he was around," Gordon says. They go on to tell me the major events of his life, ending with his death at age thirty, but all their stories are without any bridges. He served his stint in the army in Texas, but no one knows how he got there. I begin to realize that I will probably have to make up the transitions on the basis of what they tell me.

No further mention is made of "Bessie," whoever she was, and I decide it wise not to ask. At this point, I am painfully tired, and somehow I know Rob is going to show up tomorrow and tell me much more of what I need to know.

I say goodnight to them about eleven o'clock and go to my room, my head spinning with the tune of southern accents and the vision of all the grinning sepia faces in the photographs. I take some aspirin, and change into a night-gown, aching with exhaustion. But sleep will not come.

Finally, I jump up, grab a notebook from my suitcase, and write everything I can think of — all my impressions of the evening in a hell-broke-loose fashion, just to get rid of the ghosts. I had felt a strange sense of the past listening to them talk, and the pictures of them as children helped me to enter into their lives. Then my eyes grow heavy, and I am barely able to turn out the light before I slip away.

Toward morning, I awake with a start thinking someone is in my room. I put the light on and sit up out of breath. Without getting up, I hang my head over the bed and look under it, but nothing is there. Then I get up and open the closet. It is empty. Since there are no other hiding places, I lie down again, and turn out the light. The room has an eerie pale gray light, and I close my eyes to shut it out. Soon I am asleep again and I feel myself beginning to dream.

First I am floating above the ground in my nightgown, afraid that people will be able to see my nakedness under it. I try to pull it down, but the wind keeps whipping it. I start to fall and am terrified. Then I am in a house that feels like the one in the Bronx where I grew up. I walk down a long hallway toward a mirror that covers the wall straight ahead of me. The terror closes in on me like tires screeching in the night, because I cannot see my reflection no matter how deeply I peer into it. I can see the sconces on the stucco wall, the moldings and the oriental runner racing in perspective into the mirror, but I am not there at all. I run upstairs into my tiny bed, and listen for footsteps. Is Death on the prowl, coming up the stairs for me, while my mother stays on the first floor, laughing with her sisters, having no idea of my orphaned state? The phone rings, and I can hear my mother again talking to my father on the other end.

"Oh, no," I say out loud. "Please don't make me dream this again." But it goes right on. I can somehow see him standing in a phone booth, his forearm against the glass, his legs crossed, his dark hair falling on his forehead as he talks. He is asking even more questions about me, and I am delighted. "Give me, give me," I say to my mother, trying to get the phone away from her.

"Stop," she says. "I can't hear him. Be quiet." I start to cry in absolute despair, and then — Help! — the phone melts into a huge dragon, hot and wet, and oozing all over my bed.

"No!" I cry out. "Oh, God, no!" And I wake up sobbing out loud, quickly realizing where I am and hoping no one has heard me.

Then I remember that Uncle Rob is coming later.

Maybe he can make the longing go away.

Eleven

℘

A change in the wind lifts the humidity, and the next morning brings a glorious day. Uncle Rob arrives at eleven twenty-five in his haze of smoke. He is just as bold as he was the night before — even without the liquor. First he takes me on a tour of the area where they all grew up. I see the Mill Pond where they swam in summer, the roads they walked, the schoolhouse they attended, and I find myself expecting to see my father in his knickers and cap around every bend.

Then he takes me to the tiny graveyard next to Lunt's Church to see his parents' grave, quite a different place from the cemetery where my father is buried. Lush greenery hangs low and fragrant, making filigree patterns on inch-thick tombstones. They stand guard in frail, crooked arches, leaning almost in caricature, marking the lives and the pasts they cover.

And finally I see the names chiseled in the gray limestone — two waist-high monuments side by side, leaning in a little as if they'd like to catch a glimpse of each other:

Emma Rose Ruden Shields
July 13, 1894 — May 23, 1924

Barret Carter Shields
August 10, 1889 — December 25, 1933

"My mama was a pretty lady," he says. "And everybody knew I was her favorite." I start to laugh at what I think
is his joke, but then I see he is dead serious. He reads my
look of skepticism and says, "I was! It's true. I sure liked it
then, but when I grew up I realized how tough she could be
on the others — especially Carter. He was so dang stubborn,
your father, and the more he tried to please her, the more he
flubbed it up. I guess he was jealous of me. Only time he
was nice was the night she died."

He takes a mean drag on his cigarette, holding it with
his thumb and forefinger. "And there she lies. See them
flowers. Greta always kept flowers on our mama's grave —
all these years. 'Course, we had some fight to get my daddy
— you know I'm talkin' 'bout your granddaddy — buried
here. Bessie hooted and howled for days, but we bribed her
with the promise that your father'd come stay with her if she
let him — meanin' my daddy — be buried next to my mother
— Bessie was married to my daddy when he died — did I tell
you that? But she really loved Carter. Everybody knew it.
Guess you want to hear the whole story, Doll Baby."

"I certainly do!" I say, and we get back in the car. He
is maddeningly slow, and I have all I can do to contain
myself. I feel like choking it out of him.

The road is lined with trees, and the bushes are so
thick it is like going through a tunnel. He turns down a side
road to show me an old abandoned railroad station.

"Trains still work, but the station don't," he says
stopping to look at the tilting roof and weed-infested platform. "They streak through here like they don't even know
this used to be a busy place. Your daddy loved to come here.
Did you know he ran away? Lost count of how many times.
Drove my father crazy. But this is where he come." A small
boy ran out from around the side of the collapsing structure.
When he saw our truck, he stopped short, looked back at the
hiding place he came from, and ran into the woods. "Used to
ride the rails with the hoboes."

"You can't be serious!"

"Yep. Sure am. Used to come home and tell us in the

dark what he did. Where he went. Hah! Anything he could imagine, he up and did! Wished I had his nerve. He always said the trains used to call him."

"Didn't anybody try to stop him?"

"In the beginning. But I guess my daddy gave up chasing him after a while." He throws the truck into reverse, and we go back to the road. The trees thin out, and we can see houses here and there, dotting the clearings.

"There are more houses now," he says, sweeping the landscape with his cigarette, "but most of the land here is still the same." He drives into a twisting dirt road cloaked by trees on either side. After a wide turn, we come to a clearing with an old farmhouse — weather-beaten and worn out. Six white ducks and a huge German shepherd guard the walk-way. The lawn is burned and brittle.

"This was our house," he says. "Here's where we grew up and where my mamma died. They laid her out here. In those days, that's the way they did it. Hah! even when my daddy died, they did it — and we were growed by then. Yep! Right in your own house. I was only eight, I think, when she passed away. They wouldn't let me see her. Sent me to my cousin's. Only your father was allowed to the wake because he was almost thirteen. But we all went to the cemetery. I can still hear the skitterin' of the dirt when they threw it on her coffin. Never forget that sound. Don't try to get out of the truck. That dawg'll eat you." He lights a cigarette from the one he is smoking and throws the stub out the window of the pickup. The dog barks, baring his teeth. I am all goose flesh.

We drive out to the main road again and make another turn into dirt. Soon we come to another farmhouse. "Now down here is where Bessie used to live." This house is much larger than the one they had lived in. The old clap-board has been replaced with aluminum siding. The bushes are clipped and a wicker swing hangs from a huge oak. The place has a quiet rustic elegance. "She was the typical farmer's daughter, if you know what I mean. Pregnant a million times but always miscarried. Then she started getting married. All her husbands kept dying on her. Hah! That should tell you something. Married more times than me before she was finished. Lord how I hated her! But I s'pose the thing you're waiting most to hear is what it had to do with us.

"Well, my dear, the real teeth of the matter is that the first one she got her hooks on was my daddy. Mama's grave didn't even have time to grow grass. Damned bitch! She was only sixteen, but she was mean. Lord, how she made us cry with her whuppin'!" He throws the truck in reverse and screeches the tires. Dirt flies up in front of us. Then he roars forward through the fog of grit and out of the driveway. "Don't know why I came here. Just looking at that house I get all — Je-sus! I hated that woman. Still do. She's still alive too. Lives somewhere in Georgia with husband number six. Fuck her. She's the one broke up our family, and that's the truth of it — sorry, little Doll Baby — it's the way it is — don't be scareda me."

"I'm not, Rob — tell me — tell me everything. I need to know it all."

"She was so disgusting. Had no right to do what she done." I put my hand on his arm, hoping he will feel my urgency. He turns and looks at me. "I guess I should tell you that I saw you when you was about four." Then he stares straight ahead. "It was a real lonely time when the army stationed me in New York. I stayed at your grandma's house with you and your mama when they give me a leave. I remember your grandma's cooking — nothing like it not even in the South. But honey, I guess you should know I loved your mama much too much even though I was married, — she was all alone — and because I loved her, I loved you too and I still do."

How many more surprises am I in for today? "Thank you for telling me that," I say. Something in me wants to cry: "Bessie! What about Bessie?"

"Well, Jesus H. Christ, woman, you're giving me the shivers — can't concentrate if you look so pretty, nohow." And he lights another cigarette, as I slide a little away from him on the seat. I stare straight ahead, trying not to breathe his smoke — trying not to breathe his energy which now has nauseated me. Horny old bastard that he is.

"No," he says. "I won't leave nothing out. I'm going to tell you the whole ball of wax. But I hope you're ready for it. Might make you wish you hadn't — my daddy used to say,

'Be careful what you wish for — you might get it.' That could be you, after you hear it all. I think it's just fine and dandy you want to write a book and all, Doll Baby. I hope you can handle all the stuff of it, because you just might have to take your daddy off the throne you probably got him on."

His words stay with me, germinating in my soul all the way home to New York, swirling in a thousand patterns until I am quite dizzy from it all.

Only when I face my typewriter and begin the process, zoning out somewhere as the words click one by one onto the page, does anything begin to make sense. I see the pain in my father's life reflected before me. And I am Alice sliding through the looking glass, running for my own Rabbit, following his steps so closely through the luminous dream in my head, and seeing myself through the other lens of the telescope at the same time.

After several weeks of feverish writing — sometimes working sixteen hours a day, I complete the opening chapters and Federal Express them to Daniel. Then I sleep off and on through an entire groggy weekend — trying to forget my father's pain and mine.

Chapter 1

Barret picked up Carter in his arms, so the boy could watch the huge mantel clock strike the hour. He wrapped his hands around his son's little legs. Barret was a soft, gentle man. He stood a safe distance away from the fireplace and from the woman who had planted her forearm on its mantel.

"Bring him here," said Emma Rose, "right up close to it." Her veined, thin hand slapped flat and fast on the mantel, her skirt swishing half circles about her long legs, as she twisted around to her husband and son, and then back again to the clock. "I can't even begin to tell you how pleased I am to have this clock, Barret. My stars, my father sure took his good old time. I thought he would never give it up!" She saw her head bobbing in the glass dial as she spoke. Now the huge clock looked even better to her. She was in it, and that was where she belonged. "I got so tired of looking at it in his house, when it was long overdue to be here in ours." She stared at Barret. "Here, I said!"

"Not so close for him the first time," Barret said, kissing Carter's head. He stood firm about eight feet away with the baby safe in his arms. "He's never seen it happen yet."

"I declare, you don't want him to grow up." She sailed to them, plucked Carter out of his father's arms as if he were fruit on a tree, and swooped him right up to the clock. His forehead grazed against it as she thrust him forward, and he reared back, blinking at his reflection in the dial, wondering what it was doing there.

The heavy scent of lilac hung in the room. Emma Rose always cut the flowers from all parts of her Virginia farm and jammed them into every corner of the house.

"How else can he see it if we don't bring him up close? I believe in plunging my son right into the very heart of the thick of things." As she spoke she took her hand off the mantel and rubbed the curve of her stomach which was indeed ripe with her second child. She was tall and angular, and her stomach was the only round part of her. "I do hope you're not trying to spoil this occasion for me, Barret," she said, watching the minute hand, wishing it would move faster. "I've been waiting to get this clock for a very long time, and now that my daddy finally gave in — actually brung it to me — to us — hisself — did I tell you that part? — I'm sure I —"

"But if it scares him, what good is it?" Barret said. "I mean — family heirloom or not, it might just scare him when it strikes — so close I mean. He should get used to it first."

"Will he see it? Now, will he see it if he's across the room? I'd like to know that. If he is a true Ruden, I declare, he will know exactly how important this clock really is." Emma Rose bounced Carter up and down; he arched away from the mantel and from her. "And someday, who knows? It just might be yours, boy, if you can manage to deserve it."

"It's — it's almost four, Emma Rose," Barret said, taking countless steps toward her, but backing up each time. "It's going to strike."

The chimes began, echoing through the slanting shadows of the late afternoon sun.

Carter jumped a little at each tone and looked into the smooth hollows of his mother's face. Her blue eyes flashed more than usual. She cupped his chin and turned his face back to the clock.

"He doesn't like it, I told you; he's too small yet," Barret said.

"Barret, will you stop distracting him so he'll see the knight? Sakes alive."

First there was a faint buzzing, whirring sound, and then two little doors at opposite ends of the top of the dial burst open. A knight galloped out of the left one, hunched taut in the saddle, back sloped, knees bent, chin almost touching the horse's mane. He aimed his lance straight ahead. Spellbound by this creature, Carter did not see the dragon come out of the other door until the knight was almost upon her. Her fierce face, jagged with serpent scales, had flaring nostrils and a gaping mouth. And the boy saw her against the background of his own reflection in the glass dial. He thought she was coming for him and began to howl.

"Sakes alive, Emma Rose. You see he doesn't like it," yelled his father above his cries.

The dragon fell through a trap door when the lance struck her, and a second later, the knight disappeared behind the dragon's door, which shut in a blink. Carter stopped crying. His mother laughed. "I'm telling you, Barret, he will grow up in spite of you. He will fight his battles hisself — if he's any son of mine — or go down trying. You want to keep him a baby forever?"

"He's only two years old, for the love of heaven!"

"See? There — he's looking for the knight again." She rubbed the boy's nose raw with her handkerchief.

"Of course he is — he's so scared of it," Barret said. Carter looked at his father's soft, light brown eyes that were the exact color of his hair and reached out his hands. Barret took him, and he snuggled himself into his father's chest.

"Yes, but he likes it just the same. Children do love to be scared." Emma Rose always spoke in absolutes. "And he will be a fighter — bring honor to his family — yes he will!"

Barret told the story again and again even after Carter grew up. He seemed to have forgotten his dismay at the baby's fear, because he related the incident with mild amusement. "And how Carter cried the first time he saw the clock strike!"

Sakes alive.

Emma Rose's grandfather, Rolph Ruden, had made the clock in 1850 in the Black Forest and carried it all the way to Virginia on his lap, when he and his bride made the great ocean journey in steerage. Carter heard the story of his feisty great-great-grandfather, many times — how he made his new wife carry all the luggage so that his hands could be free to protect the clock. It had been his wedding gift to her and was all that he could salvage of his profession, after his possessions and land had been confiscated.

His brother owned the Petersburg farm and had done Rolph the favor of dropping dead shortly after the newlyweds arrived, leaving Rolph the property. After that, the clock was handed down to his eldest son, who left it to

Barret and Emma Rose. In a way it was lucky for Emma Rose that she had no brothers, or she probably wouldn't have inherited it. Her father, however, insisted on putting Barret's name on it instead of hers, which infuriated her. "He is the son I never had," said her father, much to her dismay.

But she was right about Carter. In spite of his fear, he begged to be picked up to see the drama of the clock again and again, until he was old enough to climb on the hassock and see it by himself. Whenever he was alone in the room, the ticking, ticking, ticking, was hypnotic. As soon as the knight, whom he called Lancelot, went back into the clock, Carter scrambled up on the overstuffed, velvet couch and straddled its fat arm. He had found a rope which he hooked around the wooden knob on the front of the arm, and then he would ride toward his own dragon, snapping those "reins" and digging his heels into the sides of his "horse." He was lost in the clip of the hoof beats and the imagined roar of the dragon. He saw her mouth shooting fire, her blood dripping to the floor, and he smiled a knight's kind of smile as the world's time came to a halt and had to wait for him as he rushed forward, forward in his own battle-air, caught in the clickety-clack of the mystical hooves.

At night he loved to hear the clock when everything was quiet. It tolled the hour and gave a round, pleasing tone that echoed through the house. There was something warming and liquid about it, even all the way upstairs, and he knew that Lance was calling to him, urging him again to ride straight ahead, to make a line that would go on and on.

But after a while he outgrew the couch,

and began to look around for a real steed.
The old horse that pulled their buggy to town
had a sagging back and only one eye. Carter
was forbidden to ride him, because he'd buck
anyone off his back — even Barret. But he got
them to town and back, and that's why they
kept him. "Sir Ron" was his name, but there
was nothing knightly about him.

"I know how you lost your eye," Carter
told him on a breathless day in the summer
before his eighth birthday. He had brought
some sugar to him in the south field, which
the horse refused to eat.

"What's the matter," said Carter. "Flies
getting to you?" There must have been fifty
small ones on Sir Ron at once. It was a
dreadful thing to see how they tortured him.
Not only did some of them crawl into the
space that used to be his eye, they crawled
into the good eye as well, so that the tear
duct was all puffed out.

"Poor, old thing," said Carter. "The
dragon got you, didn't she?"

In the meantime, there was Mabel, the
mule. Carter rode her every chance he got
that summer, because, even though she would
often stand statue-still, she was his size,
and she never bucked, and Carter pretended
first of all that she was a great horse, and
secondly that they rode to their duels at a
gallop. At first it bothered him to look
through her huge pointy ears, with their own
entourage of flies. Everybody knows horses
don't have ears like that. But then he
strained to pretend that this "horse" had
special, magic ears. They had to be bigger
than those of any other horse, so they could
hear where dragons hid. Didn't they? Even
so, he knew he was only fooling himself; he
knew deep down that Mabel really didn't work

as a horse.

Lots of things really didn't work — even though he really wanted them to — even though he prayed that they would. And that heavy kind of longing, that aching vexation of his spirit that told him things always missed a little, gnawed at his heart and followed him everywhere.

Emma Rose knew the name of every insect, weed, and animal that lived on the farm. Her father had taught her, she said, and Carter and his brothers knew they had better remember everything she taught them, too. She recited her litany of bugs and plants with little stabs of her voice, as if she were drilling the information into her children. In the fields they always walked at least three steps behind, in spite of all their efforts to fall into step next to her. If one of them was lucky enough to catch up, she managed to nudge against him, shoving him off to the side, so he fell even more behind her than he was before.

"Horn worms and sphinx moths — pick 'em off the tobacco leaves and dump them into the water pot. Flea beetles, wire worms, and cutworms are the worst 'cause you can't see them right away. Some of them burrow, and cutworms are only at night. When you are all in bed, Papa and I flame 'em." She always laughed when she told them how many cutworms they burned to death at night, the tight plait of her blue-black hair pulling her eyes to the sides of her face.

Her lessons were mechanical like the rest of her. She was never still, but seemed to focus on her children in a way that said they had better absorb everything she taught if they were to survive in this world — if they were to amount to anything; and there was always a question in her voice as to whether or not Carter would. She shot her energy out all around her as if she hoped he would catch some. But for the life of him, he could not remember her lessons, because, try as he would, he just could not care about farming.

His father's sprawling fields defined themselves in neat furrows pulled with the blade of their plow, but marked forever with the sweat of their shoulders. That's what they mean when they say you put your sweat into something, because when you walked behind that plow, your skin tight and burning in the sun, you dripped right into the earth. At first, Carter was proud to help his father with the heavy work of planting, but the pride quickly turned to fatigue and boredom at the prospect of being trapped in the cycle of chores that stretched ahead for endless years.

Most of the time they worked outdoors, and Mama stayed inside. Her labor there was never-ending too, and she had babies as well. She attacked her mountain of work with gusto and pride, looking askance at Carter whenever he tried to shirk.

By the time he was nine, there were four of them in the fields. Papa, Carter, the middle brother, Andy, who was seven, and Rob, the-five-year old. School was his only re-lief.

As soon as Emma Rose was through with one of her teaching rampages, Carter always left the room as quickly as possible. The fact that he was the oldest made it worse. She seemed to be mad at him all the time, because of his failure to remember.

One day he tried to surprise her by picking all her carrots. He knew she would be happy to see that all the work was done. There were so many, they spilled out of the basket as he scraped it up across the edges of the back steps and onto the porch.

"Mama, come see. Mama!" He held one out in his hand. The screen door clapped behind her a second before her howling began.

"Whaaaaat did you dooooo? You goose! Barret, look what this child did! Carter Shields you are a dunce. Do you hear?" Barret ran out and put himself between them.

"Now wait, Emma Rose, he —"

"Look at that! Not even half growed. Don't you ever pick anything until I tell you, hear?"

"I can put them back, Mama . . . I'm sure I can —"

"Put them back — what's the matter with you? Why can't you be like Rob. Only five and the best worker we have."

"I'll bury them again. Then they'll grow more —"

"The boy was trying, and that's what counts," said his father. His arms hung down stiff as if he didn't know where to put them. He kept moving them in little starts, trying to make a gesture, but one never materialized.

"My carrots is what counts. The whole planting is lost. It's clear that Rob is going to be the farmer in this family. You'll see he will, Barret. Now what am I supposed to do for carrots?" She slapped the back of Carter's head as he went down the steps.

It wasn't Carter's fault that he hated farming so much. Once Papa took him to Richmond, and all he needed was one look. The city was for him. They rode through Capitol

Square in the buggy. He had never seen so
many people dressed up — even in church. And
the Capitol Building looked like a giant
Greek temple. He felt important just looking
at it. And then there was the statue of
Washington on horseback, huge and imposing.

Papa knew what he was thinking. "When
you grow up, don't get stuck like me," he
said. "Trouble is — I don't know what else I
can do. Farming is all I know." He twisted
the reins around his thumb, hunching forward
and looking far away. "You know what I think
sometimes?" he said. "I think the best thing
about the South is the train heading north."
Then he grinned and winked. "But don't ever
tell your mother I said so."

How Carter loved him for telling such a
big secret. He would never get stuck. Some
day he would go some place even better than
Richmond. Maybe to Washington, DC., or even
New York. He might even stay there. He would
have a big house and his own Model T. Then
his mother would come to visit, and she would
be really impressed with what she saw.

The spring of 1925 was the warmest that
even his grandparents could remember. Everyone moved at the slowest pace, and a single
day seemed to have more than twenty-four
hours. In early April, Emma Rose's belly
started to swell again. The weather bothered
her, and she often remarked that she felt
"done in."

"Emma Rose Shields, a woman in your
condition's always ten degrees hotter than
everybody else," said his father one long
afternoon. "Come here and set a bit." The
glint in his eye made Carter want to sit
between them.

It was a steamy morning several days later when Emma Rose came in the back door carrying crape myrtle branches for forcing. Her black hair frizzed around her face, and she glistened with sweat from her walk. The hollows of her cheeks and her blue eyes were so pronounced, it looked as if someone had drawn them on her ·with a sharp pencil. She had pinned up her skirts. Carter could smell wet grass on her stockings, and it mixed with the scent of her lavender dusting powder. She had a breathiness that made her words sound like little gasps, and her steps slapped against the wooden floor.

"Carter, get me that vase — the one in the parlor — and put some water in it for me —" she said. "Hold on — were you fighting again?"

He guessed his face had a telltale bruise or something. His two brothers, Andy and Rob, stopped playing with their oatmeal. Andy, because he was the one Carter had been fighting with, and Rob, because he was glad he wasn't guilty. She freed a hand, pinched Carter's shoulder, and then twisted the pinch.

"No, owww, Ma, I wasn't." He filled the vase, leaned back to carry it against his chest, and set it on the end of the kitchen table.

"Yes he wahr too," Greta, his four-year-old sister popped up to snitch. "It was him and Andy, and they both fell off of the porch." She giggled, and skipped around him. "I catched you, Carty." Her hair was a thick auburn mess poking out of her barrettes.

"Shut up," said Andy. His pale face was often stern. He had stick-straight pale blond hair that always fell in his eyes no matter how hard Mama slicked it.

"Don't talk to your sister that way. I won't have it."

"But, Ma," he whined, "she's always spying on us."

"Now you listen here!" Why did she always look at Carter when she was angry? "I won't have you behaving like babies in my house — in front of your sister — in front of me, fighting all the time."

"Carty's too strong," said Greta. "He'll be too rough and won't know how to take care of Cousin Henry's puppy. I have to do it. You have to be good first, Carty."

Andy used this diversion to bolt for school, and Rob was fast behind him. "Bye, Mama," called Andy. Rob stopped just long enough for a kiss; his dark hair glistened with sweat.

"Mama," Greta piped. "Why're you putting sticks in there?"

"They aren't sticks, child. They're branches." She twisted the spray of crape myrtle to fit the mouth of the vase. "If I put them in water like this, the flowers will grow right out of them . . ." She stopped suddenly and held her stomach.

Greta didn't notice Mama. "Real ones or magic?"

"What's hurting you?" Carter said.

"Just a little pain . . . it will pass . . . there." She gave a quick smile and dropped her hand as if nothing had happened.

"Darn, did Papa go and get you another baby?" Her hand shot out into his face. It stung, and he could feel the heat from the slap deep in his brain. Her eyes were fierce blue pinpricks.

"I didn't mean nothin' . . ." He forced a smile.

Greta stared at them. "Where is it? Where is the baby?" she demanded. "Can I be the mama? It can have all my squash to eat."

"Now listen here, it's time for school. Carter, catch up to your brothers." He was dismissed. She got up and began to arrange the branches better in the vase.

"Can I go get Henry's pup?" Carter asked, not looking at her. "He said I could have it. And besides, I'm going to be thirteen —"

"This is April. Your birthday's not for another six months."

"I know, but the puppy needs a home now."

"You never can tell!" she said under her breath as if she didn't want him to hear. But he knew it was for him.

His cheek still felt faintly hot from her slap. She couldn't just give him something nice — like letting him have the puppy. She always had to throw in something to neutralize his joy — in this case, the slap. And it was her reluctance to give in, to say, Yes, you can certainly have the puppy. "You never can tell!" was all she could muster.

He could hear Greta singing to her dolls on the porch as he ran, "Boys are gone away — away . . . boys are gone away — and Greta's going to play — to play . . ." Her voice stuck to the breeze.

The heat continued to build, and it showered late in the afternoon almost every day. Carter helped his father. He walked behind Mabel, the mule, with the long leather leads thrown up over his shoulders, watching her pull the plow through the earth, making the dark moist furrows behind him. They were going to make yet another planting of corn. But who was in charge here? Who was being led? Was Mabel tethered or was he? He looked between her twitching ears, now no longer made of magic, or equipped to hear dragons. And he saw the flat earth ahead — smooth and blank. Nothing lay ahead. That's probably why he hated it so. Time stopped in that earth. It melted into the ground with the rain, with his sweat. And he was afraid he might get stuck in it.

He had given up asking if he could have his own horse. Besides how far could he go on a horse? But if he looked down the train tracks — well! They took you somewhere. They had direction. Time could move forward.
So whenever he could, he ran down to watch the trains. And then in school he learned about horsepower! When the chug of the engines reached his ears, he heard the sound of a thousand hooves instead. Now he saw his dreams embodied in the face of the locomotive as it ground its way down the track, faster and faster. How he envied the passengers in their fine clothes and longed to make a journey — anywhere. He could not wait to grow up.

When the spring came that year, the energy of the landscape was so heightened, you could sense it even when you were inside. It seemed to sing — each new species coming into bloom and finding its place like an instrument in an orchestra. The fierce yellow of the forsythia surged like a trumpet, calling the magnolias and dogwoods. But by the time the raging pinks of the azalea arrived, Carter no longer felt good about spring. Emma Rose's pains had grown worse.

Her skin was translucent, showing fuzzy blue veins underneath, as if she were turning inside out. Then in May, her belly stopped growing, and she was tired all the time. So strange to see her slow down. She had always raced against the slow rhythm of the farm.

"It should be kicking by now," she told Barret one night as they rocked on the porch swing in the dark. Carter was on his way out to them. He stopped and listened. "There's no kicking. It's way past time." He could hear his father sucking on his pipe; and when she stopped talking, the sucking grew louder.

"Kicking'll come soon. Maybe you didn't count right," Papa said. Carter wondered what they could have been counting.

"No, Barret, this is different. Something is wrong with this one — with me. Once I thought I even heard him cry — a terrible sob he made —"

"Oh, Emma Rose, you're makin' it up!" his father said.

"Now when have you ever known me to do that?" she huffed at him. "I heard it! One big long wail that flashed at me when I wasn't looking . . . It's saying what his life will be like some day, and he's wailing before he's even born. Don't you tsk at me. I heard it before. With Carter too — 'fore he was born — he cried like he saw all the hurt of his whole life — all at once, and gave up." Carter smelled the honeysuckle curling up from the woods near the road. It mixed with the smell of the pipe. "And I get so scared. Now, why should that be, Barret?"

Barret had stopped sucking his pipe. Carter remembered how it tasted whenever he sneaked a smoke. He thought of smoking a pipe in public some day. He thought of anything he could, so he wouldn't have to think about what Mama had said. "Well, people's minds think things sometimes," Barret said. "Pay it no mind."

"I wonder if I'm going to lose the child," said Emma Rose. "That's what I worry about the most. I guess that's why none of my children will ever mean as much to me as Rob does. To think I almost lost him when he was born — how close he came!"

"I have to wind the clock, Emma, and then I'll get us some lemonade," Barret said. "Don't fret so. Please don't fret."

Carter ran for the stairs and heard the screen door bang behind him. Then the grinding, chinking sound of the key turning the clock's gears. He tiptoed up to bed in the dark. None of her children? It was hard to breathe. None of them would ever mean as much to her as Rob? There was a huge hole in his stomach. And he shook inside with a yearning that would not go away.

The next morning he was supposed to go and get his new puppy, and this helped him forget the awful things Mama had said the night before. He had just crossed the south field and turned onto the road to Cousin Henry's; the sky was gray and leaden, and the air hung like cobwebs. There was a thick brush of tangled vines next to the road, and as he passed it, he had the feeling that he was being watched. He heard a quick swish and bent over, pretending to tie his shoe; a faint snap, a low rustle, then still. A brown toad, big with young, stretched slow leaps in front of his foot, and he kept blocking her with his hands, making her change directions. He waited, and then he knew who was there. He stood and turned suddenly, freeing his toad, and staring intently into the vines. Bessie Chadzik, the daughter of a neighboring farmer, cowered in the brush.

"Whatcha doing in there, girl, besides getting poison ivy?"

"Well, what are you supposed to be doing anyhow? How am I supposed to know you'd come along?" She was almost sixteen and very ugly, with sparse kinky hair and a nose that looked like a potato.

"Well, I sure in hell wasn't coming to see you." She brought out the worst in him — even then.

"You swearing? Now what would your Papa say if he heard you? What would he say if he known you swore 'front of a lady." Her hand jerked up and down, moving the leaves in front of her. She was scratching herself as she came a little way out of the vines, but she tried to shield her face behind creeper leaves. Bessie always scratched — as if a thousand thousand gnats were biting her incessantly.

"He wouldn't like that, but I don't see no lady around here — what would a lady be doing in the brush, huh? Killing the trees, maybe? Maybe they'll kill you." Although she was almost four years older, he was at least a foot taller. She had enormous breasts that stuck out like a shelf. And she had a way of rocking on her heels that made them bounce up and down.

"Never you mind. I just didn't have time to fix myself this morning with all them chores. So I didn't want to meet nobody just —" He wondered if he could balance something on those breasts.

"Who looks at you anyway?" But he flashed to a time two years or so before when he had wanted desperately to look at every

part of her. They were playing under Bessie's
front porch, and the blindfold she tied on
him was part of their game. He was not allowed to see — only touch. And she let him
touch her — everywhere. And even though her
skin was rough and scaly, he thrilled to
touch it — until her brother caught them with
Carter's hand in her bloomers and beat her
with a switch. Carter had escaped and run
home, expecting doom to fall on him at any
moment, but somehow Bessie had persuaded her
brother not to tell. He avoided her as best
he could after that; but for two years the
incident had sat between them like a presence
whenever they saw each other, although they
both pretended it had never happened. But
this time, he could not help but remember the
scaly, flaky feel of her thighs, and he could
smell, even now, the same musky smell of her
as he had on that day under the porch, and he
turned so she could not see his erection.
Would his nostrils ever be rid of her?

He started to run toward Cousin Henry's.
"You got big ugly tits!" he hooted, hoping
that if he jeered loud enough, he could stop
time in the present and not fall back into
the past. Then he heard the flap of her feet
and realized that she was running after him.
He turned to see her breasts bouncing, her
wide-open mouth and flaring nostrils. "Get
out of here!" he shouted. And he hated her
for the way she had of oozing herself into
his life, pretending that they both shared
some kind of bond — that they both knew how
much he liked her. But she kept coming, and
for an instant in that wild-faced look of
hers, he saw the future smoke up in front of
her.

He did not know what it was he saw down
that long arch of time, only that she was

there, and in the picture, she brought him evil that he could not stop. He fought to let the image of her go — to return to the present. And in his frenzy to rid himself of the ghost of her, he zigzagged twice, then turned and tripped her with his foot. She landed prostrate on the ground, her arms flailing, her breasts crushed into the dirt; and he sprinted away faster than he thought he could, running full throttle away from the curse that time had shown him.

Chapter 2

The heat and rain increased as the days passed that spring, but so did Emma Rose's ill health. She had taken to her bed and rarely left her room. Even the arrival of the puppy couldn't chase away the gloom that hung over the house.

It was on the last Sunday in May, when Carter came in for supper and found Andy and Rob sitting in the kitchen at an empty table. They swung their feet back and forth, making swishing sounds on the floor, afraid to look up.

Andy spoke first. "Greta's with Aunt Marion," he said. "They didn't want her here now, because Mama's so sick." He looked so forlorn, his blond hair and pale skin making him blend into the white curtains.

"Well, she should be here. It's her mother, too," Carter said, not knowing why he felt like arguing with him.

"Don't start scrapping, Carter. Doc Evans is in there with Mama," Rob interrupted, his tears on the brink. He was usually laughing about something. Now his voice was squeezed and high-pitched, and he looked like a tiny leprechaun giving out serious advice.

"Yeah, don't start with me. She's too young is all," Andy said.

"Didn't you hear what Rob said?" he said, "The doctor's in there. Mama'd say, 'Show respect.'"

"I am showing it," Andy sailed back. "I stayed here all day. Where were you? Gone to the trains again?"

"Does anyone tell you you shouldn't play ball?"

"It's okay Carter, Andy likes to play ball more than anything."

"Then he shouldn't sass about me."

"At least playing ball's good for you." Andy smiled, satisfied, his dimples puffing in and out.

"So's playing cards and meeting trains," Carter said. "That's real good too."

"Why do you care so much about meeting them trains?"

"Well now, I guess I like to know who gets on and who gets off, little brother."

"Hush your mouth. You both just hush up, ya hear?" Rob said. He saw Papa first, moving into the room like a marionette, his shoulders hunched as if a string pulled them up, his arms swinging like pendulums.

"Come," said Barret in a hollow voice, and that was all.

In the bedroom doorway, the doctor stood absolutely still, but the white flowers in the wallpaper seemed to turn slowly. The filmy curtains puffed at the windows. Mama's hair glinted in iridescent black lines spread over the pillows. A dry green film hung over her skin, and her hand was translucent in the lamplight. Her fingers twitched against the rough muslin sheets. Carter went over and held them to stop them from jerking. Andy and Rob cried, hugging Barret and touching the sheets near her feet. She looked small as if her body had shifted to a lesser shape. Her face was gaunt, and her cheeks sucked in and out.

"Carter," she said in a voice as far away as the mourning dove's, "it's okay to cry now." But he bit the insides of his mouth until they were raw.

"Nothing to cry for . . . you'll be better — you will," he said.

"Be proud of the land . . . it'll make you . . . a man." Don't say that, he thought. Say anything but that. He gripped her hand too tight and let it go. He waited, but she did not speak. Instead she looked at the ceiling, heaved a deep, dry sigh, and then lay still.

And all of them were caught in that sigh. It was a sound that was past, present, and future. He would hear it in the dark for the rest of his life. He clutched her hand again. Couldn't she say she loved him anyway, even though he couldn't love the farm? No, only Papa understood. Please say just one more thing! Say you love me!

The doctor moved like a ghost and closed her eyes. No!

Carter took his hand out of hers, and ran from the house choking. He heard Papa calling after him, but ran blindly on, only knowing he'd smother if he stayed there. She whizzed past him. Again and again! He had to outrun her — to stop seeing her face in that death bed, the same bed where he was born.

He had seven league boots. The landscape

flickered and swirled away as his feet pounded the earth, his mouth sucking for air. He reached the dog house and took the puppy off her lead. He sat behind the little house, where no one could see him. The little dog sat stone still in his lap, feeling his pain, and he could not breathe even after resting for several minutes. There was no air in him, and it was impossible to cry. He fought for breath. The trees kept rushing past, dashing and darting in his head, even though he sat still. He had bought earbobs for her birthday, which was the following week. Now he could not give them to her. What a strange thing to think of. They matched the cameo brooch that she loved, that had been in her family. She would never know how long he had been saving for them.

The sun was setting, throwing blasts of orange and pink across the sky. Mama can't see it; she'll never see it, he thought and then swore out loud — bellowing out every rotten word he'd ever heard, cursing the world fiercely, as if his voice were a weapon. The air grew darker, and he wanted to run home, but he could not move. He was afraid his feet might grow roots. Drag yourself to the house, he told himself. But as he lumbered back, something grabbed at him from wet shadows, like in a dream when someone chases you, and you can't run.

By the time he was near the house, the sky was a black hollow dome. He looked at the square light from his parents' bedroom window and felt comfort and dread from it at the same time. He could not bring himself to go in. The perfume of wet honeysuckle nauseated him. The smells of all the wetness mixed together. He went behind the barn and vomited, burning his throat even more. Then he stumbled toward the house, holding on, hand over hand, to the splintery side of the barn. It hurt to walk. The barn door was open, and Sir Ron, the one-eyed horse, shuffled his feet. He went in, and wrapping himself in her blanket, fell instantly asleep in her hay. Poor, poor Carter. Hoarse and cold and lonely and scared and wanting more than anything for the weight of death not to be real.

He awoke in the night, the figure of a ghost outlined on the soft wall of the barn. He pushed with his heels backing up into the straw, not daring to look away until he realized it was the moon playing against a hanging harness's shadow that made an elongated head with an open mouth waiting to swallow him. And even when he knew it was only a shadow, he had to get out of there because it had spooked him. Bolting out the little side door, he ran for the house just as someone was descending the porch steps — someone he never had seen before, and it made him stop short. A tall scarecrow man jolted down the porch steps to his horse and buggy.

"Bye, Barret," he said over his shoulder. Carter could see his father crouching in the doorway. "Let it set now. Don't disturb nothin'. Be back in the mornin' to take away the buckets. Least we got a start in this heat."

"I'll keep the parlor door shut." his father's voice was thin and empty.

"Jes don't let the kids in there till I finish with the buckets. Takes a while to drain." He flexed the reins, flipping them against the horse's back until it clopped away, leaving Carter with a sense of dread he could taste. Barret went inside.

Carter ran to the porch's open windows and stared inside until he could make out the form of his mother. She lay on the dining room table, the heels of her feet hanging over the edge, and a sheet draping her body. He eased himself through the door and into the room with her, and he inhaled what the man had been talking about. Under the table the four buckets stood in a row and the smell of blood smacked him like an assault. Where can I go? he thought. How will my mind ever be able to think of anything again without seeing this? The buckets under the table — the buckets of blood.

"Oh, Papa," he sobbed. "No fair."

"Carter — boy. Come out of there." Hearing his voice his father had come to the doorway. "Come. Don't never stay there. Come inside with me." And they hugged each other as they walked to the stairs. And then they cried.

He awoke in his bed to see the weak sunlight shining on Andy. At first, he remembered nothing. Half in a dream, he imagined his brother was calling him to breakfast like any ordinary day. But then it came back — that cracking pain billowing into him like smoke, and he opened his mouth to grab some air. Oh, no, don't you cry, don't cry in front of Andy.

"Get up, Carter. There's biscuits from Aunt Marion, and . . . funeral's tomorrow," he added importantly. Aunt Marion's biscuits, not Mama's, Carter wanted to say. You people are all rotten. All of you. Don't you know how bad she feels, she can't make our biscuits? But he kept silent. "They're all comin' here today — but . . ." Andy pushed his fingers back through his stick-straight hair, trying not to cry. " . . . but we're not allowed to stay — only you are. You even get long pants."

Don't they understand anything? He didn't want to be the oldest. He didn't want their goddamned pants.

The world looked different to him from that moment. The room came into a heightened focus of sharp edges. He saw the things about him in bold outline. Like pictures in a coloring book.

Papa was waiting for them in the kitchen. "Carter be good and stay here with us. Don't go away, boy." He hugged him, and they both cried all over again. Never before was he ever so close to his father, and the sad thing was that he never would be again. "Come and see her," he said, and they went into the parlor.

The infernal buckets were gone!

Now her skin was opaque and cold, as if it had finally triumphed over the heat. He could not stop his tears. He had not uttered a word yet that day, and he had forgotten the damage he'd done to his voice. His sobs came out old and cracked, making sounds in a wicked witch voice.

Aunt Marion told him to eat, but he could not. His father told him to wash and change his clothes, but Carter only stared at him as he turned to wind the clock. Barret did so with great deliberation, as if it took all his concentration. But once or twice in between winds, he stopped, stared off, and then reminded himself with a little jerk to make the next turn. Carter walked up behind him. He wanted another hug, but did not know how to ask for it. Instead he saw only his father's broad back, slumped against the mantel, and his sad, sad eyes reflected in the glass dial, seeing nothing.

He backed away from his father. "Maybe you should stop the clock," he said. "Maybe it shouldn't work while she's lying here dead." And he ran out of the room, and went upstairs, not feeling his steps against the stairs.

He hated the sight of Barret's old suit, laid out for him on the bed. It was his first pair of long pants, but he did not want to feel good about anything. He could not bear to think of the reason why he got them. He had to cinch in the waist with a wide belt to keep the pants from falling down.

On the way back to the parlor, he wondered what his mother would think of him in Papa's suit, and his tears began again. He had to guard his mother, but he did not want her to see him cry. He heard his aunt preparing food in the kitchen, walking a hundred steps back and forth across the wooden floor, and he remembered that people would be coming soon. He held his breath and walked alone into the suffocating parlor. At first he did not look at her. He heard Papa's buggy returning from taking his brothers to a neighbor. There was a fancy rattan fan on the wall opposite the casket; he took it down and fanned himself and the flies. Then he stopped and looked at the clock. He squinted his eyes so the movement blurred and grew still. The ticking faded from his consciousness. The room grew heavy, sluggish. There was no sound. No movement. No air. No time.

Now he was ready. He inched himself around to face her. Ever so slowly. He tried to tell himself that she was the same as before. She might even say something, because she knew he wouldn't ever tell. Perhaps it would be that one last thing she had forgotten to say before the doctor had closed her eyes? But she did not move. The sunlight flickered on her face. You could hear the silence of her. She lay with her dead baby still inside her. The baby whose time could never be — who could not live, and so had poisoned her with his own death.

He wanted her to touch him. Did she love him now? His lungs never fully filled up; the air was so heavy with moisture — it was like breathing in wet smoke. He could not smell her lavender. Instead the air was stale. Could that be her scent now? He moved a chair next to the coffin and sat there, staring at her hands. The veins were gone. He dared to touch her finger. It was stiff and cool like glass. It left a space inside him. A bed of ashes where nothing would grow. She was wearing her long blue taffeta skirt and white lace blouse kept for special occasions, and at her throat was her grandmother's cameo brooch. Was this a special occasion? He stared at the brooch. Papa came into the room with a bunch of lilacs.

"These will sweeten up the room," he said. Was he referring to Mama's smell? How dare he! He placed them near her, but sat across the room on the fat couch that had once served as Carter's horse. Then he looked at his son. Carter fanned. First himself and then Mama. He didn't want to look at Papa. The lilacs were too sweet.

Was this really her? Could he live without seeing his face in her eyes?

The mourners came in a line, bringing sweaty bowls of food to Aunt Marion in the kitchen and then filed into the parlor, paying their respects with stilted and empty words. He would not speak to anyone. They fluttered aimlessly like moths, sometimes touching Barret, who wept a river. Their shadows lumbered uncertainly in the oppressive room like slow ghosts. Intruders. Carter

hated them. He touched the metal handles of
the casket. They felt slimy instead of cool.
But then a squeezed and strident voice,
counterpointed against the muffled sounds of
mourners, made him quickly draw his hand
back. Bessie Chadzik came toward him. He
caught the flash of her splayed nose as her
ugliness colored the room. Her face said, see
how sad I can look? She tried to make her
bottom lip tremble. Her crepe dress made a
scratchy sound as it grated against itself.

   "Carter Shields, you dear child, I am
sooo sahr-ry for you, really I am, you poor,
dear thing." He stood, and shot her the most
burning look he could muster, and she looked
away from him, trying unsuccessfully to toss
her kinky hair which would not move. She
began scratching. First her arm and then her
stomach. She changed her focus to his father.
"Mr. Shields," she slid across to him, "I am
so so sahr-r-ry for your trouble. She was so
young, I declare." Carter wondered if her
skin flaked off as she scratched. Like so
many dragon's scales. Her piercing voice drew
everyone's attention to the other side of the
room, and her cheap cologne smelled like
cloves. Maybe if she scratched long enough,
she'd just flake away and disappear. How dare
she take so much attention away from his
mother? He wanted to hit her. He felt a
monster moving around in his chest, pulsing
against his ribs. Mama wouldn't want to hear
about this monster.

   Everyone was pinned to the scene of
Bessie and his father. Carter turned to his
mother and grabbed blindly for the brooch at
her throat, unfastening the clasp, and sticking himself sharply with the pin. He caught
his breath. The cameo was safe in his sweaty
fist, and he sucked the blood where the pin

had pricked. Tears squeezed his eyes, as he turned blindly, squaring himself to face them, knowing for certain that he would be caught.

But no one had seen him take the brooch. No one had so much as glanced in his direction.

Blinking his eyes, he finally focused and marched over to where Bessie was. "You ain't worth the powder and shot to blow you to hell," he said. Then he took the porch in three strides and was down the warped front steps before the screen door could clap shut behind him. The hot air slapped his face as he tore across the grass, tripping on his pants, feeling the freedom of solitude. And then his puppy, Mo, was there running with him, yipping and jumping, and he could hear Greta's voice in his head, "Boys are gone away, away" over and over, keeping time to his running, almost mocking himself.

"Look, Mo," he said as they were nearing the pond. "Don't want no one to find it." He turned the cameo over in his hand. "This is her favorite, so I have to keep it for her. We're going to bury it in the dog house as soon as I get me a wooden box and tar paper." He wrapped it in his handkerchief, and put it deep into the pocket of his father's pants. Then he took off all his clothes and dived into the pond. This is the first time I am going swimming since she's dead, he thought. And he knew he couldn't go home and tell her how good it was. But no tears came to his eyes. Shouldn't he be crying again? His feelings had dried up inside. He thought of pricking himself again with her pin, so he would cry.

Chapter 3

The silence in the house, on the days after the funeral, had a presence all its own, as if a separate person had moved in. The five of them walked a wide circle around the stillness of this stranger, wishing it would leave. Neighbors had continued to bring food for several days, and a week later, as the boys helped Papa prepare the table, they could hear Greta singing to her dolls on the porch. She had become very aloof, playing by herself, speaking very little, except to her dolls. "Mama's gone away — away, and me and you can play — and play, till she comes back to stay — hay, she comes back to stay." Andy's tears came in a rush, and then Rob cried too. "Don't tell the boys when she comes back. She can only stay with the girls. We can hide her in my room."

"Tell her not to say that, Lord almighty, make her stop saying that," Carter said. Barret went out to her.

"Greta," Barret said, "Greta, listen to Papa. You know that Mama was very, very sick, don't you?"

"Not very, very. Just sick," she said, putting a bonnet on her doll.

"No. Listen to me, child. Mama is up in heaven now. She was too sick to stay here, so she's up there with Jesus."

"Oh, Papa, if she wants to, she can come back. She can, you know."

"No she can't," Barret whispered. "She can't ever come back."

There was a long pause, and then, "But you never can tell . . . maybe . . ."

"No, Baby, not maybe." He stroked her

thick hair, which hung loose now with no one to pin it, and he carried her into the kitchen.

"Does she still love me?"

He kissed her forehead. "Always and always . . . she will always love you, and we will always love her."

"She might come back though, you <u>still</u> never can tell."

After dinner, Barret put her to bed and then called the boys together around the table. He told them that they would have to stay with their grandparents temporarily. The change would be good for them, and besides he had things to attend to. Greta needed a woman to take care of her, and there didn't seem to be any other choice but for them to "visit a spell at Grandpa's," whose farm was about three miles south. "Let me stay with you, Papa — just me," Carter said.

"After a time, boy, I promise you that."

"But why not now?" he whined. "You need me to do the work here. Let me stay and help. I don't belong with them." What more did Papa want? Carter was offering to do what he hated, just so they could be together.

"Soon," Barret said, "I guess there's things I have to do by myself, you know what I'm talking about? I'd like to be by myself for a while; then you can come. 'Sides, cousins are coming to help during afternoons. But after a time, just me and you. I promise you that. And if I need something, or if Granny does, you can take the buggy back and forth." And he packed them up and took them to Granny's to stay.

Carter had no way of knowing then what his mother's death had done to his father. For although she disapproved of him most of the time, she gave him a purpose and direc-

tion. Now he had none. There was a gaping
space in his soul that would never again be
filled. "She keeps me honest," Barret had
said of Emma Rose many times. By that he
meant, he had always known what to do next.
Now he had to discover it for himself, or
flounder because he missed the mark.

But Carter was unaware then of his
father's huge suffering. He was only aware of
his own. Barret first declared himself for
Emma Rose two years before their marriage
when he sent her scores of postcards. "So
fine a lady as you," he wrote over and over,
as if he thought she was too good for him.

*(Sixty years later I found those post cards when I
visited my Aunt Greta. We had gone digging in a long-
forgotten trunk in Greta's attic and had misty eyes when we
found the very words Barret had written to his bride.)*

Perhaps the elegy at the funeral should
rather have been for him, for his life now
left adrift and for the part of him that had
died.

When he returned home, Barret guided Sir
Ron up the dirt road that led to his house,
and shook when he saw a woman standing alone
on the porch. She held her hand up on the
post the way Emma Rose always did. Emma Rose
had always made it a point to be waiting on
the porch for him when he came in from his
fields. "Such a good feeling to have someone
greet you when you come home, all done in,"
she'd say. It was probably the only gentle
thing she had done for him in their years
together.

Now the horse went on his own, Barret was transfixed in his seat. Then her hand waved, and he heard the strident voice, "Halloo, Mr. Shields!" which dispelled the nightmare of a reincarnated Emma Rose; but it soon brought on a new one which proved later to be much more terrifying.

Bessie stood squarely, as if she were firmly rooted, and he realized with horror that she was welcoming him home to his own house.

"And where are your lovely children?" she sang the words in her dreadful high-pitched drawl. One hand scratched the back of the other.

"To visit . . . they're gone to stay with my folks . . . for a spell." Barret was clearly out of his element.

"Well, ain't that fine, now . . . I baked some pies and corn bread today, and I know how most folks likes my pies, so I brung some for your family." She punctuated the ends of her sentences by rocking forward and then bouncing back on her heels, making her breasts bounce when she landed. "I just knew you'd be all done in from your chores. Now, I hope it's a respectful time to come. I expected your children to be here, but I guess I can set a spell anyhow. Well now . . . I declare, I see such a frown, Barret! I mean I am sixteen with my birthday just last month and all. See here, I put them in your pantry, so you can have some pie if you like, or bread with your dinner." Her fingers were never still. Itch, itch. Scratch, scratch.

"That's fine, Bessie. That'll be just fine. Thank you for your . . . kindness." He wondered how long she would stay.

She came often after that, and he really

didn't know what to do with her. He was also
troubled by the thought of imposing his
children on his elderly parents, but he went
helplessly about his farm chores, unable to
find a solution. At night he would return
home at once dreading and somehow wanting to
find Bessie there. As unpleasant as she was,
she was some small balm for his loneliness.
She did fuss over him, and somehow, it made
him feel important.

Three weeks after the children had gone
to Granny's, Carter decided to go home and
beg Papa to let him live at home. He swung
grandpa's buggy toward the house and was
surprised to see the curtain stretchers,
usually kept in the cellar, now set up on the
side of the house. The stiff parlor curtains
were washed and impaled onto the pins, with
wet patches glinting in the sun, like dew on
a spider web. It gave him a good feeling — a
feeling of life to see them there. He called
for Barret, but there was no response, and
then he remembered that his mother would not
be there either. His shoes clumped on the
wooden porch, and he hesitated outside the
screen. The hush of the house was disturbed
by a jay scolding the cat, and it snapped him
out of his thoughts. He went in. The room was
unusually bright because of the absence of
the curtains. He looked toward the place
where the casket had been. A hazy sun gave an
alien glow to the room. A dragonfly droned
and hit the screen in little flits. The clock
ticked on and on. Was it louder than before?
His mother's big vase stood on the floor
empty like an echo, its big gaping mouth
seemed to mock him. Her absent flowers left
their presence everywhere.

Sinking onto the maroon couch, he pressed his weight against the stiff upholstery and felt the place with his hand where he used to "ride" his horse. The clock struck one. The knight came out. He and the dragon rushed toward each other, and Carter's tears came fast.

"Lord almighty, where are you, Ma?" he exploded. Punching the cushions, he rocked the back of the couch into the wall. An eerie screech ripped the air, and he jumped up sucking in his breath, shaking and terrified. The couch moved. His feet gripped the bottoms of his shoes, and then he jerked the couch away from the wall. There was Bessie hunched down behind it. He grabbed her by the wrists and twisted her up. She was moaning as loud as she could, and he wanted to kill her.

"Bitch!" he yelled. "Did you do it? Did you touch her curtains? They're Mama's. Rotten bitch! Mama's curtains!"

"You'll be punished; pu-n-n-nished for evah —" she screeched, trying to free her hands. He tried to smack her, but she bit the hand he held her with. He pushed her down onto the couch, banging her head on the wall, and as he ran out of the house, he collided with his father on the porch.

"She's here," he howled. "She took Mama's curtains and stretched them . . . there . . . on the side." He pulled Barret to the end of the porch, jabbing his finger in the air. "Lookee here." He spoke as if he had solved a crime. Then he realized that his father wasn't looking at the curtains. Didn't he understand?

"It's her curtains! . . . Papa!" Carter searched his eyes. "Say it!"

Papa's voice was so low, Carter wasn't sure he heard it.

"Carter, boy . . ." he stammered, "Bessie . . . come to . . . she come to help."

"What?" The monster was back raging her fangs at his ribs.

"She don't mean no harm to us. She come to help."

"I can help you. Whaddya need her for? Don't do it, Pa; don't let her touch Mama's things. It ain't right." He had to get her out of there.

"I'll go home now, Barret," Bessie said, coming out onto the porch. Her voice was controlled, but her fingers twitched furiously, scraping the sides of her arms. Barret did not try to stop her from leaving.

"Oh, Papa. Don't do it." Barret hugged his son until he stopped sobbing. Then he told him he had to go back to Granny's after they had lunch.

"Forget about Bessie," he said, "she don't mean no harm."

"When did she come?" Carter saw that Papa looked away from him. He knew he didn't belong at Granny's; but now he felt that he didn't belong here either.

"Just today," Barret said. He got up and crossed to the mantel. "I think the clock needs oiling." The monster dipped into Carter's stomach, churning and tearing. He knew Papa was lying. Barret accidentally moved the hand to the hour and set it off. Two gongs. Out came Lance.

"What would happen if just once Lance did it wrong?" Carter asked. "If, just once, the dragon knocked him off his horse instead of dying herself? Would the clock ever run again?" Would the mechanism fall apart forever? Does everything break down sooner or later, like love, or families? Does anything escape the erosion of time? He couldn't taste the cold meat Barret set before him, but somehow he got it down. Papa never answered his question.

After lunch, he went to Mo's doghouse and dug up his mother's brooch. He pushed it deep into his pocket and galloped the horse, all the way back to Granny's.

After the incident with Bessie and his father, he almost never dared to go home. Papa visited his children often, taking them to church and occasionally on a picnic. Sometimes Carter would learn of his visits after they occurred, because he was down at the station. Barret often scolded him for going off on his wanderings, but he did what he pleased. Why should he care what Papa wanted of him, when he didn't want him to live at home? Off he went to Cousin Henry's, to Mill Pond, but mostly he went to the trains. His adventures there became more and more frequent. He brought the harmonica Barret had given him. He sat on the edge of the platform and played whenever someone passed by.

Sometimes he took the buggy, but on a day in late July, he ran all the way to the station. He heard the triple hoo of the mourning dove float high on the wind. Who taught him to wail only three times? Other birds chirped, singing their parts together, but he was separate, alone in his misery, moaning his reverberating hoo hoo hoo; waiting a time, and then sailing his echo again into the wind.

The wail of the freight's whistle covered the dove's sound. It came Wednesdays and Thursdays at noon. The coalie came at five-thirty. The first thing you saw was the plume. A great silver puff like a squirrel's tail wagging its way behind the engine. Now, she slowed into the station and almost stopped. The loud chugging softened and was covered with sharp voices hurling obscenities into the air. Three men in an open boxcar stood pushing and scuffling with each other. Two of them were trainmen. Carter climbed a tree so he could see better, and gasped to see the man who was not in uniform thrown headlong off the train. He fell with a crack onto the powdered dirt, landing on his side and scraping a big tear in his pants.

"You lousy bum. It serves you right," yelled one of the men still on the train.

The man on the ground shook his fist at them. "You stole my food. All bulls is bastards and more bastards — that's what you are!" He did not get up, but sat there rubbing his leg as the train lurched and then gathered speed. The men laughed.

Carter waited until the train was gone, and then he ran down to him. "Are you hurt?" he said. The man smelled of decay.

He drank from a bottle he pulled from his back pocket. "Sons of bitches, bulls, stole my gear and damn near broke my leg!"

"Is it broke?" Carter half hoped it was. He had never seen a broken leg.

"Don't suppose," said the man. He stood slowly, and Carter could see blood oozing from his gaping pant leg. The man grinned, and Carter saw with disgust that part of his upper lip was missing. His smile stuck out like a leer, and his eye teeth hung in fangs, grinning stalactites chopping at his words. "Fuckin' bulls would have done me in if I wasn't sharp. But I'll get them some day. Always do. You can't pull a snake's tail without it turns around and bites you." He began patting his pockets and pulled out tobacco and paper. They both stood there baking in the sun. The man's collar bones stuck out like elbows. He was as thin as a cattail, and his knees were always bent, probably from all the bouncing he did on a moving train.

"What about water?" he said. "Any water around here?" He was probably in his forties, and looked like he had been quite agile before he got hurt.

"Station house got water to drink," Carter said. "I guess you could wash your leg there."

"Well, let's get it, young fella. Looks like you're the only friend I got right now. Come on — move." He handed Carter his flask as an offering, and so he took a tiny sip, being careful not to cough. Then he wiped his mouth roughly on his sleeve. As the man reached to take it back again, he used his other hand, and Carter saw that his pinkie finger was gone. Where might these missing pieces of anatomy be?

"Smoke?" said the man, offering a hand-rolled cigarette. Carter stretched a little taller. Then the man stared hard at the boy and put his hand up around his shoulder, but Carter twisted out of it and ran a little ahead of him. They puffed away as they headed toward the rain barrel. Carter was careful not to touch him.

The man poured water on his wound and tied it with his handkerchief. "Now, lessee," he said. "Where is a store around here? Gotta get me some supplies, and then I'll be moving again." He spat on the ground. "So wheresat store?"

"Coming up soon — ahead," said Carter. The general store was south of the railroad.

They walked toward it. Again he put his hand on Carter's shoulder; again Carter twisted away.

"Lookee," he said, "when we go in, you ask him to fit you a pair of shoes, ya hear?" This was great news. A man whom he hardly knew was going to buy him a pair of new shoes.

"Sure thing," Carter said.

"Keep him busy with your shoes." They went into the crowded store. Carter lost sight of his friend in his excitement over the shoes. He loved to get new clothes. When he finally found a pair that fit — big brown ones of smooth leather, he looked up and realized that the man was gone.

"How are the shoes?" said the store owner. Carter didn't answer. He blinked as he continued to look for the man.

"Carter! How're your shoes?" he said again.

"Uh, they . . . they hurt. Don't feel good," he said. "Try you again, sir." He switched to his own shoes and hurried out.

He saw the man limping about fifty yards ahead on the road to the station. "Hey," he called. "Why'd you go? What about my shoes?" The man laughed.

"Well, now, I told you I have to ride, didn't I boy?" His oversized shirt bulged, and he hugged himself around his stomach. "When you ride them rails, it's like you own the country. You can go anywhere. See everything. Get drunk in Chicago, sober up by time you hit Kansas City. Just clacking along." He leered. They had rounded the turn and now could see the station. "Best sound in the world. Love to hear that clacking — just as long as the bulls don't catch you." He opened his shirt and removed several items that

Carter had seen earlier in the store: a frying pan, blanket, folded knapsack, odd utensils, and several jars of food. "I'm the King of Siam when I ride the rails. I'm the President of the U-nited States. 'Course I have to get my supplies first. Whatya say? Want to come?" He put his hand on Carter's chest and rubbed it down over his stomach. Carter backed up. "Why're you so jittery now, boy?" Carter felt sick. This was the strangest and scariest man he had ever met. And he had been his accomplice. He had just helped the King of Siam rob the general store. He touched the brooch in his pocket. His mother would have cried.

"You took all that!" Carter said. His voice got very high.

"Told you I was sharp," said the man. "There's two kinds of people: them that're like you, and everybody else. Them that're like you, you help them and they help you. Them that aren't, you gotta be sharper than them. Now when do you suppose Old Dirty Face'll be coming through? Tonight maybe?"

"What's that?"

"The next freight, boy. Don't you know anything? Come with me. I'll teach you all about trains." He ran his hand down Carter's arm.

You stink, mister, he wanted to say. You really stink. "There's a freight at noon tomorrow; I can't go though — anywhere with you," was all he could manage.

The man shot his hand out and twisted Carter's wrist. His stench was nauseating.

"You're telling the truth about that train, boy. I know you're telling it, because if you fixing to tell anybody what I done, I'll get you — you know it, don't you? Like I said — don't ever pull a snake's tail."

Carter pulled his hand away and stared at the man's missing lip. Specks of his saliva sprayed on Carter's face. "You better come with me. You're making a big mistake." He put his new possessions in the knapsack. "Calvin's my real name, boy. I suppose you thought I was Calvin Coolidge." And the head went back, and he laughed in big chokes so that his fangs quivered.

"Warren's my real name, boy," Carter lied. "I suppose you thought I was Warren Harding."

"Watch out who yer callin' boy, boy," said the man. "Name ain't Coolidge. It's Jones. And nobody calls me Calvin anymore. On the rails, everybody gets a new name of their own. Mine's Hellbag Jones. That's what they call me. Now go home and see what eats you can bring old Hellbag tomorrow, and while you're there, you think about coming with me. We'll have a real time of it — I promise you that. See you in the morning before I catch out and start heading south again."

Carter started to run back down the road toward home. He turned and looked back at Hellbag, but he still moved away from him in a kind of backward run. "Heeeeey, Hellbag," he called. The man looked up. Carter stopped. He revved up his voice: "Fu-u-u-u-uck you," he roared as loud as he could and then ran home fast. His wrist hurt for several days.

Chapter 4

Fall came early that year. Mill Pond shimmered with frenzied reds and golds. Running through the swirling fiery leaves was a good distraction from the stabbing ache of his mother's death. The children were still living at Granny's despite Papa's promises to let them come home. When school started, Papa said it would be best if Granny got them ready each morning. Easier he said. Carter tried to convince Papa that he would be no trouble if he came home, but he refused. One day in school, he wrote him a note. It said, "Papa, do you love me? Check yes or no." But he threw it into the pond on his way home. It floated like a leaf.

In November, Carter turned thirteen. Granny made him a chocolate cake, and Papa brought him a copy of *Great Expectations.* Inside it he wrote: "For my dear son Carter, who I love. Papa. November 4, 1925." Carter wondered if he had found the note.

The next day while they were eating what was left of the cake, Granny told them that they were invited to a party at the Chadzik farm. When Carter protested, she said it would be bad manners for him not to attend. She smiled at him. Granny always smiled.

"I don't care about manners;" he said, "besides, the person I hate the most — of anybody — is Bessie Chadzik."

"Hate is something like quicksand," Granny said, "the harder you work at it, the deeper you sink. And then it festers inside you. Besides, in the Bible it says, 'love one another.' Try to look for something good about her."

"There isn't anything. I hate her. And you know what? Cousin Henry said he saw her, and she is trying to dress like Mama. I really hate her!"

"Shame!" said Granny. "You mustn't say that about anyone. Come on now, Carter, there has to be one thing good. You can think of it. Remember the Good Book." Her face and hair were white-gray. She always wore black.

"Well . . ." he tried.

"That's it . . ."

"She cooks good."

"There you see?"

"I won't go," he said. He felt his anger come up into his mouth as if it were a big piece of phlegm.

"Your mama would have wanted you to. She cared about manners." Unfair!

She held out a pair of his grandpa's suspenders in her arthritic hands. It was her guilt gift. She knew how much he liked to dress up and not wear farm clothes. Yet he didn't really like the suspenders. They reminded him too much of the leads that went around his shoulders when he had to walk behind Mabel. But he wore them anyway.

"You'll need new shoes too," she said. "Your feet are growing big. The party is next Sunday, so there's time." He winced when he thought of his last encounter with buying shoes.

In spite of himself, he enjoyed the party, but he made sure that he stayed far away from Bessie. Neighbors and relatives fussed over them, and several ladies — old and young — let him know in one way or another how good he looked.

"He looks like that Douglas Fairbanks one — only his hair has red in it," he heard old Mrs. Dance say to his Granny when he passed by. He had slicked his hair with Grandpa's hair tonic. He felt older. He had even shaved his fuzz of a mustache for the first time.

"Barret, your children are a picture. I just have never seen anyone with such green eyes like Carter's" Mrs. Dance continued her praise to his father. She said it a bit sorrowfully. "My stars, such beauties, tsk, tsk." No one mentioned their mother, but you could hear the sadness under the words. Carter thought it strange that his father never looked at him that day. But he was distracted by all the attention he was getting.

Cassandra Dance, a fat girl of his own age, looked at him with rapt attention. "Something ain't just so here, Carter," she said, getting up from her seat on the living room couch. Carter had always liked Cassandra. It was comfortable to be with her. "Something bad's going to happen here." She crossed to him. "I'd better stay by you, Carter," she said to him. "I'll even hold your hand if you like me to."

"Do you think I'm a baby?"

"Can't help it," Cassandra said. "Something I feel."

"What's wrong with you? Don't get weird on me." And then he turned away from his long-time friend, because at that moment he saw Violet! Her family was visiting from New York. She had a china doll face with a tiny nose and the longest blond hair he had ever seen. It made him gasp to look at her. He couldn't tell how old she was, but she had little puffs of breasts. Yes! He loved the way her dress pulled across them! Cassandra slumped into the kitchen and pretended to help with the food.

Violet stood near the back door and fussed with her hair. Whenever he looked at her, she was looking at him. He was taken in completely with all her ribbons and lace, and that name! He had heard of "Daisy" and "Lily," but imagine naming someone "Violet." Violets had personality. She smiled, turned

quickly, and went out the door into the yard.
The ducks set up a squawking, and that slowed
her down. She was obviously a city girl. Then
she was caught in the crowd of them. Carter
moved fast and went out the door behind her.

"They won't hurt you," he said. "Where
are you going?" He knew she liked his eyes.
He could tell the way she looked at them. He
shooed the ducks away.

"I just needed some fresh air," she
said. He was much taller than she was.

"Come on, I'll take you for a walk." He
took her hand. He put it in the pocket of his
coat. They got out of sight of the house
fast. He knew he didn't have much time.
"You're a real pretty girl."

"So they say." Now what kind of answer
was that? What was he supposed to say?

"Guess you have a lot of boy friends up
there in New York."

"Enough to keep me busy." Here was
someone with experience.

"Well . . . So . . . And how — uh — how do
you like kissing?" he said.

She smiled and leaned up against a tree.
"Depends on who I'm kissing." He put his
arms around her, then crushed his hand
against the tree's bark when he dived in fast
and pressed her. He was so nervous that they
bumped heads before he finally found her
mouth. A shy violet she wasn't. They stood
there pressing mouths, and she put her arms
around his neck. So this is how you do it!
This must be the Big Time, he thought. Or did
he already experience Big Time sex when he'd
had his hand in Bessie's bloomers? No. That
didn't count. Bessie was ugly. Now he had
finally arrived.

But before he could enjoy any more
bliss, he heard the gang of little kids

coming to look for them. He quickly let go of her. They broke apart. She smiled and looked away from him.

The children had been sent to bring them back inside. Greta pulled on his arm. Cassandra held her other hand. "Papa has a 'nouncement, Carty," she said.

"What is she talking about?"

"We don't know," Andy said. "They told us to bring you back in for an announcement." He looked at Cassandra, hating himself for treating her badly. She knows, he thought to himself. She always knows.

He started running back toward the house, leaving the others, even leaving Violet behind. The sense of dread fell on him like a net.

There they were — all the adults gathered around his father and Bessie, toasting with their glasses; and then he knew!

"No," he said, and Granny grabbed his arm.

"Hush, Carter," she said. "Don't say anything, child. Be very quiet and stay here with Granny." By now the other children had entered the house too, and Mr. Chadzik, Bessie's father, began to speak. He had stayed sober just long enough to get through this moment. All the while Granny held Carter close to her.

"We are happy to tell you children that you now have a new mama!" He rocked back on his heels like Bessie, bouncing his paunch up and down. "Right before we came here today, Barret and Bessie tied the knot in Lunt's Church. Isn't that swell!"

There was a hush as everyone turned to look at the children. All those faces with forced smiles, hoping that if they stared and smiled hard enough, they could wish away the hurt. Lots of yellow teeth and wide open eyes kept nodding at the children.

Carter's voice started to talk without him. "You can't do such a thing. Oh, Papa! In the same church where she's buried? You can't, you can't —" No one else was in the room or in the world just then. Just the two of them facing each other. "You didn't tell me? You didn't even tell me?" he hollered. Papa's face was pinched and hurt, but the hurt was for Carter. His eyes were empty like holes, and Carter thought he might fall in.

Andy and Rob were bawling, and Greta was howling in Granny's arms. Quite a celebration.

Carter took off the jacket he was wearing and hurled it on the floor. It was the same one he had worn to the funeral. A button flew off it and whizzed by Bessie's head like a bullet. "You can all go to hell!" he whooped and ran out of the house. A sob caught in Papa's throat, but Carter was out the door — off their property — into the woods — twigs tearing his shirt sleeves — eyes pounding and chest heaving for air.

He ran parallel to the road that led to the church, when he heard his brother's voice. Rob's little legs bobbed in a jerky staccato, and he was trying desperately to catch up.

"W-a-i-t!" His feet pounding the earth made his voice rise and fall with each hammer of his shoes.

"No," said Carter, but he did slow down.

"Where can we go?" Rob wanted to know.

"I'm running."

"I know that, but where?"

"Come and see." And they kept running, gasping for breath, until they saw the church spire through a stand of pines. "Did you ever come . . . here?   By yourself, I mean," Carter gasped. They kept on. Rob did not answer.

Then it dawned on him. "Oh, no!" said Rob. "I'm not going . . . where I think you're going." He jumped on Carter, piggy-back style, trying to stop him, trying to knock him down. But all he succeeded in doing was to wrap his legs around Carter. By this time they had cleared the trees, and Carter headed straight for the graveyard, running with Rob on his back.

"Come on," he said. "Be brave."

"Shit!" said Rob, but he stayed mounted on Carter's back. "You're dumb, not brave. It's stupid to come here."

When they reached the graveyard's gate, Carter stopped and Rob slid down. "I'm not going," Rob said as Carter held the gate open for him. He stood firm outside the tiny cemetery, distracted by the long shadows of the monuments made by the falling November sun.

"We have to tell her what Papa did," Carter said, walking between the graves toward the tall gray monument that looked something like a tower. "We have to tell her what happened."

"Shit," said Rob. "You think she don't know?" He swung the gate and ran in behind Carter. "You stupid fool. Whaddya think you're doing here?"

"Shut up, Rob," Carter said. The Ruden monument was as tall as his shoulder, and only about a foot square around. It had four equal sides, with the names of the dead Rudens on each side. The top was carved to a point. He walked around, facing his mother's name, but the sight of it caught him off guard. He sank to his knees, and heard his heart moan.

"'Smatter," said Rob, stopping behind him. "Lose your nerve? You think she don't know? And if she don't, why do you want to tell her? Why do you want to make her upset? You're so dumb, sometimes. Dumb, dumb, dumb!" Carter's back was to him, and he mistook his posture, thinking Carter was praying to their mother. "Get the hell out of here!" He jerked forward, landing next to Carter on the ground. "You hear me? You heah —" And he stopped when he saw the expression on Carter's face.

They were both silent for a time. Carter did not take his eyes off her name, and then he said, "You're right. She does know. She knows all about Bessie, and you know what? She doesn't even care. She doesn't even care where we live at all."

"You're loony as a wild dog."

"There has to be somewhere to belong —"

"Why you talking like that? Huh?" Rob interrupted.

"There has to be somewhere to belong — doesn't there?" All the while he stayed there on his knees, his eyes never left the letters of her name. "Doesn't there, Mama?"

EMMA ROSE RUDEN SHIELDS

"Stop it, Carter. She didn't tell you all this. You're just making it up. She can't talk to you. It's shit, is all. A bunch of shit."

"It's not like she said it. But I heard it just the same. I don't know who it was said it, but there's more."

"Stop! do you hear?" Rob wailed. "You better get away from that Cassandra girl. She been spookin' you."

Carter never heard him. "My letters will

never be here — the letters of my name. I
won't ever be able to look down and see the
letters on my grave."

"Who? Who for crissakes? Who told you
that?"

"I don't know," Carter said. "I just
heard it. Just now. A voice. Said there won't
be any. No name on my grave."

"I hate her and you," said Rob. And then
his tears gushed, and Carter held him, remembering something Granny had said once. "Do
you know how long you hold someone when they
cry?" she asked. "No," he said. "You hold
them as long as it takes." So Rob cried and
cried, and Carter held him as long as it
took; and bit his lip, and heard the moan
again deep in his own soul.

Granny was right about the quicksand. He
was sinking in.

After a while, Rob spoke. "Bessie said
she wanted it to be a surprise. The bitch!
Can't you think of a plan or something?"

"A plan for what?"

"For us to do. To mess up Bessie — you
know, something mean — get rid of her."

"Papa must have gone crazy. He isn't
Papa anymore."

"Of course he is!" Rob said. "Who else
is he, for crissakes?"

"Well then, put it this way, you can't
trust him. He lies."

"Everybody lies," said Rob.

"There's nobody you can count on,"
Carter said.

"There's only one thing you can count on
— is the seeds and the earth, the land when
you work it."

"I can't," said Carter. "I'll never do
that. I'll just have to find something else."

"Like what?"

"I don't know yet, but something."

"You just can't set still long enough is all." He pulled on some ferns by his foot. He tied two of them into a knot. Then he looked at Carter. "Well then, what about Bessie?"

"What about her?"

"Let's mess her up. Think of something."

"Wouldn't help. Papa still isn't Papa anymore. The family is all like a pretend game."

"Well, what is there to count on?"

Carter realized he was freezing. "I don't know. Movin', I guess. Keep on movin', little brother, is all. We have to go back to them," he said.

"No, let's go home." And so they walked back to their house, but when they got there, they hid in the barn and got warm in the horse blanket. Papa found them when he and Bessie came home. Carter could not look at him.

By this time, he was so used to having the rug pulled out from under him, that he didn't even expect the floor to be there when he landed. After that day in the cemetery, he dreamed about his mother often. Then the dreams would come to him in little pieces when he was awake. Often she haunted him from the corners of rooms or from behind flowers. He often thought he heard her whisper a quick "Carter" disguised in the rasp of another sound. But if he turned to look, there was only a space.

There was no surface where the floor had been. Instead, there was only a narrow plank to walk on. Like the oak branch that stretched across the narrow part of Mill

Pond, where he used to walk sometimes with tender steps, or sometimes hand over hand, crisscrossing over to show off. The tree which grew out of the side of the bank had always comforted him as if it gave him her "arm" to protect him. And if no one were there, he stretched himself tight and let go in the middle of the pond. That was when he allowed himself to fantasize that she was still alive — that he could still give her the earbobs he had bought, and she would smile and say how good he was, and look right into his face, as if she were taking a picture of him. And then he would fall down in the water, feeling safe and happy when it covered him. He listened to its full silence and let himself go limp until he rolled to the surface. And it wasn't until he was swimming back to the shore, that he would admit that she was gone. But all that had happened before the disastrous wedding.

And now it was too cold to swim.

Chapter 5

Barret always used to say, "Be careful what you wish for — you might get it." He was right. For months, Carter had wanted to move back home with his father. Now he got his wish. Only Bessie was there. Never in his wildest dreams could he have imagined the nightmare he would walk into, and the loneliness he would have as a result of Bessie's horrible schemes and machinations.

He could not even speak to his father if she were nearby. It was as if his father had lost his voice. Whenever anyone tried to speak to him, Bessie answered. If Greta went to him for a hug, Bessie would step in between them.

The days dragged with a pall over them. Carter wondered how they got through it all. He and Papa avoided each other. It was easier when he went to school. There he put on a good show of being carefree. It helped. He also found his way down to watch the trains more and more frequently. It got him out of the house and away from Bessie. He had to bite hard against the outrage of having her sleep in his mother's bed and touch his mother's things. He couldn't imagine his father "doing it" with her. How could he? She was so ugly and hateful. Once he even saw her half-bare. She was getting undressed in his mother's room, and she left the door wide open. He crouched down behind the old chest that held his mother's linens in the hall and told himself to go downstairs, but he kept watching. Why did she leave the door open? He finally got to see what he had touched years before in their game of Blindman's Buff. Her breasts were enormous balls with huge dark brown nipples.

Carter had been to the trains a hundred times, but on an unusually mild day toward the end of November, he made a change in his ordinary routine that affected his life forever. How he later wished it had never happened! He had taken Junie Lou, the best girl in his class, down to see the coalie train come through, because it often dropped pieces of coal, and she wanted to find some to bring home to her mother. The day was overcast, and everything looked brown and worn out. Of course, he took her through the woods, so he could get in as much kissing as possible. Normally, he walked the road to the station; but because Junie was with him, the woods it was. He was vaguely aware that he was unfamiliar with this part of the woods, but it didn't seem important. A loud and sudden voice splitting the air, singing in French made them both jump. There was no warning. Even if they had ever heard opera before, they might not have known how extraordinary it was to hear someone singing it in the woods. They ducked down in the bushes and listened to the rich tenor:

> *Ces livres sur qui tant de fois*
> *Nous avons incliné nos têtes*
> *rapprochées*

Carter slowly rose up from the brush, looked in the direction of the sound, and was astounded to see a "community" of three vagabonds, going about their business in a hodgepodge of makeshift lean-tos and other broken-down paraphernalia well shielded by the trees. He whistled in a whisper. What a terrific discovery! He saw one of the men tending a fire in a short clearing in front of the "house," and another far to the left was facing sideways away from the rude structure. He was peeing into the woods, and singing at the top of his voice.

> *Et ces armes (un jour ma min les a*
> *touchées Déja J'étais impatient Du long*
> *repos auquel J'aspire!)*
> *Pourquoi me réveiller, ô souffle du*
> *printemps?*

Junie got scared and ran home, but Carter stayed to watch. He was afraid too, but he was too fascinated to go. A third man was coming from the direction of the stream to the right. He shook several dripping utensils and a frying pan. All around the camp were wooden boxes, sticks in the ground with tin cans turned upside down on them, and various items hanging from nails that had been put in the trees: a pair of boxing gloves, a slice of a mirror with a razor strop and bowl, and a clothesline that had been strung in the back right corner behind everything. Of course, there was a woodpile. The center of attraction, however, was an old bath tub covered on top with planks of wood. He guessed it was their "table". In spite of the thrown-together nature of this place (which he later learned is called a jungle — every train yard had one, all across the country) it was relatively clean. There seemed to be some kind of order to it.

"Hello there," he called, not coming too close and hoping his voice didn't crack. "What's for dinner?"

"Lookee," said the man with the fire, "just who we need." He was turning three rabbits on a spit.

"What would you be needing me for?"

"As it turns out, we just used our last match. Have you got any? I don't feature sticking my head in that fire to light my ciggyret." He was friendly, but the smell of them was awful.

"I don't have any, but I can get you some," Carter said. "Anything else you need? I can probably get some food. I'll bring that too."

"Well now, ain't that nice?"

"No trouble," Carter said.

"You can have some rabbit when you comes back." He held out his hand. "Name here's

Mile Away. This here's Lion Hearted." He indicated the one who had the wet utensils in his hand. Lion, who had a huge shock of yellow hair that stuck out like a mane, also shook his hand. "And that there's Deadman." He was the one who had been singing and urinating. He barely grunted at Carter and sat on a box. In spite of Deadman, he felt very welcome. He told them his name, and Mile Away said it would take some time for him to get a real railroad name. "It has to come out of the action," he said. "Depends how life goes you." He wore two wool shirts, a yellow and a blue, and a dark green heavy sweater. He kept stretching its arms to cover his wrists, because he was cold. He had a puffy shape. His face was deeply lined brown leather, and his nails looked like they had rusted. His brown eyes were so bloodshot, they looked maroon, but they were friendly and smiled at Carter.

"'Course some names is a c'ruption. Take Lion Hearted here. Name used to be Lyin' Harvey. Like telling a lie, you know? Reason is women, ain't it, Lion." Lion winked. "He got so many women in so many places, he had to lie to all of them at once. Still does. But there's two ways of lying. He also got them flat on their backs most of the time, know what I mean?"

Carter laughed as loud as he could. "'Course I know," he said.

"But he changed his name to Lion Hearted. It's a c'ruption."

"Got sick of 'Harvey'," said Lion. He ran his hand over his mane. "Don't mind the lyin' part."

They even let him into their card game, which was played on the tub. Carter always thought he was a good card player, but he was no match for these pros. Deadman was the dealer, so it took forever to play. His skin was like wax, and his eyes never blinked. He couldn't turn his head, so his whole body moved if he wanted to look sideways. He rarely spoke, and when he did, Carter couldn't understand the grunts he made. The only time he made any sense was when he peed. Then his voice sang out clear as Caruso's. Since Carter had no money, when the game was over, he ran home for some goodies instead.

"Well, wash my dishes!" said Mile Away when Carter returned with matches, some food, and an old navy coat that he got from Cousin Henry. "I'll look like a goddamned sailor. Thankee, son." He put it on top of everything else he had on.

"Why don't you take off your sweater first?" Carter said.

"Well, damn," said Mile Away, "in winter time you wear everything you got. I thankee much. That's like being a son to me." He touched Carter's arm, but the boy moved away.

"Hell, I'd rather be your friend," Carter said. Mile Away had teeth only on one side of his mouth on the top, and his face looked lopsided. He spoke very slowly; in fact he did everything slowly, but he was warm and kind, unlike Hellbag.

"Now, ain't that something here. He wants to be my friend. Yes sir, kid, that's fine." He smoked a pipe and held it in the good side of his mouth. The pipe was lopsided too.

"Whose gloves are those?" Carter said, pointing to the boxing gloves on the tree.

"Anybody's," Lion said.

"Reckon I can show you how to box," Carter said. He had never boxed, but he had seen it in the movies and somehow he just knew he could.

"Gud," Deadman grunted.

"I can play the harmonica too. Sometime I'll play for you."

"Gud."

"Play it now," said Lion.

He played "Suwannee River."   Deadman sang, without peeing this time.

"Gud," he said when it was over.

Chapter 6

Christmas was coming. He could not imagine it without his mother and hated to look at the tree Bessie put up. One night about a week before the big day, the three boys and their father were playing cards in the parlor when they heard a shriek from the kitchen. Bessie ran in holding her finger.

"Feetie, Feetie — lookee — I told you Feetie, I can't cut meat by myself."   She spoke a kind of baby talk to Barret. "Feetie" was her word for "Sweetie."   She had been trying to cut up the remains of a large roast to make it into another meal. The predictable tears followed. Carter looked at her cut, which she kept shoving in his father's face.

"For heaven's sake," said Carter, "wrap it up, and be done with it — it's not deep. You make it sound like you're going to bleed to death."

"You heard him. You heard how he talks to me. Why can't he be nice? I had no one to help. You had to play your old cards."   And she sat herself on Papa's lap. Why was he putty in her hands?   Why couldn't he be a man?   Tell her what a fake she was, and get rid of her for good? She seemed to change him into something else, and he always looked sad.

He bandaged her finger accompanied by apologies and kisses, and then she insisted that he make her tea and sit with her for the remainder of the evening. So much for cards with the boys.

Carter gave her the widest berth he could for his father's sake, but father and son became more and more estranged.

One day he came home from school and found her spanking Greta's bare bottom.

"Get away from her," he roared.

"Look what she did," yelled Bessie. "Just look at that jam all over here." A jar of her preserves was smashed on the wooden floor and the jam was everywhere.

"I didn't do it," cried Greta.

"Well now, there was no one else here all day but you and me, so who do you think did it, Miss Sassy Mouth? Do you think I did it? Huh? Is that what you think?" She reached to pull Greta's hair, but Carter grabbed her arm.

"I'm telling you right now, Bessie," he said. "Don't ever touch her, or you'll be good and sorry." She let go, and Greta, yowling until she was hoarse, escaped upstairs. "You're going too far, Bessie. You're not our mother —"

"Oh, yes I am. I'm your stepmother, and you have to mind me." She started to cry. "I do try so hard for you, Carter. I declare, I make pies and cakes and nice suppers, but nobody ever likes me." He could not bear it. "Can't we try to be friends? After all, you're the oldest, and very close to my own age." He really wanted to hurt her. He took another jar of her preserves off the pantry shelf and smashed it on the floor.

"You make me sick," he said. "Tell Pa I went to Granny's." And he left her screaming out the window for his father. As he stepped off the front porch, Greta called him from her window.

"Carty, don't go." She was still blubbering. "Please stay with me." Lord, she could tear him, that baby sister. Then he saw the boys coming.

"Here's Andy and Rob. Don't worry, Baby. I'll be home after dinner." He ran for the buggy next to the barn. He hated to look at Rob's disappointed eyes. He had never made good on his promise to think of a plan to "mess up" Bessie and get rid of her.

When he returned after supper, Greta was asleep and his brothers were doing homework. Papa was reading, and Bessie was knitting something. What a picture, he thought. Home sweet home.

"Hello, Papa," he said, "what are you reading?" He knew he would have to apologize, but he tested the waters. Papa never answered him. "Okay, Bessie. I'm sorry about your jam. I'll weed your garden for you. How's that?"

"Son," began his father. His eyes looked cold and hurt. " . . . you know your mother would not want —"

"Well, now, how about some pie?" Bessie cut in. "I have some lovely pecan pie just how you like it, Barret." She shooed them into the kitchen. Carter was still hungry, and so he ate it. Bessie continued her chatter about the difficulties of keeping all her men happy and well-fed. They chewed in silence, because everyone was tired of trying to start conversations that she would finish.

That night, Papa had to go away. One of

his brothers was going to slaughter his hogs the next day. This required many hands. It was customary for several of the men to spend the night there, so they could begin as soon as dawn broke. Carter wanted to kiss his father good-bye, but he could not get up enough nerve, and then Papa was out the door and gone.

Carter went upstairs and lay on his bed. Turning out the light on his night table, he saw the crooked silver lines that the moonlight made on the floor. They had always been there in the background of his memories from the time he was a small boy. Silver lines on the floor from the moon's light, like train tracks for him to think on. He fell into a deep sleep.

He had no idea how long he slept, but some time later as he lay on his back, he was aware of his erection and a pleasurable feeling filling him all over. Gushing through his dream, water cascaded in all directions, velvet water, warm and tingling, stretching him, giddy and sprawling into rapture. But then he knew that someone was touching him, holding him there, and he tried to snap awake but he was too far gone to stop. Horror seized him as he realized his nightshirt was pulled up, and someone was there, half-lying on the bed with his penis in her mouth. Bessie! Sucking him — thrilling, swimming, and then he came.

"Oh, God," he gasped, jerking his knees up and shoving her away as hard as he could.

"Oh, Carter," she said, "Dear, dear Carter. I'm so glad." She held her hands up to her wet face.

He fought for air. "Get out of here," he thundered. "Get your fucking self out of my sight!"

"No, no, Carter, it's all right. You'll see — I want us to be close. I never had anything like this before — anything like you. I watch you all the time. This is the first time you were having the dream."

"Out!" He fixed his clothing and slid off the bed on the opposite side.

"But Uncle Ernie told me how good it is. He used to —"

"OUUUT!"

"You'll see, after you think about it. This will make everything fine between us. You are a man now, aren't you? We can have us good times and all," she said. She went around the foot of the bed and pulled her blouse up exposing her chest. He tried to run past her. "You'll change how you think about me. I know it. I can feel it, and if —" He tripped and smashed the window. Distorted triangles of glass crashed on the floor.

"Get out of here!" he screamed. "Don't you ever set your filthy feet in here. Pig. That's what you are."

"What is the matter with you?" She was on fire.

"You are a fucking pig."

"You are just crazy! You are a crazy, mean boy!" She shrieked all the way down the hallway.

His chest wheezed. Trying to stop shaking, he wrapped a cloth around his cut hand and sat on the floor. His blood pumped so hard, he could hear it. It took all his concentration to get control of himself. After a while, he went to the shelf where his books were. Finding some paper, he began to write.

Dear Papa,
    You always told me we come from
good stock. You said that when your
grandfather had to run away from Germany because they took his lands, it
was the bravest and noblest thing anybody ever did. If he had stayed there
it would have been the same thing as
letting someone beat you up without
even trying to fight back, like some
kind of sissy. Because what our family
had was so much pride and their own
place. Now if they didn't leave, you
said they wouldn't have respect for
themselves. Well now, neither do I. I
mean, for myself. I don't know how to
say it, but it's like somebody stole
something from me here, and I have to
leave. I don't belong and I can't be
proud of anything here. I still love
you, but I can't stay. You wouldn't
want to know all the reasons. Don't
come after me.

                    Your son,
                    Carter

    He put a chair under his doorknob and
lay stiff under the covers. When he finally
fell asleep, he dreamed of the clock in the
parlor. He was looking at the dial, and it
got bigger and bigger until it filled the
whole room, and then he fell into it. The
dial disappeared and so did the room. There
were hundreds of shiny silver lines floating
through space, each belonging to someone. And
he rode on his, and he couldn't get off, but
neither could anyone else. All the people
were going in the same general direction, all

lines pulling inside a blue-black tunnel. And
sometimes the lines crossed, and sometimes
converged. Lance was there too, riding his
line instead of his horse. But there was one
line with a lady on it. She was naked, and he
couldn't see her face, because she always
looked away from him. In a flash, her line
slammed into a giant Christmas tree. It
rippled and stopped, and the energy of the
jolt resounded like a sound made in a tunnel,
and it touched everyone around it. It bat-
tered some people. Others were shocked or
caught short, or they just drooped aimlessly.
There was lightning crackling around her, and
she fell away into a blackness. And all the
pine needles fell on him. Then he had to find
her. He was frantic, and he could not
breathe. He looked everywhere and tried to
ask the passing people if they knew where she
was. But as they came up close to him, their
faces were nothing but blank skin. And his
line kept on going forward, so he could never
find her. He kept looking back, sweating and
shaking, and all he saw was the face of the
clock ghosted behind him, and he was in a
cold, drafty place.

He awoke long before the sun, and taking
his clothes and boy treasures, put them in a
sheet and tied it up. Then he went to the
kitchen and packed some cold meat, jars of
peach preserves, coffee, cereal, and all of
Bessie's famous pies and bread. He hoped it
would cause her trouble — having to bake all
over again.

Then he tiptoed into her room. She lay
on her stomach in a heavy sleep. Going to her
bureau, he slid open a drawer, making no
sound. He took all her underwear out of the

drawer, and silently went downstairs. It was ten minutes to five. Bessie would be waking soon. He went outside and draped her underwear all over the porch railings. He hung frayed bloomers from the trellis where roses used to be, and yellowed brassieres from the empty hooks that had held the hanging petunias. Then he went back inside. He waited by the clock, his hand poised in front of it. When the five chimes finished, and the dragon came out, he stopped the pendulum, leaving the dragon and Lance permanently exposed. He took a ribbon off one of Bessie's camisoles and tied it around the dragon's head. Then he hooked the shoulder strap in her mouth letting the camisole swing down freely in front of the clock. Finally, he tilted her Christmas tree over slowly until it lay on its side in the middle of the parlor.

The moon had turned the ground fog silver. Trudging through the iridescence of the night was like seeing a dream move away as you passed through it. He must have looked like some weird kind of Santa Claus with the big sack of his possessions. This was going to be some Christmas! He knew he would break his father's heart, but he couldn't help it. There wasn't much left of his.

Chapter 7

Mile Away carved Carter's name on the big oak tree right under his. "Now you're a official man of the road — like me," he said. "Put your name on a tree — it's official."

Deadman had caught some fish, so they had quite a breakfast celebration. Mile Away gave him his own place to sleep. It was a lean-to made of wood and cardboard. They played lots of cards. He watched them while he played and got better and better. He played "close to the vest" like a pro.

On Christmas Eve, he got dead drunk. He alternately slept and vomited for two days. He did himself a favor, because, even though he was miserably sick, when he awoke, he realized he had missed the whole thing.

Then Mile Away told him he was going to Georgia to see his brother. "I can always hit him for some cash. He's a highfalutin' doctor down there." He spat out of the space in his mouth and rubbed himself. He even rubbed slow.

"Will Deadman and Lion stay here?" Carter asked.

"Never know."

"How long will you be gone?"

"Few days, I guess. Long as it takes to get the cabbage. What do you say, kid?"

"Well, I don't know. I guess I say, good luck."

"No, I mean, want to come?" Mile Away said.

"Come with you?" A train hooted in the distance. It was like a cue.

"There's the whistle. What do you say, friend of mine?" There were only about thirty seconds to decide. The clackety-clack rhythm of the wheels sang in Carter's head. "Don't cost nothing. That's for sure." He slung his gear which was all packed over his back.

"My stuff isn't ready," Carter said.

"That's nothing. I got plenty. Be back in two days."

"Oh, Lord almighty!" said Carter. And they ran for the tracks.

"We're catchin' out," said Mile Away.

She slowed as she made the turn. She was a long freight. "Old Dirty Face," he remembered Hellbag had called it. Mile Away headed for a boxcar that was open, and ran alongside, keeping perfect time to the train.

"Move with her, first like this; then hoist," he shouted at him. It was the only time he moved fast — when he ran for a train. He threw his gear up, and jumped on, hollering more instructions.

"Run faster. Grab the hinges! Swinghup. Ha! That's it! We're gone." Carter landed on his back, whooping and hollering, feeling like he could fly.

He knew what old Hellbag was talking about as soon as they sneaked on that train. His first ride on the rails! He too felt like the King of Siam. He was thrilled to his bones. Here was a freedom he'd never felt before. He was swept away in the roaring current of the train. The farms flew behind him like ribbons in the wind. He wished his brothers could have seen it. And then he began to feel bad that he wasn't there to protect them and Greta from Bessie. He felt them falling away from him, and then he felt terribly afraid. He was not ready to be on his own. And no one had told him not to fly too close to the sun.

"Don't you never go nowhere on a train without me," Mile Away cut into his thoughts. "There's too many things can go wrong." He had to shout over the loud cadence of the train.

"Reckon I know that," Carter said. He looked out through the frame of the open doors. "It's like a movie screen," he said.

Only the scenery here was alive. The rhythm
was so pleasing. The clackety-clack returned
to give him a kind of hope.

"But listen to me, kid," said Mile Away,
"Still, never without me, and if anybody
talks to you, you tell me, y'hear? There's
too much you don't know yet." Carter really
wasn't paying much attention to him. "Hear
me?"

"Uh . . . anybody like who?"

"Look, friend," he said, "people like
you and me is too easy for bad folks. They'll
steal you; maybe even kill you. Ever see any
really bad ones?" Carter thought immediately
of Hellbag.

"Well . . . not really," he said.

Mile Away held him with his maroon eyes.
They would not let go of him. His voice moved
to a higher, breathy pitch. "Now you listen
good, kid, and don't forget none of this. I
met the Devil once on a train," he said,
"only he didn't have horns — just a farm hat
and overalls. But it was him all the same. He
was brute mean, but he was also ver-ry
smart." His chest heaved in and out. "Much
smarter than me. There was three of us, not
Deadman and Lion, two others you don't know,
Brassbuttons and Sawbones." He became more
and more agitated as he spoke and punctuated
his words with big gestures of his hands.
"And he bet us in a game called Row, and we
don't know how he cheated, but he sure
cheated, and we had nothing left. Not a
penny." He hugged his knees, forgetting
where he was, but his breath came in shorter
and shorter gulps.

They suddenly flew into a tunnel. Carter
bolted up. There was nothing but a pit of
blackness. Mile Away was unfazed. He went
right on shouting his story. Soon they came

into the light again, but Carter was seized
with a grating terror. He moved closer to
Mile Away.

"We was in a boxcar like this, and next
thing you know, this friend of mine, Brassbuttons, gets mad and starts cussing and
accusing this Devil of cheating. So the Devil
jumps up without even using his hands — the
train is full speed, mind you. He is absolutely steady on his feet — I said absolutely
— he picks up my friend in his two hands in
one second and throws him off of the train
like you just snapped your fingers. Shoot, I
messed my pants. Sawbones and me, we said not
one word. We just stared straight ahead as if
everything was the way it was supposed to be.
And damned if that Devil didn't laugh a sound
I never heard before. It tore through your
skin like a 'lectric shock. Then he started
to pack my poor friend's gear.

"'He wont need this anymore,' he says.
He put it all in with his own. 'Time for
another game of Row,' he says. You see, evil
ain't particular who it strikes. Always
remember that! And you and me is nobody.

"'Well,' I says. 'I got no more money,
sir,' I says. I'm trying to be polite, but I
damned near don't know how to say nothin'
right.

"'That's okay,' says the Devil, 'I'll
take your gear.' I swear there was glue in
his eyes. 'You arguing with that?'

"'Oh, no,' we says.

"'And when that's gone, I'll take your
soul,' he says; and his laugh went buzzing
through us again. You could almost see it —
that laugh. It looked like lightning. That's
when I knowed for sure he was the Devil.

"Sawbones looked at me, and his eyes
said we was caught, and so we played the

cards."

"If there were two of you, why didn't you gang up on him?" Carter said.

"Well, kid, this may . . . this may be hard for you to get, but sometimes when you're scared that much — as much as we was — you can't even move. Couldn't of pulled a setting hen off her nest. That's how scared we was."

"I would have ganged up on him."

"Couldn't. You don't know what evil is till you meet him, I'm telling you. Well now, he was just about through taking all our gear. Then he done something terrible to Sawbones — you know what I mean, kid?" Carter blinked at him. "Well, what it was is — he pulled down his pants and . . . and he raped him — right then and there."

"Well, how can you rape a man?" Carter asked.

He pursed his lips and sucked his teeth. "Look, son, you heard of sodomy, don't ya? That's what he done. There's only one place he can put it, isn't there? Well, that's what he done." Carter wanted to vomit. He thought of Hellbag touching him that day.

"Now, I'm shaking to the death to think what was coming next, when, God Almighty, the train starts to slow. We was coming to a town — don't know where — too scared to think. And next thing you know, he ups and ties all our gear together.

"'Should get a nice price for this,' he says. 'You boys will never see me again, but if you do — watch out.' And a big puff of steam flies up into the car and — swear to God — he disappeared into it. And we had nothing, but at least we was alive, and he didn't get our souls. But he knows that we know he's a murderer. And I don't know if a knife can stab the Devil, but that's why I carry one." He pulled up his pant leg and showed it. "If I ever see him, I sure have to try before he gets me. Still I know sometimes — I know he'll get me. Then I changes the subject and tell myself I'm makin' it up."

"Stop it," Carter said. "Stop making it up."

He was relieved to get back home to Petersburg two days later.

But then he remembered that he didn't really have a home anymore.

"Don't you ever want to live in a real house?" Carter asked Mile Away one day the next summer.

"Hoboing's not as bad as people think. I used to live in a house. Had a woman. Never had no kids though. Wish I did. Nope, I could never go back to that. It's like reading the same newspaper every day. It means everything in here would always be the same too." He pointed to his head. Then he brushed some dirt off his coat sleeve. He loved that old Navy coat Carter had given him.

"Mile Away, do you know when I went to Georgia with you that first time, that was the first time I left Virginia?"

"Well, now," he said, "that would make you a good name. How about we call you 'Virginia Kid'?"

"Think I like Lancelot better. How about Lance for short?"

"Where'd you get that from?"

"I just like it. Ever hear of Lancelot?"

"Whatever you say, kid. How would you like to try New York?" Carter couldn't believe it. He had often dreamed of New York. But imagine New York with him in it!

He got his geography firsthand. After New York, it was Chicago, then Little Rock, then back to their jungle in Petersburg. And a week later, they were off again. They traveled the country for almost a year. Once he wrote Papa a letter telling him he was okay and not to worry. He never knew if his father tried to find him.

In October, when the crops were all laid by, he saw that Mile Away was getting ready to make another journey. "It's time for us to take our minutes," he said. That meant something like taking a vacation. "Now the best place to do that this time of year is New Orleans. What do you say?" They soon found themselves on a train bound for New Orleans.

But, oh, how he would later wish he had stayed home!

The New Orleans jungle was the closest thing to a hobo resort anybody ever saw. There was a section north of the train yard where the tracks curved off to the northeast. It was bordered by the Mississippi on the left and lots of woods on the right. Many shacks and lean-tos had been built along the river. These were right out in the open, and a few even had docks where hoboes were fishing. Other shacks were hidden away in the woods. Beyond these was a liquor still, sputtering forth some of the most foul-tasting brew Carter ever drank. He and Mile Away found an empty shack away from the sharp-smelling still and left their gear there. Mile Away wanted to fish, but Carter wanted to see the city.

"Come with me now;" Mile Away said, "tomorrow I'll show you around. Right now, we need to catch us some dinner." They headed for the river. It was much bigger than he ever imagined. It curved its way through the city like a snake, and he could see the fancy buildings in the distance. Lord, it was beautiful!

In the late afternoon, Mile Away told him to wait by the shack they had claimed. He walked into a group of hoboes who had made a fire.

"See the kid over there," he said, pointing at Carter. "He's going to box any one of ya, and I'm holdin' the bets." Mile Away moved so fast, Carter didn't know what hit him, but he was glad to see the slimmest of the hoboes, a man named Dutch take the challenge. Before he knew it, his shirt was off, and he was putting on the gloves. More and more of the men gathered to Mile Away's barking of the bets, until there was quite a crowd. Carter was very scared, but giddy at the same time. He grinned at them and flexed with his gloves in the air. He felt better when he got up close to his opponent and realized he was more afraid than Carter was.

"Ten rounds. Ten rounds is all. Place your bets," Mile Away hollered. It was starting to get dark when Carter began his boxing dance, his feet beating in a ticking rhythm. The air smelled electric. His hands shot out in mock blows. He knew he was the center of it all. He flushed into a sweat.

They faced each other, and he began to punch. The hoboes started to coach with their yells and cheers. Dutch's gloves came at him, but Carter was much faster. He let all the ticking out of him. He felt the beats leave his elbows, arms, fists. The crowd got louder.

Carter knocked him out in the second

round.

"That's my son," said Mile Away, booming over their shouts. It took Carter a while to make out what he was saying. They were all slapping him with congratulations. "My son." He heard the words again. He couldn't look at Mile Away. Why had he said that? He hated him that moment. He was filled with a longing for his father that went around him like a rope. The men drifted away to their suppers. He went off by himself a little and smoked.

A hobo named Quicksilver played a banjo and sang songs about all the people he had cheated. It was rumored that he never bathed at all. Everyone was careful not to stand downwind of him.

"He don't even like to drink water," said Mile Away who was halfway to drunk with his moonshine by now.

"Mile Away, are you getting plowed?" Carter said.

"What?" He looked right past him.

"Don't drink any more tonight, Mile Away," he said. "You'll only pass out, and you know most of the people here. I don't."

"Hoboes is hoboes. Besides now you're a hero."

"Look, I'm telling you — don't leave me alone here, Mile Away." The banjo plunked on and on. There was no moon and the only light now was from the fires which were growing lower and lower. It was a warm night.

"You ain't alone. Go to sleep. Go in the shack," he said. Quicksilver sang his way over to them before he could protest:

Beside an empty jungle on a cold December day,
Inside a rusty freight car, a dying hobo
   lay.
His pardner stood beside him with sad
   and drooping head,
A'listning to the last words the luck-
   less fellow said:"

Carter's impatience with Mile Away grew
worse. He was plunged into despair. He didn't
like Quicksilver or his song or the jungle or
anything. He wanted to go home right away. He
saw his father's face, his brothers running
across the field. He thought he could smell
Granny's bread. And then he was seized with
an ache for his mother that he had not felt
in a long time. It was hard to breathe. He
felt in his pocket for her brooch and earbobs, where they were always safely pinned.
Crawling into the shack, he lay down looking
out at the night. A lone firefly flickered
weakly at him. Mile Away came in and lit a
cigarette. He wondered if fireflies think
cigarettes are other fireflies in the dark.
   He wondered where his mother was. Had
she softened her position toward him since
that day in the cemetery? Did she care about
him now? Did it matter to her — this makeshift excuse for a home that he had found
with the hoboes?

"'I'm going to a better land where everything's bright,
Where hotdogs grow on bushes and you camp
   out every night,
Where you never have to work at all or
   even change your socks,
And little streams a' moonshine come

runnin' down the rocks.'"

Time slides like a stream beating over
rocks, and you are swept forward in it. But
what you really want to do is turn and go
upstream to see what used to be there — to
feel again what is missing, and let it rush
into you, and soothe, so you can smile.

The jungle was growing quiet as more and
more of the men either went to sleep or
passed out. Carter was not in the mood for
drinking. He strained for the sound of a
distant locomotive, but Quicksilver was all
he heard. Now his throat hurt from trying to
swallow the lump that was there. Through the
doorway he could see black trees swaying
their leaves, lonely and limp. What was he
doing here? He belonged on the farm, didn't
he? — a train whistled in the night. He hoped
it would stop. Oh, if only it would take him
— take him home. He wished he had his gear
packed so he could catch it. Maybe he could
persuade Mile Away to leave tomorrow. The
crickets pulsed louder and louder, and Quicksilver came nearer.

"'Hark, the train is coming!
I'll catch out on the fly.
Farewell, pardner, I must leave you. It
ain't so hard to die.'
The hobo stopped. His head fell back;
he'd sung his last refrain.
His pardner swiped his hat and boots and
jumped that eastbound train."

Carter became aware of a lot of commo-

tion outside which swelled over the sound of
the banjo. A group of hoboes had gotten off
the train he had just heard. A swinging
lantern led dark and jumping shadows of men
toward them. Mile Away was half asleep, but
the sounds of the men roused him. He got up
and went outside.

"I'm going to pee," he said and rose
with a great effort. The new arrivals were
milling about, trying to find empty shacks.

And then the laugh came choking through
the night, splitting the other sounds in two.
Mile Away gripped him, drunk as he was, and
froze. "It's him!" he said. "It's the Devil."
He stumbled forward toward the river, and
Carter lost sight of him. The men were coming
closer. He too recognized the laugh, and the
voice, and the bent knees as they passed his
fire. Hellbag! A good name for Mile Away's
Devil.

"Who's got a shack for me? Anybody?" he
asked. He passed Carter and looked into their
shack; his lantern swinging grotesque ghosts
over everything. The smell of silage hung on
his regular decay smell. "Well, lookee here,
a nice Navy man's coat," he said. Carter's
nerves stood up and saluted. He had to go in
and claim the coat.

"Hello," he said, sticking his head in
and looking Hellbag in the eye. "How goes
it?" Devils don't have to work in corn
fields, he said to himself, so they couldn't
possibly smell like he does.

"Well, lookee here. Where'd I see you
last, boy? Richmond was it?"

"Name's Lancelot, not Boy," Carter said.
"Sorry but there's two of us already here."

"Reckon we can fit three. Got my own
roll."

"Well, I don't know, it's pretty small,"

said Carter and moved toward the door.

"I thought we was pals. Besides, I'm only staying one night. Moving out after I see if somebody's here." He came forward and pushed Carter's hair off his forehead.

Carter backed out the door. "Got to pee," he said.

Hellbag pulled a flask from his pocket. "Stay awhile — here." He raised his four fingered hand.

"No, I — not now. Be right back." Where the hell was Mile Away? He grabbed the lantern and ran to find him. The air was thick and black. When he was far enough away from the shack, he called Mile Away's name in big whispers. He kept the lantern on him, figuring Mile Away could see him.

"Do you hear me? I know you're here, Mile Away." He was getting closer to the river.

"Kid," he heard him say, and that was all.

"What are we going to do?"

"Where is he?"

"Staying in our shack!" Carter said.

"Great God almighty!"

"I couldn't help it. He moved right in. What was I supposed to do?"

"Why didn't you tell him it was full?" Mile Away said.

"I did, but he didn't see nobody else. You left me there, remember?" He gritted his teeth.

"I told you I saw him murder somebody." Mile Away was cold sober. He kept gesturing with his hands, but no words came out. Then he said, "So. He moved in, did he? Well." They sat down on a dock. The water shone from their lantern like shiny mud. Then Mile Away said "okay" about six times as if he were

about to come up with some marvelous plan.
But each time he said it, he just sucked his
teeth and wheezed a little.

Finally, he said, "Let's wait a while.
Maybe he'll fall asleep. Then we'll get all
our stuff and get the next train out of here
no matter where it's going." He blew out the
lantern. It looked like he might get his wish
to go home and see Papa. Maybe Bessie was
gone. Now he had to pray that whatever train
they caught was going to Virginia. I'm going
to see them, he thought. He vowed never to
leave home again, until he could do it with
style. He would travel only on passenger
trains, in fine clothes, and with money in
his pocket.

They waited about two hours. He had
trouble staying awake.

Mile Away sets the lantern outside the
shack. The light throws weird shadows of
their bodies against the doorway. They leave
their shoes next to the lantern outside on
the ground. Hellbag is asleep. They can hear
the snuffing of his snores. Carter goes in
first in slow motion and hands some of their
gear out to Mile Away who sets it outside on
the ground. They don't dare to speak. Or even
breathe. A few tiny pebbles on the cardboard
floor cut into Carter's feet. He senses that
Mile Away is shaking, and the light flickers
up on the side of his face — the side without
the teeth. It makes him look like a huge
gargoyle. He enters and Carter gets close to
his ear, speaking as softly as he can: "Look
and see — is that everything?" They are
forgetting the coat which Hellbag had hung in
a different place. Mile Away points to it.
Carter takes a step toward it, and as he

reaches for it, a hand shoots out of the dark
and claps shut on his ankle. He feels the
twisting bruises and falls backward in the
shock of his pain and knocks Mile Away down.

"Stealing in the dark?" Hellbag roars.
He flies on top of Mile Away, and they roll
and pound each other. "Fuckin' thief in the
dark." Carter can't tell who is who. Hellbag
is all thrashing angles as he hisses and
writhes. Mile Away seems to be made of round
puffy air. He cannot get a grip. Carter rips
off Hellbag's shirt, trying to pull him off
Mile Away, but gets sucked into the whirlpool
of their bodies. Mile Away wheezes and fum-
bles for his knife. Hellbag now snorts in a
fiendish fury. He sees the knife. His knee
goes smack into Mile Away's windpipe, and he
grabs for it.

"Stop," Carter roars and lunges for his
arm, but he smacks Carter flat into the wall
with one blow. Carter's head hits, and he is
dazed, but he can see the horror through
filmy eyes. It is all one motion: the grabbing, the lunging, the stabbing. Hellbag rips
the knife in and out of Mile Away in big
hacking gashes, and then he slits his throat.
First there is a thin red line, like a
thread; then huge gushes of blood — a tide —
a dam bursting, springing free. It runs down
his chest and onto the floor, and his body
jerks in spasms. He twitches and throbs,
quivering and lurching. How could he take so
long to die? Carter thinks the jerking will
never stop. The blood smells hot like garbage
burning. Carter throws up all over the floor.
He knows he is going to die.

"He wasn't stealing. He lives here, you
bastard," he sobs.

"Not any more, boy . . ." Hellbag leers
and smirks. He rubs his hand on his own

genitals. "Don't you want some good fun, boy?" He opens his pants. His penis, stiff and gray, springs free. Running for the door, Carter spits in his face, but Hellbag barrels after him and grabs him by the pants, ripping them down and throwing him face down on the floor. He groans with a hard and fierce rage as Hellbag paws his backside. He mule kicks, stabbing Hellbag in the groin with his foot. Hellbag falls, cursing him. Carter wheels and pounds his face, and his fist snaps Hellbag's head back so that it catches the sharp corner of a two by four. He crumples as limp as Mile Away, as Carter gasps for air. He can still feel Hellbag's penis squish under his foot. He thinks his foot is diseased. His heart feels like it is beating outside his body, and his fear is still there even though Hellbag doesn't move. It hangs in big swallows in the room, floating in silence against the loud heaving of his breathing. He is sticky with vomit, sweat, and Mile Away's blood. The smells throb in his lungs. And the buckets of blood under his mother's body flash as fire in the back of his brain. Don't look at him. Don't turn, he tells himself. Walk out slowly. Fix your pants. Take your shoes, your things. No one will grab you. The river. Go. Yes. Now. Run!

"Oh, my God, Mile Away!" he screams and sprints blindly on. Buckets of . . . buckets of blood.

He fell in the water with his clothes on. Then he took them off and tried to scrub them. He pounded them against a pile and hurled them onto the bank. He kept diving down, scraping his foot — the foot that had touched Hellbag — on the bottom of the river. He washed himself as best he could — his hair, the inside of his mouth — for a long

time. At first it was cool and soothing. Then
he started to shake again. What if Hellbag is
somehow in the water? What if his hand comes
out and grabs my ankle and pulls me under? he
thought. Why did he want to do such terrible
things to me? Was he dead or only knocked
out? Maybe he came to already.

Carter jumped up and down on the grass
to dry off and wrung out his clothes. A pale
gray streak crept into the sky. He headed for
the yard carrying his rolled up clothes. Any
train would do. He walked soundlessly through
the breaking morning in a tense knot, trying
not to feel. He wondered if they had found
the body. Of course, they would think he did
it. And they would all remember him because
of the boxing.

The train. Think about the train. That's
all. How long before a whistle?

The mourning dove haunted him from far
away. He had to press his fists into his eyes
to keep from crying, because he could not
afford to go to pieces now. He knew Mile Away
was dead, but he still thought he was going
to see him walking toward him, saying it was
all a mistake. He hid, still naked, in a
rusted, abandoned gondola car, crouched and
aching and listening so hard, his ears
buzzed. Then the long moan of a whistle far
away. He scraped on his wet clothes and was
ready. He mounted when she slowed. He had
never been on a train without Mile Away
before. The boxcar was empty except for some
cardboard in the corner, left by the last
hobo before him. He watched the jungle pull
away and fade. A curl of smoke rose above the
trees. Someone was up early making coffee. He
thought he heard Quicksilver's banjo.

Did it really happen?

The train was heading west, farther and

farther away from home. The police might be
looking for him there. He would have to wait
a long time before he could go back. He made
a bed of the cardboard and lay down. The
motion of the train made his body hurt more.
Mile Away's words crept into his mind, "Evil
ain't particular who it strikes."   Am I evil?
he thought. He cried until he thought he'd
break in half, but then he was able to sleep.
The train beat on, rattling its rhythm into
his feverish dreams.

    His head was hot. He lay in a half
sleep. The train rode into a storm, and   he
watched the needle marks of the rain, thinking that he saw his mother's face shimmer in
the uneven lines. He remembered when she
would feel his head to see if he had a fever.
Then she would go downstairs and make him
soup. Her death haunted him, like a tiny
sound you're not quite sure you heard. He
only wanted his mama here. He wanted her to
sit on his bed and hold him so that no part
of him could want anything. And the tiny
sound turned inside out and became part of
his dream. He saw her face smaller and
smaller like swirling water when it goes down
the drain. He reached out his hands to hold
her face there, but he could not.
    He slept and woke again. The terror of
Hellbag was like choking black smoke. He was
fouled with the fiendish memory of him — a
barb in his mind. Then he shook with chills.
The cold was inside him, but his skin dripped
with sweat. Would he ever forget?   Or is
Hellbag engraved indelibly on him like some
barnacle from hell?   He could not stop his
pounding thoughts.
    The train rushed him through space,

became his enemy, wouldn't let him stop and rest. His thoughts raced and bumped with the racket of its restlessness. Its churning sound tumbled his mind into rhythmic somer-saults as faces vaulted over each other: Mile Away — Deadman — Papa — Lancelot — Greta — Hellbag — Cassandra — Mama. Oh, God. Stop — please stop. Bessie — Cousin Henry — Lion — Papa. Please Papa. Find Papa. Time whizzed past without him. He could not fit himself into it. He vomited again, this time hanging his head out of the moving car. And then he felt a dizzying thirst that made him twitch all over.

Chapter 8

Carter lost track of days and nights. Finally an excruciating thirst awakened him from his stupor, and he became fairly lucid. A hot, dry breeze slid into the car and stirred him. He sat up and felt like the inside of his mouth was swollen when he tried to swallow. It was daylight. The train slowed; the square shadows of the cars skimmed over dry, cracked earth and looked like some weird giant caterpillar. Where was he? How far had the train gone? He had to get off. His body felt foreign — repulsive to him. He was filled with the dread that he might die here, and if anyone found him, no one would know who he was.

The train continued to slow. Brown, barren mountains loomed all around. They had jutting shapes, like so many huge hobgoblins, and parts of them were layered with overlap-ping strips of flaming rock. Could they be

the wide lips of monsters who might suck him
into the center of their darkness? He heard
the fee faw fum of their waddling steps. The
land was a grating copper color with only a
few unfamiliar trees. The air smelled sulfur-
ous. And then he saw cactus plants — huge
green statues, ominous against a glassy blue
sky that was so bright, it hurt his eyes.
Parched red houses here and there, and what
looked like a general store suddenly appeared
beside him.

The train stopped. He slid weakly down
onto the hollow, wooden station platform. A
single sign, "Marathon," stood at the end of
it. Everything was dry. He shielded his eyes
from the pain of the searing light, and the
mountains took his breath away. They made him
so small and scared, as if he might disappear
at any second. He slumped toward the rain
barrel which was under the sign, and his hand
shook as he lifted the dipper. He drank very
fast in huge gulps even though the water
tasted rancid. He had to will himself to slow
down.

"You will get sick, Meester Boy." He
jumped to see a fierce looking Mexican girl
with eyes like polished glass, and next to
her stood an ugly burro. The girl wore a
dirty, white satin dress. It was cut in
jagged edges at her knees, had a nipped-in
waist, and was studded with shiny satin
roses. "You should not swallow too much."
She kept petting her burro with slow caress-
ing strokes.

"It's . . . I have not drunk anything for
a . . . for a long time," he said.

"But your stomach is still thee same
size." Her fleshy mouth twisted in a grin.
He held on to the top of the barrel. "Don't
you know this, Meester Boy? Where you come

from?" He could actually hear the stroking of the burro.

"I . . . the train just kept going . . . I fell asleep." He put his hand to his temples to try to stop the dizziness.

"Maybe you are still the baby? Babies always have to sleep."

He raised one hand in the air. "Where . . . is this place?"

"Marathon. Can't you read?" Her voice was a burr in his ears.

"Yes, can you?" he asked. Her eyes seemed to have been made for a much larger face. "Just exactly where is Marathon?" He wanted to say other, more clever things, but he was too sick to think.

"Texas. Don't you know anything?" Amazing! He had come all the way to Texas. Her eyes made him shiver.

"Of course I know it's Texas," he said. "I mean what part of Texas?"

"What you mean 'part,' Gringo?" She took the dipper from him and filled a small bucket for her burro. "You go this way is Alpine." She pointed to the northwest. "And way over there" (to the east) "is San Antonio." The burro drank from the bucket. "You see the mountain? El Muerto — is the name of that one. There." She pointed to a jagged, ominous sculpture that made him think of a dragon. "My father say — first it make men crazy, and then it make them die."

"A mountain can't make you die," said Carter.

"Chu Chu, what do you think of this boy here? He goes asleep, he does not know where he is, he wants to drink all our water, and he is not afraid of El Muerto." More stroking — down the muzzle this time. Then she turned, leading him away without so much as a good-bye.

"Hey, wait. Don't . . . go yet."

"What is for me here, Meester Boy?"

"Stop calling me that. My name's Carter."   Her eyes held him. She could not be from this earth.

"Listen . . . I . . . I'm very sick, and I don't know anyone here. Is there a doctor anywhere around?"

She made a clucking sound with her tongue. He saw its pink tip, wet and smooth. "You do not look sick, does he, Chu Chu?"

"That's because I'm trying not to."   His head felt huge. The light pounded against his eyes. He faked a cough, and spat into the dirt.

"Now look how sick is that. What you think, Chu Chu? Should we believe him?"   His fake cough made him choke, and then he really was coughing. "Maybe he is still the baby. What you think?"

"You would help me — if you were a good woman."   He liked the sound of that word — "woman,"   and hoped she did too. He didn't know what else to do, so he sat on the platform and bent way over. Maybe now she would see that he might be dying, and find some help for him, but he heard nothing, sensed no movement. Was she still there?   He was about to look up when he saw her feet from the corner of his eyes. What he did not see was the spider that had inched out of the space between the uneven platform and the ground. He grabbed his stomach and rocked, moaning a little. She stood in front of him and offered him the dipper. Did she feel sorry for him? He drank some more and gave it back to her. She had beads on her wrists which rattled when she moved. The spider crawled up his shoe and under his pant leg.

"Are you a gypsy?" he asked, looking at the bracelets. Then he felt the insect's ticklish legs.

"Ha. You think I am gypsy? I am Juana. I am more like movie star, no? You chicken? You think I put a spell on you?"

Carter jumped and shrieked when the spider stung him severely in the leg.

"*Dios mio!*" Juana yelled when she realized what had happened. The insect disappeared quickly, leaving Carter howling and bent over, clutching his leg. Juana was on her knees in an instant, pushing his hands away. "Stop! Let me get it!" she yelled, and she began sucking the sting and spitting in the street. Carter did not know what was happening, only that his pain was the most severe he'd ever had in his life.

"I think I get it out," Juana said, taking water in her mouth and spitting that too. "Now you not feel better, but you will not die. You will have the fever. I take you home with me. You come to my mother. She is *curandera*. We help you." He could not argue. Please don't let her be evil, he thought. He could not help but think of Hellbag. No. She was nothing like him.

She helped him onto the burro. Then she led him to her home, which seemed very far away. Juana talked all the way there. He felt the brush of the burro's mane. It reminded him of Mo. He closed his eyes.

"Do you know *curanderas*?"

"Ah . . . no — I —"

"Ah, Gringo, you know nothing. I forget. My family keeps the secret of *curanderas.* We know all the plants to heal you. I keep them ready. We heal all the people. They come to us from the town; sometimes even the soldiers come. I learn the healing from my mother, but

I do not want to stay here and be *curandera.*
You will see. I will tell you some day. When
you are better, maybe you will help me with
the farm until my father come back from the
army camp. And if you know how to ride the
trains, maybe you show me how."

        Their home was a two-room hut near the
foot of a low mountain. A stream ran nearby;
though most of the land was dry. There were
many goats and sheep bleating about. The
trees were short — more like bushes, but the
cactus stood fixed and menacing, as if they
watched them like so many thorny sphinxes.
Neat wheat and corn rows as well as other
crops were planted near the hut. The sky was
a sickening artificial blue.
        She brought him inside to her mother who
was as squat and round as Juana was tall and
angular. She had skin-tight hair wrapped in a
bun, and it seemed to pull all her features
to the sides of her face. Her eyes were
stretched and ringed in red. Her nose was
like a parrot's beak, and her chin came to a
point. The jagged shoes she wore grated on
the floor like rats' claws. The two women
spoke in Mexican. What if they were gypsies?
He had to hope they could help him. Juana's
mother, Maria, touched his face and lifted
his arms. He felt himself falling, and he
stumbled onto the cot in the corner of the
room. The walls were plastered with sour-
smelling mud. In the center of a windowless
wall was one of many *nichos* — a niche for a
statue of a saint. In the midst of all this
poverty, here was room for a lovely statue,
with a fat candle sputtering in front of it.
The light made it hard for him to focus. A
roof, only a little more than six feet high,

made of yucca leaves, was held up by a log in
the center of the room. Maria handed her
daughter a mortar and pestle. Then she took
down some dried herbs that were hanging from
the ceiling, and Juana mashed them. Her
rhythm was steady, beating an even time, and
he was caught up in the succession of steady
taps of the pestle. It was dizzying. His
teeth chattered. Juana began to blur. He knew
he was losing consciousness, and prayed they
would do him no evil while he slept.

He felt something hot on his chest,
something cold on his head, and his leg was
wrapped in wet cloths. He squeezed open one
eye. His clothes were gone. There was a mess
of hot white paste on his chest. A cloth
covered the bottom half of him. Juana handed
him his mother's brooch and earbobs. "I find
these in your pocket," she said. "I wash your
clothes." The harshness was gone from her
voice.

"Thank you," he said. Her eyes were soft
now.

"Who give you that?" She stared at him
without a blink.

"They were my mother's."

She smiled. "Your clothes are dry. I get
them." She went outside. Maria began spoon-
ing hot liquid down his throat. She yelled
after Juana, and all he could make out was
something about the cold compress on his
head. He thought she wanted her to change it.
Finally Juana came in with his clothes,
jerked it off him and slammed outside again.
When she returned, it was much colder and
wetter than before, but she was fiery hot.
Her anger hung in the room.

Twenty-four hours later, he was cured,

but they continued to run back and forth with their herbs, mixing this and that, and generally fussing over him which he liked.

"What did you do to me?" he asked.

"Do you think *curanderas* tell the secret?" Juana said. She touched his forehead, and he felt a thrill from her hand. He reached up and touched it. "We know how to cure you. That is enough. Now you rest." He was very curious, but he knew he was not going to learn any more.

"I feel fine now." He sat up. Maria pushed him back onto the cot.

"No, you rest." He lay there looking at Juana. How could he have been afraid of her? Her skin was a dark olive, and her shoulders stirred under strong shiny black hair. It hung loose with nothing to bind it, and it swished when she moved. She looked at him openly as if she had nothing to hide. There was a tiny quiver in her rich, full lips, and her enormous black eyes never wavered. Now she had on a dark red velvet dress. Where did she get such clothes? The tops of her breasts curved out of the low front, and there were glass buttons down the bodice. She was barefoot and sensuous, and he felt light-headed all over again. He tried to square his shoulders — which is not easy when you're lying down. He bent his knees to hide his erection. He loved her all at once. How could anything so beautiful be hidden away in this god-forsaken place?   It was exciting just to be near her. Could he take her home with him?

Then Juana and her mother argued about her dress. He could tell from their gestures that Maria wanted her to take it off, but Juana wouldn't hear of it. "*Su padre, su padre*," flew around the room, and Juana cried. But the dress stayed on her — all that day and the next.

Two days later, Carter offered to help them with their farm, and they accepted. He learned that Juana's father had gone to a military outpost with several burro loads of chino grass, a wild rough brush used for fodder for cavalry horses. The grass would then be carried by mule team to the main camp, Camp Marfa. They had no idea when he might be back. He often returned with one or more soldiers who came in search of cures or to do more trading. There was a lot of work for Juana to do while he was gone.

And although Carter was doing farm chores again, he wasn't even aware that he was working. Being with Juana made him feel so good he did not even think about what he was doing. Time flew. Often she let her guard down, and became almost tender. She had a longing in her voice, a sadness that she tried to hide. It drove him wild. He did his best to brush up against her whenever he could. He tried to pay attention to the corn fields and the goats when he had to, but all he could think of was those wild, sultry eyes. He could almost see himself in them. She was nothing like Junie Lou. This was definitely the real thing; she was a woman. Sometimes he couldn't stand the excitement of looking at her. He could feel the sweat on his temples whenever she came close. He was constantly hard. Did she know the effect she had on him? Did she know he loved her? She had cured his body, but now he was lovesick.

Every morning before light, they had to unlock one of the floodgates at the edge of the stream. They were situated so that releasing one of them allowed the water to burst forth and irrigate part of the field. They left their shoes on a high ridge. The corn was high, and its pungent stickiness mingled with Juana's earthy smell.

About two weeks after he was cured, they were working quickly one morning, directing the flow of water toward the driest part of the field. When she did her chores, Juana was so fast that she seemed to be in more than one place at a time. This day she was wearing a torn bright green dress with black lace pieces hanging down on the skirt. Again he wondered where she got these fancy clothes. He dared not mention them however, because of the angry arguments they caused her to have with her mother.

She ran from stake to stake in one motion, never stopping for a breath. Suddenly she stopped and bent to rescue a tiny lizard from the rushing water. She scooped him in two hands, making a little cradle for him to lie in. Carter looked into her dress and could see most of her taut, full breasts. He could not stand the pain in his groin.

They stood close; their work stopped by the lizard. The surge of water swirled around their ankles toward the corn. Pink cloud fingers inched across the sky as the sun neared. She stood still, holding the lizard. All her motion was replaced by a calm focus on the tiny animal. Her muscles slackened. Then a creeping gait came into her step as if she were afraid of waking someone. Airborne, drifting steps. Her arms slowly lengthened as she dawdled near the corn, holding the lizard out for idle inspection. She tickled its stomach with a long slow finger. He wondered if she would sing it a lullaby. She ambled toward the edge of the water without seeming to move. He sauntered next to her. She bent over her catch, lingering over him as she let him go toward a dry spot. He curved back and forth in a hypnotic S.

"Why are you worried about a lizard?" Carter's voice drifted among floating moun-tains, cactus, streaks of sky, and perfectly still stalks of corn prolonging the trance of the breaking morning. The idle air drowsed around his head. Her eyes were far away.

"She wants to be free and go away from here," she said.

Would she let him kiss her? His arms hung boneless at his sides. "Where do you think he will go?"

"She is a girl, and she will go to Hollywood to be movie star."

He hesitated, pulling a silky burst from the top of the corn and twirling it on her skirt. She opened her black eyes full at him. He could not look away. He could have grown roots in that spot. Time slowed more. She pushed her hair up behind her head and held the pose — all the while never shifting her gaze from his eyes. Her lips parted as if she were about to speak, but she released her hands and the hair tumbled down. The skin on her arms shimmered.

"You are the most beautiful girl I ever saw." His voice cracked.

"Beautiful like a movie star, you think?" She closed her eyes. It was like a curtain coming down.

"Far better than any I ever saw."

"Can I be movie star? Who else will say I am beautiful?" She took a step away from the house in the direction of a dry section of the corn field. She was watching her feet take deliberate, careful steps as if she were trying to make perfect prints in the oozy earth, balancing like a tightrope walker.

"Everybody will say it — once they see you."

He follows her, covering her prints with his own. "But no one sees you out here —" He touches her hair so lightly that she does not feel it. It is cool and ticklish-smooth. He touches her bare arm, and runs his fingers inside her elbow. " — out here in the middle of nowhere." She does not pull away. She turns and stares into his face. Black almond eyes that he can see right into hold him still. Yes, it is his face he sees in them. There is no hesitation, no shame. They walk on tiptoe beyond a few more rows of corn, and then go into the rows where they are hidden. She looks at him and then away. He feels her smooth, smooth skin itching to be touched before he even makes contact. Ah.

"No one is here." She says and rubs her finger tip on the electric inside of his wrist.

"No one but us . . ."

"And the birds." She lifts his hand to her breast. He cannot breathe. He moves his other hand up and down the curves of her waist. She hugs him and runs her tongue in his ear.

"Do you like birds?" she says.

"I like birds and lizards and girls named Juana." He kisses her hair, her neck, her cheek, and then he finds her mouth. They kiss for a very long time, his mouth covering the softness of her lips. He feels her tongue; his head races and explodes. She pulls her arms out of her sleeves and lets her dress fall. Then she unbuttons his shirt. It is really happening. She takes it off slowly, and caresses his shoulders. Then she

removes her underwear. Oh, Lord! She stands
fully bare before him. Her body shimmering in
the early translucent light, and then she
helps him take off his pants. She leads him
down on top of the clothes. They hold each
other's nakedness and their bodies start to
move against each other. His skin is so pale
and white next to hers. She roughly massages
his chest as if she is discovering something.

"I like you have no hair," she says. He
wonders how many men she has been with and
how hairy they might have been. He kisses her
beautiful round breasts and she moans. She
rolls herself on top of him, and in a thrust
she is everywhere; and she is wonderful. Life
is wonderful. Even here in the middle of a
Texas no man's land.

"I love you," he said.
"You are beautiful boy." Why couldn't
she have said "man"?
"Say my name, Juana."
"What you talk about?"
"You never say 'Carter.'"
"Why you care for that?"
"I don't know. I've just never heard you
say it, that's all."
Her laugh was rich and throaty. She
turned over on her back. "We have to put the
clothes back."
"Not yet. Tell me about Juana, the movie
star," he said, stroking her breast.
She smiled, and her face flashed as she
saw her dreams in her own eyes. "One day they
come here, the movie people, and I see them.
They come to Marathon to make the picture at
the railroad and out near the big mountain. A
whole train comes with all the people — and
camera — everything to make the movie — no,

you say 'shoot' the movie — like a gun —
they say 'shoot.'   So many things on the
train, and they live on the train and stay
here for two weeks. Then they go. I come
every day. I watch them, until my father — he
beat me for going there. He want me to be
farm girl and *curandera,* but I know I go to
Hollywood. I told the man 'How do I be movie
star?'   He say to go to Hollywood and see
him. But my father, he forbid me."   At the
mention of her father, her face hung in
sadness, and the music left her voice.

"Where did you get these clothes?"

"I steal them from the Hollywood man. I
go there at night and steal them. My father
forbid me to wear them, so I hide them and
put them on when he goes away. They are my
Hollywood clothes. Soon I am going."

"How? How can you get there?"

"You will show me? You go on train by
yourself. Where you go on this train here?"

"I wasn't going anywhere. I was running
away from something bad in New Orleans. I
just got on the first train I could."   His
voice became thick as he saw Mile Away twist
in his blood.

Carter thought she would ask him what
happened, but she was too preoccupied with
the thought that he might know how to get her
out of there. "So now we go on train to
Hollywood. My father will be home soon. We go
today. You will take me? Hey? Meester Boy?
You not a boy now."   She laughed again. It
was good that he did not have to tell her
about Mile Away.

"No, it's too dangerous, and you're too
beautiful. There are men — bad men on the
rails, and you — we'd never make it."

She began to kiss him, and he was hard
instantly. "Yes you must take me. We be

careful. I wear farm clothes, not my beautiful dresses and hide my hair and no one will — that's the way — I'll look like a boy."

He laughed out loud.

Then there was a huge noise like an earthquake, and fear shut its jaws on him. Hoof beats — a shrieking roar wrenched his ears, "Aaaaaahhgrrr," and a small brute of a man slid off a galloping horse and thundered at them, his wrath boiling out of him like the steam of the trains. Cornstalks fell every which way. Carter grabbed for his clothes, but the man was on him with a foaming snort. He looked as if he might explode.

"*Parete, Papa. Estas loco?*" Juana yelled. A charging bull, his hands were around Carter's neck. They clutched each other, but Carter could not breathe. Then there were two more faces behind the man's — soldiers' hats — a flash of metal, and they pulled his hands off Carter's neck. Juana's father growled and fumed, but the soldiers held him off.

"Get out," Juana screamed, "he will kill you." Carter ran, trying to put his pants on at the same time. Years later he was able to laugh at how funny he must have looked, skipping and falling into his pants, grabbing his shoes off the ridge, and trying to hold his shirt in his teeth. Juana was sobbing to the soldiers. "Hold him. Do not let him go. He will beat me again. Hold him." Carter felt awful that he was leaving her there, but he kept running.

"Oh, God, there's never a choice," he said aloud. His thoughts whirled in a spiral.

When he reached a safe distance from them, he turned and saw the soldiers leading her father into the house. Juana stood shimmering in the hot sun, her dress wrapped around her like a towel. "Come back some day, Carter," she called. It was the only time she ever said his name.

He was absolutely certain that somehow they would be together soon. He held onto that hope.

But he never saw her alive again.

One of the soldiers turned back to look at him. Carter liked the sleek look of his boots. A metal piece on the soldier's hat caught the glinting sun. He wondered what he would look like in a uniform like that. He waved to Juana and picked up his pace toward the station. Why had he dared to hope that this could be a place where he might belong?

There were two young men on the platform, probably a few years older than Carter. Their hair was slicked; their shoes were shined, and they shifted uncomfortably in their Sunday best. He skulked behind the rain barrel, ashamed of his tattered clothes. The first time that he had been dressed up in fancy clothes was at his mother's funeral.

Everyone was dressed up that day — the day when the earth was a piercing green, and steamy air clung to everything. But the image that was most acute was the silence her death had left behind.

"Oh, teach us to number our days," the Reverend had said.

"Amen," everyone said. But Carter said nothing. The dirt skittered on her casket like buckshot hitting the floor. He could not say "Amen." He shut his ears against the words. He would not let them finalize her death. How could they leave her here? How

could he bear to see that casket lowered,
when she hadn't had time to tell him she
loved him?

But now those same words of the Reverend
shouted in his ears. One of the young men on
the platform laughed. What did the Reverend
mean?   Is it now that I should number my
days? Carter thought. Make fast and furious
plans. Count and calculate the quickest way
to manhood. Ever since his mother died, his
life had been fleeting like a train out of
control. He was too busy to savor what was
important. He had squandered time. Juana
taught him how to cherish it. Oh, my perfect,
beautiful Juana, when will I see you again?
He heard one of the young men say that
Camp Marfa was a six or seven-hour ride to
the west. They had enlisted, and seemed quite
excited about going. Then it dawned on him
that they were going by passenger train, and
he would have to wait for a freight. He could
not stand his own musky smell. The army
seemed to be an obvious solution. Their train
arrived, and they boarded. As it grew smaller
in the distance, it somehow had the look of
sophistication, of maturity and success. What
if he got all the way there, and the army
wouldn't take him?   He knew he would have to
lie about his age.
A coalie streaked in at a million miles
an hour, the whistle sounding like a hoarse
owl. She did not slow at all. Her shadows
flew, scraping the ground, her smoke foaming
into the air; the spaces of the cars blinked
over him. He stood helpless. He wanted to
cry. You cannot even catch a shadow for a
second in your hand, he thought. Like time,
it will go relentlessly on without you.

"Oh, teach us to number our days."
Watch me, Mama. Never take your eyes off me — ever again.

It was two hours later before a freight came through, its steam pouring out and wrapping around his legs making him sweat. He thought of Juana the entire time — the deliciousness of her skin ran itself over him. He would ache for her, but he realized he could not have stayed there even if her father had not come home. He was tired of poverty and feeling dirty all the time. He would be sixteen on his next birthday. It was time for him to do something important. Something he could count on — something that smacked of the truth of what life was supposed to be about. You really have to hurry, because you never know what will happen next, and time may run out on you.

That is the truth of the matter. You may never get a chance to be somebody.

"Oh, teach us . . ."

He fingered the brooch in his pocket.

Twelve

℘

Truth is like an anchor. You have to pull it up out of a dark place, and if you don't watch carefully, it can slip right through your fingers, out of sight again. I see the letters, always with a capital T. Truth.

Sometimes it gets so stuck down in the mud, you can't pull it up at all. Or maybe you don't want to. What if you pulled it up and found something awful there instead of what you expected? Better not to know.

People hide the truth from children all the time probably for a thousand different reasons, but none of them are good. And children cannot be deceived. Not really. Not in their heart of hearts.

I have to stop my father's story now. His pain is too much like my own. I always knew the truth was hidden from me — even when I was little. The secrecy surrounding him gave me such a sense of foreboding, that I left the anchor deep in the water. I'm sure my father knew the truth about his mother's impending death long before it occurred, and he certainly must have known that Bessie wanted his father, although he railed against the truth of both of these things even after the fact.

And I — how I railed against the feeling of longing for him — not wanting to know anything other than the fact that he was my father — forever young, larger than life, the perfect man. I forever chased the ecstasy of him, yet hid it even from myself.

And now truth changes the focus so I can know him as he was with all his faults and sufferings. He'd experienced loss and betrayal caused by his mother's death and father's remarriage. He'd known the same kind of longing that I would later feel for him, long before I felt it. He knew how it feels to want to see and touch someone so badly, you think you'll expire if you don't, like it's part of your breath.

He is in me. His mother is in him. There are so many people in other people. And do we ever emerge from each other, like Melissa's dolls, and get free?

Everyone had made a fuss over my father's looks, just as they had over mine. When I wrote about people admiring him at Bessie's wedding, I heard the chorus of voices in my own mind echoing over and over, reminding me of my obligation to be attractive. It had been preordained.

"Once when you were a tiny baby, and you were asleep, your father cut off your eyelashes with a cuticle scissors," Aunt Dora had told me long ago, her face softening as she stared into her memory, "because he'd heard that if you do that to a child when it is very young, the lashes will grow in longer and thicker than they normally would have been." The message she thought she was giving me was, "See how much he loved you?" It is not only amazing that he did such an outrageous thing. It is equally amazing that no one questioned it, thought it a bit bizarre, or wondered why I was not good enough the way I was. It must have been imperative to him that I turn out pretty. I had to carry on his legacy. Was he afraid I wouldn't be pretty enough? I suppose it makes sense that this would have been one of his priorities — a man who had been admired for his looks all his life. But would he have loved me if I weren't pretty? Would that have been a condition? Being pretty can be a great handicap. You always wonder what else people like you for, if anything. I have had a fantasy of making love with a blind man. Then I'd know I'd be loved only for myself — not for my face.

*   *   *

When I learned of my father's attempts to win his mother's approval, I knew how he had felt when he failed. I thought of her reaction to his pulling up her carrots — how she treated it like a capital crime. I too had felt that same shame he had — the kind of shame that burns like a branding iron, and his story took me back into the past to a day when I was in the first grade.

Several of the boys in my class, much to my chagrin, said they liked me. (Was it my eyelashes?) They used to march around the playground sing-songing whatever game they were trying to get going, hoping that other kids would hang on to their little train until there was enough for a team. On this particular day, a kid named Monty started a new game. "Hang on for Christina's husband," he sang over and over, and about four other little boys hung on. They were giggling and having a grand time in spite of my flushed face, and I couldn't wait to rush home and tell Granlena. Surely she would know what to do about it. Instead, she told my aunts that night, and it became the family joke. Why did I ever tell? They laughed, repeating it over and over, and my face hurt from freezing it into a smile. So many faces to watch and please.

Then Aunt Dora took me to her office to "show me off," she said. I sensed from the beginning of this adventure that there was some impossible task for me to do — even though at that point I had no idea what it was. I felt like someone in her first acting class being asked to play Lady MacBeth. I knew I was in way over my head — but I had to do it — the show must go on.

I stood next to her on the square rug in the square office and waited for the crackling of her smile. It was scheduled to go off when her boss emerged from his office on his way to the men's room. We were positioned there to wait for him — so he couldn't possibly duck us when he came out. All the secretaries in the pool stopped typing. I was poised and tensed, waiting for the downbeat of her smile, and I knew when it began because I could hear it crack. Finally it came, and her words ricocheted off the corners of the desks, her serpent curls bobbing to the beat.

"Oh, ho, now, Mr. Wentworth, I'd like you to meet my niece."   She used a sing-song voice like the boys on the playground. Poor man. He didn't even have a script, but he was forced to be in the play too. "Tell Mr. Wentworth about the boys in your class," she said. "Wait till you hear this!" Then there was a big pause as if the room inhaled. And he was so polite and patient, while my feet pressed down into my maryjanes, because I knew I couldn't do it. I wanted to stick out my tongue. I wanted to pull my dress over my head and disappear.

And finally, because I couldn't bear it any more, my voice squeezed out, "Oh, they stink!" It was the dream actors have all their lives. They are on stage, and somehow they are in the wrong play, or they've been given the wrong script. To say such a thing in 1946 was the equivalent of saying "they suck" or "they're assholes" today.   Not exactly what you would want in polite office conversation.

Then there was so much choking laughter to cover my grave aberration — to cover everything — to smear a fog over the room so perhaps Mr. Wentworth — the big boss, mind you — didn't really hear it — only thought he heard it — so perhaps he wouldn't think too ill of us after all.

Had I really said it?   "Stinks?"   I actually said the word "stinks" in front of Mr. Wentworth!   The shame of it poured into the room like the exhaust from a bus, and I could taste it all afternoon.

My arm hurt as Dora tried to usher me into the ladies' room, still hitting everyone with the angles of her laugh as the door finally closed behind us. And her laugh just stopped like a finger snap, and all you could hear was the click of our patent leather shoes on the marble floor before all the scolding began.

I never went to her office again.

Thirteen

Although I continue to write the story of my father, I lose much of the impetus I had when I wrote the early chapters. Discouragement begins to set in. I doubt not only my ability, but the worth of the whole project. I've received no feedback from Daniel on the chapters I sent him. If he responded, would I regain my momentum? What is he waiting for? I sent him my manuscript over a month ago, and August is almost half over. Doesn't he know I have to go back to work soon?

The apartment is light and airy, and a breeze billows the gossamer curtains at my bedroom windows. Charles calls to tell me he must fly to Atlanta for the weekend. A bell rings in my head, as I remember Uncle Rob saying that Bessie is still alive and living in Georgia. When I tell him I'd like to go along, Charles sounds genuinely delighted.

"I'm leaving early Saturday and coming home Sunday afternoon," he says. "Great if you'll come, but I have meetings all day Saturday. Won't you be bored?"

"No, not at all," I say. "While you're at the meetings, I'm going to track down my long-lost step-grandmother. She lives in the suburbs of Atlanta. Surely you remember when I told you about old Bessie?"

"She's the one who married your grandfather, and

they never told the kids till it was over?"

"The one and only."

"You'd better call her first and see if it's okay." I know that, Charles. I really do.

On the plane ride I am thinking about Bessie and the frail, squeaky voice I heard on the other end of the phone. She sounded like she was dying. Didn't I know she wasn't well? Hadn't I heard from Greta about all her illnesses and operations? She then proceeded to treat me to a litany of her ailments, and just when I thought she was going to hang up, she told me it would probably be a wonderful thing if I came to see her, because, after all, I am her granddaughter and she's never seen me.

"She's on her fifth husband," I tell Charles as the wheels of the plane touch down. "Imagine — four times a widow."

"Maybe she kills them off," says Charles, gathering his things into his briefcase.

"Or they die from revulsion. Rob said she's always sick, and no one can stand to be around her, because all she talks about is the last disgusting episode of her body falling apart."

"How sick could she be, if she's outlived all her husbands?" Charles asks. "Poor slobs. They probably all tried to bump her off."

Bessie lives with a sweet and caring little man named Hans who has a thick accent, and who has my sympathy from the time I walk in. The house is a tiny four-room cottage with a different pattern of linoleum and at least a hundred knick-knacks in each room.

"Oh, Hans," she says. "Look — it's my granddaughter who I never saw before." She scratches her arms with opposite hands. The sound of it is like the steady swish of a lawn sprinkler.

"You should have known me when I was young," she says. How could I? "Hans takes care of me now. He's afraid to leave me alone. God bless him. What would I do without him?" Scratch, scratch, swish, swish. "You see, I had another operation, besides the ones I told you about on the phone. First gall bladder and then a cyst, look!" She proceeds to pull her blouse up to show me her scar. It is a surprisingly long and ugly black line extending down from beneath her sagging breast over a fat and gray, wrinkled stomach.

I don't know which way to look. I try to get away with a glance. It is so embarrassing, but I know she'll be disappointed if I don't commiserate. It's a good thing that my daughter isn't here, because if she were, we would surely laugh out loud. I keep trying to change the subject. I mean, what does one say to such a scene? "What a shame"? "Certainly is a long scar"? I am reminded of *New York Magazine* conversation-stopper contest.

Meanwhile she offers me fruitcake and a dish of licorice whips that look like shoelaces except I can't help thinking of the black line of a scar that runs down her stomach.

"Hans loves to eat these," she says when I refuse. "Here Hans," she pulls a long line of the candy out of the dish and puts the end of it into his mouth. He chews away, maneuvering the rest of it into his mouth with his teeth, not using his hands. I think I am going to be sick.

I excuse myself, and on the way to the bathroom am shocked to see a photo of my father on Bessie's dresser. He is about twelve years old and is pulling a wagon with three younger children in it. Bessie has followed and now stands behind me.

"That's my father, isn't it?"

"Yes, Oh, yes, there he is. He was the oldest and then there's Andy." She points to the sandy-haired boy whom I recognize from the photos I saw at Aunt Greta's. "Then there's Rob," she ticks them off on her fingers as if she has trouble counting them. "And the little girl is Greta. Don't you know your Aunt Greta now? Lives in Petersburg still."

"Yes, I told you, I've been to visit them, to find out about my father. Remember?"

"Did you see my clock? My clock with the dragon? It's mine, you know. But your uncles, Rob and Andy — they took it away from me and gave it to Greta. Such a brat she was, when she was little. Carter would never love me. That's where we all lived. See the house back here?" She is now back to looking at the photo, which is actually the top one of several folded together like an accordion, revealing several more frames. "I was only a girl myself. Only sixteen when I married your grandfather. Oh, we were so happy then. I didn't used to be so sick and all. Not then. Used to go in the buggy to town — 'to town, to town' I used to say. There it is. See?" She turns another frame which holds a photo of the buggy. She is sitting next to my father who is holding the reins and looks bored. "People thought I was their girlfriend after they growed. They would drive me to town, to town. Yes. I used to love that. We were all so happy."

"People thought you were whose girlfriend?" I ask.

"The boys'. Your daddy's, mostly, until he left. He left so many times. Couldn't love me. Then I was your Uncle Andy's girlfriend — just pretend. Oh, it was such a good time. Why did he have to up and leave me so many times?" Scratch, scratch. The smile came back. "So happy."

Had she told the lie for so many years, that she now believed it? Happy? I stand stone still. I cannot swallow. Her smile is hard-edged, and it doesn't stop. She is covering the pile of dirty rags in her memory with it. She waves her hand in the air in a circle and then goes back to her scratching. "Such a happy girl I was. All the children. Yes. We had such good times in our family." Something twists and flashes in her eyes for an instant. But her hand waves it away, as she scratches her face. I think of my mother's trowel smoothing and sealing the cracks in the plaster. Bessie smoothes and seals everything with her scratching and her smile. What flashed in her eyes? Was it evil?

"Wasn't it a shame he had to die so young," I say looking back at the photo. And her smile turns down at the edges as if it fell.

"Oh, yes," she says. "I always felt so bad at how he died. But he was never good to people. Always made them worry — all the time — worry, worry. Now they would say he lived in the fast lane, you know? He never stood still. Some people think he asked for it. I tried to warn him — even though he couldn't love me." Her hand dances around the photo for a second as if she is about to scratch *it*, but then she folds it up, her hand covering the top photo. Opening the top dresser drawer, she puts it in, trying to hide the top photo. "So bad. Put him away, so he won't leave me any more." As she puts it back into the drawer, she catches her breath when she sees an object wrapped in tissue paper. She looks at me quickly to see if I saw her hide it under the picture.

"What — what did you try to warn him about?" I look her straight in the eye.

"I already put him away," she says trying to close the drawer.

"Surely, you can tell me more," I say. Pretending to want to touch the picture, I put my hand in the drawer, keeping her from closing it. "But surely you —" I stop short because there I finally see the photo that is now on top of the accordion of pictures. It is a picture of my brother! "Oh," I say, "here's Carter."

"Now it is the time for Bessie to have her nap," Hans is behind us. "So sorry to tell you, but she has to have her rest now." Then he closes the drawer. "Strict orders from the doctor."

"My baby," she says over and over – "the only good one."

I ask if I may return the next day, and Hans says they are expecting company as he leads her into her bedroom.

Charles meets me back at the hotel, and I tell him about weird Bessie at dinner. But it is really her fascination with my father that I am thinking about. What exactly was contained in her pleasure of having people think she was my father's girlfriend? Why didn't she want me to see my brother's photo? I decide it best not to tell Charles this part.

Charles pushes his food around his plate into neat little piles. "Tell me how your book is going," he says.

"It was going great guns, but I seem to have slowed down a lot. That's one of the reasons I wanted to come here."

"How many pages have you written?" he asks.

"I am always amazed at how many people ask this question, as if that had anything to do with the worth of it."

"Okay, I get the point." Charles looks hurt.

"I'm sorry," I say. "I guess I want everyone to understand what this means to me. When you ask me a question like that, it seems like you have no idea where my real struggle is."

"I probably don't, but I'm trying. That's the best I can do," Charles says. "It isn't that I don't want you to write a book — if it makes you happy. But there are other things at stake here. What I really want to know is when you are going to finish it."

"Pardon me for laughing, but it's not like knitting a sweater. You don't exactly measure it in inches."

"Well, then let me ask you this — when are you coming home? I'm tired of this ridiculous arrangement. Either you come back home, or I think we should go our separate ways." His voice gets louder. A man at the next table glances over. "I'm tired of the comments, the explanations I have to make to people. I'm sure most of them think writing your book is just an excuse. And if we do split up, I'm going away. I'll relocate — maybe Florida." He is gritting his teeth now.

I am nauseated and am thrown back twenty years to the time when we were engaged to be married. It was two weeks before the wedding when I decided I didn't want to go through with it. I needed more time, I said. Let's postpone everything. Oh, no, he said. That would never do. Either we got married on the agreed-on date or we wouldn't get married at all. And if we didn't, I'd never see him again. He was going away. (Only then it was to California.) Start life over, he said. Without me. Oh, God. What could I do? What would my family think? How could I walk out on all their expectations as well as his? I could not look past the wedding day. The dark space beyond it was much too deep. Yet I knew there was a big reason why I shouldn't get married — even though I didn't know what it was. And so I let the anchor slip back into the water and went ahead with the wedding. He was so handsome. My best friend called him a sunset. We were a perfect couple. Made in heaven.

"Do you know what?" I say. "I think I married you for all the wrong reasons. You were dark and aloof — just like my father. I felt like I always had to wait until you were ready to be close to me. I held my breath for so long, running after you and dying for your approval. I held on in the only way I could. I married you. This must be very confusing, and it's certainly not very fair to you, because I no longer want you for those reasons." The wine is mellowing me, and I know it, but I can't stop.

"Too bad someone didn't warn you about all this back then. Maybe you'd have married someone else."

"No. I probably wouldn't have listened."

"How comforting. Well, how about coming home?" he says. "If you married me for the wrong reasons, maybe you can find some new ones. Better ones."

I don't answer. The words in my heart just won't come. I remember when we were dating — how I needed him to open up to me, and how much I wanted to share with him what was down deep in me! My prodding to make him reveal himself got on his nerves. I decided to cool it, because, after all, the words would certainly come after the wedding, when we would finally be close. Wouldn't they? I was certain.

I didn't see the ring until we stood at the altar. We had decided to keep the engravings a secret from each other until our wedding day. The best man took it off the satin pillow and gave it to Charles who placed it on my finger. A plain gold band — on my finger for the first time. I waited until the Communion. We had a moment to sit while the attention shifted to the priest who spoke in Latin at the altar rail, giving communion to the congregation. I sat with my hands resting on the white organza of the beautiful dress Granlena had made for me. It only took a moment to twist off the ring. I looked up at Charles, and he winked at me. I held it sideways and peeked inside, and a huge lump of disappointment rose into my throat. "More than words. Charles," it read. I died a little. How could he? His position on the subject of sharing with me was now official, and I guess he knew that such a gesture would make his resistance acceptable. After all it was set in gold. Blessed by the church.

I smiled. I swallowed the lump in my throat. Everything would be all right.

But after twenty-odd years of trying, I now have no words for him either. His responses are always so intimidating, that I no longer speak about anything important.

Later, up in our room in the hotel, we get ready for

bed in silence. I wonder if he will try to make love to me. If he does, it will be the first time in almost two years. That is when I stopped asking him. I got tired of all the rejection.

He takes a silky robe I have never seen before out of his suitcase. Then I hear him using his electric shaver in the bathroom. I realize that I have no desire for him. Muffled by running water, I hear him coughing. Then it sounds like he is wheezing. Quite out of breath, he finally comes out, clean shaven and wearing the new robe.

"Something is wrong with me," he gasps. "I can't get my breath."

"Maybe you should lie down."

"Yes, let me rest a minute. Maybe it's some kind of anxiety attack." He puffs his chest in and out.

"Better?" I ask after a few minutes.

"I guess. Boy! This never happened to me before."

"Do you think I should call someone?"

"Someone like who?"

"I don't know — a doctor maybe?"

"Of course not." Puff, puff.

"Well, I was only —"

"Don't be ridiculous."

"Sorry."

"I'll be fine —"

"Good."

"— in the morning." Puff.

No more words. It's okay. You don't have to make love to me. I don't mind anymore. Well, maybe just a little. I stare at the ceiling, wrapped in the profound silence of marriage. Then I am overcome with tears at what my life has become, but I hide them from him. I learned a long time ago how to cry without making any noise. The bathroom further hides the end of my cry. When I come out, he appears to be asleep. Careful not to touch him, I crawl soundlessly into the bed beside him in slow motion.

I dream of sitting up in a beautiful tree with bright pink blossoms, but something is trying to pull me out of it. I hold on to the bumpy trunk, but it is as if there is a crack, a rupture, and I am propelled deathward into a black abyss. There is no hope, and death is all around me. I see a coffin in the middle of a desolate cave. Next to it is a table all set with fancy plates and silver, but when I go up to it, the food on the plates is nothing but bitter ashes and cobwebs. Gray air is all around everything. The coffin opens, and my father is in it. He wears a navy blue suit — double breasted — and his hair is slicked back. Then there is a rushing noise, and I know that the hooded figure is prowling close by in all the dreariness looking for me.

Everything changes, and I am in my lonely bed back in the Bronx in the little house, waiting for my mother to come up the stairs. My eyes are heavy, but I must force them open to keep watching the head of the stairs, because if I don't, *He* might come instead of my mother. The same Death that was looking for me in the cave. I lie exhausted. I cannot bear it. "What do I care anymore?" I say. "Come and get me!" But what if Death does come for me, and takes me away to his lair, and my father isn't there when I arrive?

My father. Why did he leave his mark on me — deep in my center — a wild pain left there, so I would chase his ghost forever?

The next morning I tell Charles I'll come home, but not until the end of September, because I need to give some kind of notice to the apartment management. I realize in spite of myself that if he were out of my life for good, I still could not look at the space beyond. It is too dark and too deep.

Fourteen

§

Standing between the suitcases in my tiny living room, I look at this wonderful hiding place that I have made for myself. Only two rooms, but I have grown to love them. How can I give them up?

The blinking light on my answering machine catches my eye and interrupts my thoughts. Daniel's voice makes me want to cry again. No need to call him back, he says, because he is on his way here. And the best part is that he loves my book. I check the clock and realize he could be here in as little as an hour. Then an express train gallops through the station and sounds its warning whistle. Be careful, Christina. What was it Barret had said? Be careful what you wish for. You might get it.

And soon it is my own doorbell that I hear, and an ice cube forms in my stomach when I let Daniel in.

"It's wonderful to see you," I say. He kisses his fingers and touches them to my face.

"Oh, how can I bear not to have you. I am like Odysseus passing the Sirens."

"Shall I tie you to the mast?"

"Not a chance, but consider yourself warned."

"I've been on my own journey — this time to see Bessie you'll be glad to know, but the bad news is that —"

He stops me with a kiss, and I have to pull away from him. "Don't," I say.   "Don't make this any harder than it is."   I brush tears out of my eyes and am shocked to find them there. I have thought this through. I know what I'm doing.

"What's wrong?" he says.

"Nothing at all. I've made some decisions — I suppose the most important one is that I've decided to go back to Charles."

"Oh," he says. "Oh, that! Nothing to it, I suppose."

"Sarcasm doesn't become you."

"Well,? Are you going to tell me next that you really want to?" he asks. He gets up from the couch and leaves me sitting there.   "Is that what I'm supposed to think?" I draw my knees up to my chin. I cannot look at him.

"I'm not sure if it's wanting to or feeling that I should. Please — you're making this so much worse."

"Worse than what? What could be worse than this — maybe if someone died. Maybe that would be worse."

"Oh, God, Daniel! What are you trying to do?"

"You really haven't resolved anything, have you?" he says, looking out the window. "I mean nothing has changed. So who are you kidding? What's to keep everything from sliding right back to where it was before? Happy marriage number forty thousand, three hundred and seventy-six!"

"He seemed to really want me back."

He turns and leans against the window sill, his long legs crossing at the ankles. "He'd have to be out of his mind not to," he says ever so slowly and keeps his marvelous eyes steady on mine.

"But he means well. Please sit here," I say, patting my hand down on the couch next to me. He stays at the window.

"You sound like you're stuck in some kind of trap. You don't have to stay in it."

"I don't want to talk about this."

"Christina, listen to what I have to say. Please don't make a decision until I finish. I — I'd like you to do something first. Then I promise, I'll never bother you again. I've thought about this all the way here, and even though you've told me this awful news, I'm still going to ask you. It's — here it is: come away with me. Just for a week — less if you like. But stay with me. School will start soon. And if you go back to him then, we may never have this chance again. We may never be able to touch again — ever in our lives. And maybe — just maybe — it'll help you to know better what to do."

"You're hoping I'll fall in love with you and leave him."

"No. I'm hoping that we'll both find out what the truth is here for both of us. Besides, haven't you ever wanted to run away — even for a little while — do something wild and so far out of the ordinary that — "

"Of course I have, but — "

"But what?"

"It's not my style."

"Are you absolutely certain?" His eyes plead.

"No," I say. I wish he'd touch me.

"Then come with me. Here's your chance to look at your life from a new angle." He rubs the back of his neck.

"Where would we go — if I can, I mean?"

"St. Croix. A friend of mine has a place right on the beach. I told him I was going to ask you to come. He said to tell you he hopes you say yes. He's waiting for my answer right now, because he's going to Europe, and he needs to know."

"You know this is absolutely crazy."

"Of course it is, but it's so good, Chris. I already have two plane tickets. That's how much I know we need to do this."

"Oh, Daniel, I want to! I really do — only — "

He comes across the room, and pulls me up off the couch. "Only this. Come with me. He has a big house, with servants, no less!" He puts his hands on my shoulders, massages the back of my neck with his fingers. "And that's all I have to say. Except that I'd like to kiss you for about three hours." He hugs me to him. "That's all for now, just kissing. How long will it take you to make up your mind? But don't forget, we can read your manuscript together."

"I have three more chapters to show you— how did you know? I'll have to call my daughter. I'll give her the address, and — "

"Why? Why do you have to tell anyone? You'll be back before they'll even know you're gone."

"No. I couldn't do that. I couldn't just leave and not

let at least Melissa know. She won't have to know I'm going with you — only just where I am. I'll tell her not to tell anyone else, except if it's an emergency."

"Okay, but I think it's a mistake. I'm going to my brother's now, because I want you to be absolutely sure you want to do this. If I stay any longer, we'll both be blinded by — " In a second I am in his arms. "I want to make love to you. Do you know how much?"

I know that I can feel him inside me already — but I'm so afraid. We kiss for a long time.

"I have to think more — I —" I pull away from him.

"Then think. I'll go. But I'll be here in the morning and you can tell me then. Please, don't call anyone."

"No. It'll be better if I do. If I call her now and tell her I'm leaving tomorrow, then when she writes down my address, it will kind of make it official."

"Are you afraid you'll change your mind?"

"Yes, very. But I'm also afraid I won't."

Chapter 9

"Hello? This is the army recruiting office, Camp Marfa, Texas, here. We are trying to reach a Mr. Barret Shields. Is this his residence?" It was a young stocky lieutenant who made the call. Wade was his name. He talked out of the side of his mouth.

"Yes, it surely is," said Bessie.

"Well, then, ma'am, I'd like to speak to him," Wade said. "Is he there?" He tried not to move, because he didn't want to start sweating again. He had been on his way to a secret meeting with Sergeant Wheeley's wife when Carter found his heavy-footed way into the camp.

"No, he ain't here now, but this here's Mrs. Shields, you know."

"It's his mother," the lieutenant told Sergeant Wheeley, who stood next to Carter, grinning.

"Please, she's *not* . . ." Carter didn't know what to say for fear of jinxing himself — she could ruin everything. But maybe it was better if they thought she was his mother. He gripped the edge of Wade's desk.

"That's good enough," said the sergeant.

"We have a young man here — Carter Shields, says he's your son; is that right?" Wade asked.

"Texas? He's in Texas?" Bessie seemed excited. "Well, I declare!"

"Seems to be some static on the line." It probably wasn't static at all. More likely it was the sound of Bessie scratching herself. "Is he your son?" The lieutenant reached for the water pitcher. He had indeed begun to sweat. He glared at Carter.

"Well, yes, he is," Bessie said.

"Now, ma'am, he's asking to enlist, but we don't know if he's old enough." Wade's voice mocked Carter; he spoke to Bessie as if she were a child. "He could be seventeen, I reckon, but we're not sure. Could we have some verification, Mrs. Shields?"

"He's as old as he says he is;" Bessie said. Then after a pause she added, "Is that all you want?"

"Well, I guess it is, for —"

"Can I talk to my father?" Carter interrupted, his sweat making his hand slip off the desk.

Wade covered the mouthpiece with his beefy hand. "She says he's not there now, little boy."

"He's there. I know he is," said Carter.

"I can't hear — no wait."

"I know he's there. I know he is." Carter's voice rose.

"It must be a bad connection . . ." Wade pumped the cradle up and down. "Operator?" *Click, click, click.* "She seems to have hung up, little boy."

(My uncle, Andy Shields, told me of this incident in 1988. Of Carter's lying about his age and Bessie saying, "He's as old as he says he is." Now I step into a past where I only dreamed before. There are scraps and shreds of half-remembered thoughts poking out of the darkness. I have lived in the cover of this book far too long — tucked away in the fly leaf of a story I have never been able to tell. Hurry! Get it onto the pages. Stop looking over your shoulder. You only think the eyes are there watching. Confront the ghost and perhaps it will become real.

Or disappear.

It must be a bad connection.

He's there. I know he is.

In the pages, time has no dominion. It tumbles over itself out of control — a whirligig of intermissions, of incessant lost moments, waiting for someone to rewind the clock. The pages flip. I can enter here and walk through the fields of my pre-existence; span those yesterdays that separate me from my father, Carter Shields. Our stories crisscross, but we will know each other from two separate timetables. We will look across the open space of our mortality and call to each other. We do not hold onto the memories. They hold onto us.
I am Carter's daughter.
I wonder if he has ever heard me calling.)

Chapter 10

After Bessie hung up, he was subsequently fed, scrubbed, sheared, and outfitted. And when his training period was over, three painful months of aching muscles and lots of blisters, at the age of (almost) sixteen, his primary task was to patrol the Mexican border on horseback in a stiff and careful uniform. Quite a jump from riding freights in rags. He loved the secret of being so much younger than everyone there and still being able to outperform many of them. He loved the rich feeling the uniform gave him. A "new man" feeling, he told himself. But most of all, he thrilled at the thought of having his own horse at last! And he had fooled them all.

Poor Carter! How many dragons must he slay? Riding tight against the rich saddle under him, boots of supple, smooth leather lacing all the way to his knees, he streaked through the still air, the sky flapping behind him like a flag as he raced for the border — back sloped, knees bent, chin jutting forward — almost touching the horse's mane. Would he ever run out of dragons?

He was on his way into Lieutenant Wade's office at dusk one night while he was still in training, when he heard Wade's voice (the same one who had made the phone call to Bessie) trail out of the window.

"Did you hear about that new recruit we got?" he told the sergeant. "Shields's his name. Can't get over him. I thought he was going to be a dud. Passed all his tests first time around. Should see him ride too. Like he's racin' the clock all the time. Don't much like him though."

"You don't much like nobody," said the sergeant.

For the first time since his mother died, Carter felt safe. There was something very reassuring about the military. He quickly fell into the routine and liked the idea of the orderliness of the place, of everything having a purpose and of there not being anything extra, of the newness and perfection of the clothes, and of the fact that everything about the life there from the meals to the schedule could be absolutely depended on.

But he never forgot about Juana, and resolved to visit her as soon as he got a leave. He could not wait to show up clean, with money in his pockets, so she would see what a fine man he had become.

August 2, 1927

Dear Papa,

I am sending you this letter by way of Cousin Henry. I wrote to him and asked him to deliver it into your hands, because since Bessie wouldn't let me talk to you on the phone, I figured she might throw away my letter and not let you see it. Did she tell you I called? I'm in the army at Camp Marfa in Texas. My training is almost over. They call me Private Shields. Here is a picture of me with my troop. I like being here and doing my job, but I miss you so much, Papa.

Sometimes it's hard to believe what happened to us, isn't it? We used to talk so much when Mama was here. I guess that's what I miss most. How we talked. But when Bessie came, there was no more talking, so it wouldn't do me any good to come home.

Someday I'll come home though. I love you, Papa, and Greta and the boys. Please tell them for me. When I get paid, I'm going to send them presents. There's a town near here called Marfa. It has a wide street with some stores, so I'll find something for them. Lots of things happened to me since I left home. Some of them were good and some were very bad. But I'm fine, and I guess I'm growing up. If you can, please send me my books, especially *Great Expectations* and *The Odyssey.* I like to read at night sometimes. I miss reading too. I'm sorry I ran away, but I had to go. Please write to me.

Your son,
Carter

"The prisoner is to pick up and remove all the garbage from the entire camp," said Lieutenant Wade. His eyes were like brown buttons. They had no pupils. He made Carter stand at attention, while he relaxed at his desk, shrouded by smoke from his cigarette.

"Yes, sir," Carter said. Lord, he was tired.

Wade got up and walked to the window. He moved slowly, because he would soon be on his way to visit the sergeant's wife again. He did not want to sweat before he got there.

"You are to ride shotgun on the side of the wagon and see to it that all the garbage is collected and burned at the incineration location. Is that clear?" Wade said. Carter wondered why Wade had ever joined the army. He looked like he belonged in a gambling hall, with lots of cigars and cheap girls, exactly the place where Sergeant Wheeley had met his wife. Carter had Wade typed pretty well, even though he knew nothing about his affair with Mrs. Wheeley.

"Yes, sir." He had played cards the night before, and he had only had four hours of sleep. He stifled a yawn. His ears popped.

"If the prisoner refuses to obey, you are to report that. But if he should decide to make a run for it, you are to shoot him," Wade said. He saw the sergeant come out of his house and cross to the stables.

Carter gulped. "Are you sure?"

"Something wrong with your ears, Private?"

"Sir . . . no sir."   Shoot him?   Was he kidding?   He was a boy like Carter. A fellow soldier who had gotten in trouble for something. He wasn't the enemy, for crissakes.

"Private Wassermann will drive the wagon, and you will guard. Now has your slow southern head taken all this in?"   He massaged his cigarette before he put it in his mouth.

"My head may be southern, but it isn't slow, sir," Carter said.

"You will answer yes or no when addressed by a superior!" His cigarette broke. He started to sweat.

"Yes, sir."

He smiled and threw it into Carter's face. "Now, it seems you owe me a cigarette." Carter did not flinch. It fell to the floor.

"Yes, sir."

"Do you have any?"

"Yes, sir."

"Well, then, let's have one."   Carter took out a half-smoked pack and put it on his desk.

"Get out of here, Shields, you jackass, and keep that big rebel mouth of yours shut."

"Yes, sir." Carter was half out the door. He looked out the window again and saw the lights flash on and off in the Wheeley house.

"Do they call you Shield-Face?   Instead of Shit-face?" Wade said.

"No, sir."   Carter kept on going. Wade went out the back door to his rendezvous.

Fuck him, thought Carter. He found Private Paul Wassermann, the horse-drawn wagon, and the prisoner waiting for him outside Lieutenant Wade's office. Paul was driving and the prisoner sat in the open seat behind him. Carter swung into the seat next

to Paul who was slim and very tall, at least
six feet three, with sandy hair and light
blue eyes. His face was thin and friendly.
There was a smoothness about him that Carter
liked.

"Turn around," he said. "I think you can
shoot him better that way."

"Sure," Carter said, "I was going to."

"Is this your first assignment?"

"Sort of. But after this I get to patrol
the border."

Paul laughed. "Wade is a fucking bastard. He likes to put greenhorns on tough
detail the first time around."

"I'm no greenhorn. I passed everything
first time."

"Take it easy," Paul said.

"Besides, I'm not even supposed to be
doing this. I'm a bugler."

"Since when?"

"Since the other bugler got transferred
and I volunteered."

"Where did you learn?"

"I didn't yet. But I can play the harmonica. I can learn it fast."

"You sure got balls," Paul said.

"I sure do."

They drove through the officers' quarters, and saw the back of Lieutenant Wade as
he disappeared into the back door of the
sergeant's house.

"What do you think of that?" Paul asked.

"Very interesting," Carter said.

"Everybody knows about it except Sergeant Wheeler."

"Bastard. I hate him," said Carter. But
he was more interested in keeping a careful
watch on his prisoner, a young man named
Craig Davis. He was nervous about this assignment. What he didn't know was that Craig

was Paul's friend. The prisoner was short but
handsome, with quick, green eyes and a serious expression, but he looked like he might
explode any minute. There was a tense energy
that he tried to hold in check. He was somehow always in motion even when he was sitting
still. He and Paul had enlisted together.
Both of them were doing well, until four
months before when Craig had failed to shoot
rum runners at the Mexican border. Sergeant
Wheeley had seen him deliberately shoot over
their heads. He had served four of his six
months stockade already. But Carter didn't
know that then. He kept looking at him,
knowing he couldn't shoot him either and
praying that he wouldn't try anything, so
Carter wouldn't have to prove himself. His
head was fuzzy; he yawned to clear it. Craig
kept looking at him. He tried to look tough.
Paul drove the wagon to the mess hall. He got
out and started to go inside.

"Now hold onto everything while I'm
gone, you hear?" he said and disappeared.
Craig looked hard at Carter and went about
picking up the garbage. Their eyes kept
catching each other. The harder he stared,
the more tired Carter felt. Sleep came over
him like a wave. He couldn't get control. It
was so hot.

He felt Paul nudge him. Craig was sitting on the ground in the shade of the wagon.
He had finished all the garbage.

"What a fuckin' face," said Paul. "Hey,
Craig, why didn't you run away? Hot shot
here couldn't shoot you either."

"Oh, Lord," Carter said. "You could have
run." Carter looked at Paul. "He's still
here. I fell asleep."

"No kidding?" Paul said.

"I didn't do it for you," said Craig.

"You don't have to kiss me for it. Think I'm stupid? I only have two months left, jerk." He said this with a very stern face, but then he broke it into a grin.

Paul roared. "You two are a pair."

"Oh, he ain't so bad!" Craig said. He chewed on what was left of his nails.

When Craig's time in the stockade was up, the three of them stayed together whenever they could. But they were careful not to let Lieutenant Wade see their friendship. He would try to keep them apart if he knew. Paul and Craig were good to Carter, especially when Wade was on his back for something. He didn't know why Wade hated him so much. He always called him "Shields Face" or "Shields Baby." One afternoon he caught Carter smoking in his bed. He raged for him to go outside the barracks. This was so more people could hear his tirade, and Carter could best be humiliated. Craig came out behind them when he heard Wade's voice. They both jumped to attention.

"'Smatter, Shields, you tired? You feel like relaxing with a smoke? I think it's high time you woke up. You need something to wake you up. Something with some energy to it. Let's see you dance. We can call you the Dancin' Baby with a bugle. Come on, now, dance!"

"I can't, sir," Carter protested. "I don't know how."

"Well, now, that sounds insubordinate to me, don't it to you, Davis?" Carter ground his teeth; his rage sizzled behind his eyes.

"Begging the lieutenant's pardon, sir," Craig said, "but the fact is, Shields don't know how. When it comes to dancing, he is a mess, sir, Lieutenant, sir. Why I was just saying to someone the other day, that Shields — he can't dance worth a hill 'o beans, sir," he said.

"Shut up, Davis. You're full of shit. Now, Shields, you can dance here or in the stockade. I don't care which." Carter bit a piece off the inside of his mouth. He danced. He wondered who was watching. Son of a bitch.

"That's it, Boy. Isn't he cute?" Wade was hacking out the side of his mouth.

Then a voice rang out through the bull-horn from somewhere behind the barracks. "Wade thinks of Shields when he beats his meat!"

Carter was sure it was Paul's, even though the horn disguised it. It was followed by lots of whistles from all over the camp. Wade frothed over instantly. He turned fiery red. Carter wished he would have a heart attack.

"Who said that?" he fumed. But he knew it was futile. He'd never find out.

"Now you just go right on dancing," he choked and sputtered like a spitting cauldron. Carter shuffled his feet, seething and hating him, wondering how many of the men saw him. He was close to the breaking point, and Craig knew it. "You think you got friends here?" Wade went on. "You got no friends. No one wants to talk to you, Shields Face. Remember how when we called your house, even your little Mommy wouldn't talk to you. Now doesn't she love her little sweetums any-more?"

He roared and walked away from them. In his fury, Carter saw the back of his ugly head, and started to run after him. He proba-bly would have killed him, if Craig had not stuck out his foot, tripping Carter and

making him fall face down in the dirt. Then
Craig fell on top of him, his hands snapping
shut on his arms. Wade whirled around.

"How clumsy of me, sir," said Craig.
"Begging your pardon, sir. Don't trouble
yourself. I'll just help Private Shields to
his feet, and we'll be on our way. No, that's
perfectly all right, sir. You just go on
about your business, and Private Shields'n
me'll be just fine, sir." He gripped him in
the tightest clutch Carter ever felt, and
although he was shorter and slighter, he
managed to push him clear to the other side
of the yard.

"Up your mother's box," said Wade over
his shoulder as he walked away. Craig clamped
his fist into Carter's mouth.

"Don't! Don't you say nothing. You hear
me?   Not one word. Now let your steam out
easy. Okay?"   He stared into Carter's eyes.
When he finally nodded, Craig took his hand
away.

"I want to kill him," Carter said. "He
needs killing."

"Maybe, but not by you. Just wait. Bide
your time. You'll get your chance."

The town of Marfa was a treeless place
with red adobe houses dotting the maroon
earth arranged as if they were a throw of so
many dice about the unpaved street. The
mountains in the distance were made more
severe by the angles of the cactus, which
stood everywhere, as if posing for a camera.
They were as much as four times taller than a
man. Strange to see them — instead of trees.

When the three friends got their first
passes together, they went to town. It was a
little over a mile walk to the one decrepit

hotel.

"First we have to see if the speakeasy still works," Paul said. He had been there before and knew his way around. They ducked through an alley behind the hotel. A dilapidated Indian stood smoking in the sun near the small door in the side of a wooden building. Paul tried the knob. It wouldn't move.

"You need liquor, maybe?" the Indian said. He looked like he had just stepped out of the movies. He actually had a blanket wrapped around him. He leaned against an old cart and spat into the dirt. The high-heeled boots of the cattlemen clumped across the wooden "sidewalk" at the opposite end of the alley making hollow sounds.

"Got some?" asked Paul.

"Pay the Indian."

Carter took out a dollar. "That's all you get," said the Indian showing them a Ball jar — the kind used to put up preserves — which he had hidden under his blanket. The dollar disappeared. They drank it fast. Then they went into the lobby of the hotel. Four girls stood up, like paintings coming to life, and immediately showed their wares.

"Upstairs for a dollar?" was all one of them said. Carter wished he could have said he didn't want to do this, but he was the first one to go upstairs for a dollar. He thought he should have been with Juana, not this cheap whore. She never even talked. Just did her job and then left. How different from Juana. The whore made his body feel good, but he didn't think about anything. There was no ecstasy. But it did let him slow down for a while. The world waited while he sailed in space.

Afterward they compared stories. Only some of them were true. Craig said he had taken two of them at once.

"There were two left after you guys went." He shrugged. "I didn't want her to feel like a leftover." Carter pretended he thought all of this was great, but he felt awful. He realized how far away he was from anyone who loved him. May your dick fall off if you ever do it again, he thought. But of course, he did. He could not turn away from the thought of all that warm skin against his. There was something about skin against skin, flesh against flesh, that he couldn't resist. And besides what would the guys think, if he said he didn't like it?

"I think I hate the army more than I ever hated anything. More than anyone can hate anything," said Craig. "That's why the fucking is so good. It's the only good thing." They walked into a candy store. Carter bought cigarettes and a paper.

"I know, but what else can we do?" he said. "If we quit the army, we can't get work. There isn't any. For myself, I can't even go home. Besides I make more money here, than I ever could on our farm. Someday I'm going to live in a big city with a house and a car and a lot of girls."

Paul laughed. "You mean you didn't make twenty-one dollars a month farming?" His father owned a small grocery store in the Bronx. What did he know?

"You don't make anything farming," Carter said. "You just walk through the seasons with the crops, hope you get enough rain, make your mortgage and get enough food, if you're lucky. And then it starts all over again. The worst part is — it's always the same. You never go anywhere."

"You better put the cigarettes back and save your money," said Craig.

"I can't save all of it," Carter said. "I'll save some. It kills me to buy cigarettes. All that free tobacco on my father's farm, and here I am buying Spuds."

"Well, why not hit the old man for a tin or two," said Paul. "He'll send it to you if you ask, won't he? Then we can all save more."

"I'm saving fifty percent of my salary," said Craig. Fifty? Fifty would never be enough, Carter thought.

"No, ninety," he said. "I'm going to save ninety. Look here," he opened the paper. "'A Hupmobile car for $1060 . . . not the expected power, but abnormal power; not the regular speeds, but extremely high speeds. Two passenger with a rumble seat, beige fabric convertible top.' This is what I need." Upstairs for a dollar? He'd have to start cutting down, he thought. The girls were too expensive. "Think I'll roll my own cigs from now on. Until my pop comes through." Lobo Negro tobacco was only five cents a bag.

"Let's go for a swim," said Paul. "There's a salt lake near here." They went past the front of the hotel. Then they heard a far-away whistle. A sloping, western sun threw an eerie red glow behind a strange figure of a man coming into the town. He had a huge hat like a Mexican, but wore dirty black baggy pants and a shirt. Slung over his shoulder was a horn-of-plenty basket which he kept dipping his hand into, and appeared to scatter something on the ground. His body shook as if he were laughing, but they heard no sound.

"Come on, Carter, what do you say? Did

you hear me?" said Paul.

"I'm coming," he said but could not look away from the man. What was he throwing out of the basket? Suddenly the Indian was next to them.

"You see the crazy man," he said. Now Paul stopped to watch too. "What's in his basket?"

"He crazy man."

"Hey, what's doing with you guys? It's just an old man," said Craig.

"It looks like plain old dirt," Carter said. But inside he gave a shudder that he felt down to his bones.

"What a loony bird. Gives you the creeps." Paul threw his cigarette pack up and down like a ball. They were so busy watching, that none of them saw the group of tough looking cowboys come out of the hotel.

"It's just plain old dirt, isn't it?" Carter asked Craig, but somewhere in his soul, he felt like he had seen something like death.

"Why don't you go and ask him," said the tallest of the cowboys. He may have been part Indian, because his cheek bones stuck out below black eyes, his hair hung like wires, long below his collar. His boots were worn and dirty. "What you come here for? You all like to watch maniacs?" He made it clear that he did not want them here at all. He snatched Craig's cigarettes out of the air. Then he tossed them up and down. "We like cowboys in this town, not soldier boys. Not with those smacked-ass haircuts." His friends laughed, laughed on his cue. "Let's see you ask the old man what's in his bas- ket." Craig chewed his nails. Carter made a grab for the cigarettes, but missed. The old man moved closer and closer on noiseless feet.

"You scared?" the cowboy jeered.

The old man never looked up, but seemed to laugh to himself. Now he was directly opposite them. For a moment they were all caught in his spell and forgot their sparring. His actions seemed to say: You know what I'm doing — everyone knows. Don't ask me — I will only laugh.

And just then he did laugh. It was very soft. A sort of hee hee hee, hee hee hee.

"He crazy man," said the Indian. "Pay the Indian and he tell future." The spell was over.

Craig's cigarette pack flew through the air and struck the old man's hat. The cigarettes spilled over the street. Carter was on that bastard cowboy in a second.

"Stay the hell in your fucking barracks, and leave our girls alone," he bellowed, but Carter kept pounding him.

"You can keep your fucking girls. They stink, like you," Carter said. Paul and Craig dragged him off. The cowboy's friends dragged him away, too.

"I was winning," he said. They pushed him down the street.

"Listen, big shot, how much trouble are you looking to get into?" Paul said. "You're in uniform, jerk."

"Wait," said the Indian. "You need liquor? Pay the Indian." He held up a jar wrapped in cloth. "Two dollar. And I tell future, too." It was the same size jar as before.

"Fuck you," said Craig.

Carter paid. His eye had started to burn and swell up where the cowboy had hit him. "You're going to get in trouble if you don't get some ice on that eye soon," said Paul.

"Soon as I hear my future," he said.

"Don't buy car," the Indian said.

"And?" Carter demanded.

"That is future."

"Lousy bum," he said. "I paid a dollar for that?"

"Forget it," said Paul. "You're going to be in enough trouble with that eye. Let's go."

"Shit," Carter said, but allowed himself to be persuaded back to the base. As they walked, they saw an antelope dart like wind across the mesa. He was heading for the shelter of the chino grass at the foot of a low mountain.

"What did the deer say to the antelope?" said Craig.

"I'll bite," Paul said.

"'I just heard a discouraging word.'" Paul hit him.

> October 12, 1927
> Dear Carter,
> I cannot tell you how glad I was to get your letter. I cried, boy. Cried like a baby. Everyone in Petersburg is so happy to know you're safe and sound. I sure was proud to see your picture. Greta clapped her hands and said, "Carter is my boyfriend." Andy and Rob said they are going to join the army when they get old enough. Aunt Marion is sending you her best biscuits. Granny is sending muffins, and Bessie is sending you a pie. And she did tell me when you called. I had went to town, and she couldn't remember where you were so I couldn't call you back.
> Now, it's been so long since I

gave you a present that you are getting one very soon. I am sending you
lots of tobacco and a whole bunch of
new books. What's the point of sending
the ones you already read? Write
soon.

> Love,
>   Your Papa

*   *   *

November 1, 1927

Dear Carter,
        I asked your Papa not to tell
you, so I could do it. Grandpa passed
away three months ago. You know how
he had a bad heart and all. So be sure
you pray for him at night when you say
your prayers. Now don't forget. Bless
your heart. And here is his watch for
you. Now you will always know what
time it is.
        This is his wrist watch that
I gave him for a Christmas present.
His pocket watch is here for you when
you come back. Now be so so careful,
dear, dear Carter, and come see Granny
soon.

> Love,
>   Granny

It was the first time he heard something
from his family in two years. He read those
letters a thousand times. In fact he was

never without them. He carried them, limp
with the dampness of his body, in his hip
pocket until they finally fell apart. Reading
them was like somehow touching Papa and
Granny. How he ached for them!   Neither
letter had mentioned anything about the
police looking for him, so he guessed the
news of Mile Away's death had never gone
anywhere. Mile Away!   You poor old soul, he
thought. It is almost a year since you died.
Where are you now?   Then he wondered if
Hellbag were dead too, and he shuddered.

Chapter 11

     In January, Craig was assigned to the
infirmary, while Carter and Paul rode down to
the border to catch rum runners. Carter loved
the feel of the rock-hard leather under him.
It made him feel so . . . old . . . was the word.
But then he remembered all too quickly how he
felt when he had to guard Craig that day, and
how easy it must have been for him to get
thrown into the stockade for not being able
to shoot a man. They were under the stars for
three days, eating rations and camping out.
They played a lot of poker in those days.
     On a murky day late in the month, Carter
saw a reed with a lot of sticks and debris
flat around it sticking vertically out of the
water, moving slowly across the river.
     "Paul," he said, and pointed to it.
     "Yup. It is," he said. They waited. He
took his canteen and stood flat against a
boulder that overhung the water. When the
reed got very close to the edge, he poured
his water in a gush down the reed. A short,

squat Mexican sputtered out of the water. He had bottles of liquor tied all over him. They were amazed that he had managed to swim across with all that weight. They took some of his bottles and hid them in among the boulders for themselves. As long as the Mexican didn't try to run, they didn't have to shoot him. They made sure he had no other options but to be captured.

"Look at his leg," he said. His pants were torn away to reveal a festering sore as big as a half dollar. His eyes filled with fear as he tried to cover it. "Don't worry, old man," said Carter. He gave him some rations. "We take good care of our prisoners. We'll take you back tomorrow to camp, and our friend Craig will fix you up in the infirmary."

"Poor guy. How would you like Craig taking care of you? What the hell does he know about anything? Let's call him 'Crack' instead of 'Craig'," said Paul.

"*Dr.* Crack," Carter said.

"Dr. Crack Quack," said Paul.

"Well, someone there better know what to do."

"Yeah, but not Craig." They tied his hands, and by late afternoon the next day he was safely in the hands of "Dr. Quack." The three of them stood talking in the infirmary anteroom after the Mexican had been taken inside.

"You'll never guess who's in here," said Craig. "Your favorite lieutenant."

"Don't tell me?" squealed Paul. "Oh, I'm so upset."

"What's he got?" Carter asked.

"Probably the clap," Paul said.

"No. It seems he was visiting his lady friend, Mrs. Wheeley," Craig said. "The two

of them were cavorting in their birthday
suits when her wedding ring came off and
rolled under the table. She asks him to get
it for her, and he's on his hands and knees
under the table when her dog comes in and
licks his balls. It gave him such a shock, he
jumps up, hits his head so hard, he passes
out. She thinks he's dead and comes over here
and bribes me to come and get him outa there
before her husband comes home."

"Couldn't happen to nicer guy," cried
Paul through his laughter.

"This is the only chance we may ever get
to give it to him good," said Carter. "Look,"
he pointed to a small American flag held by a
stick that was about a foot long. "Do your
nurses take bribes?"

"Doesn't everybody?" said Craig.

"Okay, here it is," Carter said. "Get
one of them to tell Wade he has to have his
temperature taken by a . . . let's call it a
new procedure. Then, we bribe her again to
stay out of the way, one of us puts on a
mask, goes in there and tells him it's a
special kind of temperature we have to take,
and he has to stay there for a half hour
while it's taking. And we take his temperature with this!"

"Son of a bitch!" Craig's eyes watered
when he laughed hard. He could hardly talk.
He jumped over the counter and landed in a
chair. "Wait. We have to take a picture. We
want everyone to know how patriotic he is!"

"But I can't be the one who does it,"
said Paul. "I'm too tall. He'd know me.
Carter, you got to do it."

"Oh, my God," Carter said. "I'd die
first."

"Well, it was your idea."

"No, I'll make that nurse an offer she

can't refuse. She'll do it. I'm not going to contaminate myself."

It was the talk of the entire camp. There was Wade, lying face down on a cot with a flag sticking out of his ass. Word spread. The whole camp tiptoed by for a look. Wade thought Carter was still on rum patrol, and never found out who did it. The best part was that someone even went to get Mrs. Wheeley to come by for a look. That was the end of their affair.

Several months later, Carter saw the old man again. The maniac on noiseless feet with the soft-sounding laugh and vacant eyes. That same night he dreamed of him. He saw the old skeleton of a man fallen face down in the street. He saw himself go to help him. First he turned him over, and screamed to see his eyes were two holes that went all the way through his skull. There was nothing in them. Carter cried out in his sleep. The recruit in the next bed shouted for him to shut up.

Chapter 12

In May of '28, Carter was given his first full month's furlough. He took a train bound for Marathon, no longer afraid to see Juana's father, because he knew he'd never recognize him in his uniform. Besides he was at least two inches taller.

"What will you do when you find her?"
Paul had asked him. Carter grinned. "Besides
that."

"I'll give her money and put her on a
train, so she can go to Hollywood. It's what
she wants."

Carter bought a horse from a drunken
cowboy at the station for five dollars. He
hoped to sell it for more than that when he
returned.

Maria was tending the goats when Carter
rode up. She was bent over into a circle, but
she straightened when she heard the hoof
beats.

"He not here. He out to get the chino
grass," she said.

"Maria, don't you know me?"

"*Dios*! You? So, you are a man." She
laughed and held out her hand. He felt mature
and important. Just a teen-aged kid, but able
to look at least like twenty.

"Where is Juana?"

Her face grayed and slackened. "She go
away. She leave me." Sadness hung on her
like a veil. "I beg her not to go. Her father
— he bad man — he beat her. So she go. I give
her what I steal from him." They went into
the house.

"When did she leave?"

"When you go, she wait, but cry olla
time. Two months back, she go."

"Did she write to you?"

"I no read."

"But it's almost a year. You don't know
where she is?"

"I pray to the Virgin." She walked over
to the *nicho*. "I light the candle. She will
find the Hollywood man. Come, eat. You eat?"

"How did she know where to go?"

"She say she ride to next town — not Marathon, so no one know her — so no one tell her father that she gets on the train. Then she will get on the train in the next town."

"But how do you know if she ever got on the train? That country is so deserted out there."

"Juana very strong. She do what she please to do."

Carter left. He watered his horse at the station and then rode west following the tracks. It was a barren wasteland, an empty landscape. In the distance he could see the jagged, skinny mountains, sepia skeletons that seemed to frown down at him. El Muerto towered and colored the air. And the buckets of blood came back, like the time when the night settled on New Orleans, and Hellbag killed Mile Away. The day ebbed. The shadows lengthened. The cactus seemed to laugh, raising their arms in mockery.

He went four miles, maybe five, and off to the south of the tracks he saw something move, something flap in the wind — cloth of some kind, shredded and bleached in the sun, and he guided his horse there. Her skeleton lay in the sand, left by vultures and bleached white from the sun, still wearing the dress, the red dress — the red, now faded and visible only in the folds, with all its softness in uneven tendrils, flecks of lace crackling dry over the worn nap of the velvet, stick-straight bones thrusting out of the hem, the pieces of tattered cloth wrapped flat around the bones of the chest and the skull grinning up to the sky.

The wind kept flapping the cloth like scarves blowing on a beach, making her look like she shivered. He could not bear it and exploded his wrath in horrible curses, roaring to the laughing ghost, the keeper of time who scattered his dust and brought these two together in torment. He shrieked his anguish — the sound thundering all the way to the mountains, howling, yelping — until his voice was gone.

And El Muerto laughed back.

His mother heard him. Emma Rose heard his cries long before they ever sounded. She had told Barret that night on the porch in the dark, " . . . one big long wail that flashes at me when I'm not looking . . . it's saying what his life will be like some day, and he's wailing before he's even born . . ."

(And many years later, I heard the same sound. It was my own baby, Carter's grandchild, safe in my womb, yet crying for her life. Did my mother hear mine, and did she call him over to hear? "Carter, the baby is crying. Come and hear the baby cry." Did he put his ear to her stomach? Did he hear me then from another dimension, just as I have heard him call me from beyond his grave?

"My father is dead, Sister Mary Catherine."
"Say deceased, dear. Never say dead."
"Does that mean he's dead?" I said.
"Yes, of course. He's with God. God wanted him," Sister said.
"Why did God want him so much?"
"We must never question God, Christina."
"Then who can I question?")

Fifteen

℘

At thirty thousand feet we are sucked through the universe, and the lives we knew fade fast behind us. I see my husband's and daughter's faces in the blank air outside the window, and then those of the women in my family who molded my life — the Chorus of Shoulds. I let them go. Daniel kisses my finger tips and then sucks them. I think I might die.

"I want to touch you," he whispers, then turns to see a kinky-haired flight attendant halting at each seat, as she moves like a bride down the aisle. She turns her head back and forth like a sort of pendulum as she checks her passengers. Daniel stops her. "I wonder if you might have a blanket among your store of goodies back there," he says. She stares, smiling for a beat, then disappears.

"What are you doing?" I ask ever so softly, afraid I might laugh out loud. He doesn't get a chance to answer because she whisks herself back down the aisle, carrying a folded blanket over her head like a tray of food.

"My wife is having cold flashes," he says. "Thanks ever so much." I turn my head out the window, so she can't see my face collapse. "These attacks are awful. Look how she shakes." He turns back to the stewardess. "My dear," he says, "you've been too kind — whatever they're paying you, it isn't enough." She smiles her professional smile and leaves us. Daniel opens the folds of the blanket and spreads it over us.

"Come out, come out, wherever you are," he whispers to me. "The coast, as they say, is now clear." Then he starts to put his hand up my dress. I jump about a foot, and try to stifle a giggle, stopping his hand. "Relax," he says.

His other hand strokes my breasts, my thighs. I cannot bear it. "Wait," I whisper. "I'll never survive."

"No one can see."

"That's true." I'm close to silent hysteria and fight for control. I finally stop him altogether, holding both his hands in mine. "But I am going to be on fire by the time we get to St. Croix."

Then he starts to chuckle. "So what's so terrible? Maybe all this heavy breathing will make the plane go faster."

"Either that, or we'll use up all the oxygen."

"I'll wire ahead and have a cab waiting, so we can whisk ourselves right into bed," he says, "before we both explode."

"I thought you were going to read my manuscript," I manage to get out.

"Have no fear. I'll appreciate it more in this — this heightened state. How's that for a euphemism. Heightened state — whew." Taking my hand, he looks at me with serious eyes, his face an inch away from mine as we both lean back on the high seats.

I can hardly hear him as he whispers, "I want to kiss your ankles, your knees, your thighs. I want to undress you, suck you, turn you in all kinds of positions. Slowly — so slowly, so you can enjoy it that much more. I want to penetrate you and I want you to come over and over." And no love making I have ever had has ever excited me as much as his words. And then we are kissing. He makes a little moan, so low it is barely there, and then we both pull away from each other, knowing we have to stop. The cushion of the seat is so welcome, because I am as limp as a rag, and we stare at each other for a bit, only knowing the moment. Then we move apart.

He pulls himself up stiffly and pulls his glasses out of his pocket. "My dear, I told you I wanted to read your manuscript, and I wish you would stop this shameful behavior and let me have it."

"I'll try to control myself."

We do not even see the house, the rooms, as we pass through them on our way into the bedroom. We sink together in the dark of the bedroom, against a blue haze of cool sheets. He explores me with his finger tips, and then his tongue, as if I am glass — as if I am the most precious thing he has ever discovered. He licks me in little circles, and the stirrings begin there, but then they spiral all the way inside — down my throat and into my stomach — way inside to a deep golden place that I didn't even know was there. His energy builds. But the most wondrous thing about his mouth is not only the way it caresses me. It is that he talks while he makes love. And words for me, I soon realize, are the biggest turn-on of all. And Daniel's words wash over my body and into my spirit and I am ablaze.

"You are like some kind of music for me," he says. "So, so sweet . . . pouring into me and out." Meanwhile his fingers are never still, and I know that I am the only thing in his consciousness right now. He sees me with his whole self. Me. He wants to get in, so I can be so close — all around him at once. Oh, yes.

At first we are still, as if we are counting all the parts of ourselves. Then we rise and fall. There are long lines of pleasure that continue down pathways — down through my limbs and end in my toes, fingers, ears, and in places that hide in the back of my spine, of my mind, and then wind back again, and in the dimness I can see that he looks into my eyes the whole time. He never stops looking. I am tight all around him, wet and tight, memorizing his hardness, as it trembles in me.

"You are the most thrilling — the most beautiful woman I have ever known." There are a thousand diamonds all around us on a black velvet cloth. Back and forth, they move with us, back and forth; and I know that death cannot prowl here.

I try to speak. There are many words deep in the golden place, but few emerge. Because of you there is only now, I think. The past fades into itself like a black hole and the future is impossible — not even a flicker of a thought. "There is only right now," I finally manage to get out, "and you have made me beautiful."

Morning seeps into the room which is done all in blues and whites with lots of wicker and chintz, and white wooden shutters make the light slant in pale stripes.

We waken with arms and legs entwined. I can still feel him inside me when I think of it. I want to make love all over again — to fall back into the dream where the past has no power over us.

He kisses my forehead good morning. "I think we've been together like this before somewhere," he says. "Don't you? I know we've done this before."

I stroke his thick hair, push my fingers into its coolness. "I think something in me remembers you from eons ago. Is this why you're here now — why you came into my life?"

"You brought me into it somehow. Why did you do that?"

"Did I?"

"If you can believe there are no accidents — then, yes, that's what you did," he says. "And now you have to free yourself. You are too beautiful to stay in a cage."

"I have to go back and end it myself, don't I?" He does not answer. "I don't know how. Everybody is going to get so caught in the undergrowth of my problem. None of the family even knows there is a problem, except Melissa." I get up and walk naked to the window. "I guess I just have to *do it*, as they say in the commercials." I open the shutters and the light spills in. I see the clear aqua surf. In a minute, Daniel is behind me, wrapping me in his arms.

"Let's swim before breakfast," he says, "just as we are."

"Will anyone see us?"

"Who cares? Let's let the water heal us."

"Can I look for shells too?"

"I'll find you a thousand shells, if you like. I'll make you a necklace. I'll put them in your hair."

*   *   *

After a naked swim, we wrap ourselves in white terry robes and walk along the water in a pink sunrise. It is only the second day we are here, yet I am completely at home.

A strange creature crawls under the water a foot from the edge of the wave.

"A sea anemone," Daniel says. "Beautiful."

"It looks like a flower," I say, daring to touch its pink petallike tentacles which wave to the rhythm of the sea.

"Look," says Daniel, picking it up and revealing a shell underneath it. "It's attached to the top of this shell, which is really the home of a hermit crab. Ah hah! There he is." And a small crab, with long legs and pincers, struggles to find water. "The anemone attaches itself to the back of the shell. Even when the hermit grows too big for its shell and moves to a new one, it takes the anemone with it, and transplants it onto its new home." The crab claws and scratches the air more violently, trying to gain a foothold. "They are always found like this, living together, never alone."

"Good grief," I say. I don't want to touch it anymore. "Will they die if they're separated?"

"I don't know," Daniel answers, "maybe. Maybe they'll die of broken hearts."

"Or relief." Now the crab is becoming more frantic. He finally thrusts himself all the way out of the shell and spills into the water, taking off at breakneck speed. "Oh, no, come back," I say. "You left your anemone all alone. What will become of her?"

"She'll probably be just fine," says Daniel. "She may like living alone, or she may find a better crab. Who knows?" He holds out the empty shell to me. "Want to take her home?"

"No. She'll die. Leave her here where she belongs." He puts her back into the water.

As we approach the house, we see the maid ahead of us, crossing the verandah and carrying fruit in a basket on her hip. Daniel halloos to her, and she turns to greet us. She is an earthy, huge black woman with quarter-inch hair and wonderful cheekbones. She is barefoot in her cotton dress, and stands now with one foot turned outward, her heel resting on the instep of her other foot. Two long earrings, made of a thousand tiny iridescent beads, hang from her ears, giving her face a gypsy flair.

"You see the water," she says. "Eat the fruit. Then go and swim in the water. Here lady." She holds the fruit out to me, huge mangoes that she had peeled and sliced for us.

"Oh, thank you," I say to her. "You are lovely and so kind." I take some fruit and give it to Daniel.

"Your earrings," he says to her. "Where did you get them?"

"I make them," she says. "I string the beads with the magic hair of the holy man's goats."

"Can you make yourself another pair?" Daniel asks.

"The other week, perhaps. When you go home, and I don't work then."

"Good. Then sell me these. I want them for my lady."

"Oh, Daniel," I say. "Don't ask her to do that."

"'Sokay," she answers. "He knows the magic when he sees it." She takes them out of her ears and gives them to him. Then she disappears before I know it.

"Daniel, I don't wear earrings like these. I never wear anything this long — I think they would look nice on Melissa, maybe, but I —"

"Maybe it's time you did. What's the matter, do you think you're too old?"

"It's not that — it's — I don't know what it is actually, I just know they're not my style of —" He leans me against the wall of the house, and puts them in my ears. Then he starts to kiss my neck.

"Now, my dear, you are wilder than ever. You are a gypsy, you are Nefertiti, Cleopatra, and I'm hard as a rock, and we are going upstairs, and I am going to make love to you again, and this time you are going to keep those earrings on!"

For two more days, we revel in the sensuous island. And then it is time to leave. I am feeling blue as I try to wrap my damp swim suit in a towel before I put it in my suitcase.

"I'm scared to go home," I say.

"Then let's stay," he answers.   He leads me to the main room of the house, a rustic sitting room with dark wooden beams and a fireplace, and pours us some wine before we go out for our final lunch.   "Christina, remember that I told you I loved you. Perhaps because it happened in the height of passion, you might think that that doesn't count. Now I'm going to tell you while I'm cold sober. Yes, in spite of the wine. Not only do I love you, but what is more important, I want to grow old with you. How do you like that, even though I know I have no right to say it?"

"Right is not the issue," I say.   "I'm just not ready for this now. Please think of what is ahead of me."

"I know, my darling. I guess I never should have said it. Forget it for now, but when it comes back to you later, think about it and remember."

But then we are both startled by a sharp knock at the door. Daniel strides across the room and extends his hand toward the door knob.

"Wait," I say.   "Ask who it is."

"This isn't New York, Christina," he says, and flings it open.

Dora!

I want to die on the spot. Her tiny frame stands at the peak of its fury, and her venom sprays as if she were a mini volcano. "How could you do this to your family? What would Granlena say if she knew?" she roars. Daniel is thrown back by her swift and voracious entrance, her hair wild and flying into serpent tendrils.

"You think you can blacken our name like this? No telephone, Melissa said. Hah! Do you think I was born yesterday? I got the truth out of her. You have to come home now. Now!" She is in a frenzy of spittle and tears, and she oozes all over us. Her face is juicy red — you can see the corpuscles sticking out of her cheeks. Her hand covers her glass eye. She storms into the bedroom, with us running after her.

"Excuse me," Daniel says.   "But you can't just burst in here and —"

"Wait a minute," I break in.   "What do you mean, you got the truth out of her? What truth?"

Dora hasn't even heard us.   "Granlena must never

find out. But you can't hide from me. I have eyes in the back
of my head, remember? You think I couldn't figure out that
you're having an affair? I got it out of Melissa. She may be
your daughter, but I'm the one she trusts." A huge lump on
her neck begins to pulse in and out.

"You may have confused trust with bribery," I snap.
"I can feel the anger rip through me. "Get out! Get out of
here right now!"

"No, don't even try — don't even so much as ta-rye to
excuse yourself, because you can't. I got it out of her. You
can't escape my vigilance." The swollen blob gets bigger on
her neck. She suddenly gasps and clutches her head.

"Just get out I said!" I shriek at her.

"She looks like she's going to blow up," Daniel says,
with a warning in his voice.

"Look, Aunt Dora, sit down a minute — okay, okay —
you don't look —"

"Don't you 'Aunt Dora' me. Who do you think —"
Now she is wheezing and can't talk. She bites at the air,
spitting and blasting out random grunts and sounds.

A sudden chill stops me cold. "Aunt Dora, you have
to stop. For your own sake. Please sit down — lie
down . . ."

"Bessie . . . did it," she chokes. The lump on her
neck is enormous. "I . . . loved him, but . . . Bessie did it
— you'll . . . see." She clutches her chest. Her face is blue
and swollen. Then the lump turns blue, bounces in a final
pulse, and disappears as her glass eye flies out of her head
and lands on our bed. It keeps going, falls off the edge and
then rolls under the bed as Dora sinks to the floor. She falls
down on herself like a beach chair collapsing. Then she is
still, staring at the ceiling with her only remaining eye — her
mouth open and forehead in pinched frowns.

"Oh, God, Daniel — don't tell me —"

"I think she's dead. I'm so sorry, Chris . . ."

I put my hand on her chest which is wet with her spit
and perspiration, and then I see the stain of urine spread
under her on the floor.

"Looks like she exploded — some kind of stroke, I
guess," Daniel says. I sink on the edge of the bed and sob.

He immediately turns practical. "We have to get her out of here," he says. "We have to figure out a way to get her home."

"Home? But she's dead."

"Yes, but we can't let anyone know she died here. This is not the way for your family to find out about us."

"But what else can we do?" I stare at her, afraid to move, fighting panic.

"You can't take a body out of St. Croix without all kinds of red tape. It could take forever, and it will inevitably involve publicity."

"Well, then what?"

He stares at her a moment. "She is very small and light." He hesitates. "Please don't be offended by this, but since she's so small . . . I can probably carry her . . ."

What is he talking about? "Carry her?"

"In the — in the suitcase — the big one . . ."

"Oh, God, Daniel! Please — *no* —"

"But what else? Listen to me. There's no alternative. Do you want your daughter and everyone to know where you are?"

"No but — we'll never get away with it."

"It's a choice: Either sneak her out of here, or let everyone know. And once the government gets wind of a death, we'd be stuck here for days, maybe weeks. Please trust me, Christina." He goes to my big suitcase and empties it; then he gathers up her slack body.

"Oh, my God, no. We can't. We just can't do this to her."

"It's beyond our control, Christina," he replies grimly. "There's nothing else to do now." He puts Dora in the suitcase, bending her knees up, but keeping her back as straight as he can. Then he reaches under the bed for her eye. He holds it gingerly, and it looks at me. We can't help it. We laugh uncontrollably as he puts it into the suitcase and zips it up.

"I'm sorry, baby," he says when we manage to calm down. "But think a minute, what was that she said about Bessie?"

"Bessie?" I try to think. "She said something like, 'Bessie did it' — what ever 'it' is. Did what, I wonder?"

"You don't know?"

I shake my head.   I can't think straight.   Later perhaps I'll be able to make sense out of it.

We have to leave some of our things behind and divide the essentials into the other suitcases.

"We have to keep this with us," Daniel says, testing the wheels of the suitcase that has Dora in it, and making them roll back and forth.   "Roll it right into our seat.   Besides I can carry it if I have to.   I just hope the handle holds out. She couldn't weigh more than ninety pounds."

"Aren't you going to check your bag, sir?" says the Red Cap, just doing his job, hoping for a tip.   Does he suspect us?   We ignore him and get on the plane.   But it is after we land that there is a problem, because now we have to go through customs.   Cursory inspection, of course, because St. Croix is a US possession, but still . . .

"Now's when we need your tears, Christina," Daniel whispers.   "Let yourself go, and cry.   That's all you have to do and try to keep it up when we have to pass the customs official."   By now it's easy for me to cry and as my tears flow, Daniel ushers me across the floor.   His right arm is around me, and his left is pulling Aunt Dora.

"I'm sorry," he says to the customs officer.   "Her father just died, and she can't stop crying."   I sob away.   A Red Cap follows us with our other bags.

"Go ahead," says the official, glancing at our short list of purchases.   "No need to stop here."

"Good girl," Daniel whispers.   We then push past the crowd and go out onto the street where we get ourselves into a cab — Daniel, and Dora, and I.

Sixteen
℘

"Last week, my grandmother went upstate to visit my other aunt — Aunt Julie — the one who has the farm," I tell Daniel in the cab leaving Kennedy as darkness falls. "I just hope she's still up there. What if we get to the apartment, and she's home?" We speak in hushed tones.

"Maybe you should call and check," he says. He tells the driver to stop at the next gas station, and I force myself to get out in the midst of traffic chaos and belching brakes, as huge tractor-trailers inch their way in for gas. It is difficult to walk. The air is thick with fumes. I feel as if I weigh three hundred pounds, pushing myself through this barrier of heavy air. The phone is slimy in my hands.

"No answer," I say collapsing onto the seat next to Daniel. "Are you sure? I mean, can we do this?" I whisper. I keep seeing Dora folded into the suitcase. "What if she's not really dead? Isn't that possible?" I listen for sounds from the suitcase and then start to cry again.

"You know she is. You would like to think this never happened. So would I. Don't make yourself feel worse."

"But I mean, we can't just leave her in the apartment, can we?"

"We're not going to just leave her there. Lean on me," Daniel says. "I can think straighter than you can now. It will be all right."

"You guys ready yet?" says the driver, chawing on a wad of gum. "All the same to me. Meter's runnin'." He is a fat, greasy-looking man with no neck.

"You'd better give him directions to her apartment from here," says Daniel. I do, and soon we are on the Hutchinson River Parkway, almost home.

"I think she's starting to smell," I whisper.

"She's only dead six hours. Don't worry."

It's dark when we get to Dora's apartment. Daniel hides our other suitcases in the bushes near the side door. Then we cross the lawn and let ourselves into the lobby with her keys.

"One flight up," I whisper, and Daniel precedes me, lugging the suitcase up the stairs. We do not speak. I try to whistle a tune, lagging behind Daniel, looking to see if there is mail in Dora's mailbox. I don't want anyone to see us together, although the odds of meeting someone in this small apartment house are almost nil. He has only gained half a dozen steps when the door of a first-floor apartment opens, and my aunt's elderly neighbor, Anderson, sticks his head out. With that, the suitcase's handle breaks off in Daniel's hand, and he cannot stop the suitcase from sliding back down the stairs, knocking me down and finally hitting the wall.

"Easy does it," Anderson says, helping me up. He ignores the suitcase, which is now behind him. "Boy, they sure don't make these things the way they used to, that's for sure. You okay? But then, they don't make nothin' the way they used to."

Daniel is trying to get past us to get to the suitcase. "I'm so sorry," he says, "I hope I didn't hurt you, miss." He is still clutching the handle.

"No, I'm fine, really," I say, trying not to look at him. Daniel hoists the suitcase, hugging it with both arms, trying to smile as he heads for the stairs, trying to make it look as if it isn't heavy.

"Well, good luck," I say to him as he disappears around the curve of the banister.

"Odd sort," says Anderson. I wait a bit, to give Daniel some time. "We sure get some strange ones in here now and then. Who do you suppose he's visiting?"

"I'm sure I don't know," I say and start up the stairs.

"They don't make people the way they used to neither. Oh, by the way," he waves his hand the way my students do in class. "How's your aunt's African violets? I gave her some; did she show you?"

"No, but I'm sure they're fine. I'll let you know next time I see you."

"Maybe I can come up now and check them," he says. "I raise 'em you know. Hobby of mine."

"Well, that's lovely," I say over my shoulder. "But this really wouldn't be a good time. She's expecting me for dinner, and I'm late now."

"Don't think she's home. Saw her leave at five this morning and haven't heard her come back."

I stop short, not knowing what to say to that, so I laugh a little. "Oh, there you go keeping tabs on her. Let me know if she has any new boyfriends, will you?"

"She don't," he says.

"I'm sure you just missed her when she came back."

"Oughta be tendin' her violets. There's a secret to 'em, you know. Gotta keep em wet."

"Oh, good." I am gripping the banister to keep me from running up the stairs.

"Most people don't know that. Let 'em get too dry. I ought to know — been raising 'em for years. I'll give you one. Want one?"

"Some other time would be just fine. I promise to ring your bell one of these days." And I finally escape.

"Yeah, go ahead — always in a hurry. Everybody's in a hurry."

"Thanks again, Anderson," I call back and turn to find Daniel leaning on my aunt's door, wheezing for air. He puts his finger to his lips, and I open the door. He moves Dora silently into the apartment. We bring the suitcase into the living room and unzip it.

Don't look at her, I say in my head, but I do, in spite of myself. She is gray and pasty with all her frowns still intact, and her clothes are damp and wrinkled, as if pressed

into more frowns. Daniel pulls her out, and her body tips
over onto the floor, still curled up.

"Shit!" he says.

"I forgot about Anderson. He probably listens to every
footstep up here."

"I'm sorry," Daniel says.

I cannot bear another moment. I am going to be sick.

When I come back from the bathroom, he is bent over
Dora. "I can't straighten her out any more than that," he
says. "Does it look like she could have fallen here in this
position?"

"Oh, God, I don't know. How long before — before —"

"Rigor mortis passes off? I don't know. Some hours,
anyway."

I take her hat and gloves, put them away in her room,
and go through her purse to remove any evidence of her trip.

Daniel goes into the kitchen to wash his hands. I
follow him, because I am in great need of a hug, and besides I
really don't want to be alone in the room with her. "I'll take
all your things to your apartment," he explains. "Call me a
cab. As soon as it comes, call the police and her doctor and
wait for them to come. They'll know what to do. Then you
can leave and come home."

"But can't they tell that she's been dead a while?"

"Sure, but you will say you just came here and found
her this way," he says. "You have no idea when she died.
You spoke to her last night, and she invited you for dinner.
You came at the time you agreed on and found her."

"How did I get in?"

"Let them assume you have your own set of keys."

"There is a set of keys here in her jewelry box," I say.

"Good. Take them, have a set made for yourself
tomorrow, and then put this other set back in her purse. I'll
wait for you at your apartment. Will you be all right?"

"I think so. I guess I have to be."

"I'll go down and take all of our things to your house.
Call the cab."

While I wait for the police, I cannot take my eyes off
her. She lies distorted in her wrinkled clothing, like an old

canvas beach chair that no one can open. I decide to take her dress off her, because all those wrinkles might look suspicious to the police.

I sit immobile on the floor, not wanting to touch her, and try finally to touch only the garment, not her skin. But as I struggle to get her arm out of the sleeve, her fingers brush against me. They are stiff and cool, like wood. Do I have to do this? Perhaps I am not only concerned about what the police will think. Maybe it is a way for me to make her seem more comfortable. It is something I can do for her, assuage some of my guilt.

Finally I get the dress off. I throw it in her hamper. Now she is in her slip. Is she still angry with me? She spent most of her life being angry. Has she let go of it in death? The silence in the room seems to breathe in and out, as I look at this woman who had a hand in shaping my life. Why did she distort the truth so? Why was everything about my father so sacred to her, so secret from me? Daniel has put the glass eye in, closed her eye lids, yet I feel she is still watching me.

Now we are face to face, my Medusa and I. No more need to pretend. What do you think of me now? You know that I am an adulteress? People in our family don't do that. Or do they? Did you ever? But what about before my memory? Who might you have loved? "I loved him," you said. Did you mean my father? Let us assume so. You also implied that Bessie didn't love him. What else do you know of Bessie and the whole situation forty-odd years ago? "Bessie did it," you said. Did what? I don't care what you think of me anymore. I don't care if you see me cry. It is so hard to breathe in here.

Shall I open a window, spray air freshener? But it is not just the air that is heavy. You will be glad to know that now that I am alone and have a chance to think, I realize that I cannot leave Charles. You came to accuse me, and so I stand condemned. I will return to the bosom of the family, and perhaps then all the pain I am feeling will stop.

Now I remember your box of photographs. Several years ago I started to look through them on a rainy afternoon, but you came into the room and distracted me, making it clear that you didn't want me to look. I played into your

game and stopped as I was wont to do — always trying to
please you. What is it, Dora? What do you know? I'm going
to the chest where I know you keep them. Here is the old
Lord & Taylor box filled with photos on thick black paper,
brittle as autumn leaves. Just as I begin to leaf through
them, the buzzer sounds, making me jump. I cover the box
and put it near my purse. I will take it home with me.

"Good-bye Dora," I say out loud. "I'm so so sorry for
you. So sorry for me." And I grit my teeth to stop my eyes
from welling up. The police are here.

Soon the ordeal is over, and I am finally in my own
apartment, in Daniel's arms, all cried out. He is kissing me,
and I stop him.

"I have to tell you something," I say. "I don't think I
can go ahead with my plans now. I mean — I know what I
said about leaving Charles for good and everything, but now
— with all this — I —"

"Don't tell me you're superstitious," he says, stroking
my hair.

"It's not superstition, but — look at it this way: I go
away with you and look what happens. You have to admit, it
seems a bit of an omen to say the least —"

"Come on, Christina, you're not serious. What is it?
Do you think God is punishing you or something? It only
works that way in the medieval minds of very troubled
people."

"I can't help it. It's just that I am so terribly afraid.
I've never been alone in a crisis before and —"

"But you weren't alone. I was there, wasn't I?"

"I know, but —"

"But I'm not Charles, am I? Tell me, would he have
taken charge better than I did? Is it because he has more
money than I do? Goddamnit, Christina —"

"Now, you're the one being ridiculous."

His face falls, and he softens. "I know, but you make
me feel so safe. I'm so afraid of losing you. Tell me. Tell me
what it is. Make me understand why you have to do this.
Oh, God, Christina, don't leave — don't let this happen."

"There is something here that is so scary — I wish I
could tell you, but I don't really know myself what it is. I just
know I can't bear it. It's too much."

"You said you thought we were together before in another life."

"Oh, yes," I say, "for sure."

"Doesn't that count for something? I thought our coming together was so predestined — there has to be a way for us. I want us to grow and learn and love together."

I cannot look at him. "I can't," I say.

"This is your journey through the underworld — you're halfway there for God sakes. Don't turn around and go back!" Oh, please don't say this to me, I think to myself. I refuse to listen.

"It's actually a physical feeling," I say. "I had it in the hotel room when I told you I was going to leave him. Every time I think of being on my own, it happens. It's such a breathless thing, like I can't get enough air, and there are actual pains up and down my legs — I can't say any more — please —"

"And staying with Charles is better than an unknown terror, is that it?"

"Stop it!" I say.

"No really. Is what you describe worse than what you had at home with him? You told me what it was like. Do you really want to live with it again?"

"Maybe it's my karma. Maybe I wasn't meant to be happy."

"There are no Furies, Christina, only the ones we create and believe in."

"I don't know what the reasons are, okay? I'm telling you all these things — all these reasons why I think I can't leave him, and I'm not really sure myself what the real one is — what the one thing is that stops me. I only know I can't do it; and that's the long and the short of it. Life is a trade-off, and I guess this is it for me."

"You said you'd never felt a connection like ours with anyone else."

"That's right."

"Was it true?"

"Yes."

"Then how can you do this? Suppose I were to tell you that it's my karma to be with you?"

"I'm not ready to let you in."

"Perhaps my usefulness is over, and we will have a missed connection which is a thousand times worse than no connection, because the after-shock will always haunt us."

Now I am crying uncontrollably. His voice breaks.

"Good-bye Christina. I have to go." He reaches for the door.

"Wait. You have to know that I do love you — but I have to finish what I started — until I find out what it is I'm searching for. If only this had been another time —"

"I don't believe in 'if onlys.' I hope you can get it together. I'm giving you back to yourself. I'll be okay. Maybe we'll get another chance the next time around. Maybe one more lifetime will do it — maybe then we'll fix this missed connection." He closes the door.

I do not try to stop him again. I cannot stop any of this destiny as it rolls me back to my stuck place in the universe. Why can't I write my own story? Change the script to a happy one? Or have I already written this life of mine?

Seventeen

℘

"I can't get over it! Wherever did you get them?" Melissa squealed at my earrings. "They're fabulous! It's about time you started dressing your age. So many things you wear are so 'old-lady school-teachery'."

"Thanks," I tell her. She is wearing her new rose-colored suede jacket "for fall" that we just bought. We have shopped all morning in Bloomingdale's and are having lunch in their little restaurant.

"No really, I always tell you to dress the part of the vital woman that you are."

"It's wonderful to have my own fashion consultant."

"Come on, Mom!"

"Tell the truth — you don't think they may be just a touch too wild?" I say, fingering the little beads on my right earring. It is the first time I am wearing them since I had worn them in St. Croix.

"Absolutely not. They suit you better than anything. How come you didn't buy me a pair?"

"Next time I go," I say. I think I can hear the sea when I touch them. It's better than holding a sea shell up to your ear. Maybe I should buy a new outfit to go with them. Something that's not too "old-lady school-teachery." Something that won't make me think too much of Daniel.

"So who were you with down there?"

"I told you — just my friend Doris and her relatives."

"I saw Doris in the city day before yesterday," Melissa says. "Funny she didn't look tan."

"She hates the sun."

"Really."

"How're rehearsals going?" I ask.

"So, so."

"You don't seem that excited to have the part," I say. "It is the lead after all."

"Yes, but she's sort of droopy," she says.

"Well, wouldn't you be if you had to bury a brother who had already started to rot?" Oh, God — Dora!

"Mom, you're making it sound like farce. *Antigone* is serious stuff."

"Of course it is, and I'll be there in the front row, cheering you on —" I hope she didn't see me wince.

"Actually, you should be able to relate to it better than I anyway," Melissa says. "Her father is dead, like yours."

And your father isn't, I think to myself. But he might as well be, because he never was present for you. How I had always wished that my daughter would have a wonderful father! That Charles would have been the model father. The father I never had. How epidemic is fatherlessness?

"'Course, I suppose you can relate to it on a husband level too — poor Oedipus, having to marry Jocasta. What a dirty trick. How is Daddy these days?"

"My God, you have a way with words. He's trying," I tell her. "What more can I expect?"

"Trying what?" she says. "What makes you think he's going to be any different? Nothing has changed. Are you really expecting home sweet home? Oh, and that's a great word — 'trying'," she goes on. "Is he 'trying' to ridicule you any less, 'trying' not to make you feel like shit quite so often?"

"That is quite enough."

"Look, you moved out to write your book, and to try to work out some of your differences, you said." Let go, Melissa. Please let go. I cannot bear your truth. "You admit that nothing got resolved, yet you think things will be okay now. Sounds to me like you're living in a dream world."

"Do you think that it is absolutely necessary for you

to say these things to me?" I say. How did we get into this? What would she say if she knew about Daniel?

"Sorry."

"No, you're not."

"You're right, I'm not," she says. "I just can't stand to see you unhappy — to see him push you around and make you so afraid to open your mouth — to be yourself, for heaven's sake. I guess what I'm trying to say is that I love you too much. Enough is enough."

"Thank you," I say and cannot speak for a few minutes. Finally, I add, "I'm very touched by what you've said, and I really can't ask you to understand. You're just going to have to try to trust my decision. It will work, because I'll make it work. Look, I don't have all the answers, I just know that he appears to really be aware of our marriage — of keeping tension out of the house."

"How long have you been home? Give him time. He'll be screaming in no time," she says as she cuts her quiche into little squares. "Finding everything wrong with everything all over again — he can't help himself. He has to do it."

"That is no way to talk about your father," I say looking for the waitress, because my yogurt tastes sour.

"Even though it's true."

"Melissa, I've made a really tough decision here — really, really tough. Can't you help? What I've done — moving back — is the right thing for me now. I've settled in — I've gotten on with my writing. After Dora's death, it slowed down — it is so hard, you have no idea, and I have several more chapters to write — but it's over a month already, and Daddy seems to understand that finishing my book is really important to me. His attitude toward it is much better."

"Better than what? I hate this restaurant. It's so Yuppie." The waitress arrives, and I ask her to replace my yogurt.

"My book. I said my book is — why do you turn off every time I bring it up?"

"No big deal? I didn't say anything about it."

"I know. You never do."

"Well, I did ask you once if I could read it, and you said no."

"It's not ready for anyone to read." And I see Daniel's face in the house in St. Croix — saying yes over and over as he reads — approving, loving, and affirming both the manuscript and me. Where have you gone, my love? What have I done?

"Could it be that you won't let me read it, because you know I want you to write about something else?"

"What in the world — ?"

Tears well in her huge hazel eyes — poised and ready to fall, coating her in a feverish glow. "I need you to tell everybody about me," she says. "I mean what happened to me. You always had such a loud voice, Mom." She rubs her eyes and the tears run down, taking some of her plum eye shadow with them. "When the city decided to dump near our property, you wouldn't stand for it. You went to City Hall with the petition that you got hundreds of people to sign. And you won because of that voice. The newspaper heard you and printed the story. When you directed plays in school, I heard you at rehearsals. That voice again — coming out of the dark, from the back of the theater — that voice: instructing, commanding, informing — and everybody always listened. How come you never told anyone about me? What happened to your voice when Daddy beat me? Why did that have to be a secret?"

The silence closes like a trap. My mind races and tries to squash down the pain. Is that how I have hurt this child? I thought I was the parent who protected her. Why am I being blamed for something someone else did?

The waitress finally arrives and replaces my yogurt. It gives me a chance to breathe.

"I think it's time for me to go," she says, getting up.

"Don't . . . please."

"I don't know why you have to protect him." Her eyes blaze at me.

"I tried to do the best I could."

"I guess it's not enough for me. Or maybe it's just that I hate to see you waste so much energy on him."

"You'd like some of it for yourself?"

"Not anymore — well, maybe just a little." She sobs audibly and sinks back in her chair. "Yes. Yes, I'd like a lot of it for myself even though I'm grown up now. I guess I'd

like you to use some of it for yourself too. But there's
something else. Everyone I know — all my friends — everybody comes to me with all their problems. I sit and I listen to
them and take them on. But I have nowhere to go with mine.
Sometimes I wish I could be your little girl again. All those
times when it was just you and me — when he wasn't home."

I take her hand across the table. "I love you, Melissa,"
I say, "and I am so very very sorry."

She clutches my hand, and her crying subsides.
"Really. No. I'm the one who's sorry. I shouldn't have said
those things."

"Yes you should have."

"But they hurt."

"Yes, even so. I think the worst regret a person can
have is that they failed a child. I know I failed you. I was a
victim too, but nevertheless I failed you. And the worst part
is that I can never go back and do it over — I'll never have the
chance to make it right. Nothing else a mother does in life
means very much once that blight is on her record. Distrac-
tions can take away the sadness for a time. But the guilt
always comes back and brings the sadness with it."

"Oh, please. Please don't talk this way. I love you.
I'm sorry. Don't say these things." Melissa is trying hard not
to cry anymore.

"Oh, baby you're right. Please forget I said — any of
this. I'm fine really, and I hope I can help you to be fine too."

We are both quiet for a time. Melissa takes out her
lipstick and applies it. Then her hands fall into her lap. She
looks at me hard and says, "You deserve someone who
appreciates you, and someone who knows how to laugh. You
say Daddy's changed. Before, you used to say that whenever
you tried to write, he'd come into the room and ask you
something, even when you had a 'DO NOT DISTURB' sign on
the door. Are you going to tell me he doesn't do that anymore?"

"Not nearly as much."

"But the fact is — he does do it."

"That isn't the point."

"What is?"

"Well, the day I moved back, there were flowers
waiting for me. He took me out to dinner that night to

celebrate."

But he still hasn't made love to me, I think to myself. I guess I could ask him — but then —

"Does that do it for you? Does he ever show you — really show you that he loves you?"

"Now *I* think it's time to go."

"Okay, fine," she says, "but I have to say just one more thing. You need someone else, someone who — you know — showed some affection and could appreciate all your good qualities. Think about it."

When I get home, after dropping her off at the train station, I reach up to my right ear and realize that I have lost one of the earrings. I scream like a banshee, knowing there is no one there to hear.

Then later I walk through the house, looking at all the things I'd chosen and placed there, these china lamps, that bronze statue of a young girl; trying to make the place beautiful, trying to make it mine — trying desperately to feel like I belonged in it.

Did I write this book too? How did I get into this story? So it goes. I guess this has to do it for me, Melissa. Here I am. Home. Whatever that is. Whatever that means. "Home is the place where, when you have to go there, they have to take you in." Is that all there is to it? There's got to be more. Change the story.

I have looked everywhere for my lost earring. Perhaps I lost it because I think maybe I don't deserve it. Oh, Daniel, where are you?

The season changes. Fall always seems like a new year to me. Starting over. A good time. Right? The leaves are falling. I think of Shelley. I always teach him at this time of year. Falling leaves — or are they driven " . . . like ghosts from an enchanter fleeing,/ Yellow, and black, and pale, and hectic red,/ Pestilence-stricken multitudes . . . " I revel in the smell of autumn and the snap of smoky Hallow-een air. I love the rushing clouds. I push Daniel's face out of my mind — spare myself the pain of the loss of him as I write of my father. Yet it is Daniel's face I see when I try to visualize dear old Dad as he runs for a train, makes love to Juana, joins the army. I try to catch myself. Push him away. This is my father's book, not Daniel's. I will think only of my father. I have managed to let him grow up, get married for the first time and have a son — my brother, the boy I didn't know about until I was eighteen.

It is moving closer to the time of my birth — his death. How will I write this? What can I use for a reference? I think I am putting on weight. I don't jog anymore. I must get back to it.

The company Daniel works for has sent another man to do the school video at Daniel's request. It proceeds without incident, until one day in late October when the man walks in to my classroom with a package. "Somebody in the mailroom told me to give this to you. I don't know why they didn't mail it themselves."

I know why. "Who sent this?" I ask. I can't breathe. I see the thick brown envelope and my stomach does a little dance. There is no return address, yet I know it's from Daniel. It is typically him. "Who sent this?" Of course. Why would he mail something when he can have it hand delivered.

He shrugs. "They said it came from out of state with instructions to give it to you."

"Where did it come from?"

"I know as much as you do — that's all."

"Thank you," I say and walk all the way to my classroom before I open it. Why is he contacting me? Don't do this. I have succeeded in getting you out of my mind — a little — and I know I shouldn't even open this. Christina! Get hold of yourself. Don't look at it. Throw it away or at least save it until you're stronger — until you finish the book . . . I'm glad to be back home, do you hear? I am supposed to be married to Charles and not think of anyone else. Maybe we'll even start making love again. Who knows? Charles and I?

I get to the doorway and close the door behind me. I lean against the door. The empty desks laugh. The room echoes in hollow silence. My hands move without me and rip the manila flap, not even opening the little silver clasp. I want to holler — to not make a sound. There is only a piece of plastic inside — a plastic bag from the super market, white with some letters on it: "I love New York." And then the note falls out on my desk, and I see him utterly. "I hate not being in New York in the fall," he writes. "I was hoping I could ask you a favor. It's the leaves, you know. I remember the leaves being so beautiful last year, that it broke my heart to see them. But now that I can't see them at all, it's breaking my heart even more. Would you send me some? Just put a few in this bag, maybe, and send them to me? I'm in an airless air-conditioned office in Galveston, and if you send them, maybe it will help me to see your face again. Then perhaps I won't miss you quite so much."

I go home, but I don't know how I get here, because I have no memory of driving my car. I can only see Daniel's face. I take a huge empty box from the attic and rush to the backyard. Then I take the most beautifully colored leaves I can find and fill the box to overflowing. Yes, yellow and black and pale and hectic red. Maples and oaks, sycamores and elms. I love the leathery feel of them, the ashy smell. I fill up the box and send it — with no note. It is impossible to write even a word. He has turned a light on in me. I take a good look at the" pestilence-stricken multitudes" of my life.

Where is he?   Is Galveston near Marathon?   Oh, Daniel!

Perhaps the leaves will be enough. Perhaps when you get them, it will be all the connection you'll need.

Or ever will have.

Somehow, the days pass, and I am able to write, at the same time making a wrenching effort not to think of Daniel. Thanksgiving races into place. Charles goes to visit his mother. I am delighted at the prospect of not having to cook and of being alone. This will give me four days to write with no one to bother me. But as I am getting nearer the end of the story, I find myself distracted by the tiniest things. The plants need watering. I see that my ficus is outgrowing its pot and spend an hour repotting it. I don't want to think of the end of the story — to visualize my father dying. Soon I will come to that part of his tale. How can I let him die again? No. Each time I try to write it, I get the same feeling I had when I tried to think of leaving Charles for good. It is a desperation like nothing else. A tolling of utter and final nothingness. Beyond death.

Chapter 13

When his hitch was up, in 1931, Carter re-enlisted. He had earned the rank of Private First Class, and Wade had been transferred, making life much easier. He felt as though he could make a success of himself in the army. Besides, the Depression was worse than ever, and his success in the army seemed assured. But the best part was that he felt he had finally found the place where he really belonged. What would he do if he left? He could never risk being a hobo again. Maybe in three more years, when his second hitch was up, he would be able to find a job. Maybe something would happen to save the economy and there would be jobs again. Or maybe he would never leave the army. He might make corporal then, maybe sergeant; that sounded good to him.

In June of that year, he was sent to the stables to check on the grooming of the horses, right after breakfast. Two new recruits who had frequently been in trouble had been assigned the detail. He could hear the whinnying of the horses before he even got inside. The two men were fighting, throwing themselves and their gear about the stables and upsetting the horses. Carter hollered for them to stop, but they were caught in the fury of their own pounding and cursing. He grabbed a rifle and fired it. The sound stopped the men, but made the horses even more excited.

"Get out of here," he shouted. "Get out before you're done for." The horse that had been caught in the fray — Carter's own horse — whinnied and danced away from him, not knowing where to go. He tried to steady her as another mare who had gotten loose came and knocked into him broadside. "Whoooa, Babe," he said. "Easy girl." He mounted her quickly in an effort to gain control of both of them, but it was the wrong move. She would not be calmed and reared up, catching Carter off guard and throwing him backward. His head hit a support beam, and he fell to the floor. All he remembered was the back of the horse's head coming up at him, her black shiny mane swishing furiously.

He awoke in the infirmary to find out that he had had a kind of seizure after his head hit the ground. It was later diagnosed as epilepsy.

He was exhausted and sore. The doctor explained what had happened. He said he had to stay there to make sure he was not going to have another seizure. He had another the next day. This time he felt it coming. First he felt lots of energy flow into him. It was clear and pleasing, and there was a harmony all around him. But then his thoughts were interrupted, and he was in a dreamy state; he flew back through other years. He could see his mind leave — fly off, and he could not catch it. Then the light was so intense, it nauseated him. It swirled down in a kind of gyro, and he fell into it. He awoke this time with the doctor and nurse holding on to him. The whole thing only lasted about three minutes, but to him it felt much longer.

The doctor gave him medication, and told him that his condition was not serious, but that he should be extremely careful not to fall or bump his head.

However, about two weeks later, the army hit him with the big news.

He was told to report to his immediate superior officer, who was all business, even though Carter had played cards with him only the night before.

"I have your papers here, Shields."

"What papers?" The officer would not look at him.

"Discharge papers. You heard about this didn't you?"

"No, sir."

"You know you can't stay in the army with epilepsy." He might as well have slapped him in the face. He stood stunned. "Sign here."

"Uh, could we talk this over, sir?" he said.

"These are not my orders. There's nothing to say. Army regulations. You really didn't know?"

"No, sir. Sir, if you don't mind me saying this, I — this place is like home to me now."

"Well, you have to sign," he said. "It's an honorable discharge. Nothing to be ashamed of."

"I'm not ashamed, but I — then what do I do?"

"You clear out." He finally looked at him and then his face softened. "I don't know what else to say."

"You can't do this to me. You just can't."

"You have to clear out. Sorry," said the officer.

He passed the stables on his way back to the barracks. He heard a loud whinny. The horse he had wanted all his life! Had she

done this to him on purpose? Then he saw his
father's face, heard his words. "Be careful
what you wish for; you might get it."

It was November 1932, and he was on his
way home. He felt even more disoriented to
see how many new buildings had gone up in
Petersburg since he had left. The town felt
alien, but what was worse — he felt alien to
himself. Here he was, involuntarily thrown
into a new phase of life. Again. Lord, he was
tired of it.

He decided to wear his uniform home. Why
not? It was his armor, and it was what he
had become, even though the army didn't want
him anymore. It would protect him from the
past that he was returning to. He had told no
one of his homecoming.

He threw his bags into a cab at the
station, and then got in himself.

"Where ya comin' from, soldier?" said
the cabby. He had no teeth.

"Texas," he said. "Do you know where the
Shields' farm is from here?"

"Henry Shields?"

"No, Barret Shields. It's three miles
past Henry's — on the same road." Of course,
he knew. Why, he didn't really know Barret,
but knew Henry, and wasn't it interesting the
way you could know some parts of a family and
not others . . . there were so many Shields
around these parts . . . He droned on and on.
Carter tuned him out. He was hyperventilating
— overwhelmed with a twisted image of his
home. He could not straighten it out. Perhaps
it had changed so much during the years he
was gone, that it would be all right now.
Maybe they could make amends. Be at peace.

The cab rounded the bend that led to the

farm, when he saw one of his mother's old geranium pots smashed in the road. The flowers were still alive. He told the cabby to stop. Mama would have hung them upside down in her root cellar by now. What a strange thing to remember. Why was it here, smashed on the road? A young girl appeared from nowhere sprinting down the road, running toward Carter like a track star. She looked about ten or eleven years old. Her legs were long like a young stallion's. Her feet dug the ground. As she came nearer, he saw that she was crying, screaming near hysteria, and he looked past her to see if someone were chasing her. No one appeared. By now she had caught up to the cab. Her hair thumped down her back in a heavy braid. There was a grace — almost a frailty about her that he found beautiful and touching. She never looked at him or the cab.

"Stop," he said, and got out, so fast he scared her. She ran past him.

"No," she said over and over. "Don't do it. Don't do it, Papa. Noooo!" And then he knew. He barreled after her.

"Greta!" She turned her head in terror and ran faster. "Greta, wait! It's Carter." She stopped, and her eyes were enormous. Her chest heaved up and down. He squatted down in front of her and held out his hand. She stood for several seconds looking at him, as if he had returned from the dead.

"It's me, baby. Who is hurting you?" She took his hand and then fell onto him. Her crying began all over again. He carried her to the cab.

He told her not to speak, to try to calm herself. He held her for a long time. She kept saying, "Oh, Carty, Oh, Carty," the way she used to. Finally, she quieted.

"They're going to send me away," she said. "They want me to live in the Thompson house and clean and cook and stuff, and take care of their creepy daughter and not be with Papa. Papa is the whole thing — to me, I mean. I even farm with him when Bessie lets me. Andy and Rob help me with my chores a lot when she's not around. I hate her; she's so bad to me. Look what she did — smashed Mama's geranium pots to punish me. She did it here so Papa wouldn't see. And if I tell him, she'll say I did it. Don't make me go back there. I'm going to run away like you did. Now I have to."

"No, baby, you can't run away. But . . ." She began to cry all over again. "No, no, no listen to me. Shhh. First let me talk to Papa," Carter said. "Let me see what's what. Don't worry, I won't let her touch you."

"She broke Mama's flowers just to make me cry."

He told the cab to go. What had happened to this family? It was like an erosion. All the bonds slowly worn away until all he could hear was the moan deep in his heart.

Bessie stood on the front porch. "Well, I declare, look at the likes of you," she said. "A growed-up soldier boy."

"Where's my father?" Carter said, putting a foot up on the steps and leaning his elbow on the handrail. He looked at her directly.

"He's out on his tractor. Aren't you just a little bit glad to see me?" she said, pushing her hair behind her ears.

"Well sure, I am. But can you answer my

question?"

Bessie huffed and took off her apron, showing her great shelf of bosom. "Where else would he be? Bet you think you look rich as a bitch in them clothes!" She sashayed down to him, touching the fabric on the side of his breeches.

"Let's get something straight right now, Bessie. Maybe you think you can talk mean to everybody around here. Well, you're not going to do it to me."

"Now, Carter, when you talk like that to me, I liked to die — don't you know it? I'm being as nice as I can — under these trying circumstances. And you're not being very sensitive to my loss, I have to say." She puckered her bottom lip and lowered her eyes. Why do I have to play her way? Carter thought. How does she manage to get me all confused — still, like she used to?

Okay, he decided to play. "Bessie, you old . . . ah . . . sugar plum . . ." He gritted his teeth, "how about telling me when my father will be back?"

"You mean you're not even going to ask me about it — my loss? You did hear me say, 'my loss,' now didn't you?"

Carter smiled. He tried to look friendly. "Certainly wish you'd tell me right now," he gave a little bow, "— all about it — Miss Bessie."

She moved her lips up and down until they quivered. She was able to accomplish this by beating her teeth together several times. "Oh — I tell you — I am nothing now but an orphan. My mama passed two years ago and now it's my daddy. He's passed on too — just last winter — and that means I have to decide what to do with all their things and all. It is such a horror — such a horror — I tell you!"

"What do you mean — 'all their things'?"

"Why, their farm and things — all those things." She scratched her left arm with her right hand, then ran it over her breasts.

"You've inherited everything? Is that what you're trying to say?"

"Well, yes I have, and it is such a horror — to know what to do with everything, and all?" Now her tongue came out and wet her top lip.

"Somehow, I'm sure you'll be able to figure it out," Carter said.

"Well, it is all so confusing to me, you know — with my dearest daddy gone and all."

"Your dearest daddy beat the shit out of you when you were under his roof, so forget it. Why not sell everything and be rich. I remember how you hated your father. Cut the baloney!"

"Now that is a dreadful thing to say to me — a dreadful thing. I declare, you are a hateful boy, Carter Shields!"

"Bessie, how about just telling me when my father will be in from the fields?"

Her hand went back to her breasts. "How should I know?" He grabbed her wrist and held it fast, up and out, so she couldn't touch herself.

"When?" he said.

"I don't know," she smiled and talked as low as she could. "Still a hateful boy by many standards, I do declare."

"He won't be back till dinner," said Greta from the doorway.

"Well, then, let's walk out and find him," he said, turning to Greta.

"She can't go. She hasn't done her chores."

"Bessie, it's almost six years since

I've been home. Her chores can wait. She's coming with me." And he and Greta walked out of the house toward the south field.

"Oh, Carty," Greta said and gripped his hand.

"Hope you enjoy all those 'things' from dearest daddy, Bessie, old girl," he said over his shoulder as they walked down the dirt road arm in arm.

His father's tractor was stopped and unmanned in the middle of the south field. Carter didn't see him right away, because Barret was bending over the tobacco plants.

"There he is," said Greta. She pointed to a dot of a man half a mile away. Her voice had a heaviness to it, no matter what she said. All her sparkle was gone. They walked a little faster. He smiled at her, but she just looked up at him wondering why he was smiling. He saw the little skipping girl of earlier years, kicking her feet in Mill Pond, making the water rise in frantic splashes as high as she could. "I'm making rainbows Carty," she used to say. "Look at my rainbows!" He remembered the wild flyaway ringlets poking over her head. What had become of her? How did they break her spirit? Now her hair was severely tied to her head, confined into a tight braid. Was Bessie afraid she'd be too pretty if her hair were loose? The rainbows faded one by one into the mist of his memory.

"You're beautiful. Do you know that, Greta?" Carter said. She jumped up into his arms, the way she used to whenever he wanted to pick her up.

"I love you, Carty. You're still my boyfriend."

"Are you kidding?" he said. "In a few years, you're going to have so many boyfriends, you won't be able to count them all." She jumped down. Her face clouded, and she looked away from him.

"Don't keep foolin' me — the way they do."

"This isn't foolin'," Carter said. "One thing you can be sure of. I'm the one you can trust, no matter what. Remember that."

"Are you sure?"

"Positive."

"Oh, I just love you, Carty. Papa still doesn't see us. Look there's Andy and Rob." It was amazing to see them. Two grown up boys. They were working about another eighth mile below their father. Even at that distance, he could see the seriousness of Rob's posture in the field. Rob, just as he used to be, completely rapt in the business of the soil, standing and staring at the ground and then squatting to attend to something. He still loved the farm. Bessie had not been able to kill that in him. Carter guessed that when Rob turned the dirt in his hand, he did so as if he were fondling a woman.

They kept walking. "He's going to love that you're here, Carty. Once I even heard him crying about you. It was after Henry brought him a letter you wrote. He was in the barn. It was after Henry left. I guess he forgot I was still in the hay loft. Uuup! Now he sees us. Look! But I bet he don't know it's you."

They began to run toward him. He had taken some bales out of the back of the tractor for mulch, and he was turning back again when they caught his eye. He stood for a moment, hand on hip like he always did, and then his posture changed as recognition came.

His arm went slack. He dropped his pick, took a step, waited a bit, and then he was running too.

"It's me, Papa!" Carter yelled and threw his head back and laughed.

"It's him. Carty is back," squealed Greta, sounding like herself for a minute.

The three of them hugged, and Papa cried. There they stood in the middle of a tobacco field, feeling like they belonged to each other, and loving how that felt. Soon Andy and Rob were there too. It was like pieces fitting into a puzzle. They asked Carter a thousand questions, never seeming to be satisfied with the answers, because they wanted to know more and more. They all admired his uniform, especially his corporal stripes, the badge for expert rifleman, and the patch for bugling.

"No more work today. We're celebrating," said Papa. "Let's go back to the house and ask Bessie to cook early. And I have some homemade wine."

The memories took hold of him as they entered the house, and he saw old familiar things again. The parlor made a stab in his stomach, as he saw his mother lying there dead, but it lasted only a second. Then Lance came out of the clock, and Carter smiled to see him. He thought of the hours he'd spent in that room when no one was around, going on all sorts of adventures with Lance, slaying dragon after dragon.

There was no way he could persuade Papa to keep Greta at home instead of hiring her out as a domestic. He thought it was Bessie's idea, but then found out it was Papa's.

"But how can you do such a thing to

her?" Carter said.

"It's not how you think," said Barret. "Bessie and her don't get on together, you know. These people are good ones. Our Reverend knows them. They're fine people; got a sickly daughter. Only want Greta for some cleaning and as a companion and tutor for the daughter. It'd be much better for her than to stay here with Bessie."

"But she'll be away from you too, Pa," Carter said. "She is really hurting. She thinks you don't want her here."

"Talk to her," said Barret. "Tell her it will be better for her. Tell her how much I don't want her to hurt no more. Maybe when you say it, she'll believe it."

Carter kept Greta close to him, and told her when he thought the time was right. And for the remainder of his visit, he made it absolutely clear to Bessie that while he was there, it was to be Greta's vacation. Bessie said very little to him after that. Most of the time, she ignored him.

On Sunday, he put his uniform on to wear to the service at Lunt's Church. He hoped it would protect him from the memories that might be lurking in the mustiness of the dark corners. But first he went to the graveyard. He needed to find out if the same thing that happened to him that day when he went there with Rob would happen again.

The tower-shaped tombstone rose above the others, bleak and cold. A chickadee sat on it and then scolded him as she flew away. There was the inscription: Emma Rose Ruden Shields, Wife of Barret Shields, Born April 9, 1895. Died May 25, 1925. And there was Papa's poem engraved on the front:

IN LOVE SHE LIVED
IN PEACE SHE DIED
HER LIFE WAS CRAVED
BUT GOD DENIED.

That's how Barret had seen it. He was too grief stricken at the time to be angry.

How could you have done that to us, God? Carter thought. Where is your heart? You could have left her alone long enough so she could get to know me — you could have at least done that?

But this time he saw no visions of his own grave. Perhaps he was too angry with God to allow them in.

He left the graveyard which was to the left of the church and headed for the service only after all the congregation had gone inside.

His mother's casket flashed in his mind for a moment as he entered the church, but he was soon distracted by the attention he got from old friends and relatives. "It's Carter," he heard people whisper as they came in. Bessie was the first one in the pew. She had on a ridiculous straw hat, bigger than her head so you could see air between the sides of her head and the crown. What an embarrassment! She scratched all through the service. Carter sat on the aisle. He recognized most of the congregation. Many there were old-timers, but then he turned to see some new people gathering in the rear of the church. A man and woman, somewhere in their fifties, came down the aisle, helping a teenaged girl who walked on crutches.

"That's her — the girl Papa wants me to stay with," whispered Greta who sat next to him. "It's Louise, is her name." She became anxious and held his hand. The family stopped and entered the pew directly across from them. Behind the three of them was a young man about twenty escorting a beautiful wisp of a girl.

"It's Hanna. Don't look at her, Carty," said Greta. "I don't want you to think she's pretty. It's Louise's big sister. I don't want you to like her."

"I'll never like her as much as I love you," he said.

Hanna! She was tall and thin, and looked like a picture he saw of a twenties' flapper in a magazine. Her skirt was shockingly short, and the fabric was so thin, you could see the shape of her legs through it as she walked. Greta knew what she was talking about. The skirt rippled over her and made him want to touch her all over right then and there. She smiled at him. Her hair was short and wisped around her face, and she had high cheek bones. The hollows in her face seduced him even more; he wanted to kiss them. Her gray eyes were wide and cat-pointed. They shone with something electric.

The two came closer down the aisle; she stopped when she saw him, smiled again and got into the pew after her parents. But the young man with her got in after her, so Carter couldn't see her directly. It was probably just as well. The Reverend might have thrown them out for indecently looking at each other. A few times he caught her eye, visible for a second before and after the shifting body of the young man who did not seem to be aware of her at all.

"Who's he?" Carter asked Greta.

"It's her brother," she said. Wonderful news! Carter thought he might have been her boyfriend. He and Hanna kept on looking. Then her brother got up and went out for a minute.

While he was gone, she appeared to be furiously writing something in the back of the prayer book. No one else seemed to notice. Her body shook as she wrote, faster and faster. She made one final gesture with her pencil and closed the book. Her brother came back. When the service was over, she came out of her pew, crossed the aisle to where Carter held his breath and only looked up at him the last second — when she was close to him. She smiled, handed him the book and left without a word. Only Greta saw it. He put it under his arm as if this were a matter of routine. He didn't want anyone to question him. Least of all, Bessie. Later he took it out. It was a sketch of him, and the contour of his uniform, exaggerated on the page, made his biceps look bigger than they were. He could not control his grinning and wondered if anyone saw or figured out what had happened. Down at the bottom of the drawing was her name: Hanna Thompson. What class!

The Thompsons lived in Silver Hills, the wealthy part of Petersburg, northwest of the railroad in a place Carter had never seen. He had heard that her father was "in publishing," and had no idea what that meant; but from the look of their house, publishing must have been good. That afternoon, Barret had to go to their home to discuss arrangements for Greta. Carter went with him. The house was a huge Victorian with a high porch that wrapped all around it. Inside, the ceilings were high and lofty, but every square inch was decorated with ornate and expensive clutter. The furnishings were plush and overstuffed, and the walls were covered with paintings and drawings in the style of the sketch Hanna had drawn of him.

They talked with her father over tea, and then Hanna came into the room. Carter had no air. She walked directly to Barret. "Mr. Shields, how grand to see you again," she said, her back straight, yet supple.

"This is my son, Carter," Barret said. He looked proud.

Her posture softened as she shifted her gaze to Carter. She wet her lips. "I do believe we met in church, in a manner of speakin'." She held out her hand to Carter. When he took it, he realized from the way she held hers, that he was supposed to kiss it. He did so with a louder smack than he intended.

"Well, Mr. Carter, how impulsive you are." Her tongue rolled over her top lip. Was there a slight derision in her voice? He guessed he wasn't supposed to make a noise when he kissed. Shit.

"I was admiring" — just then his voice cracked, and he thought he'd die — "the pictures in this room, Miss Hanna."

"Well isn't that grand of you. You must have guessed that they are mine, now did you? Do you like the landscapes or the portraits? I'm best at doin' people, don't you think?" The gray eyes lowered.

Her father cut in, "We are very proud of Hanna's art. We are thinking of sending her to art school in Richmond."

"My daddy thinks I'm too young to go to Washington to live by myself, so that does leave Richmond, now doesn't it? Have you been to Washington, Mr. Carter?"

"I'm . . . the fact is, I'm . . . I was thinking of going there to look for a job soon."

"How clever of you. You know my daddy

knows lots of people there. He could probably put in lots of good words for you." A white fluff of Persian kitten bounced into the room. Hanna squealed. "Oooooo, there you are, such a little precious!" She scooped him up and kissed his face. Carter wondered if anyone saw the bulge in his pants. His father was making his good-byes. He had to move fast.

"Miss Hanna, do you think I might visit you again?" he said.

"Why whatever for? Of course, I can see that we have a lot in common, because of the way you like artistic things. But I am prom- ised, you know — to a man of very high stand- ing!" Her tongue came out again. "Maybe you can sit for me sometime. I love to do hand- some men." She licked the point of the kitten's ear. Thank God his pants were tight. He wished he could die.

His world was now further divided be- tween those with money and those without. Hanna had made it all too clear that he was not a "man of very high standing." He would show her. He would make his fortune in Wash- ington and come back standing high! Or so he told himself, but deep down he doubted he'd ever have her.

He knew he had to get a job fast. He had saved five hundred dollars from his army pay. He could live on that for quite a while, but he didn't want to spend it. At the same time, he guessed there wasn't much call for a bugler, horse groomer, or catcher of rum runners in Washington.

*   *   *

Saying good-bye to Greta was tough. He had tried to convince her that staying with the Thompsons was the best thing for her, but she was extremely distrustful of Mrs. Thompson.

"What if she hits me like Bessie? Where will I go?"

"I'm sure she won't. Look everyone's not like Bessie."

"Lots of mothers like to hit."

"Our mother didn't," Carter said.

"Are you crazy? She hit you all the time. Don't you remember?"

"It was only once in a while when I needed it."

"Why are you fooling with me?" she said. "I don't think anyone needs it. What good does hitting do? It only makes you cry and get oh, so lonely." She was like a tender flower.

"Greta, trust me. You will like it at the Thompsons," Carter said. "I bet you, you'll have less to do there than here. And you'll like their little girl too. I met her, and she can't wait for you to come."

"Are you sure Papa doesn't want to get rid of me? That's what Bessie said." A yellow tiger lily, bursting with intense color, but oh, so fragile.

"No, she said it because she's only out for trouble. She doesn't want any of us."

"Oh, yes she does. She wants you, Carter. I can tell."

"Don't you ever say that, do you hear?"

"Okay," she said. "But someday I'm going to spoil all my children, because I want plenty of people around me — laughing all the time. We're just going to love each other, Carty. That's all anybody has to do." He hugged her. She was so beautiful.

"Papa is going to come to see you every Sunday," he said.

"When he comes to see me, I want him to take me out somewhere."

"If he agrees to that, will you go and stay there?"

"He said I have to," said Greta.

"But if we make him promise to spend every Sunday afternoon with you — just you, won't that make it better?"

"I think I love you best, Carty, next to Papa." They hugged again. She said she would write to him in Washington, so he would know everything that was going on with her. And although he promised to answer her letters, he seldom did.

Chapter 14

He had the names of several Washington contacts in his wallet. He also had the name of a rooming house. He found it soon after getting off the train. The street lights came on, yellow balls of light shimmering in the puddles on the concrete. The tiny house was wedged between a garage and a row of stores. It was dirty and tired looking. He rang the bell. You could smell garlic even before the door was opened. Everything about the house was in shades of dingy gray-green. Two men dressed in homburgs and spats came out of the front door. They looked too fancy for that moldy place. He wished he could dress the way they did.

"Think it over, old woman," one said over his shoulder. She stood there — a dwarf of a woman — the most repulsive person Carter

had ever seen. "We'll be back," said the man.
They faded into the yellow glow. She looked
at Carter. She knew what he was there for.

"Three dollars, two meals, two meals for
you, no pets," she said. "Three dollars every
Friday, every Friday, three dollars."   She
laughed and shook her stooped, squat body.
"Sssst, sssst, sssst."   It was more like a
rasp than a laugh; her skin was gray; her
clothes a dingy green. She had a pointy chin,
and there was a red mark where her nose
should have been; it looked like someone had
pushed it into her face.

"I guess I'll take the room," Carter
said. He did not know where else to go.

She held the key in front of him. When
he started to take it, she whisked her hand
back. She hacked out her laugh again, shaking
her whole body. "Sssst, sssst, sssst. Three
dollars for me. Three dollars for me. Sssst."
He gave it to her, being careful to drop it
into her hand, so as not to touch her skin.
How much did that leave in his shoe?   She
showed her crooked green teeth and that made
her drool. He went to the room with a throb-
bing pain in his head.

The light from the hallway spilled into
his room. It was all squalid paleness with a
lumpy looking bed. A cracked linoleum floor
had huge horrible pink flowers grinning up at
him through lots of dirt. There was an old
bureau with a lamp on it, a colorless arm
chair, a streaked mirror, and a hook on the
wall with two hangers on it. The lamp had a
singed orange paper shade. And when he
switched it on, roaches scurried every which
way and disappeared into the cracks. The
light sent an orange gloom into the room like
the glow of a witch's candle.

He stood for a long time, not knowing

why he couldn't move. He told himself to put his things away, but it was a great effort. His arms were sluggish as he put his bags on the bed. The air was dingy as lead. His clothes weighed him down. He took off his jacket and arranged his things in the bureau as best he could, but it took forever. Razor, soap, talc, after shave, shirts, underwear, his grandfather's watch, his mother's brooch. He stood his books in a line on top of the bureau and threaded his uniform on the hanger, fastening all the buttons and hanging it on the hook. He pressed out his tie. He moved like a shadow, knowing that after he finished setting up the room, there would be nothing else left to do.

He lit a cigarette and lay in the dark. Is this what it means to make your way in the world? He didn't think he was strong enough. If only he could have stayed in the army. Nothing had prepared him for this. He only let himself cry because it was pitch dark, and he made no sound. He had learned how to do that in the army. He knew he couldn't possibly be homesick for the farm, so he guessed it was a longing for what might have been.

The next day wasn't much better. It was cold and gray with a damp air that stung. He went job hunting in his uniform. He thought it might help. How else could anyone get a job in 1931?

It didn't help. Most of the people he went to wouldn't even see him. Those who did all said the same thing. Nothing now. At the end of a week, he had run through all his leads. He washed dishes for two weeks. The restaurant gave him a free meal, and that meant he didn't have to eat Mrs. Gargoyle Greenface's disgusting food. But how was he

ever going to make something of himself, so
he could show Hanna what a man he was?
Someday he had to give her his mother's
brooch. Was it ever going to happen?

When he came home the next day, the two
men he had seen when he first arrived there
stood on the front steps arguing with the
green landlady. He could not hear what they
were saying, and they stopped when they saw
him. Jesus, he liked their clothes.

"Good evening," he said and went to his
room.

Every night when he came home, the ugly
landlady would meet him at the front door.
She smelled like mold. He hated to see her
face, but he knew it would always be there.
And then she would infuriate him by making
him play her stupid slow guessing game.

"Mail for you? Mail for you? Sssst,
sssst, sssst." The scratch of her voice made
him want to kill her. At first he was polite.
He smiled and looked puzzled. "Ask me, ask
me," she rasped.

"Okay," he said. "Did I get any mail?"

"Maybe." She crinkled something in her
pocket. "Rustle, rustle, rustle, rustle goes
the mail. Sssst." She shook her shoulders.

"Can I have it?"

"It smells pretty. Like perfume."

"Please!" he yelled. Could Hanna have
written to him?

"Take it, take it." She pulled it out
as fast as a magician. He took it and bolted
for his room. "Sssst, sssst." Her game was
over until the next time he came home.

In the safety of his squalid room, he
opened it only to find disappointment once
more. Bessie! She had written to say that
nothing was new, except for her gall bladder
attacks, but she just thought she'd let him

know how much "everyone" missed him. What in the world is she up to, thought Carter. And why did she perfume the letter? He burned it in his ashtray. Good.

One night in January as he approached the rooming house he was overcome with nausea at the thought of facing the disgusting woman. He knew he had to find somewhere else to live. But it was a frightening thing to think about. Finding a place. A place to belong. Maybe he was afraid he would never belong anywhere.

She stood slightly behind the door. He shouted at her in her own words before she had a chance to say anything. "Mail for you! Mail for you! Let's have it, old woman. Give it to me now, before I kill you." He thought she was going to cry. Her mouth jerked wide. He spoiled her game; she seemed lost. He held out his hand. She gave him the letter. He ran.

"No perfume," she called after him. Damn her! He imagined her standing behind him spilling sawdust out of her mouth. He was sure it lay scattered about on the floor all around her.

The letter was from his father, and it disturbed him to see how shaky his handwriting had become. Was he sick? He called home right away only to be told by Rob that yes indeed, Barret was not feeling well. No one thing, mind you — just a general malaise. Inside the letter, Barret had enclosed another one — one that had been sent to the farm from Paul, Carter's army buddy. Carter was thrilled to hear from him and even more thrilled to learn that Paul was on his way to also make his "fortune" in Washington.

He moved into Carter's rooming house and, like Carter, soon made a dollar a day washing dishes. They each earned six dollars a week, twenty-four a month, almost half of which went for rent. Every day before he went to the restaurant, Carter tried a different place for a better job. The answer was still the same. Nothing now.

"It's humiliating," Carter told Paul on the way home one night.

"Listen," said Paul. "Times are tough. We're lucky to have the jobs we got."

"You call this lucky? I don't. How can you feel like you're somebody washing dishes?"

"Hey don't get your dander up with me. Lots of people have no jobs," he said.

"Yeah, and they jump out of windows. Something has to break for me. I wish I could have stayed in the army."

He dressed in his only good suit, because Paul and he had found some girls to go out with that night. It was double-breasted, navy blue with pin stripes. As they turned the corner of his old musty street, he recognized the man with the homburg walking a few feet ahead of him. He was one of the men whom he had seen arguing with the landlady. He was short and square with a toupee that looked like black patent leather. He stopped to light a cigarette, and Carter caught up to him.

"Hello there," Carter said. "Could it be we're coming from the same place?" They walked together; Paul dropped behind.

"Zat so?" the man asked, not looking at Carter. "You live there?"

"Yes. But I am hating that hellhole more

and more."

"What are you in?" the man asked, glancing over his shoulder at Paul.

"Uh, fine china," Carter said. "But I'm interested in moving up." He was glad he was dressed up.

"You know what?" said the man. "I like your style. Name's Kincaid."

"A man has to be a man," Carter said. "I'm Carter Shields."

"Too bad you can't make some real money."

"I could if I had a few good connections," said Carter. "Do you know anybody that I should see?"

"I might," said the man. "I could probably set something up. As a matter of fact, my operation could use somebody like you."

"I'm all ears."

"Sometimes it gets rough though."

"If you can't stand the heat, you shouldn't be baking muffins," Carter said, lighting a cigarette.

"You know," said Kincaid, "you have a good attitude, but how do I know I can trust you?"

"Listen, I was four years patrolling the Mexican border on horseback when most people my age were still in knee pants. I did okay. I saved a bunch of money in the army. I'm good with it. I play it close to the vest. If you can't trust me, it's your loss."

"Well, Carter, do you like boots — or shoes with your liquor?" So that's how come they were dressed like dandies. Carter whistled and stared at him for a second.

"Boots it is!" he said.

"Think you could do with something not quite legal?"

"It might be just what I'm looking for."

Bootleggers! "If it's whiskey, count me in."
He was terrified. Stealing from Mexican
rumrunners was one thing. This was big time.

     Kincaid and his cronies had talked the
old landlady into keeping a portable copper
still going in her basement. For ten dollars
a day, old gargoyle face had to keep it
stoked and strain off the distillate. Actually, these guys had hundreds of small tene-
ment stills all over Washington, an impres-
sive network of chugging alcohol cookers
instead of one big plant, which could be
closed down in one police raid. These were
much harder for the cops to keep track of.
Once a week, big vats of the stuff had to be
collected and hauled to a warehouse where it
was cut, bottled, and then sold as whiskey to
speakeasies or to anyone who wanted it.
     Carter thought the number of people who
drank was quite remarkable in view of the
fact that the sale of liquor was illegal. It
was quite universal. Everybody had drink
fever. People called it by a hundred names:
tarantula juice, rotgut, coffin varnish,
hooch, strike-me-dead, and on and on. He
loved the excitement of it all.
     Carter's role in all this became that of
a delivery man. He drove an "ice" truck from
one still to another, dropping off supplies
and picking up the product. The ice was his
cover. He dressed in faded khaki pants, old
shirt, and peaked cap as he hauled the vats
onto his truck. But he made fifteen dollars a
day, so he had plenty to spend on fancy duds
to wear at night. And he bought them all: the
spats, shirts with detachable collars, three-
piece suits, a homburg, sleeve garters, a new
watch chain, gold cuff links with blue stones

in them, and several pairs of shiny shoes. It sure beat washing dishes.

In her next letter, Bessie wanted to know when he would be arriving for Christmas. He felt a rush of nostalgia as he realized how long it had been since he had a real Christmas in a real house. He suddenly became a child again. Oh, he wanted it to be perfect. He took the next Saturday off and spent the whole day shopping — perfume for Bessie, a bunny-fur jacket for Greta, a lighter for Papa, books for his brothers. He tipped the salesgirl to wrap them for him in the fanciest shiny red paper and lace ribbon the store sold. He could not wait to go home. In the fairy tale daze of shopping for Christmas, a thought had worked its way into his brain. He suddenly realized that he had made a decision. He would ask Hanna to marry him, "promised" or not. He was now up to twenty dollars a day. What did he have to lose?

The next day, there was a telegram waiting for him when he got home. The old Greenface ran halfway down the street to meet him, waving it in her hand. I've got her well-trained, he thought. No more of her stupid games.

But when he opened it, he kind of wished she hadn't given it to him. It was from Bessie.

Barret was dead.

Chapter 15

If he were to take all the Christmases of his life and add them up, they wouldn't amount to much. And now this one was going to be a non-Christmas. Carter returned home to the gloom of death knowing that his father's passing would have been far less painful had it occurred at some other time of year. He didn't even bother to take the presents out of his car. Everyone's preparations stood still. Still he found himself holding up the expectations of the season against all the memories that he collected and stored all his life of what Christmas should be. When would there be a good one? Imagine having a wake on Christmas Eve instead of a celebration. The funeral was to be December twenty-sixth. This was hardly the time to propose to Hanna. Would she come to the funeral? He doubted it.

Rob came in from the barn, and Greta opened the front door, just as Carter walked up the wooden steps to the porch. She said nothing — just cried and cried in his arms. Bessie sat in the rocker in the parlor. She did not greet him. The casket was against the far wall, exactly where his mother's had been. At the window was a half-trimmed Christmas tree. "He died while we were trimming it," she said. "I didn't know what else to do with it, so I just left it there."

"It's okay, Bessie," Carter said.

Later the mourners came into the house — again in a line — many of the faces the same that had come to his mother's funeral. They came to see his father, his wonderful father lying stiff and silent in his coffin, his hands folded on his gray pin-striped suit, his hair slicked over a waxy forehead. And they talked about a dead man who had once been so alive for Carter: his hero, his larger-than-life father who had loved and protected him from — he thought of finishing his thought with the word "mother" but pushed it out of his mind.

He was annoyed that they were having the wake in the house. People don't do that anymore, he thought, and his father deserved the dignity of a funeral parlor. He had assumed that Bessie would have taken care of it. He remembered his shock when he had spoken to Rob on the phone.

"What do you mean you couldn't stop her?" Carter said. "It's ridiculous. People don't have wakes at home anymore."

Rob sounded tired. He didn't feel like arguing with Carter, or like defending something that was someone else's decision. He and Andy had fought with Bessie over the site of their father's wake, and she had won. "She does what she damn well pleases and ain't no one could tell that bitch what to do, ever, — especially now that she got so much money," he said. "Hell, it'll all be over in two days. Don't bust a gut over it — she ain't worth it." Yet Rob had cried when he saw Carter drive in from the main road. "He left her the farm," he said. "Can you imagine? How could he do that to me? Wonder who she thinks is gonna work it, 'cause it ain't gonna be me."

Now Carter sat with Greta at his father's feet. He stared at the half-trimmed tree. Most of the time Greta looked at Papa; the rest of the time she cried in big sobbing gasps. Bessie, on the other hand, was unusually controlled. She greeted her sympathizers with dignity, thanking them for coming, and glancing at Carter every once in a while. He knew that there was never any love lost between her and his father, but he still thought for sure that she would act the part of the howling, bereaved widow, ready to throw herself headlong on the body at any moment. It was not the case. He looked back at the tree, remembering the time long ago when he had wrecked Bessie's tree. Lord almighty!

By ten-thirty that night, the last of the mourners had gone. Greta had been put to bed with a sedative. Andy went to Cousin Henry's. Rob sat in the kitchen with his arm bent on the table, cradling a jar of Cousin Henry's moonshine in the crook of his elbow. He looked up at Carter who stood chain-smoking at the window.

"How 'bout we join our daddy for a bit and get drunk out to never-never land?"

"I'm halfway there, little brother. Been juicing the wheels already," Carter said.

"Whatever is he saying?" Bessie asked fussing with her black dress. It was a heavy crepe and weighed her down. "Carter, did you hear him?   Do you hear what your brother is saying?"   She saw herself taking it off right there in the kitchen, right in front of Carter in her mind's eye, but controlled her need by scratching her hips. "Rob, you are cuckoo crazy, I declare."

"Pay him no mind, Bessie," Carter said. "Pay nobody no mind tonight. Nobody — least of all him — is going to make any sense tonight."

"And how about you?   Do we include you in that?" she said to Carter lowering her eyes. "Or are you going to talk sense?   Are you going to offer me any comfort like you did your sister all day long?   We do have soooo much to talk about — you and me."

"Aw, have a drink and shut up for crissakes, Bessie," Rob said. He took huge gulps of the liquor and "ahhhhed" when he swallowed. Carter poured himself some more.

"Do you think it was wrong of me to leave up the Christmas decorations?" she said unpinning her hair and wishing it would fall free. "I mean, who knew he was going to drop dead? I already had them all done, you know. All hung up and sparkling — to say nothing of my beautiful tree. Now you don't suppose they expected me to take it all down, do you? Even though I never finished the tree?"

"A drink, I said. Have a drink, Bessie old girl," Rob said, belching out his liquor breath.

"Shut up, Rob. You just shut up, hear?" she hollered. "You and your silly talk of joining your father. Go on up to bed. What I have to discuss with Carter, I'm saying, has nothing to do with you."

"Did Papa plan on this happening tonight, do you think?" Carter asked Rob. Then he turned to Bessie. "It has nothing to do with you either," he said to her, pouring himself still another glass of moonshine and downing it. He sat on the windowsill, his legs out straight and crossed at the ankles, his tie hanging loose, and his collar unfastened. He looked squarely at her.

"Well, now, Carter, I surely think it does." She fanned herself and posed her arms for him. "It certainly does, and I'm sure if you examine all the circumstances surrounding us here, now you'll have to agree that we both have to discuss the way fate has taken her time with us."

"Why, whatever do you mean?" Rob said, mocking her tone of voice. "I am so confused!"

She turned to Rob with clenched teeth.

"I told you to shut up." She fussed with her kinky hair. Then said, "Carter, I am thinking we should go inside. Shall we talk about this inside?"

"Never mind where you go, bitch that you are. Why don't you go sit on my father's lap and talk?" Rob said.

"However can you speak that way to me?" she shrieked. "I am still your stepmother, whether you like it or not."

Rob stood up. He looked like he was going to hit her. Then he began a slow cough. "A stepmother who still owns my farm. Isn't that what you really want to say? I'd better watch my step? Isn't that what you mean?" His words were slow and steady and punctuated by the coughing.

"Are you going to let this go on?" Bessie yelled to Carter.

Rob was not going to quit. "But you have your own daddy's farm too," he said. "Isn't one enough? How many do you think you can work at once?"

"Maybe you two should settle this another time, Rob," said Carter. "Maybe you should wait until our Papa is in the ground." The liquor made him warm, and he felt a humming inside. "He's still in the fucking parlor for the love of heaven!"

Rob sighed. His nose was running, and he cleaned it with the back of his sleeve. "I'm going to Henry's," he said, "and maybe get drunk enough to see Papa. You can finish this, Carter. See you all at the cemetery . . . we have to stick together you know . . ." When he got to the door, he turned and shot his words back at Bessie like they were bullets. "Now that we are orphans — and all."

Bessie brushed something off her shoulder, using her hand like a whisk broom, her strokes coinciding with Rob's steps as he left the house. Then she fussed with her hair, trying to pull it straight. "Is that the way you think, too?" she asked, sitting at the table across from where Rob had sat. She faced Carter's long legs. She lowered herself even more into the chair so she could look up his body — so her view of him made him taller, bigger, longer. "Do you feel like an orphan?" Carter just looked at her. She jerked forward, reaching for the glass Rob had used and poured herself a drink into it. The liquor was working nicely on him. She held up the jar, and her gaze asked if he wanted more. He unfolded his legs and crossed to her, putting his glass out so she could pour. She smiled. Her hand touched his as she moved the jar away.

"Your husband is lying dead in the next room," Carter said. "Do you think it's all right for you to be drinking with me?" He took another swallow.

"I'm sure it is," she said. "It's only to calm myself down. We do have more jars of this somewhere — now I'll have to try to remember where I put them." She removed her earrings and put them on the table.

"Are you going to smoke too?" asked Carter, taking his glass back to his spot on the window sill. He lit another cigarette.

"Well, of course, you know I don't smoke. I am a lady, Carter, after all, and . . ." He smiled. "Uuup! I can tell you're just teasing me. Now why do you suppose you're doing that?" Her laugh was soft and low.

"Why don't you let Rob have the farm, Bessie. He's the only one of us who should."

"Now why would I let him have it?"

"He loves it like his life. You know that. Why do you think he's so upset? The

farm never meant anything to any of us —
including Papa."

"That's a terrible thing to say."

"No it isn't. It's a true thing to say."
His words were slightly slurred; still he was
aware of everything he was saying. He emptied
his glass.

She got up slowly, putting her two hands
on the table, making her elbows very straight
so her breasts stuck out, squeezed between
them. "Is that what we're doing here? Are we
here for our own true words?" She crossed to
him, sitting herself next to him on the sill.
"Still it seems to me that earlier you said
nobody was going to make any sense tonight.
Isn't that what you said?" She rubbed her
cool glass against her forehead back and
forth, back and forth, and then rolled it
against his arm. He looked at it, feeling the
coolness through his shirt.

"Depends on what you mean by sense," he
said.

"Well, I do suppose that's true."

"Makes no sense to me how all of us got
to here."

"Whatever do you mean?"

"The four of us 'children' — now orphaned. Left without parents. And then, you.
How did we all wind up here? You've lost your
parents and now your husband, and you seem
just fine. How is that? You seem to come out
from under — and you're smiling." His own
glass went down on the stove, and he put his
cigarette out in the ring of wetness remaining in the bottom of it. She continued to
roll her glass on him. "How did our Papa
manage to go and leave, and have it all turn
out like this, do you think?"

"Why, I told you fate has had her way
with us, now hasn't she gone and done that?"

Bessie said.

She put her fingers in the liquor and rubbed them wet against his sweating fore-head. But he darted like a deer, and, her glass dropped, not breaking, and rolled next to the ice box. He had her dress up and the length of his body flat on hers, down on the floor, in about three seconds. She clung to him in a death grip, and he ripped her pant-ies into two pieces, his mouth covering hers, and then he had it out and rammed into her in a huge thrust.

She clutched him with her hands, her mouth — all the while squeezing him so hard with her muscles down there that he came in only about nine or ten more thrusts. Then she pretended to come too, moaning like an ani-mal, and in her fake ecstasy she thought that he — that all of it had something to do with love. Stupid girl.

"Ohhhh Carter, my darling, I was right," she said to his now slack body. "I was right. Fate has certainly taken her time with us. She has. Oh, she has, and I am so happy." Her hands moved up and down his back. His face was still partially on hers. Then she began scratching him, but the itch was really her own. "Are you not speaking because you are so overcome by us together, my darling, darling Carter — at last, my Carter."

He still did not move, nor did he speak. Wherever he was, he did not see his father. All he saw in his blackout was a huge void. Her impatience grew, because she could not move under him, but then she felt first a slight twitch, a kind of ripple in him, a jerk, and hoped that he was about to tell her all the sweet nothings she longed to hear.

She felt some movement in his stomach, although he did not shift his weight. She
thrilled, waiting, feeling his hot breath on
her cheek.

"Carter, you are just starting to hurt a
little, my love. Can you move just a —"

And the rumbling came up from his stomach into his chest. She gripped him tighter
and smiled, but the warm force that moved
through him finally exploded in vomit that
poured out of him all over her face and into
her mouth which was still open.

Yet still he did not come to, and she
thought she was going to drown. She alternately howled and choked, but managed to push
his face off hers. His arms were spread-
eagle, collapsed onto the floor on either
side of her which made it almost impossible
for her to get free of him, so she slid down
under him to get free of his arms, keeping
her head turned sideways and trying to scrape
his vomit off her and onto his shirt. Finally
she was able to get one of her spread open
legs under both of his and using her hips,
she rolled him off her. She moaned and cried
as she got to her feet and ran for the bathroom, leaving Carter still out cold in a heap
on the kitchen floor.

And then it was midnight, and Lance came
out of the clock. Merry Christmas to all, he
seemed to say, and to all a good night.

It was two months later when she showed
up at his rooming house in Washington. He had
disappeared from her life as soon as he was
washed and mobile enough early on that awful
Christmas morning, throwing his possessions
into a bag and sneaking out into the fog,
relieved that no one saw him go. But tonight

he came home later than usual only to find
her in the hallway asleep in a chair that the
landlady had reluctantly given her. She still
wore her black crepe dress and a small pill-
box hat with a veil.

"Do you suppose there is somewhere we
can go to talk?" Bessie said after waking
with a start at his entrance. "You can imagine I have something of the utmost importance
to speak to you about, or I wouldn't be here."

"What is it Bessie?" Carter asked,
wishing she would disappear.

"This isn't a good place to talk, now is
it?"

"Okay," he said, showing her the door.
"We'll go to a diner." She moved through it
with dignity, careful not to touch him as she
brushed by.

She buttered a muffin as she sat across
from him in the greasy all-night restaurant.
His face was all hard lines, and he found it
difficult to look at her. "I am going to
speak very calmly to you, Carter and I hope
you will do the same," she began. "I am
extremely distressed — still after all this
time — about what happened to us that — that
time. Still I am willing to be fair, and I do
certainly hope that you are sufficiently
distressed also. Things happen sometimes that
we have no control over, and sometimes it's
best if we can forget them or at least make
the most of them — if you know what I mean."

"Look, Bessie. I'm sorry for what happened, I really am. And I would like to
forget about it. That's why I haven't answered
your letters. You certainly didn't have to
come all the way up here to —"

"Well, I certainly am glad to hear that
you are sorry. That makes it much easier for
me to say what I have to say, Carter dar-

ling." He bristled, but tried to look calm.

"There's a lot more to this than you can imagine," she went on. "I have done a lot of thinking these last few weeks, and I have made lots of decisions. You probably know that I now have a lot of property. The farm my daddy left me is worth more than I thought, because some company or other wants to build something or other on it, and they have offered me a very nice price. I will be just fine, you see. Then of course there's the farm your father left me."

She glanced at him, giving him a chance to comment, and when he remained stone-faced, she hurried on: "I know that you have had to struggle here, Carter, so I am hoping it would be a good thing if you and me could settle down together. Does that make any sense to you? Why I do hope it does."

"Isn't it a little soon for the grieving widow to think of settling down again?"

"I know you weren't happy with farming, but I thought you're older now, and maybe you'd like to give it another try."

"Farming never was and never will be for me. Give Rob the farm. I told you that before. It's not for me."

"My problem is not who to give it to. I am looking to settle down *with someone.* Are you hearing me?"

"Now, Bessie, you and I don't exactly have a history of getting along well, do we?"

"But this is different. I am talking about a much larger picture, and I'm talking about soon."

"I'm afraid you'll have to find someone else. I'm not the man you need."

"Well, you just are that very man, and I hope you will reconsider, because this is very important to our family. There is nothing wrong with a stepmother marrying her stepson — absolutely nothing wrong whatsoever."

"If he wants to."

"And you're saying you don't?"

"Yes, Bessie. That's just what I'm saying."

"Well, that is unfortunate, my dear Carter. I was hoping you would say yes on your own."

"How else could I say it?"

"I mean I was hoping you'd say yes, before I told you our very important news." She slurped her coffee off the top, because it was so hot. Then she opened the jam pot and began to spread the watery jam all over her second muffin. "Do you want some of this?" she asked. Carter shook his head and blew smoke out of his nose.

"Bessie, I'm real tired and I think we should get back. I'll see if the landlady has a room for you tonight and —"

"Carter, listen to this — just listen one more time. It's — that night when we did it — it worked. Oh, Carter, I am so so happy. All those years with your father, and I never had any babies. He always pulled it out, you see. Well, now you didn't. And I am . . . the baby I mean. I am going to have yours, and it has made me so happy, even though I know people are going to frown on us. I don't even care any more. But if we can get married fast, we'll tell them that we had a secret marriage back then, and after a while no one will be counting months any more anyway."

And he felt a huge choking bubble like a rubber sheeting pulled over his head. It closed tighter and tighter making him sweat, making something bang inside his head, and he wondered what he could ever do to make it go away.

Chapter 16

Bessie stood at the table in her kitchen, her rolling pin attacking a lump of dough the way someone might squash a bug. Little puffs of flour flew out from under its sides each time the rolling pin made contact. "You have crushed me to the quick," she said, "after all the time I have dee-voted to you!" She stretched the dough into a thin, perfect circle — the basis of a new pie. Bessie baked her life away in pies. He wondered how many she was allotted. When all her pies were up, would she die?

"It will be better for the baby if I'm not here — if I go back to Washington and come to see him only on weekends."

"He is all you care about."

"I'll take him and Greta out every week-end."

"You have never ever cared about me. Evah!"

"Didn't I marry you for crissakes?" Carter said.

"You know what I mean. Do you think I am stupid? I am talking about real caring. And besides look how long it took you! My stomach out to here —" Bessie shrieked, "having to go to church that way with everybody *knowing*."

"It didn't seem to bother you — all you did was show off."

"Whatever do you think they were thinking about? If you knew what caring really was, you never would have made me wait .so long, so everyone could see."

"Shut up, Bessie. I am so damn tired of this. You'll never know how tired. You make me sick, you know that?"

"I have taken away all your cares, and that makes you sick? If you think about it, you'll know what I am saying is true. All your worries — gone like rain in the ground," she said. "You don't even have to think about providing for us or even for yourself."

"Right. All I have to think about is farming — the thing I hate most," Carter said. "I have more worries now than I ever did. How am I supposed to stay with a woman who only knows how to scream? And how much longer am I supposed to grit my teeth so my baby doesn't hear us fighting?"

"Heaven knows you only married me because I am now considered well-to-do. I think it's time that we called a spade a spade, don't you?"

"My sister used to say that when you married Papa, he lost his voice. You'd like that to happen again, wouldn't you? You'd like me to be meek as a lamb, and yes you to death. Well, it ain't gonna happen that way. Nobody is gonna do that to me — least of all you."

"You will never speak those words to me again. Heah? You will never say those horrid things. And that is my very last word on the subject."

"Or what?" Carter demanded.

"Or what, what?"

"What will happen if I do? Will you throw me out?" He felt he might be on to something. He did not even care about the money anymore.

"Well, that probably is what you would like, now wouldn't you?" Bessie jibed.

"What do you say? Is it a deal?"

"You will always be here with me — that is the only deal." Her breasts were bigger than ever, and she bounced them even more when she got excited, rocking herself up and down on her heels. It reminded him of how she looked prancing down the aisle a year ago with her breasts bouncing on the shelf of a stomach which was "out to here" on their wedding day.

She had worn some horrible pale green lace dress that she had seen in a store window in Richmond, and they had to let out the seams all the way to the edge, because she was in her fifth month by the time he agreed to marry her.

He'd had plenty to drink that day — starting in the morning. It was the only way his brothers could get him there, and they knew it. So after he was well-armored with liquor, he just smiled at everyone, feeling like he was somewhere else, and indeed he was, because throughout the entire ceremony, he couldn't stop the flow of scenes from his past. He saw the Texas sky and Juana lying on top of him and then later there she was, dead, on her back in the desert. He saw Lieutenant Wade lying with a flag sticking out of his ass. He saw Mile Away lying dead in his own blood and felt Hellbag's hot breath on himself — so much so that it made him cry when he faced the minister at the altar, not seeing him at all only smelling the smoke from the trains of his past. Hearing the whistle and wishing he could get on so they could take him far, far from there — far from Bessie. Oh, God!

*   *   *

Bessie's second wedding day!

She had acted like she had just swum the English Channel. She was the Perle Mesta of Lunt's Church, greeting her guests amidst the beautiful flowers, and holding Carter's arm and showing him off — as if he were some kind of trophy. And after the liquor wore off, he would feel the way he had ten years ago when he had awakened to find her mouth shut tight on his cock. It was a kind of claustrophobia, trapping him in the half-light in air as heavy as cement. He could not breathe it then or now. And the layers of clouds around him formed lots of dusty corners, making him wonder if he would ever be free of them again, even when he got sober. He was tethered like Mabel, his old mule — only it felt more like a noose.

When the ceremony was over, Bessie turned and faced the small congregation. "Now I want to thank everyone heah for coming, and I have to tell you that I have so many fresh pies that I baked myself — all waiting for y'all in my kitchen right now. So come on, I declare!" She pulled him back down the aisle and gestured to all her guests with an inviting wave. He stumbled along next to her, leading the procession back to the farm, a vacant grin on his face, but under it he wished that she would die.

The miracle happened in September, two months before his twenty-fourth birthday. Never in all his life was anything so extraordinary as the birth of his own son! He couldn't believe it. There he was at the hospital every day. He was not allowed to touch the baby, but he could peek at him through a window. Bessie had to stay in the hospital for twelve days. He was grateful for the peace in the farmhouse. But he had to wait twelve days to touch his own son. And when he finally looked into his face, he saw himself in miniature! There was his life starting over again. Maybe this time it would be right. He had been extended. He would go on and on.

"I am biding my time until I can figure out a way to get out of here and come back to Washington," Carter wrote in a letter to Paul. "Something very strange has happened. We used to fight all the time. Now there is nothing but silence. My father used to say, 'Some people can touch each other without words, some can never touch — even with them.' He was right, of course. Even though I admire his wisdom, I am so afraid that I'm going to change and become like him."

(Of course, I know what he meant about silence. There is nothing lonelier than the silence of marriage. It resounds like the silence of the grave. I often lie awake in the middle of the night, staring at the ceiling. I cannot bear it.

Perhaps it is my legacy. Like Carter who stared at his ceiling, I, too, wish there were someone to touch — to tell — just a little of me.

Don't touch that, Christina."
"Don't cry, Christina."
"You mustn't ask so many questions about your father. After all, you never knew him. How can you miss something you never had?"
"You must be always happy."

Instead, my obsession stays. Is my longing a portent of something else? Do I know that someday in another life I'll see him again? Will he ever let go of me? Perhaps it's his soul's wandering that I feel. Why has he chosen to haunt me, his daughter, and not Carter his son?

"Smile, Christina, don't cry!")

If only there were a way for him to keep the boy without her. Sometimes he imagined her death. He saw people standing around her coffin telling him how sorry they were, and he wondered if he would be able to conceal a smile.

Maybe she'd fall down the stairs, or — better — into the well, so he'd never have to see her again. How come we can never decide when someone dies? he thought. How can there be something as profound as death, something that affects us like nothing else in our lives, and we have absolutely nothing to say about it? His thoughts scared him. He had to get away from her. Would she let him go? Would she ever become interested in someone else and want to divorce him? He thought of a plan of persuading Cousin Henry to court Bessie. It might work, because Henry's farm had recently been foreclosed. Henry loved farming and would be right for Bessie. Besides, he was drunk most of the time and wouldn't have to listen to her.

It was with these thoughts that he armed himself to visit his boyhood friend, Cassandra Dance, in the hopes that she might have a solution for him.

"Bessie'll never go for it," she said. "Have some tea, my darlin' Carter. Such a sight for these eyes you are!"

"Think of something," Carter said. "You always had a way of knowing what to do. You always knew what was best for me."

"And that's what I'm telling you now. But you're not hearing me."

"You're not saying anything."

"You find yourself in an impossible situation."

"Can't you read your tea leaves or whatever it is you do?"

"You want to know the future? I won't tell you. Just know this. The only way out is through. You must go through what you must go through. You have a son. You have to follow your own instincts. Part of you knows how to handle this already."

"No, it doesn't. If it did I wouldn't be here talking to you about it. I'd only have come to talk about old times."

"Think some more. Take some time. The answer will come to you."

"I have no time. I never had any."

"Dear, dear Carter — always in a rush."

"I have to be," he said. "What if time runs out on me before I get to do all my stuff? I guess I'll just have to leave her and hope that she doesn't do anything to try to keep me from my son."

That night he packed his bag, kissed his baby, and walked out on the wailing Bessie, who could not contain her rage and broke her silence.

"I put a curse on you," she screeched, throwing a pie down the front steps after him. "Do you hear that? You are cursed forever! I'll find you, and you will — you will be sorry!"

Half a mile down the road he took a Bisodol. Then he pulled over to the side of the road and cried.

*   *   *

On December 5, 1933, people stood six or seven deep at the bars. Prohibition was over. Everyone had known it was coming. Liquor companies and bars prepared for months. Now — here it was! Corks popped. Music blared. Laughter swelled like swirls of smoke through the saloons and out onto the streets. Carter celebrated with his friends in Washington, but inside him was pure panic. He knew he couldn't continue to earn the twenty-five a day that he had been making driving the bootleg truck, now that liquor was legal. Kincaid, his old boss, who was delighted to have him back, told him it didn't matter — that there would always be a market for bootleg liquor, but Carter knew his days in it were numbered. His habits had become increasingly expensive, and he would probably have to give them up. And although he knew Bessie had plenty of money, he still wanted to feel like he was supporting his son.

On the other hand, he thought, maybe the repeal was a mixed blessing. He was tired of being on the wrong side of the law. The bootleg trade continued, because the bootleggers undersold to the speakeasies, which had now gone legitimate; but Carter was afraid that sooner or later the investigations of the liquor companies would eventually blow the trade wide open. He got dressed up every day and went out early looking for a job, doing the only thing he felt he knew something about — selling liquor. He made his rounds twice a week, putting on his best gray pin stripe and hitting all the companies several times. If they were tired of seeing his face, he pretended not to notice. Then he realized he'd have to use the only other thing he knew something about.

He became friendly with the receptionist at I. W. Harper's. She liked him.

"I told you, I'm not allowed to let anyone in," she said smiling.

"Can't you say I'm an old friend of yours?"

"I don't even know you," she said. He leaned over the desk and kissed her. She didn't pull away. He probed her teeth with his tongue. She opened her mouth.

"Now you do," he said. He hypnotized her with his tongue. She seemed to fall into another dimension. She was very tall — as tall as he — with stick-straight heavy blond hair which she tied on top of her head with a purple ribbon. The hair spilled out of it like a fountain.

"What time do you leave?" he said.

"I can probably leave right now." She never took her eyes off him. They misted over, and Carter was afraid they would drip. First they went out to dinner. Then they went back to her place.

"Oh, Carter," she said after he made her come so many times she was sore, "no one has ever made me feel like you do." He had started to put on his clothes. "When can you come back here again?"

"Well, the thing is," he said, "I'm very busy. I have a job, but I also spend a lot of time looking for a new one. That's like having two jobs. Maybe if I could get in to see Mr. Big Brass at Harper's . . ."

"You mean then you would have more time for me?"

"Well, I might. I might be able to arrange that."

The next day she finagled an appointment. A week later, he had the job. Liquor salesman. Thirty a week to start, plus commission. A big comedown from twenty-five a day. But he knew eventually he had to get out of bootlegging. He would, however, keep up those deliveries at night for a while and do his new job during the day. He began to sock a lot of money away, so that when he made the transition, it would be smooth.

By November of '34, he was making fifty a week with Harper's, and he had enough saved to quit bootlegging altogether.

Maybe things were improving for him. He began to whistle. Christmas was coming. Decorations appeared in store windows. He stopped and bought a glass angel for a Christmas tree. Who could he give it to, this harbinger of peace and joy? Could he spin himself into a sugar plum dream? Ridiculous. Why should this one be any different and how could he dare to think it might be better than others? It was at Christmas time when he first ran away from home. That was the Christmas he missed — he slept right through it in a drunken haze with the hobos. Maybe he should do it again now. No, he had to stay sober for the sake of his son.

He drove up to Bessie's farmhouse on an icy blue night. Greta ran out to meet him with baby Carter in her arms. She got into the car and held him on her lap. There was a silly grin on her face. She played with the baby, covering his eyes with his hands and popping them off again. "Bessie is out at Cousin Henry's," said Greta. "He'll be bringing her back soon."

"Good. Then we'll drive for a while."

"Carter, Carter go away. Carter, Carter stay to play," she sang. The baby giggled and put his hands on her eyes.

"Hey," he said. "You called him Carter."

"That's his name, isn't it?"

"No, I mean you always said 'Carty' not 'Carter,'" he said. "At least that's what you always called me."

"That's when I was a child."

"Oh, I see. Now you're an adult."

"Well, practically. I mean I am seventeen."

"And never been kissed?"

"Oh, Carty . . ." she blushed.

"Don't tell me! You have a boyfriend?"

"Well, you even said I would, you know."

"Of course, I'm only kidding. What's his name?"

"Gordon." She was grinning so hard, she started to giggle.

"And?"

"And what?"

"What else do you have to tell me?"

"Oh, I'm so confused. Do you know what?"

"What?"

She covered her own eyes with her hands, and spoke in a half-hysteria, "He wants to marry me. Oooo!"

"Whoooa! Hold on," he said. "You're much too young for that."

"No. Lots of people get married now. And I'll get away from Bessie. Besides I really love him." By now she had draped her scarf over her head so you couldn't see her at all. "He says I'm very mature."

"Oh, crap," Carter said. "Listen, you didn't — he didn't try to — you know — do anything to you, did he?"

"You mean . . . well, he kisses me a lot on the . . . on the . . ."

"On the what?" He stopped the car and pulled her scarf off.

"On the porch. Bessie won't let me go anywhere with him."

"God bless Bessie," he said.

"I guess it's because he's so old."

"How old is he?"

She got all gooey again. "Twenty-three. Can you imagine that? Twenty-three years old, and he wants me!"

"I think I'd better have a talk with him as soon as possible."

"Oh, Carty, please don't be mad at me. I'm so happy. For the first time in such a long time! Me — can you believe it? I'm happy." He hugged her. Her eyes sparkled in the glow from the moon.

"I'm happy for you, little girl. It's just that I want things to go right for you. I don't want you to make a mistake. Look what happened to me. For that matter, look what happened to Papa when he married Bessie and how all of us were hurt by it. I love you, little baby. I don't want you to hurt ever again."

"Just talk to him then. I know you'll like him. He even wants me to finish school first. See? He cares about me. I told you." Her beauty gave Carter a lift. What a delight she was.

"You know what?" he said. "You are like a Christmas present." He kissed her and gave her the angel. "You made this day just fine for me."

Greta and Gordon were married the following Thanksgiving, and Carter gave her away. She was a truly magnificent bride. How he prayed for her to be happy! For Gordon to treat her right. His beautiful baby sister.

For the next two years, he brought lots

of women home so he wouldn't have to sleep
alone — just to have someone there. But every
morning he wanted them to disappear. He could
handle being alone in daylight. But by night-
fall, he had such an ache inside — as if
everyone in the world had gone away, and he
shuddered in the dark.

"What's the matter with you?" said Paul
one night after a card game.

"Nothing. Nothing at all. I don't like
losing, though."

"You kept staring off into space all
night. Looks like you lost your best friend."

"Just tired."

"Who're you kidding?   You need a good
roll in the hay."

"It's not the same. I mean it doesn't
seem to help."

"Help what?"

"I don't know — chase away the blues, I
guess."

"Listen, pal, whenever you walk in
anywhere, women just about throw themselves
on the floor and spread their legs open,"
Paul said. "If that won't chase away your
blues, I don't know what will. Why won't it
happen to me?"

"It's that I want somebody somewhere to
care what's inside here," Carter pointed to
his chest, "not just what's in my pants."

"I don't get you," he said. "With your
looks you can have anybody you want . . ."

"That's the problem. I wonder if I had an
accident and got disfigured or something,
would they still like me?"

"You're nuts," said Paul.

He began to think maybe he was. If not
nuts, then marked in some way. Singled out by
some grand master planner as the lonely joker
in the pack. He did not want to believe it,

but the more he thought about the events of his life, the truth of it seemed more and more certain. Always alone, surrounded by the fragments of what might have been. He had played his feelings close to the vest all his life and wondered if this trap that he found himself in would ever change.

He made his rounds of the bars and hotels, taking orders and trying to push the booze in the same way he had always done. Getting into his routine was good for him, because he had to be on stage in a way, and the energy of his performance helped him forget how sad he felt. The company had come out with a new sample kit. The little bottles were much flashier and had a darker green glass. He thought they were classy and would probably increase his orders. Inside the cover of the kit was a diagram showing how grain was made into alcohol. Hell, anybody who had ever seen a still already knew that.

When he went home at night, however, the loneliness settled in like fog, covering even the corners of his room. If he could not find a woman, he often went down to the basement of the building of his rental to work with wood. There was a forgotten work bench there with many tools intact. Sometimes he made a toy for baby Carter and sometimes something for himself — a tie rack, a bread box, a carved frame for a picture.

Winter started early in 1937 with icy force. He had a hard time keeping his car on course, the wind was so strong. Sometimes it was hard to walk without getting slammed into a building. Bars did a windfall business as people took refuge from the cold. Pace Setters, one of the classier local hangouts, had added dancing girls to its entertainment. Several other clubs picked up the idea, and this brought a new crop of females into the city. Tap dancing was the most popular, and Carter was fascinated watching these beauties as they went through their paces. The sound of the rhythm was as regular as the ticking of the old clock from his boyhood, and the constant percussion of the taps cheered him up.

Pace Setters' floor show started at ten. He tried to have his rounds finished in all the other clubs, so he could wind up there in time to catch the show. Ten girls from New York in silver tap shoes and blue sequined costumes with long silver strings hanging around their legs like a skirt! These skirts parted with only the slightest swish of their legs. Beautiful girls with pulsating feet and just the right bounce to their breasts. Because they did so much business together, Fat Costello, the owner, often saved him a seat up front at his postage stamp table. Costello jumped up and down importantly at the end of every act to introduce the next one, smiling through his sweat and talking too close to the microphone. He constantly tugged at his shirt collar which was too tight. He was a cigar-chewing, back-slapping loudmouth who was not to be trusted, but business was business.

It was on December 12 of that year that he met Emelia. He remembered the date, because Costello had been announcing since the beginning of December that his Christmas show would start on December 12. He stood in the doorway waiting for a mediocre torch singer to finish her number, when he saw that Costello had someone else at his table. Costello waved to him.

"Pl'up a chair," he said. "This here's Tony — B'loney I calls him. Meet Carter. Tony's with Shenley's."

"Ever hear of us?" said Tony laughing. His face had a constant smile on it. Shenley was Harper's biggest competitor.

"Once or twice," Carter said, lighting a cigarette. Half-hearted applause ended the singer's performance.

"Zat so?" Tony said.

"Waita sec," said Costello. "Gotta bring on m' girls." His hair was as thick as grass. But he had no hair on his fingers or arms. He bounced onto the stage, his jowls shaking.

"Do lotta business here?" Tony asked. He had a cleft in his chin that looked like he had been hit with a bullet.

"Enough," Carter said.

"Could be, you'll hafta share it with me." His smile looked like a crescent roll. His lips were fleshy.

"Zat so?" said Carter, mimicking the way he talked. By now Costello had finished with his introduction of the "best ten most beeeooodeeful goils from ol' New York." The music blared, the girls tapped out, and Costello bounced back to their table.

"Catch that on the end." Tony pointed to the last girl on the right who had the face of an angel. He licked his grin. "Ever see a face like that?"

"Ya surprise me," said Costello. "Thought ya'd go for more chest." He pointed his cigar at the taller, more buxom girls in the middle of the line.

"Too easy," Tony said. "I like a challenge." The taps got faster and more complicated. There was something very pleasing about their steady pulse.

Chapter 17

They watched the dancing for a while. Toward the end of the act, Tony leaned over and asked Costello to invite the "piece" on the end of the line to join them.

"Watch how you talk about m' girls. I keep em' away from creeps like you."

"But we're business associates," Tony said.

"Not yet." Costello relit his cigar, blowing puffs of smoke in angry snorts. He threw the burnt match on the floor. "'Sides, this ain't no whorehouse."

"Hey," Tony's smile never wavered. "I only wanted to meet her, that's all." He got up as soon as the girls finished, smiling a good-bye. He left his card. "Gimme a call," he said. "I'm at the Russell Hotel. No hard feelings."

"Good riddance," Carter said to Costello when Tony was out of earshot.

"Not m' kind," Costello agreed.

When the show was over, Carter had one more drink, then said good night to Costello. He got his coat and walked out into the icy air. At the east end of the club was the delivery entrance. The performers and kitchen help used it as well. Standing there with his collar pulled up against the cold was Tony. He hung back against the wall and waited. Soon the girls came out. Tony fell into step with the girl who had been on the end of the line. Carter followed right behind, but Tony was too engrossed to notice him.

"'Scuse me," he said to her, handing her his card. "I'm one of Mr. Costello's business associates, Tony Marchata, and I have singled you out as one of the most talented of all the lovely ladies here tonight, and I think I could help your career, because I have some great connections that you should know about." He slathered his fast words with his oozing smile. Carter caught up to them. "How about if we talk about this some —"

"Tony, Costello told you no go." Carter put his hand on the man's shoulder. "Now get lost." The girl's eyes were huge.

"Listen, fella," Tony said. "This has nothing to do with you." He twisted away from Carter and tried to take the girl's arm.

"Beat it!" Carter shouted. Tony came at him swinging, but Carter hit him squarely in the nose. Tony staggered back against the building. The girl screamed. Carter took her arm and ushered her back inside the club, leaving the bleeding Tony outside. "Don't worry, it's okay," he said. "Mr. Costello warned him not to bother you. I was —"

Costello came running over. "Whatcha do?" he said.

"It's your Shenley salesman. He was trying to put the make on her. I hit him." The girl began to cry. He gave her his handkerchief.

"Don't worry, sweetheart," Costello said. "He won't bother you no more. What's your name?"

"Emelia," she said. Her face was open and innocent. "Mr. Costello, can I go home now?" She bit her lip and fought for control.

"I'll take her home," Carter said.

"No!" she said. He saw that she was afraid of him too. She could not have been over twenty.

"Tell you what," said Carter. "How about

if I put you in a cab? It's on me." He could
not even get a smile out of her. "Stay here
with Mr. Costello. I'll get you one." One
pulled up to deliver a customer, and he
hailed it. He gave the driver two dollars.
Emelia rushed into it, her face still in
Carter's handkerchief.

"By the way, my name's Carter," he said
to the air as the cab sped away. Rose, the
hat check girl, came out the front door.

"Going my way?" she said. He took her
home. They had been to bed a few times. He
thought about Emelia all the way there. She
was so unusual. Beautiful dark eyes, cherub
face. Such innocence was hard to find. And
she wanted nothing to do with him. He and
Rose got very drunk.

The next morning he couldn't remember
what else he had done. He went home for some
more sleep. Emelia came back into his mind.
He had to keep taking deep breaths, because
he could not fully fill up his lungs with
air. His feelings exhausted him. Loneliness
uses up a lot of energy.

On his way home, he bought a mirror in
the five and ten. He stopped by the Russell
Hotel and tipped a bell boy to deliver it to
Tony.

If Emelia saw him sitting at Costello's
table the next night, she pretended not to.
He could not take his eyes off her. Trixie,
the dance captain, came over and sat down.
She was a chubby has-been of about forty who
acted like a mother hen to the girls.

"Hello, handsome," she said. "Whaddya
say?"

"He's not interested," said Costello.
"Has his eye on the little brunette on the

end."

"Who, Emelia?" she laughed. "Fat chance you'd have with her."

"Who does she go out with?"

"Nobody around here. Has a boyfriend back home in the Bronx. Besides she said she promised her mother she wouldn't go out with no bums she met in the clubs. Ha! That's you, Carter!"

"What's her last name?"

"Gentilesco."

"Good grief."

"What's wrong with an Itralian name?" Costello said. "Listen Carter, you can have any girl you want here. Forget about her."

"I'm sick of all those girls. They're all the same."

"Thanks a lot, jerk," Trixie said. "Leave her alone. She's only seventeen."

Seventeen? It was getting worse. "Give me her address. I want to send her flowers."

"He's got a bad case," said Trixie. She got up to go. "Say hello to Big Al for me." Big Al was his boss at Harper's. She left before he had a chance to ask her how she knew him.

He looked at Costello. "Well?"

"Look, Carter," he said "I'm not telling you where she's staying, so forget about it."

"What do you think I am?" he said. "She's afraid of me. I'm not going to go there. I just want to send flowers for crissakes. I think you owe me one. How many times did I cover for you when you were getting the hooch from the bootleggers?"

"Never saw you go so nuts over a dame. They're stayin' at the Bow and Arrow Roomin' House on Missouri. Jesus Christ."

"What's the Bronx?" Carter asked.

He looked up at Emelia. Was it his

imagination or did she look away fast? Had she been looking at him? He went home alone that night. No hat check girls or other easy marks for him. He sent one dozen red and one dozen white roses to her the next day. He wrote the card, "Sorry about the other night." He signed it, "The man with the cab and the handkerchief, named Carter." It was on a Monday, and the club was closed that night. Later he went to the rooming house. She had gone out with her friends to the movies.

The next day he sent violets. "Shy and beautiful, like you. Carter," he wrote on the card.

He went back to Pace Setters that afternoon to see if a shipment of whisky had arrived. The chairs were upside down on the tables. The place looked gloomy in the weak December daylight and the stale smell of smoke and booze was sickening. Costello was in his shirt sleeves with a two day beard, barking orders to a black youth who was trying to swab the floors.

"Open some windows. It stinks in here," he said.

"It always stinks in here. Whaddya think I'm tryin' to do?" said the boy.

"Ya jerk, you're usin' dirty water to mop with." He put his face right into the kid's and yelled at him. "How can you get rid of the stink with goddamn dirty water, jerk?" The boy went outside to empty the bucket. "Get some Pine-Sol, jerk!" he yelled after him.

He turned to Carter. "Whaddya want?" he said to him.

"Good to see you too, Costello," Carter said.

"Yeah, well —"

"I came to see if my order arrived."

"Well, it didn't. Again!"

"Well then, I guess I'll just have to check on it, now won't I?" Carter headed for the pay phone in the lobby.

"'Sorright, use m' phone," he said.

"Wouldn't think to trouble you, old man." He no sooner got his nickel out when Emelia came in the front door followed by four or five of the other dancers. She was even more beautiful in daylight with no makeup on. There was a freshness to her face as if she had a new way of looking at the world. Her light brown eyes were transparent. He could see into them, and they were clear and oh, so pleasing.

"Oh," she said when she saw him, but kept on going.

"Wait, please, Emelia just a second." The other girls passed her, wondering at him. She turned.

"Oh, uh thank you for the flowers, but you mustn't do —"

"It's okay, I wanted to really. Do you think —"

"I have to go," she said. "We have to rehearse."

"Emelia, please, just give me two minutes —"

"I have to teach a new girl, because I'm going home." The Bronx. He remembered.

"Then, could we have dinner? I mean if you're going home, there's no harm in that."

"It's just for Christmas — going home I mean."

"How about an early Christmas celebration dinner?"

"I'm sorry, I just can't. I have to go." And she did. Boy, was she tough! Why did he care so much about someone who was obviously much too young and not at all interested in him? He stood there wondering why he had a nickel in his hand.

He remembered that Trixie had said something about Big Al. He called him. "Listen, I hear you know a friend of mine. Trixie sends you her best."

"Trixie who?" Oh, Lord, he did not know her last name.

"Well, now, how many Trixies can there be? I'm talking about red hot Trixie at Pace Setters."

"You mean dancing Trixie with the boobs?"

"None other. Listen I think she's got hot pants for you."

"Yeah? Look, Shields, I got work to do."

"So do I. I want to talk to you about some new ideas I have for better promotion in this area. Why don't we have dinner?"

"Talk to me now."

"No, I got to show you some things I've worked out on paper. You know, boss, I think you work too hard. You need some relaxation. How about if I arrange a nice dinner for us with a couple of girls from Pace Setters. Let's enjoy ourselves first, and we can talk business after they leave for the show. Doesn't Trixie sound good to you? Come on, admit it?"

"Yeah, you're probably right."

"I'll check with them and call you back."

He didn't know how she did it, but Trixie pulled it off. Somehow, she managed to convince Emelia that it was okay to go out with him. Maybe she felt safe because Trixie was going to be there. They were supposed to meet at the Russell Hotel's dining room for dinner and then take them back to the club for the show.

He and Big Al got there a half hour early, and the girls were an hour late. By the time the girls arrived, Carter and Big Al had had a few too many, and they were deep into a discussion of Carter's ideas. He had not wanted to tell him about his ideas then, but one thing led to another and before you knew it, he was asking for a promotion, assured that Al would think his plans were ingenious.

"It won't work," Al said.

"How do you know?" Carter tried not to yell.

"Because we've never done it that way before."

"What a stupid reason!" That's when the girls arrived. What timing! Carter was annoyed at them, because if they had been on time, the discussion would never have gotten started, and now it had to be left hanging. The meal was very tense. He tried not to glower at Al. Emelia looked like she was sorry she had come. When the coffee came, Carter could not stand it any longer.

"If you ladies will excuse us for a minute, Al and I have something we have to settle." Carter knew he was tipsy, but he had to finish with Big Al.

They went into the bar, which was off the lobby.

"Look, Carter," said Al, "this is a stand-off. We can't settle it now. Let's go back inside and tomorrow morning, we'll meet in my office." Carter hated him. He had used him to get to see Emelia, but everything had gone wrong. They got up to go back to the girls, when whom should they see in the lobby with their coats on but Emelia and Trixie.

"Oh, no," said Emelia.

"What's going on?" Al said.

"We thought . . . we didn't know if you were coming back . . . we . . ." Trixie was beet red. She stammered.

"Make sense," said Al.

"They thought they'd get stuck with the check," Carter said. It struck him as funny. He got his coat and hailed a cab. Al settled the check. The girls were dying with embarrassment.

"You are a couple of cheap broads," Al said, feeling his liquor. "You must be used to cheap guys."

"How did we know what you were up to?" Emelia snapped.

"You must be used to sneaks, if you have to be sneaky yourself." He couldn't believe that these words came out of his mouth; this was the woman he had been trying to impress. The cab driver began to speed.

"Shut up, Carter," said Big Al.

"Yes, sir, Big Al, sir! Anything I can do for you, sir? Kiss your ass for you, sir?"

"Go to hell."

"Well, I'm not like your other lackeys. Count me out."

"That's just what I'm going to do."

"Couple of cheap dames!" Al said.

What had he done? The next day he went to her rooming house. Of course she wouldn't see him. He stood outside her window and threw little pebbles until she finally opened it.

"If you don't go away, I'm calling the police," she hollered down at him. A soft snow had started to fall.

"Just listen to my explanation. That's

all I ask. Please. Just give me a chance to apologize."

"No. There's no reason. Just be done with it."

"Emelia, I lost my job over it, please just give me one chance to explain."

"You really did?" Her eyes widened.

"Yes."

"Okay, go ahead, talk."

"Here?"

"You said, just give you one chance. Okay, I'm giving it to you."

"Can't we go someplace and talk? I can't talk to you here. Besides I'm getting snowed on, and I'm freezing."

"Well, if you're afraid of getting snowed on, talk fast, so you can go someplace to get warm."

How could she be so quick? Seventeen years old? "Okay, last night, I had too much to drink. I had started a conversation with my boss about my prospects, and my timing was awful, because I should have been concentrating on you and not my job. The whole thing was a big mistake, and I'm sorry, and I'd like to make it up to you. I feel really awful about it."

"Your apology is accepted."

"Can we go out again? Please? Nothing bad will happen, I promise you that."

"No, I can't. I really can't do that. I have to go." And she closed the window and pulled down the shade.

He went to the club every night. He sent more flowers. He sent word through her friends that he had to see her. He even sent telegrams. No dice.

She was going home for Christmas. Before she left, there was a big crying scene with Costello, who had a fit when he heard she was leaving. He told her she was fired. Carter saw his chance to compensate for what he'd done, and talked Costello into letting her return after the holidays.

He found out when her train was leaving and went to the station. Snow had started to fall again, and this time the weatherman promised a blizzard. She was standing on the platform with a kerchief tied around her head. On her hands were white fuzzy mittens. A huge suitcase stood next to her as she waited for her train. He wanted to hug her.

"Hi," he said, "I wanted to wish you a merry Christmas."

"Oh," she said. "Thank you."

"I'm sorry for what happened."

"I know you are."

"Emelia, it's not easy for me to say I'm sorry. What I mean is — I — you are very — I can't stop thinking about you, is what's the problem."

"Why?" It was said without guile. "I mean we have had nothing but trouble, so why aren't you relieved that I'm going away? I am."

"Because you don't understand. Because I'm trying to tell you that I'll make it up to you, and I'll never treat you badly again."

"You have made it up to me. You got me my job back."

"But I'd like to do more than that. I'd like to see you and care for you. Please trust me. Say you'll see me when you come back?" A train came blasting through, covering them with its enormous sound. They waited in the steam. He grinned and looked into her eyes. She lowered hers, but she smiled too.

"Did you get your job back?"

"No. But I got another one. I now work for Shenley's."

"Is it good?"

"Yes, in fact it's better. But you have not answered my question."

"I probably shouldn't, but, yes," she said. "I'll see you then. I mean it is Christmas, and I can't have anything bad in my heart." He kissed her cheek. She didn't pull away.

"I can't wait for Christmas," she said. "I just had to go home to my family. We have a terrific time of it in my house."

"Is it a big family?"

"I have three sisters. My mother makes a big fuss and everything. She's a great cook." Her eyes smiled.

"Well, that's just great. Say hello to Mama for me." He was a kid again, and he knew he was blushing.

"Lena. We call her Lena. Everybody does."

"How about your father?"

Her face clouded. "He . . . he's sick, and he can't come home. We go to see him in the hospital." Tears gushed out of her eyes so suddenly she had not even had time for a sob. "Oh, I'm sorry; I didn't mean to . . ." He held her. What a fragile child she was. Something good was happening between them, and he knew she felt it too.

"You poor baby, it's okay." He kissed the top of the kerchief. The snow was getting heavier. He pulled her collar up. He wanted so much to kiss her mouth. He didn't know how he controlled himself. She stopped crying. He gave her his handkerchief again. This made her laugh. It was like the sun coming out after a sudden shower.

"I guess I should call you the handkerchief man. Thank you for being kind. Are you going to send me a bill for all these handkerchiefs?"

"No. But I'll take one of yours."

"They're home. I forgot to bring them with me."

"You can mail it. To remind me of you. Then we'll be even."

"What are you doing, for Christmas I mean? Where's your mom?" she asked.

"Oh, well, she's a . . . she died a long time ago, but I still have a — there's still a big farm in Virginia. It's a . . . you'd like it — it's real pretty there." An enormous hard lump came into his throat, and at the same time a train came out of nowhere. He cleared his throat. "That must be yours," he said as it slowed into the station.

"Oh, yes, it is!" Her excitement was like a child's. He picked up her suitcase.

"Can I call you? Please?" he said through the steam. He boarded first and swung the suitcase on a rack. She stepped up behind him.

"'Boaaaard!" called the conductor. He had to get off.

"Okay," she yelled. "It's Olenville 2312." He jumped on the platform. She ran to a window.

"I got it!" he waved. She waved back as the train started.

"Merry Christmas!" He moved his lips so she could read them.

"Merry Christmas!" She did it back to him. He blew her a kiss, sending it through the snow and wet steam. The train took her away. Olenville 2312. He would wait until Christmas Eve to call. He didn't want her to think he was too anxious.

He called her that night.

He spent Christmas at Greta and Gordon's and thought about Emelia. He played with baby Carter and thought about Emelia. It was habit forming. He missed her with a terrible longing. He wondered what it would be like when she came back. But because he was so filled with her, Christmas turned out to be a good one, even though she was far away. "You're so beautiful," he said out loud.

When she came back after Christmas, they spent as much time together as she would allow. The thought of any other woman never crossed his mind. He knew she was a virgin, and he did not try to force himself on her. She came back to Pace Setters in January. He met her train. There were flowers waiting at her rooming house, and they saw each other steadily for about a month. Some time in February Trixie announced that she was taking the troupe on the road. That would include Baltimore, Philadelphia, and finally New York.

"If I hadn't met you, I'd be so happy now to be going closer to home," Emelia said.

"And now that you have?"

"I think I'm going to miss you."   He kissed her.

"You know what I think?" he said.

"What?"

"I think I love you."   He knew he had to tell her he was married, but he was dreading it. He kept waiting for the right moment.

"You don't really know me well yet," she said.

"I know plenty. It's so easy to know you, because you say what's on your mind. You never play games like some girls. You never try to hide things or pout or do so many of those other dumb things girls do." There was never going to be a right moment. He simply had to do it.

"Well, maybe you can visit me when I get to New York," she said.

"There's something else I better tell you though. I should have told you before this, but I was so afraid. It's — Emelia, I was married once. I'm separated now, but my wife doesn't want to give me a divorce. And I have a little boy." He gritted his teeth and waited for the ax to fall. There was a good possibility that she would never see him again.

"I know," she said.

"You know?"

"Yes."

"Oh, God, why didn't you tell me?"

"I figured maybe you'd tell me."

"You knew, and you didn't run away?"

"I thought about it, but you made it hard to do," she said. She started to go into her uncontrollable grin. She played with the button on his shirt.

He kissed her finger. "How did I do that?"

"Well I guess it's all those flowers you . . ."

"Uh huh."

"And the phone calls when I was home . . ."

"Uh huh."

"And the telegrams."

"Uh huh."

"And the notes under my door when I get home at night."

"And I love you, Emelia.

She was only in Baltimore two weeks when

he came walking into the club where she was dancing. How the sound of those taps lifted his spirits! He blew her a kiss.

He did the same thing two months later in Philly. She never missed a step though. Just did the whole dance with that grin she saved only for him.

In June, he asked her to marry him. He had no qualms about making another mistake. Emelia was the best thing that ever happened to him. She was perfect.

She was still dancing in Philly.

"Oh, Carter, I really want to. I don't know if I can though. My family is Catholic, and, oh, I just don't know." He had forgotten about that. Italian Catholics.

"Tell you what. How soon are you going to New York?"

"Two weeks. Oh, I can't wait. In two weeks, I can go home."

"The club is close enough for you to live at home?" he asked.

"I don't know exactly. But we're not dancing for a month. We have a month off in between. So I'm going home."

"I guess I'll have to become a Catholic."

She looked at him for a minute. "You would do that?"

"Baby, I think I would do anything." She should only know about his celibate ass. "I guess I'll have to talk to your — to Lena," he said.

He pulled up in front of the Gentilesco's small two-family house in the middle of a quiet street on a Friday night. There was only one other car besides his parked a few houses down. A tiny young woman came bounding down the front stoop to greet him. She had a square face and wore her black hair in a pompadour.

"Hi!" she said. "Dora here. Have a tough trip? I'm the big sister you talked to on the phone. I bet you were expecting someone taller for a big sister. That's my joke, because I'm not big, get it?" She was probably four feet ten or thereabouts.

"Well, Dora, I like your joke, and I'm just real happy to finally meet —"

"Actually, as you can see, I'm much closer to your age than Emelia is."

"Well, is that the truth?" He began taking his luggage out of the car.

"Well, I only mention it — not for any other reason — I only mention it to assure you that if you have any problems while you're here, why then you can certainly come to me. Because of our ages. I mean, we probably have a lot in common, and everything like that."

"Uh, where might Emelia be now?" Carter said, wondering why she wasn't there to greet him. "Didn't you give her my message?"

"Sure I did. But I couldn't remember exactly when you said you'd be here. She went bowling with my cousin. I told her not to worry about time." She took Carter's bag and started up the steps with it.

"Wait," he said, but she'd whisked herself and the bag away.

"Besides I'm sure she knows I can take care of you till she gets back."

"Did you tell her that?" he asked, stepping fast to keep up with her.

"I'm sure she knows." They reached the front door, and she pushed it open.

"Well, this is great — uh — thanks." I guess I'm supposed to say thanks, he thought, but he felt terribly confused by this woman.

"Now you're in for it. Now you have to meet my sisters." She ushered him across a walled-in porch to the inside front door which was ajar. "He's here girls, and much better looking than Emelia ever said." Emelia's other two sisters, Babe and Julie came into the living room from the kitchen as Carter and Dora entered. Julie who was only fifteen and still in pigtails simply said, "Oooo," while Babe put her hand out and said, "How do you do?"

"Well, what a bevy of beauties," Carter said. "I never knew I would be in for such a treat as this."

"Where's Emelia?" said Lena who appeared in the doorway. "Hello, I'm the mother," she said to Carter. He shook her hand.

"Dora told her the wrong time," said Julie, "so she'd go bowling and —"

"What is the matter with you?" Dora cut in. "No one knew exactly when he'd be coming anyway."

"You did," said Julie.

"That's enough," Lena said. "Go and set the table."

"Dora did it already," Julie said. "And guess what? Cloth napkins!"

"She said get out of here," Dora raised her voice. The "she" meant Lena.

"No, she didn't," Julie said.

"That's what she meant." Dora glared at her, but softened to face Carter. "How about sitting down while Babe gets you a drink? You must have had a tough time of it driving all that way." But when Emelia came bounding through the door at that moment, he moved in to kiss her right in front of all of them.

"Time for dinner," said Lena.

Emelia was right about Lena. What a special lady! She was thin with gray hair that she tied up on her head. Her eyes were big and brown like Emelia's. She seldom sat, because she always seemed to be working on something. Yet with all the activity there was something fragile about her — that she had somehow known much pain in her life, but had endured and gone on. She had prepared home-made macaroni, the best meat balls he ever tasted, and apple pie. The macaroni was so light, he ate far more than he should have. The pie was even better than Bessie's.

"Mrs. Gentilesco, I have to tell you that nobody — and I do mean nobody — cooks like this down south." He tried to make his accent a little heavier than usual.

"Is that so?" She tried to look stern, but broke into a laugh. Dora hovered near him like a hummingbird, asking him if he "required" more, filling his glass and saying, "No trouble," when he thanked her. She remained poised, ready to spring to any need — real or imaginary that she might pick up from him.

"Did you ever play chess?" he asked. She smiled and looked away, not getting it.

Lena asked him to stay overnight.

"You've had a long ride," she said. "You can sleep on the couch."

"Well, now I thank you, beautiful lady," he said.

"Don't thank me," she said. "I'm doing it for Emelia."

"Well, did I pass inspection?" he said to Emelia later when they went out for a walk after dinner. He had his arm around her.

"Did you think you wouldn't? How could you not? There haven't been too many men around here like you. In fact there haven't been any." There was a cemetery at the end of her street with a high wrought iron fence all around it. They walked along it. Emelia took a stick and snapped it along the bars.

"Now what?" he said.

"Now what, what?"

"How do I ask her if we can get married?"

"I already did."

"Well, baby, why are you doing this to me? Now you have to tell me something as important as that."

"I couldn't tell you, because she wasn't happy about it. I said, 'Lena, this is the one,' and she raised her voice and said, 'What do you mean this is the one? You're only eighteen, young lady.' If I told you, you might have been too nervous. I knew when she saw you, she'd change her mind. I'm sure she has."

"What did she say when you told her I was married before?"

"One thing at a time, Carter," she said.

"Oh, boy, wait'll she hears that one."

"First things first," she said. She didn't seem worried.

Chapter 18

Later that night, they walked over to a pretty section of the Bronx called Wakefield, to visit Emelia's uncle, a brusque man who lived alone in his big house after his wife had died. Uncle Peter offered them coffee and

then disappeared into his garden. "Make
yourself at home; probably your only chance
to be alone," he had whispered to Carter,
"Wish somebody had given me the chance when I
was young," he added as he left them on the
window seat in his living room. It faced the
front of the house, and was well out of his
sight and earshot when he was tending plants
in the backyard.

Carter put his cup down, and then took
Emelia's out of her hands. His kiss was wet
and hot, and sent her reeling. She did not
stop him from touching her breasts and bending her back, laying her down on the window
seat, so that in an instant, he was on top of
her. "Let me do it, Emelia," he said, running
his fingers under the edges of her panties.
"I want you so much."

She did not answer, but did not protest.
"Yes," she finally said. "I want it too. I
can't wait anymore either." He kissed her
hard, and then opened his pants. He took her
panties off and touched her ever so gently at
first. Then he put his fingers in and
thrilled to hear her moan with pleasure.

He entered her as gently as he could.
She loved it and wondered what all the talk
about it "hurting" had been, because it felt
wonderful to her right from the beginning. He
began to thrust himself in and out, and she
came right before he did.

"Oh, Carter," she whispered when it was
over, "It's so good. I had no idea anything
could be that wonderful."

God bless Uncle Peter, he thought. God
bless Emelia, and God bless this window seat.
"And we have the rest of our lives for more,"
he said.

Although the couch in Emelia's house was comfortable, he didn't sleep well. He wanted Emelia even more now that they had made love. It was about three in the morning, when he heard someone in the kitchen. He held his breath, listening and hoping she would come to him. Perhaps they could have a few kisses in the middle of the night, perhaps more? A second later, his thoughts soured when he saw Dora in the doorway. He closed his eyes quickly, wondering if she saw him do it. Her whisper was more like a rasp and reminded him of his first landlady in Washington.

"Are you awake, dear dear Carter?" She stayed where she was in the doorway. He dared not breathe, and in a second heard a rustling behind her that turned out to be a blessing.

"Dora, what are you doing?" Babe said in a low voice.

"Shhh! Go away," Dora whispered.

"Come back inside," urged Babe.

"Why do you suppose he thinks he wants Emelia? Isn't that something? He should have someone his own age, don't you think?"

"Lots of men like younger girls, Dora."

"Isn't that something?"

"Dora, come on."

"Do you know what?" Dora said not taking her eyes off him. "I would sleep with him if he asked me. It would be a mortal sin, but I wouldn't care."

"How can you say such a thing? Besides, he's not going to ask you, thank God. He loves Emelia."

"I bet she won't sleep with him. Ha! She won't and I will, and he picks her. Isn't that something!"

"Stop saying it! You're going to spend your whole life making up for this sin," said Babe and she yanked Dora back inside.

"Go to hell!" said Dora, and she turned so quickly that she failed to see a nail that had been left on the wall after a picture had been taken down. It ripped across her eye when she jerked herself away from Babe, rendering the eye useless for the rest of her life.

Once it was accepted that he was going to marry Emelia, he found it hard to stay away from her home. They treated him like a king, and except for his run-ins with Dora, he liked being there. For the first time since he was little, he had a sense of family. His car got quite a workout that summer. He would often start to write her a letter, and he'd get so lonesome in the middle of it, that he would get in the car and drive to her instead. Sometimes he didn't arrive until three in the morning. He often drove the distance like a madman, tearing along with the gas pedal down to the floor. He did not want to waste any more time being lonely. He had to close the distance.

With each visit, he and Emelia went as often as possible to visit Uncle Peter, and spent many more hours on the window seat. He even told his brothers about his good luck and the magical place they had for their rendezvous. Once Uncle Peter returned sooner than expected, and there was no time for Emelia to put her panties back on. They both jumped up; he quickly opened the long window seat, and she dropped them in. Rob and Andy howled when he told them the story. "Hah! I bet old Uncle Peter found them," said Andy.

"Yup," Rob added. "He probably put them under his pillow."

They were married on September 30, 1939

with full Italian regalia. Lena made Emelia's wedding gown, Dora was the maid of honor, all her relatives were there, and Carter was happier than he had ever been.

Right before the wedding, Carter's company had given him a transfer. He was now the Bronx district manager for Shenley's. He and Emelia had a one-bedroom apartment a few miles from Lena's house. They had a one-night honeymoon at the Waldorf Astoria Hotel.

(And now, I am about to be born. Time has pushed forward, spun around to the time of my birth. Out of the silence of a night, two people reach for each other to fill the black hole of loneliness, and soon I am born.

"Oh, how he loved you, Christina!"
"He carried pictures of you in his car. Mounted them right onto the dashboard."
"Thought you were so pretty.")

Emelia was as intoxicating as a bouquet of lily of the valley as she came down the aisle of the little Bronx Catholic church. Carter had to catch his breath when he saw her. There she was, looking as if flowers and birds were all around her. But a look of sadness fell on her face for a moment when her Uncle Peter kissed her to give her away, because she ached for her father, who was still in the hospital and would never be released. When the whole thing was over, she looked relieved. We got away with it, she thought. They had never told the priest that Carter had been married before. No one else knew about it, so they just kept it a secret. Even though he had finally succeeded in talking Bessie into a divorce, they still were not free to marry in the Catholic Church.

The roses were still blooming along with the chrysanthemums in Uncle Peter's back yard, where everyone had adjourned for a garden reception; and the weather was wonderfully warm, although it was near the end of September.

Carter was happy to see his and Emelia's families' getting to know each other. He was especially proud to show off Greta, who had grown more beautiful in her married life. Most of the relatives and friends, however, were on Emelia's side of the family, and were charmed by the southern accents and easy pace of the Shields family.

But shortly after the cake was brought out, someone came huffing around the side of the house toward the backyard. What's she doing here? Carter thought in a panic. She agreed to the divorce. Most of the guests hardly even got a chance to see Bessie, because Andy and Rob descended on her in an instant and blocked her from view. But she glared at Carter from between their heads, the air whistling through her nose in a noisy wheeze. "I had hoped to do this quietly before the ceremony," she cried, "but I got stuck in a damned taxi in the airport." Without missing a step, Rob took one arm, and Andy the other, and they ushered her back out to the street before most of the guests realized the intrusion.

"It won't do you no good to take me out, because I'm coming right back. They are going to know. They are all going to know that he belongs to me. He tricked me."

"You agreed to the divorce, you stupid bitch. How is that tricky?" Rob snapped.

"I thought if I was nice and gave him the divorce, he'd realize I'd do anything for him, and want me back." Rob clamped his hand over her mouth, but she bit it.

"Bitch," he cried, rubbing his hand. They stood in front of the house on the sidewalk.

"How did you manage to find out about this, I'd like to know?" Andy said.

"Wasn't hard, my sweet little middle son. I heard that the two of you went to New York. Now, why else would you and Rob be doin' that? I ain't as dumb as you think."

"Of all the bitches I ever met, Bessie, old girl, you sure are the queen of them," Rob said. "What was it Carter used to say? Ain't worth the powder and shot to blow to hell!"

"Is that any way to talk to me after I raised you — hard as you was. Now you just hear me! I just told you, and you'd better mind — you are not going to keep me from getting what's mine. He's not going to get away with this. Never!"

"Where are we going to put her?" Rob asked his brother.

Andy looked around. "We could lock her in a car."

"Don't you even say such things to me!"

Bessie was screaming by now, and Rob had to raise his voice to be heard: "She'd get out!"

"You are crazy! You'll do no such thing. I am calling the police."

"Ah hah!" Andy's face lighted up. "The famous window seat! The place of intrigue and romance!"

"The window seat it is!" Rob cried. They began tugging her in that direction — up the front steps and into the house, Bessie struggling against them with every step.

In the living room, Rob opened the window seat with a flourish, and they both pushed her in, ignoring her screams. Andy fastened the latches, and Rob sat down on it.

"My, my, my, who would think this window seat would come in this handy again?"

"I wonder if Emelia's panties are still in it?" Rob said.

"Should we just let her scream?"

"Sure. No one will be able to hear her all the way in the backyard. Make sure the door leading inside is locked."

And that's where Bessie stayed for the rest of the reception. But her rage grew, and her determination to undermine Carter's new life increased like flood waters rising. They could hear her muffled hollering as they went back outside to join Carter.

"You will nevah be free of me — do you hear, Carter Shields? I shall nevah give you up! You will rue the day you walked out on me! But I shall get you, Carter Shields. Every time you so much as look in a mirror, you'll see me standing behind you!"

"It's okay," said Andy. "No one will ever hear her!"

"Least of all Carter, so who cares?" Rob said. When all the guests had gone, and Carter and Emelia had left for their honeymoon, they let her out, gave her a meal, and drove her to the airport.

Carter loved Emelia more than he had ever loved anyone. And he loved their new baby, Christina. He'd look into her face and hope to find the means there to still the disquieting voice nagging at him from somewhere in a dark space. Like hearing a song far away: you know you hear music, but you cannot make out the words. But it should not be there anymore, he argued with himself. For the first time, his life now seemed to be the way he had always wanted it. Please give me some answers, he thought, looking into the baby's face.

Maybe it was the responsibility of his new home, his new family. Of knowing he had to work for the rest of his life to support them, and of wishing he could give them more than he had. There was guilt about baby Carter, too. There he was in Virginia. Here was his father in New York. What would he think of his father so far away?

Working forever? Was that the dilemma? Once he awoke in the middle of the night, sweating from a dream. He could not remember it, but pieces of it flitted across his memory. It had something to do with being chained to a fence and there was a face without eyes far away on the tip of his mind. But when he tried to remember, it faded, like he lost its scent. In its place was a muddle of fog swirling into frenzy that left him hanging somewhere, and he felt something like vertigo before the seizure ended in oblivion.

It was the only one he'd had since he met Emelia, but he knew that it was different from the others. He didn't think the dream had anything to do with it. There was something deep inside him that was very troubled. He didn't think it was fair. He had paid his dues. He would fight to ignore it. It had no business being here. He would ask for a raise. They would move to a better apartment. They would go out more, invite friends over for dinner and cards. None of this trouble and suspense for him. Besides, Christmas was coming. At last he would have a good one in the bosom of a loving family with his wife and baby at his side. He had made Emelia a crèche out of wood, using the workbench in Lena's home. How Emelia treasured it! He decided to get her a watch for Christmas. She had never had one, she said, and he knew it would be the perfect gift.

He made a down payment on it at a jewelry store that he passed every night on his way home. He had arranged to pick it up after work two weeks before Christmas. He knew she would love it. She kept some jewelry that had been her mother's in a velvet box for "very special times," she said. There was a reverence in her hands when she opened the box — in fact when she touched most things — that reminded Carter of his father. She made him feel so important. He wondered if he could ever be all that she thought he was. This too weighed him down.

Eighteen

℘

I thought my Christmas vacation would never end. Keeping a smile on my face in front of Charles really weighed me down. The only good thing about the vacation was that I made lots of progress on my book during the days — while Charles was at work. I guess it is just about finished except for the last chapter, which I cannot seem to write. Finally school has begun again, and I now have Daniel's Galveston phone number in my hands. At last! I had to wait for all those days to pass, before I could get it, because I had left it in my desk in school, and couldn't remember the name of his company.

I had decided to call him on the morning after Christmas. I lay in bed pretending to be asleep until I heard the garage door rumble down and Charles's car accelerate down the driveway. I didn't want to have to kiss him good-bye. I lay there waiting for the tears to come, waiting for the blue bruise to rise in my heart, the one I had managed to keep invisible for more than twenty four hours — that's what it took to get through the worst Christmas of my life, without anyone in my family finding out about it.

Charles had sucked his teeth as we neared the

church on Christmas Eve (all of us late for the vigil Mass, because Melissa was delayed getting up from the city). He was beside himself worrying that we wouldn't get a seat.

"A real tree?" said Melissa. "You mean you waited till after I left home not to put up that lousy artificial thing?"

"It happens to be a beautiful tree — for all you know," said Charles.

She lagged behind us up the vestibule steps. "God, I hope you threw it away."

"Will you stop this bullshit and hurry?" Charles said to her over his shoulder. "Because of you, we're late. Have you ever been on time for anything in your life?"

She tuned him out and went on, "I can't believe it — you finally got a real tree after I begged you for years."

"I just went out and bought it," I said. "Just impulsive I guess. No big deal."

"It is to me, and who are you kidding, Mom. You always wanted a real tree," Melissa said.

"I, for one, am not standing through this whole Mass," said Charles. "If you don't hurry — if we don't get a seat, I'll meet you at the restaurant." He had come to church at my insistence. I'm the one who wanted to come. I had even gone to confession. I thought I could clean my soul. I thought I could take away my infidelity and make things right with Charles again. (With God again?)

"Bless me, Father, for I have sinned . . ." But was I really sorry? I choked out the words of my adultery.

"And why did you do this?" the priest had asked from behind his sliding screen.

"Why?" I said. "Isn't it enough that I'm here. I came because I want forgiveness."

"Absolution isn't that simple for a sin as severe and offensive as adultery. You'll have to give me the reasons."

In other words, I'm not going to get off that easy, I said to myself.

He harrumphed a few times.

"Okay," I said, not knowing what I would say. "I did it because I live with an abusive man who is no longer interested in me or capable of love." Oh, dear. That's really it, isn't it. "Our marriage isn't really a marriage anymore. And I met someone who does love me," my voice went on without me.

"So, the reason for your indiscretion still exists."

"Yes, I guess it does."

"Then what is to prevent this from happening again?"

"Well, I did try to improve things at home."

"How did you do that?"

"It's not any one thing, exactly. I'm trying to go out of my way to overlook things." I realized as soon as I said this that I have always overlooked things since the day I got married.

"Is he?" asks the priest.

"I don't really know. I guess not."

"So?"

"So you're saying I'm going to do it again, aren't you?"

"Looks that way to me."

"I think this was a mistake, Father. I think I'd better go. I don't feel guilty anymore."

"That's not an acceptable solution," he said.

"Acceptable to whom? I think you've already given me a solution," I said and left the confessional.

Bless me, Father.

The truth is I didn't know what my final solution was going to be. I just knew that Charles and I were not going to work. In the meantime, I would hold on by my fingernails until I could figure out what to do.

Bless, oh please bless me, Father.

The church was crowded. The usher signaled to us like a traffic cop, chin up and strutting, and pulled the three of us in different directions. He finally crowded us into separate pews. We could not sit together for Christmas Mass, and it was all Melissa's fault!

"The Lord be with you," echoed down from the altar and slid along the stone walls.

With whom? Me? Charles? Melissa?

If He were indeed with us, would we be sitting separately? Yes, perhaps it was best. Perhaps He was trying to tell us something — or trying to protect us from each other.

Has this same Lord forgiven my adultery?

Have I?

"And also with you."

Is the Lord with Daniel?

I looked right past the priest and the altar and the whole reality of the place and saw Daniel's nakedness as he leaned over me, saw myself kissing him. *Bless me, Father.*

And later we moved quietly into the restaurant, again waiting for someone to usher us into seats. Would we be separated again? Would we sit at separate tables? An interesting idea for a new kind of restaurant. Separate tables for families whose destiny it is to fight all the time, who cannot sit together or get through a meal without at least one argument, a few tears.

"Smoking or nonsmoking?" the hostess said.

"Oh, nonsmoking, of course," I said, laughing — wishing I hadn't said it so loud.

"Nonsmoking? Is this a joke?" asked Melissa.

"Shhh, he stopped two months ago," I whispered. "Don't say anything."

"You're kidding!" she said out loud. I nudged her with my elbow.

Come on, God. Now's Your chance. Put us back together. Isn't that what tonight was supposed to be? A new beginning! A real tree waiting for us at home — one we would later plant in the ground. Yes. Here we were eating together for the first time in a year. Maybe we could be a family — if only for one night. Wouldn't that be a wonderful thing to take home and cherish? Not only to get through a meal without a problem, but actually to have — something we've never had before — a gathering together of spirits with the breaking of bread. (Charles had more often than not brought Melissa or me to tears at the dinner table, but maybe that is all over with. Maybe the monster is dead.) Then we could go home and open presents. Maybe there would exist some feeling of love between us — to heal some of the scars of the past — to flow freely around the room, warm the air. Maybe it's not too late.

"It's really great that you stopped smoking, Daddy," Melissa said, trying to score points. He did not reply. He stared at the menu instead.

"I said it's great that you've stopped smoking," she repeated, her voice rising a little.

"So you did," he said. Her face fell.

I said, "Oh, I'm sure you meant it as a compliment. I'm sure Daddy appreciates it."

"Is that what that was? A compliment? Says you!" he said.

Her face slid into taut lines. "Of course, it must be easy to stop smoking," she said. "You've done it so many times."

"Melissa, I don't think that was very kind," I said.

"The truth, wise ass" — Charles glared at her — "is that I realize now that I don't think I ever convinced myself those other times that I really wanted to quit."

"I don't understand," Melissa said. "How could you not want to quit?"

"Well, of course, he wanted to quit," I said, smiling brightly. "Everyone wants to quit. Daddy meant on an unconscious level, didn't you, Charles? I'm sure it's not easy. This is a great victory. You should be proud of your father, Melissa."

"I don't need a spokesman, Christina!" The edge in his voice got sharper and sharper, and his jaw locked. "— or a psychiatrist. I just got done saying that in retrospect — in retrospect, I don't think I had convinced myself that I really wanted to quit — a whole separate issue, obvious to anyone who knows how to listen." Higher and higher. Sharper and sharper. And then his finger aimed at me. If it had been a gun, it would have fired right between my eyes. "Look here, isn't that what I said? Isn't it?"

A pain began under my ribs, and I widened my smile, trying to ignore the cut of his words. I could not protest that perhaps I misunderstood him, could not run the risk of his capricious anger exploding and knocking the wind out of us.

"Oh, for goodness sake," cried Melissa. "Why do we have to do this over and over?"

"Go screw yourself," he said to her. "You always ruin everything for me."

"Charles, what a terrible thing to say."

"She always has, hasn't she, Christina. Tell her the truth, Christina. Tell her how she ruined my life — our lives —"

A pall settled over her face. She swallowed, stared at the table, and said nothing.

"How we never had what we wanted after she came into the picture — how could anybody even think of giving up smoking? It was impossible with her around."

The waitress arrived with three bowls of soup — the first course of this family-style meal. The three of us averted our eyes and shook in the shattered Christmas air, left jagged by his words.

He stood up, tense as a tree trunk, and when he spoke, his taut words sprayed spit on the soup. "Christina, do you have your Master Card with you?" As I nodded, he smiled, gritting his teeth. "Good, because I'm leaving. I'll walk home. You two stay and eat. Enjoy yourselves." And out he walked.

Tell me, God. Will I always have to love her by myself?

Finally after a long time, I said, "I wonder how this happened? What did we do?"

"Why do you automatically assume we did anything?" Melissa said, the tears already coursing down her face. "I should have known. There's no way we can be together. He really hates me. Merry Christmas to all and to all a good night."

"Try to eat something," I said. "Let's stay here a while and then go home. Maybe he'll be all right, and we can still —"

"Still what? Open our presents? Kiss each other goodnight? Are you kidding? This is incredible."

What she meant was — *I* was incredible, and she was right. Even after we arrived home, doggie bag in hand, I was still hoping that somehow this wasn't real. That somehow Charles might have mellowed — hoping that he would have realized how horrible this was, and that we'd probably remember it forever. He can't, I thought. He's not really going to ruin Christmas.

What do we do with the presents?

He was nowhere to be seen. I was sure he was up in bed watching TV.

"I'll talk to him," I said. The door to our bedroom was shut tight at the end of the hall. I could see it from halfway up the stairs.

"Charles," I called, knocking gently. "Charles, isn't there some way we can resolve this?" I opened the door and stood in the doorway.

"Go away," he said. He was watching *Lolita*.

"It is Christmas, though, and —"

"Shit," he said. "I want nothing to do with you."

"What did I do?"

"It's what you didn't do. You always have to side with her."

"Oh, I didn't, really Charles, I didn't. I tried to keep you both on friendly terms. But you can't do this, now — I mean, how can we leave Christmas in this mess?"

"Get out."

"Oh, please —"

"Get out of this room." He leaped out of bed. Stand your ground, I said to myself. He came across the room at me.

Stand your ground, I said as I flew down the hall. Might he hit me too, the way he had hit Melissa? He slammed the door so hard, paint chips fell off the wall. I went back and kicked the door as hard as I could. It hurt my foot. Then I went downstairs, and Melissa hugged me. We both cried.

"Drive me to the train," she said. "I can't stay here tonight."

"What about tomorrow? Please don't make me go through Christmas alone," I said. "Besides what'll I tell everybody?"

"I'll come back when all the people come," she said. "Oh, God. Does this mean we have to sit there in front of the whole family and pretend everything is fine?"

"What else can we do?" I said. "I don't want them to know. My family must never know."

"For God's sake, why not?"

*   *   *

I slept on the couch that night and dreamed of a long line of connecting rooms angled off a central corridor; and as I entered each one, I knew that my father was in the one just ahead of me. I ran faster and faster trying to catch up to him, knowing that any minute I would see his face, see him alive in front of me. Finally I managed to be in the same room with him. He was walking toward a window, his back to me. I laughed aloud as I reached out, clutching and grasping his arm, straining to turn him to face me. And as he did so, his face wasn't his at all. It was Charles! Charles in all his fury, snorting and bellowing his snarls of hatred. And I awoke in a cloud of utter sadness.

Christmas Day became the biggest teeth-gritting day of all time. I had invited all the aunts, my mother, grand- mother, for Christmas dinner. Was I still expected to entertain them? Pretend everything was fine?

Of course, and that is exactly what I did. What will they think when they find out my marriage had failed — that I haven't tried hard enough?

And all those people came and sat and opened presents and ate and said isn't it wonderful to be together on Christmas? And I kept squashing down the bruise so they wouldn't see it. Charles was charming, the perfect host. He and Melissa and I opened our presents in the safety of all these relatives so everyone could oooo and ahhhh, and we didn't have to say a word about last night to each other.

And in the middle of the whole thing, I got a phone call from Aunt Greta, wishing me a merry Christmas, and giving me some bad news about Uncle Gordon's ill health. I wondered about Christmas in the South, about all the terrible Christmases my father had spent there. Daniel, I thought to myself late that night, what kind of a Christmas did you have?

Daniel. I thought to myself the second I awoke the next morning as I lay in bed. Oh, how I wish I could talk to you. Maybe then I could start a plan in my mind. I'm sure it would work. Sort out my thoughts. You were so good at helping me do that.

First, I'll call your company, and they'll surely tell me your whereabouts. As soon as I get dressed, I thought, I'll drive to school and — oh, no! That's when I remembered that school was closed. I wouldn't even find a custodian there until January second.

Even though I knew Charles had gone to work and I was alone in the house, even though his presence was gone, I tiptoed down the stairs the morning after Christmas. The mode of tiptoe was so ingrained in me, I could not shake it off. I even tiptoed when I spoke. My head was hot, although I shivered in my nightgown and bare feet. I moved both my hands down the banister in a sliding grip. Then I stood breathless at the bottom of the stairs and tried to hear the silence, hoping it would chase away the ghost of Melissa's tears.

My nightgown caught on the bottom step, and as I bent to free it, I looked up at the tree in the living room. Instead, I saw only the space it had left behind. There on the floor was our Christmas tree. The first real one! " . . . instead of that lousy artificial thing." It lay in silence on its side with a halo of broken ornaments and needles around it. Did it fall over by itself? I wondered why it had decided to die on me. I wondered if it had made a sound, since no one was there to hear it when it fell.

I didn't know how I was going to pull it off, or what it meant exactly, but in that moment, I promised myself that I would never again have another Christmas like this one. I swore out loud that I would never go through this or anything like it again.

The truth is I just don't deserve it.

Open your eyes and stop kidding yourself, I thought. This person you're married to needs a great deal of help, and you are not the one who can give it. You are not obligated in any way to be his whipping post, his buffer, or his therapy anymore.

Nineteen
ϱ

Aunt Greta's voice on the phone had filled me with a longing to return to Virginia. She sounded a little forlorn when she told me Gordon was in the hospital, and perhaps it was the thought of her alone in the house that made me want to be with her. Perhaps we could have some serious girl talk. Since there is no way for me to reach Daniel until January, I decide to go. Besides the prospect of getting away from Charles and spending a few days of my Christmas vacation with her is too good to pass up.

"I'll only be gone two days," I tell him.

"Don't do me any favors," he says.

Greta's house is warm and full of Christmas. "After he went into the hospital, I felt like I really didn't want to decorate," she tells me while we sip tea on her screened-in porch, which Gordon had sealed in with huge sheets of plastic. "I really wasn't sure I even wanted to live. But every day when I went to see him, he kept asking me if I had done anything. Did I buy a tree? The colored man who does our gardening would put it up for me. Did I make my wreath for the door yet? What would our children think if they came to visit, and Mama's wreath wasn't on the door? So then I thought, well, maybe it isn't really so bad, and he'll come home in time for New Year's Eve, and then he'd be so disappointed if there was nothing there. So I did it, I did it all as you can see, and then some, but now I don't know if he's coming home at all."

And when her lower lip trembles, I think of her chubby little face staring out of her childhood snapshots. "It doesn't look good. I don't know what I can possibly do in this world without him. Why must women always outlive their men?" She jumps up to get us some Christmas cookies that she made, and I realize that she isn't looking for an answer. Her chatter continues as she returns with the cookies, offers me one, and sits with her legs curled under her. "Everything we do where they are concerned is just one big long wait. Stop and think about it. First we wait for them to marry us. Then we go right on waiting for them all our lives together. We wait for them to make up their minds, to talk to us, to talk to the children, to come home, to go out. Then when we get finished with all that waiting — then they die. Well, my stars, honey, it's then that we don't know what to do with ourselves. Guess we still keep waiting. We wait to be with them again — we wait to die too."

"Oh, Greta — stop! You don't know for sure that he's going to die."

"Yes, I surely do. I do know it. I just do."

"But who's to say you can't go on. There are tons of things you can do. I know this is not the time to think about them, but you will, and I'll help you. You can even come to stay with me for a while if you like."

"You just go on and stop coddling me." She is up again and running for the bathroom, probably to cry a little. I hear the water running and wonder if I should try to be of some comfort. But then I see she has bounded out of there and pulls a cord that is hanging from the ceiling in the hallway. A ladder swings down, and she seems to run up the length of it on cat feet. She bangs on a flat overhead door that leads to the attic with the palm of her hand. "Come on," she says, pushing herself through the narrow doorway. "I just knew you would want to see these things up here." I am behind her in a flash. "It was when I went up here to the attic to get the Christmas trimmings for Gordon, that I found them."

"Found what?" I ask.

"Surprises and more surprises."

"Isn't it a good thing you made yourself decorate even though you weren't in the mood." Greta twists a bare bulb that swings from the rafters, sending shadows all around the slanting walls.

"Look at this," she says. She hands me a box, at least two feet long and almost a foot deep, its cardboard top brittle with dust, and as we speak, a tiny spider crawls out of a crack in the corner and flees in the shock of the light. Has he seen what's inside? The box is porous and peeling with the years of attic heat it has endured. As I carefully begin to separate the top from the bottom half, at least fifty more newly-hatched spiders seep out of the layers of peeling cardboard and scurry in all directions. I yelp and drop the box to the floor, brushing spiders off my knees and legs.

"My stars," says Greta. "I am sorry. Gordon says we should show them the deed, so they'll know we belong here and they don't." She sits on the floor and finishes opening the box for me. "Don't worry, they won't stay around long, you can sit," she says, and dusts off an old trunk with her apron. I sit and she takes the treasures out one by one.

First she hands me what looks like a cardboard tube that turns out to be a large rolled-up photo of my father standing in the middle of his platoon. I am stunned as I unroll the long line of young men in their boots and breeches. They all have funny looking haircuts that shaved away the bottom part of their hair high around the ears. "This is when he was in the army. You remember when Rob told you about that, don't you?" I hardly hear Greta. All of the soldiers have a restless look in their eyes except for him. I am afraid to take my eyes away, even to blink. I am afraid that if I do, when I look back, he may be gone. There may be only a blank space where he was.

"He is the only one smiling," I say. "Look at that."

"But wait," Greta says. "I have something even better. Just look, a picture of him holding you!" My stomach knots as I see his chiseled profile looking and smiling at the baby in his arms, because in all the memorabilia given to me by my mother, nowhere is there a single photo of the two of us —

not once were we ever photographed together.

"Oh, dear," I say. "This isn't me. It must be his son."

"Are you sure?"

"Absolutely. My mother has a million pictures of me. I know what I looked like as a baby. Besides, this baby is too old. I was only five months when he died."

"Oh, dear, I did so want you to be thrilled with this."

We go on and she takes out several packs of post-cards, some plain, some decorated with cherubs and hearts. These were love messages that my grandfather had sent to my grandmother. It was the way people courted back then.

And then a kaleidoscope of images, through the stacks of sepia photos I have never seen before. The last time I visited her, Greta had showed me her childhood albums. The photos in this box were of a later vintage. Here they were as teenagers — my father back into the scene in his army uniform — home, I am told, after his discharge from his stint in the army. He stands here smiling outside a cab, his arm around Greta, his bugle hanging from his waist. But with them is another young girl, very tall and fat, and probably no more than a few years older than Greta. She holds his other hand and smiles at him.

"Was that his girlfriend?" I ask.

"No, that is Cassandra Dance. We all grew up together. They liked each other a heap of beans, but there was no romance, I'm sure of that. She still lives only a mile or so from here."

"Really!" I am riveted to her. "Why was she so special?"

"I don't know what to call it. She was a simple girl, but ever so wise. She seemed to know things before they happened. I never liked to talk to her too much, because she scared me a lot — not that I ever told her. I mean, she didn't mean to. It wasn't that she went around scaring little kids. See her here, next to your father. See how she holds his hand. Wouldn't let go of him that day at all. She thought he was only home for a visit, and she begged him not to go back. She told him something bad was going to happen to him. 'Don't go near any horses just the same,' she said even after we told her he wasn't going back. I remember how she cried. Hah! And he made so light of it, just like he always did.

"'It already happened to me and I'm fine, Miss Dancin' Dance,' he said. Always called her that. 'I got thrown off the horse and had a seizure fit. How do you like that?' Then he twirled her around. 'Aren't you goin' to dance for me? Let me see how you're a-goin' to dance.' He could always get her to laugh and forget what she was talking about, because he really cared about her. It may sound like he was making fun of her, but he wasn't, and she knew it. She knew he cared about her — but this time his charm didn't work.

"'Carter, you listen here,' she shouted at him. 'Don't you ever go near a horse's power, and there ain't nothin' else for me to say.'" Greta's eyes look off as she lives again in her childhood. The still-swinging ceiling light makes a circle around her, and the shadows move her away back into the past. "Cassandra was so upset. 'Maybe the power is in the horn,' she said referring to the bugle he wore on his waist. Clearly she was seeing something that day. I didn't figure it out until years later. Then she ran at your father, knocked him down, and ripped the bugle from his waist. Then she runs with it all the way to Mill Pond, her fat flapping up and down. He is yelling after her, for her to bring it back, and so am I, because we have figured out by now what she aims to do. So the three of us run all the way to the pond; her first, then Carter, and then me — don't forget I'm still only about twelve. Well, he finally catches her just at the pond side. Who would have thought she could run so fast with all that weight? Lord! He is trying to get the bugle away from her, but she throws it to me. Of course, I'd have given it right to Carter, but she starts yelling at me. 'Don't let him have it' she says. 'It's going to bring him badness. Run! Throw it into the pond! Greta! It will bring him the badness. That horn and the horse power —' She was spinning way out of control. 'Bring him harm. Bring him harm. Listen to me!' And I don't know what to do, so I run closer to the pond, and just as I bring my arm back to throw it, Carter swoops down on me and grabs the bugle away."

"You really would have thrown it?"

"Oh, I don't know," Greta says. "I think I really was going to, because she was so fierce, but maybe I knew he'd be there in time to save it. He was furious with both of us. 'What is the matter with you dumb women anyway? I'll never

figure you out if I live to be a hundred. You drive me crazy,
you know that?' he said, and rubbed his bugle on his pants
like we had contaminated it or something. 'You dumb stupid
girls!'

"Why was she was so frantic about the bugle? He had
already gotten hurt from the horse. You think she somehow
saw his death?"

"He was riding out on his horse to sound the bugle for
something or other when he got hurt. I never got that part
straight. I just know it was the bugle and the horse that she
thought she was warning him about. But if you look at it
another way, it was a car that killed him. And cars have
horse power and horns. She kept calling the bugle a horn.
In those days, the horns on some cars did look exactly like
bugles.

"Oh, my God, do you think — could he have had a
seizure when he — I think I feel sick."

"Calm down, my dear, and take deep breaths."

"Aunt Greta, think about it! Doesn't it make sense?
They say they don't know what caused the accident. He gets
a seizure and loses control of the car!"

"Who knows what she meant? We'll never know, I
guess."

I wish that she would share some of my enthusiasm
for my discovery. Please tell me I'm right. Don't let me have
this revelation and kick it aside.

"This Cassandra Dance, you say she's still alive?"

"Very much so — fatter than ever and just as
strange."

"I don't think she will seem strange to me. I like her
already, and I think she's someone I should know. Can we
visit her?"

"You can, my dear. If she'll see you. I really don't
care to go. Too much on my mind right now, you know."
And we look at the rest of the photos, but there are no more
of Miss Dance.

Her house looks more like a trailer than a house.
Long and skinny and temporary looking, as if a tow truck
might take it to a new spot any minute if Miss Dance had a

mind to live somewhere else. There are no trees or shrubs about it, just some brown grass, and a few misshapen flagstones in front. A plastic wreath on the door seems to welcome me in spite of its shabbiness. And then a mountain of a woman in a brown floral house dress opens the door for me.

"I'm happy to meet you, Miss Dance. My aunt has told me a lot about —"

"She called and told me," she says. "I probably knew it already. If I check to see, I can tell you for sure, but I like to save my stuff for the important things." She ushers me inside, and we sit in a brown room with Persian rugs and dozens of knickknacks everywhere. "My stuff. That's what I like to call it. Did they tell you about my stuff — about the way I see things?" She laughs and lowers herself into a chair in a smooth motion that ends in an "ooof," as she hits bottom, all the while fingering the crystal beads around her neck. I sit on a roughly textured couch with antimacassars and cat hair scattered about — although I don't see any cats. The walls are covered with pictures and bric-a-brac, and centered over the couch is a print of the Mona Lisa.

She looks deeply at me. "Why are you here, my dear? Carter's daughter? I declare, I am touched that you came to me. I loved him like my own. Like my own blood. Why did you come? I know all about him. I knew he would die when he did. He never listened to me. I always knew he would die young."

"What about me?" I say. "Do you know when I will die?"

"Yes, I can tell you that. Some I can't, you know. You will be very old. And you will just open up. Your heart will open up with love." My heart sinks to hear this. I do not want to live a long time. I do not want to spend a long time in all this sadness.

Miss Dance goes on. "You have much love in there. So much still locked up. Why? Love. I feel it. Who do you love now?" She waits and then smiles. "Oh, he thinks of you. He thinks of you all the time. You two are connected. Yes, well-connected. You think of each other at the same time. But he is far away — thousands of miles — hot there. All the time you keep thinking of him. Well. What do you know about that?" Each time she asks a question, she goes right on with an answer or some other speculation, and I soon realize that she is asking these questions not of me, but of herself. "You are so easy because you have Carter's blood."

"Miss Dance," I say, "thank you so much for letting me come. I — it's thrilling for me to know you now."

Suddenly she stops her gaze at me and calls out, "Lettie, bring us the tea, hear?" I am shocked, because I was unaware that anyone else was in the house.

A voice from the kitchen begins its sing-song answer before the body carrying the tray made its way out the door. "Ah know all 'bout it, Missy Daaaynce. Why you gwon tell me when you know Ah know all 'bout it evey time — evey time you gwon tell me 'gain. Tired of it Missy Daaaynce. Tired of it all." She is a young black woman, thin as a stick, and she serves us the tea; then walks back into the kitchen on her toes. She manages to time her speech so that the last word coincides with the last step back into the kitchen.

Miss Dance makes no explanation or apologies for Lettie, but goes on as if the tea had spontaneously appeared on the coffee table by itself. "This is going to make you tired," she says, pouring the tea into my cup. I notice that there are two pots. She serves herself a different brew. "It will help you to see things. Do you want to do this now?"

"I'm not sure. I didn't know that —"

"It's why you're here. Why you have come. Even though you aren't sure of anything. But who is?"

"I'm not sure I even know what you're talking about," I say.

"You must decide whether to trust me or not."

"Trust you?"

"Of course. I can't tell you nothing more than that. It's how my stuff works. What will happen? Well, how do I know? What will you learn about your father? Have no idea. None. But I do know you will learn much. It's why you came here to me.

"My stuff is the only thing I can trust. It's never failed me yet," she says.

"I saw your picture with my father when you both were young. Still in your teens," I say. "I guess I knew then — when I saw it — that I could trust you."

"Did they tell you about his horn?"

"Yes, they did."

"What they didn't tell you was that I knew it would hurt him. They thought he had already had the accident — meaning the one in the army, but I knew there was more. That was the only beginning of it all — when he fell off the horse. I didn't know what I was seeing then, the connection, I mean."

"I thought he had epilepsy. Is that how he died? Could he have had a seizure in the car?"

"Drink the tea," she says, and waits for me to do so. The house is strangely quiet. There is a clock ticking somewhere. Miss Dance puts a pink crystal in my hand.

"Do you want to close your eyes yet?" she asks.

"Not really, but I will if you think it will help." She gets up and puts a clean pillow under my head. I can still taste the minty flavor of the tea. I tell myself that I can open my eyes anytime I want. I am peaceful and hear the ticking, ticking . . .

"Can you see anything, now?"

"No," I say. "Well, I guess maybe, for some reason I still see the Mona Lisa that you have on the wall."

"What is she doing — that old Mona Lisa. What is she doing in your picture? The one you see in your own dream now."

"She isn't smiling — not anymore."

"Hmmmm."

"No. Now she is laughing, and I don't like her to laugh. I don't want to see her, then. She won't look at me anymore. She is looking away from me."

I am vaguely aware that Miss Dance's voice has become lower, smoother, and very soothing. "You don't have to see her if you don't want to. But you have to try harder and harder. Try to see something else. Is there something else in your own picture. The dream you have there now? What do you see there?"

The good feeling bobs away, like it is floating in the ocean, and I become anxious. "A car. Now there is a car there."

"Ahhh," she says. "Are you in the car?"

"No. It's him. It's my father in the car."

"What is he doing?"

"Nothing. He can't do anything."

"Why not?"

"He's dead."

"You can see him? You're sure?"

"Yes."

"It is surely him?"

"Yes. And I see something else. A big, big bug —
hovering, flying, waiting. Waiting over my father's head —
No! It's going to come and bite me."

"Where are you? Where are you watching him from?"
she asks.

"I'm home. I'm in my crib," I tell her, "and I can see
me — I am only a baby now; but I see my father. He gazes
down at me over the crib rail. Smiles, but . . . his face —
changes. The smile goes away . . . " I am sweating all
over.

"What do you see on his face? What is there?"

"I don't — it — fear . . . I see it — just the fear on his
face."

"What are you doing there in the crib?"

"Nothing." Now I start to cry. "I'm hurting. I hurt all
over. The pain bug comes. I can feel it even now."

"Why don't you tell someone?" says Miss Dance. "Call
someone and tell them that you hurt."

"I can't. He goes away. But leaves the fear with me."

"Where is your mother?"

"She is next to me, but her face is turned away. She
won't look at me. She sees the bug waiting."

"Call to her. Tell her what you need."

"I can't. I can't talk yet. I'm just a little baby."

"Why are you crying now?"

In the name of the Father and of the – I am sinking
down, not wanting to talk any more yet knowing I have to go
back up . . . help me . . . *bless me Father*, I have to talk I
think I am talking again . . . it hurts all over. "My legs, my
arms hurt up and down in the crib. No one knows it. I hear
them crying. All of them are crying because he's dead. They
think I don't know it, but I do. I know he's gone — even then
I know. But no one can hear me think it feel it before anyone
even tells them it happened. I already knew it the minute he

crashed before the cops came and told them. They're all crying. My mother and Granlena, Dora, Julie, and Babe . . . all of them, she wants to die too, mother does."

"Don't cry, Christina. Not to cry no more. The hurting will stop." Miss Dance's voice is soothing, sliding over me like honey. My sobs continue; then subside. "You are not a baby now. The baby is gone — all growed up — you! See you now. No more baby. Such a lady you are — not a baby.

"Go to the crib now and see the baby there. See her. Walk there now."

"Yes."

"Can you?"

"Yes."

"Do you see the baby there?"

"Yes."

"Touch her. Lean into the crib and touch the baby."

"Oh, no, I can't. I can't do that."

"Try. Try to touch the baby. That baby wants you to touch her." And Miss Dance leans over and touches my hand.

"No. I still can't do that."

"Try. I'm having the sense that you want to."

"Yes. But I'm so afraid. I think I should open my eyes."

"You can do that any time you want. But I think you'd like to touch that baby first."

"Yes."

"Do it. Touch that baby's foot. Touch her leg."

"Yes. I'm doing it. She is soft."

"Yes. Now it will be better for you. But see first — see if you can pick her up — just for a little while."

"Oh, no, I don't think I can do that."

"Now you can. Try. Try to pick up the baby."

"Someone is here. Someone is next to me."

"Someone you know?"

"Yes. My friend. He is there next to me. Daniel."

"Does he speak to you?"

"No."

"Help you?"

"No. He is just there. He just smiles at me." My eyes

are still shut tight. It takes a long time.

Then Miss Dance speaks again. "What are you going to do?" she asks.

"Now I am picking her up."

"Can you feel her?"

"Yes, and she has stopped hurting." And I am picking her up and hugging her, warm now, so wonderful.

I don't want to open my eyes yet. Miss Dance says nothing else. I am not sure even if she is still in the room with me, but it feels so good to sprawl into the cushions of the couch, that I just stay where I am, breathing easily, yet still a little shaky. Daniel is still in my thoughts. He watched me when I put the baby back into her crib. We walked away together from that place – that hazy place, wherever it was in my dreamy mind. Now he seems to be gone from my vision. Why was he there at all? What happened to me? I hear a rustling of sorts, then I am aware that someone is standing next to me. I open my eyes a little at a time. Lettie is there with a tray. Miss Dance is gone, and so is the crystal she had placed in my hand.

"You're spose to drink this," Lettie says, handing me what looks like a cup of water. "Gotta drink the water. Gots pepper in there. Missy says it's spose to ground you."

"How do you feel," says Miss Dance, suddenly appearing in the doorway from a back room and waving Lettie away. "You've been asleep for over an hour."

"Oh, no. Are you sure?" I say, trying to get up.

"Stay, my dear," she says, coming toward me and placing her hand on my shoulder.

"I had no idea I fell asleep – it just felt like I –"

"You've had quite a spell of it. You and Carter must have been connected like the crook of a tree."

"I'm afraid maybe we still are."

"Probably not as much as you think – at least not anywhere near as much as you were before. You'll see."

"The pains that I felt. What do you know about them?"

"Did you recognize them?"

"The thing is, I never knew that's where they came

from. Yes, I've felt them many times. But they always came — they only happen when – my God."

"Keep going, my dear."

"They happened when I wanted to leave my husband. I kind of left him once, but not really. I was able to only when I told myself it was only temporary, and I made sure we still saw each other often. When he gave me an ultimatum and said I had to move back or we wouldn't see each other again, I did. I couldn't bear it – the pain again."

"What about your mother in the dream? Why do you suppose she wouldn't look at you? Weren't you close to her?"

"Maybe she felt guilty."

"Strange."

"She gave it to me. I was feeling what she was feeling – lots of her pain, and she couldn't help me."

"What does that mean?" Miss Dance asks.

"I don't know, but I don't like it. And I don't like that my father was dead the whole time I was in the trance or whatever it was – I mean, why couldn't he have been awake, so maybe he could have told me something."

"Could be that you already know it."

"What do you mean?"

"Well, you keep wanting to know more and more about him. I think you've learned all there is to know. Maybe now all there is left to learn is what you don't know about yourself. Unless that's the part you don't want to know."

"Well, can't you tell me more? How come you don't know more of what went on the night he died?"

"Who says I don't? I can tell you more. But it's Bessie you want to talk to. Bessie and your mama and your aunts — everybody. Go see them. Talk and talk, and you'll figure it all out yourself – better that way."

"Bessie. She knows more than she pretends to. I only met her once, but I could tell she was full of secrets even so."

"Lordy," says Miss Dance, "I'd never want to meet up with her again. She was like catching something stuck under your fingernail. Couldn't take to her at all."

"Yes, but she may know what I need."

*   *   *

Greta stands in the front doorway as I get out of my car, and I feel as tired as a rag as I walk up to greet her. I expect her to be bursting with questions about my visit to Miss Dance. Instead she greets me with a small velvet box in her hands. "Look what I have for you," she says, handing me the box. I open the plushy top to find a pair of men's gold cuff links inside. "These belonged to your father," she says, ushering me inside to the living room couch, "and I've decided to give them to you."

"Oh, Greta, what a wonderful thing to do. Thank you so much, but –"

"But nothing, I want you to have them, that's all." I turn them over in my hand, loving to touch something that once touched him. But she doesn't notice me. "That's not all," she says and a heavy sigh escapes from her.

"Where did you get the cuff links?" I ask, then aware of her deep distress.

She sighs again, starts to form her words and stops. "Your mother gave them to me at his funeral."

"Why would she do that?" A knot forms in my throat. "Why would she give them to you? It makes no sense. Why didn't she save them to give to me? Oh, I can't stand this. I really am furious with my family. It seems so unfair." I get up and go to the window. By now it is dark outside and the street lamps make silver rings in the rain that has just begun. "At the funeral. She gave you these at the funeral? Why ever for?"

"Maybe you should tell me about Miss Dance."

"I'm sorry. It's just that so much seems to be happening – so fast."

"Tell me," Greta says.

"She said I will find out more about the night he died when I talk to Bessie, as well as my mother's side of the family. Even when I told her Dora was dead, she seemed to think there was still something to be discovered if I went to her house. I don't know what to do first."

"My dear Christina, I don't know how to say this to you, because I never told anyone before. But when I went to the funeral, Gordon and I stayed several days. And when I was up there in New York, during those days, during all that time of his death, there was something in the air. Something I picked up, but didn't want to hear, I guess. Your Aunt Dora, she – it was so obvious to me that she loved him. I mean, everyone was grieving, but hers – I don't know how to say it. Hers was different. She was wiped out. She wailed and wailed and carried on so."

"Well, it doesn't surprise me," I say. "Considering the way she talked about him."

"The second night of the wake, Gordon and I went back to the house early, because I was so tired. Everyone was at the funeral parlor that night, except Dora. She was conspicuously missing, but everyone was relieved at the same time. We went in the front door, and we could hear her in her bedroom. She made so much noise with her crying that she never heard us come in – I'm sure she thought she was alone, and we didn't know what to do – didn't know if we should call to her or not, because we knew we were eaves-dropping. 'A watch?' she kept saying over and over. 'Why is everything for her? Why couldn't you buy me a watch? Why can't it be for me?' And her wailing and carrying on went on forever. Gordon and I decided to go out for coffee, and come back later. She never knew we heard her. And we never told anyone else what we heard."

"Well what did it mean? What about the watch?"

"Seems he had bought a watch for your mother for Christmas. That much they knew, because he had stopped to pick it up on the way home from work. He had told someone in the office that he was going to bring it home with him that night. The police checked and sure enough, he had gone to the jewelers."

"Why didn't my mother ever tell me about it?"

"Why didn't they tell you any of the things they should have – to protect you, I guess."

"I mean how come she never showed it to me – it's something I would have liked to have, like the cufflinks"

"It's gone, Christina. When they found him in the car, there was no watch. She never got it."

"How did – someone took it? Oh, my God!"

"That's part of the mystery. There were other things missing too. His wallet and a beautiful car blanket that your mother had given him for his birthday."

"Maybe someone caused his death – actually did it?" I am numb. "And since Dora is dead, she can't tell us anything."

"Are you tired, dear?" Aunt Greta asks after a long silence.

"Yes, it's time for me to sleep," I finally answer her. "And when I wake up, I guess it will be time for me to go home, dear, dear Aunt Greta." I reach out my hand to her, and she holds mine in hers. I look at her and hope she knows how grateful I am. "I haven't been able to write the end of the book. It has haunted me for – well, I guess somehow it has haunted me all my life. But now – well, maybe now I can – after one more go round."

"Well, my stars, this has been something terribly important for you, now hasn't it? I do hate to see you go. You sure have been a great comfort to me with Gordon sick and all, but I guess it's time."

"There is one other thing she told me – Miss Dance, I mean. I'm still trying to puzzle it out. Something about staying connected to something spiritual, no matter what. 'Get rid of everything in your life that keeps you from seeing into yourself,' she said, 'even if it means leaving someone behind.' Can you imagine? She doesn't even know me. Doesn't even know about my terrible marriage to Charles."

"It holds you back?" Greta asks.

"Oh, yes," I say, "in so many ways."

"Well, bless your heart. I wish I could help you, but I guess no one can," she says.

"No one but me."

"I'm sure you're right. Perhaps you need to sleep on this. Let's go to bed, now, shall we?" Greta says.

"I'll probably wake up very early if I sleep now. I think I'd like to leave then, even if it's in the wee hours. I won't disturb you. You'll need your sleep."

"That will be just fine. Goodnight, my darling girl. And may you have a safe, safe journey. Rest now," Greta says in the softest voice I ever heard.

Twenty

℘

I have waited until I am certain that Granlena is out visiting my mother, and now that the coast is clear, I enter hers and Dora's apartment with the keys I took when Dora died. I fully expect to see Dora's twisted body still on the living room floor, her watchful eye following me. I walk around the spot where she had lain – where I had spoken to her – told her all my hidden things. I cross to the window. The air smells of dust, of death. Her things are still intact as she left them, Granlena cannot bear to change anything. I throw open the window and snap off two fingernails as my fingers slip off the bottom of the sash. I am afraid to look back into the room, but I make myself whirl around to face her, and, there, see only an empty space.

"Are you here?" I say and hear my own echo. I take a step, my sore finger tips now in my mouth, determined not to walk around the spot this time. "So you loved him, did you? So did I. We have that in common – both of us spent most of our lives longing for him. Well, I'm tired of it, you hear? I'm sick of it as a matter of fact. I'd like to go on without him, if you please." I walk back in big steps thumping across the living room and tramp on the spot where she had lain dead. For a moment, I think her hand may reach up out of the carpet and grab my ankle, so I quicken my steps to the other side of the room – safe like in hopscotch, in the neutral zone – then I sit in the big wing chair by the doorway that leads to her bedroom. "Go away," I say. "Go away and leave me once and for all, and let go of him too. I can do it, can you?" Then I remember Miss Dance and wonder if this is what she meant when she said I would "feel" something here in Dora's house.

I guess I should go through her things – her clothes and everything, and maybe find some kind of clue. This is absurd. What do you think you're going to find here? Your mother's watch that she never received for Christmas forty-odd years ago? You are being ridiculous. How are you going to feel when you go through all her belongings, and you don't find it?

How are you going to feel if you do?

Shall I look in her dresser drawers? I realize that I am afraid to do this. Might there be scraps of her in them? Might there be scraps of me there too? I stand paralyzed in air that won't move.

I pull open a drawer – the top one on the left with the little metal ring that clanks down when you let go of it. Her handkerchiefs, all ironed in a row are next to neck scarves, gloves. I can't do this. Melissa will do it. I'm sure she will.

No. I can't drag her into this. Come on, just look in once more. Oh, hell. Open them all. One by one. None of them messy. Fabric in the bottom one. Knits and silks that she probably intended to turn into dresses for Melissa, blouses for me. Melissa never liked her to sew for her, because she always thought her dresses were too short or too revealing, and never made them the way she wanted. Look at this wild thing on the bottom of everything. Who would wear it? Some kind of leopard print, sheer and silky and obviously very old. And folded inside it, an ancient paper dress pattern with a picture on the envelope of a sexy looking young girl in a tight fitting dress with hairdo and platform shoes circa 1940. Was Dora intending to make this for herself? Would she have worn it for my father?

One by one, I go through the rest of her drawers, then into the book shelves, the corners, behind and under furniture, even between the mattress and box spring. There is nothing here of any consequence, except the photographs, which I'd decided to leave here the night she died, but they reveal nothing new – nothing that I have not seen or felt before.

"You're not the one, are you?" I speak to Dora again. "You weren't there when he died. I thought you knew something when Greta told me what she heard you say about the watch. But . . ." I stop because there are some pages torn out of a diary and stuck inside the back cover of the photo album.

"January, 1941. I went to see her, and she had it. I know it – even though she wouldn't let me in. It was written all over her face. I called her a bitch and said I knew she had the watch, because Cousin Vince saw her at the railroad that night. What would she be doing in New York when she lives in Virginia? Someday I hope they find the watch on her. May she rot in hell." I close the book.

"It's not you, Dora. It never was. Good-bye, my dear. I hope you work out your karma."

And I close the door softly behind me.

I ride next to Melissa on the plane to Bessie's and remember that the last time I was on a plane, I shared the seat with Daniel. How I ache for him!

"When are you going to leave Daddy?" Melissa startles me.

"Oh, please," I say. "I don't want to talk about him."

"Why not? Maybe I can help you to reach a decision. Talk about fence-sitting," she says with a slight curl to her lip.

"You don't have to speak with such contempt," I say gritting my teeth.

"It's not contempt. It's irony. You should have left him when I was little. I couldn't ask you to then. Now that it can't do me any good – I don't have to live with him – I'm telling you to for your own good."

"Why can't you forgive me?"

"Why can't you live with my unforgiveness? In the meantime I'm working on it. At least you have my love."

"You don't get it," I say to her, "not even a little bit. Just remember what I said to you that day in Bloomingdale's. Because I didn't protect you – it makes any accomplishment I may have had seem insignificant. It's as if – you get one shot at the most important job in the world – being a parent, I mean – and if you blow it – nothing else really matters."

"But it does," Melissa says.

"The other mothers I know aren't guilt-ridden like me. They don't have to live with the gnawing grief that they didn't protect their children."

"But I bet they can't write books."

"What has that got to do with it?"

"Just because you made a mistake, doesn't mean the rest of you isn't worth anything," she says. "Start over. Leave him. Get a boyfriend – someone who can appreciate you, and then finish your book."

We look at each other for a while. "Do you think that might do it?" I ask.

"Worth a try. Isn't that why we're on this plane anyway? Aren't we supposed to find out whatever you need to know to write the last chapter?"

"Yes, my little chick," I say, feeling lighter. "You are going to keep old Bessie busy, while I snoop."

"Bessie busy? Keep old busybody Bessie busy? It means I'm going to have to look at her scar, doesn't it?"

"Nah – that'll never –"

"Come on, don't give me that. You know it – come on."

"Look at it?" We are both having such a good laugh. "I think you're going to have to tell her you want to photograph it for *Life* magazine. I'll pretend I'm going to the bathroom, and disappear while you admire all Bessie's ailments. 'Stall' is the key word."

"Goody. Stalling over Bessie. The Bessie Show and Tell Show! I'll probably remember this all my life." Melissa is holding her stomach. "Have you forgotten that I can't stand talking about disgusting things. It completely grosses me out."

"I hope you don't have to touch her scars. Be thankful for small favors."

"'Scuse me. I'm going to throw up."

A health care worker greets us at the door of Bessie's

house. Bessie, at seventy eight, has recently had a hip replacement following a bad fall. We enter the musty smelling house, and Bessie doesn't even say hello.

"Look at me walk with this silly contraption," she says referring to her walker. She looks frail and pinched sitting in an arm chair piled high with cushions. "Give it here," she directs Joe, the health care worker.

"All right," he says, "but it's getting to be time for me to go."

"That's okay," Melissa says. "We'll help her; you can leave now."

"When will Hans be back?" I ask.

"Oh, soon, soon," says Bessie, heaving herself up out of her chair and gripping the arms of the walker. She is wearing a Kmart Special house coat. Her stockings are rolled down around her ankles above her orthopedic shoes. "He knows he has to be back when Joe leaves, isn't that right, Joe?"

"Not to worry," Melissa says with a Cheshire smile. "I'm right here!" She stands next to Bessie who inches along with her walker. Melissa smiles even harder. "Bet you never thought you'd get to see me, your great-granddaughter," she goes on, trying to charm old Bessie.

Joe takes his cue and is out the door. Melissa winks at me. "You're doing just great," she tells Bessie. They are walking around and around the living room.

"I have to use the bathroom," I say and disappear to the back of the house, making a detour into Bessie's bedroom.

Bessie is delighted to have Melissa's attention. "Well, you are a sweet child, I declare," I hear her tell Melissa. They continue their baby step stroll while I proceed to snoop in her dresser drawers. "But my feet stink all the time now. You didn't bring me any powder, did you? I need powder for my feet."

"I'll send you some as soon as I get home," Melissa says. "I promise. How about deodorant powder?"

Now that she has a captive audience, Bessie pulls out all the stops. "Ever since I fell, I can't stop my feet from stinking. How about my scar? I'll have to show you this new one from my hip. Sit me down now so I can show you. Look at my gallbladder one. See, it's old. The new one is nice and fresh — still all puffy. Do you smell my feet? I was so constipated with all this gas, you know? So Hans boiled me up my prunes and then in the middle of the night — whew! I couldn't even make it to the bowl. Now I guess you know what I mean? But the worst thing of all was the doctor in the hospital. Not my doctor. The hospital doctor. Told me he had to examine me, and, boy! Did he ever. Whew! My stars. Stuck his finger right into my rear end. First time that ever happened to me. My doctor'd never do that, I declare. 'Least he used a glove. Lordy, lordy. Don't want any of his germs goin' up there. You can bring me my prune juice. Get it in the Frigidaire."

"Sure thing," I hear Melissa say and can picture her bolting for the kitchen so she can retch. But Bessie goes right on even though no one is in the room with her, as I keep digging, digging in the bedroom drawers.

"You have to know just how much prune juice to drink, I declare, to keep the pipes up to the right speed. I can't keep missing the bowl, now can I? Still it's no good if I'm all packed up inside like a pound of bricks . . ."

Our visit is a huge success. Bessie really comes through, although she has no idea what we are up to. But between Melissa's diversionary tactics and my snooping, I now have everything I need — all the missing pieces — so I can finally write Carter's story all the way through to the end.

And Melissa, I owe you one — big time.

And now I face my typewriter, finally with all the information I need about my father to conclude my book, but I still can feel my resistance overpowering me. I stall and stall some more.

If I finish it, might he disappear for good?

I sit staring into space. There is nothing there. A blank looking-glass for me to write on. I would rather fall into it and disappear.

I press the first key. Wonder of wonders, I am still alive! Then I plod along, one key at a time. Each time I finish a sentence, I wait for the thunder bolt. And when it doesn't come, that gives me strength.

And then I cannot bear this monster tearing pieces off my soul any longer. This is it. I face the dragon and fall over the edge, where I howl and sob all the way through to the end of the book.

It is done.

Chapter 19

*Carter left me some of his pessimism. No one knows
that but me, because no one knew he had it. Not even Emelia,
my mother. He kept it from her — from everyone; played it
close to the vest as his mother had taught him. "You must
always be ready for a lady — to present yourself as her
protector . . . Don't show your hurts ever to a lady. Now,
how can you be strong?" Her lesson had taken well on him.
In trying to please her, he had buried pieces of himself so
deeply, that even he could not find them. Her standards were
impossible. What a shame that he had to try to meet them all
his life in one way or another.*

*It was a few days before Christmas on a rainy night in
1940 that it happened. The story was told to me many times
over, depending on whom I'd asked, but I was only given the
bare facts — never any details.*
But now I have them. They're mine forever.

He had left the Riverdale office later
than usual, about six-thirty, and driven to
the jewelry store to pick up the watch. He
did not notice the cab that followed his car
and stopped half a block away, after he had
parked in front of the store, because he was
in a hurry to get the watch and get home. He
did not notice the small woman trying to
reach past her huge breasts to pay the cabby.
     The watch was a beauty. It had a
rectangular face set in gleaming marcasites
that made a kind of filigree pattern around
it and then branched off to join with a
silver watch band.
     "A beauty," Carter said. He put it up to
his ear.

Tic, tic, tic, tic, tic, tic . . .

Outside, the woman climbed into the back seat of Carter's car.

The jeweler was bald with heavy jowls and a bulbous nose. His left eye had permanent creases all around it from constantly looking into the loupe to do his work. His face looked like crumpled paper.

"Did I tell you?" he said to Carter. "Listen to Moishy. Moishy knows. I should never give ya bum steer. Never ever. Ya like th'engraving?"

Tic, tic, tic . . .

"Moishy, you've outdone yourself." He touched the tiny heart on the back of the watch. "Carter & Emelia" was written inside it in the tiniest of letters.

"So's this for a girlfriend or a wife?"

"Both," Carter said. He lit a cigarette. He wanted to get going.

"Ha! Ya want another one maybe?"

"No, I mean she's my wife, but she's like a girlfriend too."

"Ya got that mixed up? Listen to Moishy: Ya needja head examined. Here's the watch. Take. Take it."

"Listen, Moishy, can you wrap it? I don't want anyone peeking before Christmas."

"Peek? She would peek? I'd kill her if she did that." Carter drummed his fingers on the glass counter.

Tic, tic, tic, tic, tic, tic, tic . . .

"Sadie, get in here, wrap the watch."

The woman outside in the car scrunched herself down behind the seat. She covered herself with the car robe that Emelia had given Carter for his birthday.

"What?" said a voice from behind a curtain that led to the back of the store.

"Wrap, Wrap! You heard me say 'wrap'."

"I never heard you." His wife came out, a thin bird of a woman.

Moishy waved the watch in her face. "Don't tell me you never heard me. Y'always heard me. I'm telling you, wrap this watch . . . for the gentleman."

"Listen that's okay, Moishy, forget it. I can wrap it myself."

"You think I can't wrap it for you? Sadie, get it here. The man is in a hurry. Ya don't hear?" She began to wrap it. Moishy winked at Carter. "He has to get home to his girlfriend. Heh heh. Know what I mean? Heh heh." Carter counted the bills on the counter.

"You wanna ribbon?" said Sadie, leaving the wrapped present on the counter.

"Of course he wants a ribbon. Ya stupid. Get him a ribbon for Pete's sake." Tic,tic,tic . . .

"No that's okay," Carter said. He picked up the gift, tipped his hat and hurried out of the store.

"Merry Christmas," he said over his shoulder. Tic,tic,tic,tic . . .

"Ya see? Ya see what ya did?" Moishy shouted again at poor Sadie.

Outside it had started to rain. Wish it were snow, he thought, smelling the wetness and trying to dispel its gloom as he got into the car. The woman in the back seat did not move. He thought of Christmas angels, of his new baby girl. She's really too young to understand it. But he would still buy her something nice. A doll maybe. A doll named Claudia. He had already bought her that. Emelia sat it on the windowsill — a big baby doll with fat wooden legs that clapped together when you carried her. Christina was too little to play with her, but he liked to think that Claudia watched over his baby — that she was waiting for Christina to grow up. What would she be like when she grew up? he thought. Will she be like me?

He put the watch on the seat next to him. The windshield wiper scraped a steady rhythm. The rain made the hood ornament gleam and become distorted in its reflection on the hood. He thought it looked like a lizard. Or maybe a dragon. The beads of rain made serpent's scales. He turned the car onto Mosholu Parkway. No, it was more like a lizard after all. The lizard made him think of Juana, and he wondered where she was. Would he see her when he died? Would she remember him?

The car lurched over a hole in the road. He reached to steady the watch. If you held it to your ear now, could you hear it through the paper? Through the box? Tic,tic,tic,tic tic,tic,tic . . . He heard it in his head. He opened the window a little. Was that a train whistle? Was that Mile Away calling him? The cars swished past on the opposite side of the road. I wonder if they're going home — all those people driving in their cars, he thought. I wonder if they've bought watches for their wives, if they have baby daughters living here, and five year old sons named after them living far away.

Do they wonder if they'll ever get to where it is they think they're going? Can you ever reach the horizon? Tic,tic,tic,tic,tic tic,tic,tic . . .

The parkway became curvy without warning. He knew it well; he had traveled it a hundred times. But he also knew he should slow down. The steering felt a little loose. He would have it checked next time. It was hard to slow down. He saw the elevated subway off to the south. A train rattled along it. Mile Away! Is that you? Tic,tic,tic,tic . . . He remembered how he used to race his buggy on the farm, giddyapping to his father's horse; then on Mile Away's trains, then on his own horse in the army, now with his car with all its horsepower.

The woman sat up in the back seat, peeking from her hiding place. She sensed he was going much too fast. He had opened the window all the way. Don't let time get you, he thought. Make noise. Prove yourself. Chase away the ghosts. How many more dragons can there be?

"Stop!" she shrieked. "Slow down." Her voice thunderclappped him into a panic, and the recognition flashed before him!

"Bitch! You screaming, fucking bitch!" A car came toward him over the line.

Bessie tried to grab the wheel. "You are going to kill us — you stupid thing. Come to your senses, I saaaay!" Then he threw her back into the seat in his fury and at the same time swerved to the right to avoid the oncoming car. But there was also a car on his right. The horn blared. Bessie bounced off the seat and hit the door which flew open, and she was thrown out onto the shoulder.

For Carter it was a series of poor judgments. He pulled back to the left, but too far. There was a skid, a spin, a side-swipe of another oncoming car. He careened forward — then off to the right. Off the road. The steering wheel rattled. He went into another skid, facing the wrong way just as the left side of his car hit a lone pine tree. And it fell, smashing against the roof of the car, crushing the metal into his head, fracturing his skull. Buckets of . . . buckets of . . . blood . . . his ribs crushed against the horn and its blaring dirge wailed out into the night. And Death covered him up, filling his warmth with leaden cold.

He felt the jolt, the pain for only a second. Then his brain exploded with a thousand lights, and then the lines came back. The lines that had always been in all his dreams. Running, ticking along, meeting, crisscrossing into a web, then bursting in all directions. Finally a path, a road, tracks . . . And he saw the Horsemen bounding forward, pounding next to one another — big heavy heaving horses, with riders having no eyes; one of them looked like Lance — and then Carter fell through all the lines, breaking them into darkness.

The rain had turned to pelting ice. It came through the window and melted when it hit his blood.

Bessie dragged herself back to the car. She cried and kept checking herself for broken bones, but everything seemed to work. Somehow, that disappointed her.

"Do you see what you've done to us? You wicked, wicked man!" She picked up her purse and the wrapped present off the floor in the front. She tried to look at him, but squinted her eyes so she couldn't see the blood — so it would just be a blur.

"Why won't you answer me? Are you all right, dear Carter? I am so sorry. I certainly hope you are fine. I know sooner or later you'll come to your senses." She looked around, becoming uneasy as she realized her predicament. "It hurts to leave you. I don't want to leave you here, but I certainly don't want anyone to think — I mean — I would never hurt you — you know that, don't you? Everybody knows I'm still mad for you. I don't really think you're wicked. I was just fibbin' that." She fingered the box, narrow as a ribbon and wrapped in jeweler's paper, and as she spoke, she put it in her purse.

"Carter? Do you hear? Do you hear me? I have to go." Then she took his wallet and the car robe and left the car.

She scraped her feet so as not to slip on the fast-icing pavement as she minced her steps along the side of the road, heading for the intersection ahead of her. The sleet grew more intense stinging her face and making it hard to see; yet still she could hear its staccato sounds on the roof of the crumbled car she left behind. She'd get a cab. Take it to the station. No one knew she was here. No one would ever have to know.

Twenty-one

By the time she called the police, it was far too late. Might she have saved him if she had gotten help right away? Goddamn you, Bessie! I scream your name to infinity.

I look at my watch in the spirit-ridden light of early morning. It is four-fifteen. The windows reflect my image like so many mirrors, since there is no light outside, only in here from my desk lamp. My husband is upstairs sleeping. The shadows are deep set. I feel the hush of silence — of being the only one awake here in this house — maybe in the world. I can hear my own breathing and look past my typewriter, past the stucco walls of my studio and gaze finally at my father's story without falling apart.

Yes. Finally.

Can I leave now? Walk out of the pages and close the book? Wait a minute, whose book am I talking about — his or mine?

Perhaps somehow, he stands here in my studio room, looking in wonder at the manuscript, smiling at me at my desk — proud of what I have done, but most of all, glad that we can both move on. I look up at the window and feel a catch as I see his reflection next to mine. It lasts for a second, maybe two. He has on the same khaki shirt, his dark red hair curling in all directions. He smiles, but then is gone. It's okay, because something just occurred to me for the first time.

What if he's tired of all this? What if he too feels terribly bogged down with the far-reaching connection we have? Perhaps we were lovers in a former life. Gypsies. Russian peasants leading wild, wild lives with consummate abandon, imprisoning each other with lust and obsession.

Always I have wanted to see your face — just once, just one more time. I wanted to tell you what you mean to me, wanted to read in that face all my missing pieces, all my directions of what to do, wanted to find there in your eyes the secret to my perfect fantasy of a life. Now that I have written your story, perhaps I really have looked into your face — only to discover, after all, that the answers aren't there.

I no longer need to need you — as if a curtain were lifted just now when I wrote that last sentence and edited the whole thing through for the last time. Bless me, bless me, Father — I release you.

I close the door to my studio, go up to the bedroom, and pretend to sleep, waiting for Charles to get up and leave for work. I am not going to work today. I lie on my side, facing the east window and watch the pink fingers of dawn creep across the sky, heralding the light of a brilliant new day. How beautiful, I think, overcome with tears. I am airy-light and floating on butterfly wings. I close my eyes and see my pain fly out like a big, hovering June bug. It hangs in the air, and I am free.

Then I hear Charles' alarm. "Taking a shower?" he yawns.

"No. I'm not going in."

"Tough job," he says.

I doze off and awaken when I hear his car pull out of the driveway. I am fully awake and dash downstairs to pack: The small stuff first — framed photographs and bric-a-brac — and decide that I do not need to look every day at all those pictures of you, my father, images of your childhood, of your army days, your wedding. They don't have to be out on my dresser. If I put them in an album, it will do just fine. Then I will paste in all the pictures of my life, and turn the page.

The only photo I will leave out for display is Melissa's. I will look at her face again and again. Read there all my hopes for the future. She will be my life going on and on.

I run to the phone and call the real estate agent, only to discover that I cannot get my old apartment back. It's been rented to someone else. I wonder if the new tenant found any of the old dreams I left there when I moved back in with Charles. Guess it doesn't matter. I'll make some new ones. Better ones. I finish packing all my things. The boxes will have to sit in the dining room of the house and wait, while I go apartment hunting after school each day.

Charles is livid when he comes home from work. "What's that supposed to be?" he says, pointing into the dining room.

"I guess I should have warned you," I say, "but there really wasn't much time," realizing that I have forgotten to pack the nesting Russian dolls Melissa gave me when I was in my apartment. I pick them up from the table in the hallway, and we both stand there — I, with my dolls in my hand, Charles, with his hat on, holding his briefcase.

"Quickie decision?" he asks with a smirk.

"No, that's not what I meant. I made this decision years ago, Charles. I just couldn't do anything about it then. You used to say — whenever we had a fight — you used to say that if I couldn't see things your way, you thought we should go our separate ways. Well, now I think you were right. I always became very frightened and gave in to you when you said those things, because I was so afraid that I couldn't exist without you. But it is time to go our separate ways."

"So now you're not afraid anymore? Is that it?" he asks, the brim of his hat trembling.

"It isn't just that, I'm still afraid, but it's different," I answer.

"Then I think I have a right to know why you are doing this."

"I have to leave you, because we are so utterly alone."

"You are so full of shit, Christina," he says. "Why are you doing this? I want an answer that makes sense."

"I'm not trying to be cute, I truly mean what I'm saying."

"Oh, don't give me that shit. 'I have to be perfectly honest.' More damage has been done under the guise of honesty than any other foolhardy emotion." He drops his briefcase with a loud bang and comes closer and closer, pointing his finger. "You'd better have a good story ready or —"

"Or what?"

He says nothing, just fumes and breathes so heavily, I think I will see smoke. I am afraid he might blow up like Dora. I take the dolls apart, twisting them in my hand, looking at them, not at Charles. "The other reason," I say, "is that you beat my daughter. There," I say looking up at him and trying not to tremble. "I finally said it out loud."

"Oh, aren't you wonderful — you finally said it! What does that make you some kind of hero or something? You're going to leave now for something that happened years ago? You're sickening; do you know that?"

"Look, I never stood up to you for her. I never let her know she mattered enough for me to stand up to you. But better late than never — now I am!"

"Biiiiig hero, aren't you. Do you think you're a hero now? Huh, huh?"

He grabs me by the shoulders and starts to shake me. "Damn you to hell." The shaking makes his hat fall off, and this gives me the chance to twist out of his grip, dropping the dolls on the floor. I am able to run for the door, because he trips over the dolls. That, plus the possibility of his hat getting dirty, sends him into a frenzy. Now I can no longer stay under the same roof with him ever again. I can hear the cursing outside even after I slam the front door.

Now it's official. Charles and I both have lawyers. He'll stay in the house until it's sold, and then we'll split everything, clean and simple. Do you want the corner table in the hallway? I'll take the Tiffany lamp. No hassles. My lawyer handles all of this for me as the days lengthen into spring.

I stay with friends. I go to my classroom each day and greet my students. Some of them — the really clever ones — lift my spirits. The others — the ones with no lights on when you look in their eyes — wear me down. I was never much good at remediating.

I pick up the first paper, written by a student named Dimsdale McTeek. Dimsdale has trouble with English even though it is the only language he has ever known. However he has just won a scholarship to college, because he happens to be 230 pounds and captain of the football team. "Ralph Ellison wroat *Invisible Man* in 1952," he writes. Interesting spelling. "Who is the invissibal man where do he com from. what does he whant? Dont he realy know where I live right know?"

Why doesn't the intercom ring? Why doesn't that gloating secretary with the blue eyelids call and tell me Daniel is here? I need him to come and save me from all this lunacy. "How does he field about being invissibal. What it like been invisabal. I bet he still put on one foot of pants like everbody else"

The bell finally rings, and class is over. Students slide their feet out the door and burst out of the classrooms as people do when subway doors open.

It is over for a while. I have two periods free.

I go to the cafeteria for three dollars worth of quarters and then find the only pay phone in the building whose earphone is not smeared with mayonnaise and that has a reasonable amount of privacy. I stare at the Galveston number and rehearse several opening lines.

"Fuck it, Christina. Take a chance for once in your life," I say and dial with no idea of what I will say to him. "Daniel Wexler, please," I tell the receptionist.

"Who?" she says.

"Daniel Wexler. He's with Video Cats." She puts me on hold.

He has to be there.

"He's there; I know he is," I say to no one in particular. She connects me with three other people, before I learn that the job he was working on there was over several months ago. I get more quarters and then call his central office in California. I feel like I'm playing the slot machines. Wexler's in New York, they tell me. He's been here for at least a month. They give me the number.

He's been here that long and never called me? Do I

dare?

I go back to my house during the day when Charles isn't home. On my way there, I stop in Bloomingdale's and buy a bottle of Oscar de la Renta creme perfume. I had worn it with Daniel when we went to St. Croix. He loved it. Said it really turned him on. I left the bottle there in the confusion of getting Dora out of the country. The perfume is creamy and translucent. It reminds me of him. I will put it all over my neck and breasts, the way he did in St. Croix

I stand in my dining room for the last time. I look at the room, the fireplace, with its heavy mantel. We have a clock on it — not nearly as interesting as Carter's, but good nevertheless. Unfortunately, I agreed to let Charles keep it. There is a bronze figure of Mercury getting ready to run, next to the dial. I take off my wedding ring, the one with "More than words, Charles" engraved inside it and place it on Mercury's head like a crown. Then I pat my hand on the mantel and think of Emma Rose's hand doing the same thing on her mantel eons ago.

The next day is moving day and I finally do it — another apartment, even nicer than the last one, but I wonder if I will ever feel like I belong in whichever domicile I happen to find myself. Will I ever feel that the home I'm living in is a place I'm going to stay and put down roots? How I need to have that feeling about a place! I remember when we moved into our house some twenty years ago. How I catalogued all my dreams into it, and how they eroded one by one until the house meant nothing. It had become a place for me to tiptoe in — a temporary stop-over to hide myself.

Now, wonder of wonders, I am beginning to realize that the home I seek must be in my heart — I think I have finally started to learn this. Perhaps this is why I have felt homeless for so long. I had always looked in the wrong place.

This time I pay the movers to unpack, and on the first night in the new place, I go out to pick up the Chinese food I ordered, and return to discover that the overhead light in the foyer has burned out. I leave the front door open, so I can see by the outside hallway light to find the light next to the couch. After fumbling for the switch, I see that there is no bulb in it. The movers must have removed it for safety. A noise behind me makes me turn quickly to the open door leading to the outside hall. There is no one there. Stupid of me to have left it wide open; now I am spooked. Anyone could have walked in behind me. I quickly run to the bedroom, turn on the light and return to close the outside door, when the ringing of the phone makes me jump. It can't be him. There is no way he could get my number this fast. Could he? No one is there. It must be the phone company testing the line. Is someone here? In the room? Who is the invisible man? Does he know where I live?

Daniel! I can't stand this anymore. Please come back. I know what I told you when we parted, but that's all changed now.

Stop it, Christina. Get hold of yourself.

It is I who have become invisible. I used to look at Charles to see if I could see my reflection — I wanted him to be my mirror — but his face was empty of me. Did my father's early death let me taste my own invisibility — imprint me with the need to constantly seek my reflection in another man's eyes? Shall I look behind to see if my feet make footprints in the sand? Oh hateful curse! Take it from me. I would rather die than have to check someone's eyes for proof that I exist.

The foreign sound of the doorbell makes me jump again. The peephole reveals my mother's face, and it stays in my mind's eye in that tiny frame as I let her in. The wonderful Emelia — here in the flesh. I notice she is looking older, although I love her silvery hair.

"For you," she says, handing me a small bouquet of daisies. I stare at her. She is wearing her old plaid winter coat although it is quite warm outside. "Do you want me to come in?" Her tone is mellow, accepting — that of the wise woman stirring her cauldron, waiting for her child to grow up.

"Of course," I say, and she does. I put the daisies in a bottle of water, and we sit on the couch.

"The daisies are only a part of your gift. I have something else for you," she says. "It will be here soon. Melissa's picking it up for me."

"Why should you bring me gifts at all?" I ask.

"I guess I've finally understood what happened to you, and why you did what you did. Celebration is in order, I think."

"You mean my being here — the apartment?"

"The apartment, yes, the divorce, and, of course, the book," she says. "The only thing I'm not sure about is how everything seemed to happen at the same time. What else do you have up your sleeve?"

"I didn't think you'd be happy for me. I thought — well, I'm glad you are."

"But you're not answering me," she says.

"I don't know — nothing happens in a vacuum, I guess. Perhaps I spent the first forty-five years of my life running away from my fate, and now —"

"Which is?"

"What do you think?" I say, pulling a daisy out of the bottle. "Something to do with men, I'm sure. Picking ones who'll leave me in one way or another. Maybe when I was born, some oracle or other decreed that I was so marked."

She takes a daisy too and begins to pull off the petals. "Is that my fate also, do you think?" she asks, not looking at me.

"Could be, you know," I say. "First your father leaves to be sick forever. Then your husband dies in a blink. What do we do now?"

She turns and looks at me with great tenderness. "All these changes in your life," she says, "are you — do you think you have reversed your fate? Is that what you're doing?"

"I ran away from the truth of my father all my life. I used to blame you for it, but the truth is I could have stopped to question. I could have insisted that you tell me what happened. I didn't have to be so passive and accept the silence handed me. For forty-five years I did not look at it, and in trying to escape the pain of his loss, I ran right to Charles. Don't you see?"

"Perhaps everyone does do it somehow — run toward the thing you think you are escaping. And now?" she asks, her flower bare, the petals scattered on the coffee table. "Have you reversed it?" The doorbell rings.

"Perhaps," I say, getting up to answer it. "There is — oh, dear — so hard to say. There is another man, Mother. I hope he is of a different ilk. I guess we'll have to let time decide. Shh. Don't tell Melissa." I open the door to admit Melissa who carries a large box in with her.

"Hi, guys. Hurry this weighs a ton. Nice apartment. Did Grandmom give you the flowers?" She puts the box on the coffee table. "Open it. I'm dying to see what it is." She wears ripped jeans and cowboy boots, a headband tied around her forehead with tails that hang all the way to her waist. My mother kisses her, and so do I. She looks adorable as she begins opening my present, knowing I won't mind.

"My favorite grandchild! What are you up to?" my mother says.

"Look! Will you look at this?" says Melissa, finally getting the box open. My mother starts the mechanism.

And there on my coffee table is the most unusual and funny clock I have ever seen. It is made entirely of thick copper wiring, the guts of the clock all exposed, and there, dancing all over it are — what are they? — some kind of cartoon character bugs with funny faces made out of the wire — who look like they are having the time of their lives. One is hanging by his knees and swinging back and forth to the rhythm of the ticking. One is turning a big wheel. Two are walking a tightrope. Several more perform their chores with big smiles on their wonderful faces.

"It's a flea clock," says my mother. "Isn't it fantastic? Now you'll get over your fear of bugs."

"Fleas! It's — I don't know what to say," I say.

"For the first time in her life," Melissa says.

The truth is — they will never know why I am so pleased. My Furies are now cartoons embodied in this clock. "What is this for?" I ask. "I mean — why are you giving me this now — I can't believe it. It is absolutely the most wonderful thing I have ever seen or could ever imagine —"

"That's exactly what it's for," my mother says. "It's to remind you to have the most wonderful time you could ever imagine in your life."

"Ditto for me," says Melissa.   "Even though I didn't pay for it."

"Well, I guess this is as good a time . . . I have a gift for you, Mother," I say, rummaging in my dresser drawer.   I hand my mother the watch that Bessie stole, still wrapped in the tissue she had kept it in.

"It's about time," Melissa says.

Emelia is stunned beyond words as the realization dawns of what she is holding in her hands.   "Oh, my God," is all she can get out with her tears.   We sit on my new couch and Melissa and I tell her the story.   Finally, she says, "You mean, it's not too late?"

"I guess nothing is ever too late," I say.

"I used to think it was too late for me," says Melissa.

"What?" I cry.

"I mean, I used to get so sad after it happened — what Daddy did," she goes on.   "I guess now that I know that all I need is about fifteen more years of therapy — I can relax. What a relief!" We all laugh and hug, and after tea, they both leave to go home.

"I'd like to hear more about that person we talked about before," my mother says over her shoulder.

"By all means," I answer.   "Maybe tomorrow."

I reach for the phone, still smiling at my clock across the room, and learn that the number they gave me earlier for Daniel has been disconnected, and then I remember that he has a brother.   I am finally successful in getting his number, but when I dial, all I get is an answering machine.   Oh, God. "This is Christina Fitzsimmons.   I've been trying to reach your brother, Daniel.   I'd appreciate it if you'd give him my number as soon as possible . . . " I know my voice must sound corny and stilted, because I'm trying to be business-like and not let anyone hear the near-hysteria that lies so close to the surface.

It is one o'clock in the morning when he finally calls. The phone wakes me.

"I just got your message," he says.   "Is it really you?"

"It's really me," I say. I am wearing the gossamer nightgown that I bought to go away with him to St. Croix. I love the way it slides on my skin.

"Oh, jees, it's —it's great to hear your voice again." I wonder if he can hear my blood racing. "Where are you?" he says. "Where am I calling? This isn't your old number."

"No, it isn't. I've moved out again. Another apartment." I stop because I've run out of saliva. He doesn't say anything. "I finally did it," I manage to get out. "The divorce is in the works."

"Well, how about that! I guess I should say 'congrats' or something. Well. And how are you?"

"Numb. Scared. I don't know."

"But you did it."

"Yes. Somehow, I finally did." Then neither of us says anything for a long while, until he breaks the silence and asks:

"Do I get to see you?"

"Think it's a good idea? I wouldn't blame you if you'd rather not," I say, twisting a curl of telephone cord around my finger.

"You mean because I got burned once?"

"I guess so."

"Wouldn't hurt to meet and talk," he says.

"I guess not. I think you may be a kind of magic genie. Did I rub a lamp once upon a time when I wasn't looking?"

"Sure, and out I came. Your wish — my command and all that stuff. But do you have the courage to ask?"

"Probably not," I say.

"Well then, just tell me when you would like to meet."

"Perhaps later in the week, or —"

" — now."

"Oh, no. That wouldn't be wise. It really —"

"Where is your apartment?"

"Daniel, it's one in the morning."

"So?"

I rush to dress, and he is here in about twenty minutes, and has his arms around me, before the door can

even close behind him.   We stand in the darkened entrance-
way.   "I can't stand to pretend," he says, kissing my neck.   "I
haven't been fully sane since you left. Thank God you called,
Christina. That's all there is to it. It's like I memorized you
way back when, and you've never left my mind."

"Make love to me," I say with my mouth on his.   He
slides his hand down into my jeans. "It's too dark out here," I
say moving toward the bedroom. "I want you to do it with all
the lights on. I want you to see me. To look at every part of
me.   Charles and I — whenever it was that we made love —
eons ago — it was always in the dark. I need you to look at
me. No, see into me."

"Don't ever speak his name — I don't want to hear it."
He drops his jeans jacket on the floor, and I unbutton his
shirt. He pulls my loose-fitting sweater off my shoulders, and
drops it to the floor. I lift his head to my mouth. I need his
mouth, his tongue touching mine. We kiss for a long time,
before we lie down naked on the bed.

"I think you probably need a license to carry a mouth
like that," I say and I laugh, but then feel it take me away.

We hold each other for a long, long time, and I think I
must have dozed.   He moves a little, and I feel the grip of his
hard, hard thighs around my leg — the silky softness of his
hair. "Did you fall asleep too?" I ask. "Imagine that we can
actually sleep like this, all wrapped around each other, I
mean. Daniel, I do love your body so much."

"I don't ever want to sleep without you again. It's so
clear to me. We have to spend our lives together. So what if
the details aren't here yet — they aren't important." I have no
idea how to respond to what he says, so I close my eyes and
sleep again.

When I awaken, I realize he is not beside me. He is
standing near the bed, leaning against my dresser with his
arms folded, a towel around him. "What are you doing?"

"Thinking," he says.

"Come here and think. I want to touch you." And we
hold each other again.   "Tell me," I say, kissing his chest.
"Tell me your heart, or the secret of life, or the whole world —
whichever comes first."

"Christina, I'm just trying to figure out the best way to do this — be together I mean. I only know that we have to be. I just can't figure out how yet."

"I don't know that I'm really ready to go that step yet. I just found the wherewithal to leave an impossible life, something I should have done years ago, but couldn't. And now I'm here, but —"

"I don't see what one has to do with the other."

"Everything. It has everything to do with it. Yes, I want to be with you — a great deal — but there are things I have to do before I can live with anyone again. I don't want to give you a wounded woman."

"You are the most wonderful woman I've ever known. I'll take you in any condition." He probably feels me stiffen. "But what are all these things that you have to do first?"

"I'm not sure at all. Sometimes the past is so heavy on me, and the present so uncertain, that I want to give up — erase all of it." I feel the ache in my throat. No. I am not going to cry. "Wouldn't it be great if a person could write a new book — the story of a wonderful life with happy memories instead of those that absolutely knock the life out of you and then just jump into the pages?"

"Maybe you can. Maybe we can together. Do you want me there with you?"

"Oh, my love," I say, kissing him again. "There's no one I'd rather be with. But not just yet."

"The irony is that I can't begin to tell you how many times I've thought about what it would be like to be married to you, all the time you were gone," he says.

"Strange coming from you — in light of what you told me about yourself, about not being able to commit to someone."

"I know it, but now there's you. So it's all changed."

"I don't know if I can ever marry again. How could I ever say those vows? Give someone the chance to betray me again. Do you see? Do you see how wounded I am — the fact that I'm talking this way?"

"Wounds can heal."

"I know you're right. But right now, all I feel is that I want to go home. I just don't know where home is."

"I'd like to help you look."

And I am thrown headlong into my father's story, remembering how a place to belong was something he had never found.

Daniel strokes my hair as we continue to hold each other, but I drift far far away. I hear him say something about wanting to grow old with me, but I am too caught up in my father's predicament. Daniel must sense it, because he grows silent and waits for me. Oh, my dear, dear father! That's it, isn't it? If I can find it — the place to belong — where I'll never have to tiptoe, where everything is right out there in front of everyone, and we can smile and say yes . . .

I will find it, and when I do, I'll call to you across time, across the gulf that both separates and unites us as we gaze across its span — and then I'll know I'll have found home.

Bless me, Father; my dear, dear Father.
I release you.
Go.